Char
Plans

M. K. Sheehan

M. K. Sheehan

Copyright © 2016 M. K. Sheehan

ISBN: 069279980X
ISBN-13: 9780692799802

DEDICATION

For my magnificent children.

M. K. Sheehan

CONTENTS

	Acknowledgments	i
1	Arrival	1
2	Clyde's	11
3	Orientation	25
4	First Date	35
5	Strategy	48
6	Fall Semester, August 2009	57
7	Competition	64
8	Turkey Day Eve	75
9	Thanksgiving	84
10	Nashville Winter	95
11	Working	105
12	First Semester Finals	117
13	Christmas Break	127
14	Spring Semester	134
15	Goal Setting	144
16	Making Nice or Not	155
17	A New Project	162
18	Bounce Back	175
19	A New Solution	182
20	Freshman Year Ends	187

21	Home	194
22	July 4, 2010	198
23	Confrontation	219
24	Sophomore Year	232
25	Building	240
26	Revelations	254
27	Investors	261
28	Awakening	271
29	Decision Making	280

ACKNOWLEDGMENTS

I could not have written this book without the constant love and support of my amazing husband, Kevin, your roots have given me wings. I love you.

Thank you to my glorious daughter, Emma, who gives me courage every day to be the truest and most honest version of myself.

Thank you to my wonderful son, Oliver, who reminds me that beauty and art take time and though the process may be arduous the results are entirely worth it.

The following people read this work and made it better with their comments, suggestions, and ideas. Leah Charney made the characters real by asking tough literary questions. Jane Johnson made Lilly stronger with every edit. Mary Pietrzyk assured every voice rang true to the South. Angela Billancini read my first clumsy draft and insisted I punctuate properly. Melissa Laubenthal, Leslie Prusinski, Constance Miller, Caroline Beck, and Mary Jackman, your talent and optimism made the text better and gave me the courage to forge ahead. Ladies, everything you touch is more beautiful, thank you for making this work and me better.

1. ARRIVAL

Vanderbilt's campus was a bustling depot of unchecked momentum. People and boxes tumbled out of cars and into the bright August sunlight. Perky college freshmen, giddy with excitement, unloaded vehicles parked on Horton Avenue. Outside of Crawford House, her new dormitory, Lilly silently stared out of the car window, watching the commotion and mentally preparing for the jarring moment when she would inevitably exit the turquoise Ford Taurus. A pint-sized RA with a constellation of blemishes littering his face opened the trunk and began hastily throwing her carefully packed boxes of sheets, shoes, clothes, and toiletries into an large orange bin on rollers. Lilly grabbed her navy blue duffel bag from the seat beside her and stepped out into the sweltering August heat. The air was muggy and thick, hot steam rising from an iron. A building loomed behind her, draped with a flimsy black sign rippling in the wind, "Welcome Class of 2014!" The chipper RAs in their matching gold T-shirts pushed bins haphazardly, wheels rattling as they clashed against cracks in the pavement.

Noise polluted the already heavy air. Vanderbilt looked like a postcard, manicured lawns, preppy kids, and forced smiles on every face. Lilly looked at her mother; Melanie's clothes were wrinkled and she seemed haggard as though the mere effort of standing was too much for her. Lilly tugged at her own white T-shirt as though making herself look more presentable might inspire her mother to do the same.

Sophia, Lilly's younger sister, carried debris from their journey to a nearby trash receptacle and pitched it. Lilly stood awkwardly by the trunk as the pimply faced boy unloaded the last of her possessions. When he was done, he hollered and two gold T-shirts came to push the bin into the building.

The new helpers were almost exact opposites. The first was tall and lanky, with black curly hair. His caramel colored skin shiny with sweat and his shirt billowing around his slim body in the breeze. The second was thick and short with closely buzzed blonde hair. His marigold shirt seemed to be painted onto his generous frame and heavy sweat stains dripped down his back and under his arms. The tall boy took command of Lilly's bin of belongings and spoke to Melanie with a slow southern twang.

"Ma'am you're going to need to move your vehicle. We have other students waiting their turn to unload."

"Thank you," Lilly said to the boy loudly, hoping her mother would catch the hint and repeat the sentiment.

"I'll park the car," Melanie announced vaguely.

Lilly shot her sister an expectant look.

"I'll drive," Sophia said begrudgingly, reluctantly taking the hint.

"I'll meet up with you for dinner?" Lilly asked straining her face muscles to keep her appearance composed. She had imagined a more ceremonious transition. She realized in the moment that she wanted a hug or a lingering look that said I love you and know you will do well. But that was not to be.

"I'm pretty tired," Melanie said with a sigh as her shoulders slumped forward. It was four o'clock. They had been on the road all day, driving from Cleveland to Nashville.

"We'll just go to the hotel," Sophia said with resignation, not waiting for her mother to get to the point. Lilly's grandmother had given them enough money for gas and two nights at a cheap hotel. Trying to stretch the limited funds, Melanie had reserved a room at a hotel in the suburbs far away from the campus and the city.

Lilly could tell Sophia did not relish her new position in the family. Sophia resented the fact that she would need to take care of their mother. A role Lilly fulfilled with a sense of duty, quietly believing it gave her some control over their unwieldy existence. Lilly hugged Sophia apologetically as Melanie walked to the front passenger seat, fell back into it, and closed the door. Melanie's arms were crossed as she stared ahead. Lilly knocked on the window. Melanie rolled it down, still staring straight ahead.

"I'll see you tomorrow." Lilly instructed, she put the duffel bag down on the ground beside her and squatted so she could see her mother's face.

Melanie stared ahead blankly.

Lilly continued, "Your day starts back here at eight, you'll need to get up at seven and I won't be with you, I have my own schedule. But, you can call or text me if you get lost."

"Ma'am, I'm going to need you to pull out," the pimple-faced boy yelled.

"She's going!" Lilly shouted and glared at him to shut him up. Startled by her angry reaction he quickly turned away, mortified. Returning her attention to the window, Lilly asked, "Ok, Mom?" in a more controlled tone.

"Fine," Melanie said with a pout.

"Ok, good. Call me if you need anything," Lilly stood up and hoisted her bag back on her shoulder, stepping back to the curb.

"See ya, Lills," Sophia said as she put the car in gear.

"Bye," Lilly said quietly as she watched her family pull away.

Lilly could feel her eyes stinging with the beginnings of tears but she held them back. Masking her sadness with anger Lilly shot a final glare at the acne encrusted RA, who deliberately avoided her gaze, and followed the bin of her belongings into the dorm. Her skin was sticky with sweat as she waited her turn to have her picture taken and student ID badge printed. Once done, she evaluated the picture as she walked down the hall. She should have taken her hair down; the hair around her face was wet with sweat and the florescent lighting made her already copper hair look brassy, but overall she looked pretty. Her eyes were bright and shining blue; the white of her T-shirt made her skin look tanned. Lilly pocketed the ID, satisfied with the results. Lilly awkwardly stood by her bin in line for the elevator.

"This should be fun," a boy in line ahead of her said sarcastically as he raked his fingers through his dark hair.

Lilly nodded and kept her mouth in a straight line. She didn't want to encourage conversation.

"I'm Max." He gave her a rakish grin. Max had warm brown eyes that looked like chocolate morsels.

"Lilly," she said, allowing her eyes to wander to his bin, overflowing with garbage bags. She was relieved when the elevator doors opened and he boarded first leaving no room for her. She took a moment in the silence to breathe, counting her breaths to calm herself as she waited, one-one-thousand, two-one-thousand, three.

The elevator opened, it was Lilly's turn. The elevator was silent and cold; like entering a grocery store freezer. She could smell the two mismatched RAs sweating the alcohol they drank the night before. Emanating a yellow, bourbony smell Lilly recognized immediately, the sickly sweet of yesterday's Wild Turkey. The elevator lurched to a stop, a rush of cold air and a chemical smell, like floor cleaner and bleach pushed through the open elevator doors. The RAs pushed Lilly's bin roughly out of the elevator and down the corridor. Packing materials littered the hallway, trash bins overflowed with empty boxes and crumpled newspapers. Lilly opened the door to the sound of comfortable laughter and three girls turned to stare at her expectantly.

"Hi … I'm Lilly." She scanned the room for a face she might recognize.

A girl in a neon pink and green dress printed with palm trees stepped forward and brightly announced, "I'm Emily, your roommate. I'm so glad to finally meet you, Lilly. Let me help you with that bag." She snatched the navy duffle bag off of Lilly's shoulder and placed it on a desk chair. She kept talking as she flitted across the room like a hummingbird, "This is Porter and that's Celia. We all went to Harpeth Hall together here in Nashville. They're my best friends in the whole world and they live at the other end of the hall." She chirped the last sentence as if it were a victory for all of them.

Rich girls, Lilly thought to herself and fought the urge to roll her eyes. Out loud she said, "Nice to meet you."

The room was small and hospital white. To Lilly's right there was a small mirror and a sink with a cupboard underneath it. There was a slender bookshelf next to the first bed that supported an exposed mattress. A wardrobe with a single door stood between the two headboards. The the bed closest to the window had been claimed already. Emily had covered it with a floral print duvet and two rosy pink gingham throw pillows featuring her initials embroidered in bright green thread. The bed alone suggested an optimism and wealth that Lilly had only seen in magazines. A large window took up the entire back wall and to Lilly's left there were two desks with a small walkway between the foot of the beds and the desk chairs. The room was distinctly organized; half of the space was beautifully furnished, the other half was Lilly's.

The RAs quickly emptied the bin and left.

"Where did you say you were from?" Emily quizzed with a polite Southern lilt in her voice. Deep brown eyes straddled either side of her tiny upturned nose. Her hair hung past her shoulders in thick brown curls. Each movement and the deliberate way she carried herself conveyed authority. Lilly wondered if anyone had ever dared to tell Emily she couldn't have something she wanted.

"Cleveland, Ohio," Lilly answered, scanning the room.

"Where did you go to school?"

"Magnificat," she answered. Lilly could tell Emily wasn't listening. She suspected the questions were for the benefit of of Celia and Porter.

"Catholic school?" Celia asked, her crisp polo shirt folding gently around her stick-like frame, from her perch on one of the desk chairs.

"Yes," Lilly nodded. She could tell the girls were scrutinizing her and her answers.

"All-girls school?" Celia said with a confident smile, her teeth a bright white row of Chicklets.

Lilly nodded quietly and agreed, "Yes."

Celia had sharp features and clear blue eyes. Her golden blonde hair was cut into a sharp bob right at her chin. She wore a bright green polo shirt and pink gingham shorts with tiny green leaves embroidered on them. She looked like a watermelon. She asked brightly, "Have you ever been to Nashville before?"

"No." Lilly admitted with some embarrassment. She had never been to Tennessee or anywhere outside of Ohio, really. She rubbed the toe of her right shoe onto the inside of her left ankle.

"What did you say your major was?" Emily asked as she leaned against her desk next to Celia.

Lilly scratched her bare arm nervously, "I'm a double major in history of art and also mathematics. I'm in the honors program. What's yours?"

Emily answered promptly and assertively, "Communications."

Celia added, in her sprightly chirp, "I'm in history, I didn't even know they had an honors program, that's awesome Lilly."

Lilly smiled and nodded, proud of her accomplishment and pleased to have it recognized.

Porter yawned behind her hand and spoke in smooth low tones, "I'm a theater major but only because Vanderbilt doesn't offer a focus in music. I'm a classically trained opera singer." With her long, dark hair and curvaceous body, Porter was the most exotic of the group; she was also the tallest, her long legs dangling loosely over the side of the bed like limp spaghetti. She wore a loose-fitting colorful tunic and had gold bangles stacked up both of her forearms. The bracelets made a light tinkling sound like a wind chime whenever she moved.

"You sing opera?" Lilly raised her eyebrows with fascination.

"I'd rather sing country. I write my own music and lyrics," Porter added casually inspecting her manicure as she spoke.

Lilly was impressed. "That's awesome."

Celia asked, "Are a lot of your friends coming to Vanderbilt?"

"No. I'm the only one from my school," Lilly explained. She twisted a ring on her right ring finger.

"Well, you can always hang out with us," Emily offered generously.

"You can keep in touch with your friends from home online too," Celia added.

"Yeah," Lilly agreed. "I will." She smiled at Celia. Lilly already liked her.

"Did you play any sports?" Celia asked curiously.

"I played lacrosse," Lilly offered.

"Me too," Emily beamed. "I played center."

Lilly nodded, "Point."

"So, you're not aggressive?" Emily suggested with an arched eyebrow.

"I'm more strategic," Lilly explained.

"Your signet ring is pretty," Emily complimented.

"My what?" Lilly asked with a wrinkled forehead.

"The silver ring you're twisting right off of that finger," Emily nodded her head towards Lilly's fidgety hands.

"Oh," Lilly stopped playing. The ring was a simple silver band with her great-grandmother's initials engraved onto the face in an ornate script. It was the only family relic she had and whenever Lilly was stressed she found playing with it irresistible. "Thank you."

"Your freckles are adorable," Celia added trying too hard.

"It's the right amount," Porter asserted, getting up from the bed and moving past Lilly to the mirror. "It's like a Jackson Pollack splatter across the bridge of your nose."

Unable to stop herself, Lilly said, "Jackson Pollack used a drip technique. He didn't splatter paint he dripped it from above onto the canvas using a variety of unconventional tools."

Porter looked at Emily in the mirror and rolled her eyes at the reflection. Emily rambled on as though Lilly hadn't spoken. "I hope you don't mind, I took all the furniture towards the back of the room."

"That's fine," Lilly answered. She was looking forward to having her own space. She didn't care if it was in the front or the back of the room, as long as it was hers. She pulled clothes out of the her duffel bag and started sliding them into the drawers of the empty dresser. There wasn't much to unpack, but Lilly busied herself picking out where to place personal belongings and trying to predict where she might look for things.

Several minutes later Emily said, "We share a wardrobe. I don't know how they think that is enough space for two people," clearly trying to restart conversation with her roommate.

"Cool," Lilly said as she hung up three dresses, leaving plenty of room on her side of the closet.

"We're going to the bar tonight, do you want to come?" Emily asked again, attempting to interrupt Lilly from her task.

"No, thanks."

"Have you ever even been to a bar?" Porter asked with a condescending tone.

"I've gone to bars for dinner with my family."

"We mean to go out. You know drink, meet guys, that sort of thing," Emily explained, clearly trying to sell Lilly on the idea. She had a hopeful look on her face.

Lilly stalled, hoping to end the conversation, "I don't have a fake ID."

"Don't even worry about it, we'll pass one back. We'll go in and then send someone out to meet you and bring you one of the ones we already used. It'll be fun. You're coming," Emily asserted.

"You can borrow one of Porter's outfits," Celia volunteered as Porter shot her a death stare.

Before Lilly could come up with another excuse, her phone rang, it was her mother. She watched Emily and Porter share a judgmental look when she flipped open her phone but turned her attention to her conversation.

"Hey Mom," Lilly said, relieved to escape the conversation.

"Our hotel is across town," her mother said breathlessly as if she had just run there. "Sophia and I haven't eaten. It took us forever to get here and I don't think we'll be coming back for dinner." Lilly could picture her mother patting her hair absentmindedly, the nervous expression on her face as she waited for Lilly's response.

Lilly sighed aloud, "Ok, I'll figure it out." Lilly was disappointed but not caught off guard. The call was really just a formality. Something Melanie did to pretend she was a normal functioning adult, not a high functioning alcoholic. Lilly did not need to be physically there to see Melanie wringing her hands. Her tongue heavy, her yellowed teeth chewing together as she pursed her cracked lips for another sip. Lilly could clearly picture Sophia checking her phone, appearing distracted but actually keeping vigilant watch, as Lilly had for most of their lives.

Melanie answered brightly, relieved Lilly had not questioned her decision. "That sounds good. We'll see you in the morning."

"Ok," Lilly said, at least her mom remembered that she needed to be back at school in the morning.

"I love you," Melanie said desperately, attempting to confirm in words that her daughter did in fact still love her.

"I love you too," Lilly answered begrudgingly, giving in to her mother's need for reassurance even though it was entirely undeserved. Lilly clicked the phone closed slowly, thinking about what to do next.

"Is everything alright?" Emily asked brightly, shattering Lilly's reflective moment.

"Oh," Lilly shook her head, bringing her awareness back to the ivory room, the florescent lights, and the aggressive smell of expensive perfume. "Uh, my mom and sister just got to the hotel. They're not coming back tonight."

"Well that settles it," Emily said perkily with a smile. "Now you can come out with us!"

Celia smiled warmly as Porter looked down at her iPhone.

Lilly nodded her head up and down slowly, her lips a tight line pressed together. *She walked right into that one.*

Celia and Emily dressed Lilly in a sleeveless sage green shirt dress and pulled her hair into a full and messy topknot. They even stabbed a heavy pair of pearls in her ears. Even as a child, Lilly could not remember someone combing through her hair or caring what she wore. She didn't understand these people. They pressed as far as they could go and then began negotiations, overtaking her schedule, her dress, and her physical appearance in a single day. Lilly had to admit she liked feeling taken care of; it was nice. Still she was unsure how she felt about people so comfortable making decisions for her, demanding only that she partake in their plans, play their game, and follow their rules.

Walking across campus to the bar, Lilly couldn't help but be distracted by

9

the lush greenery of the trees and the grandeur of the corinthian columns. The sun had set and the air was cool and pink. There was a warm rosy electricity on campus that excited and charmed Lilly to no end. A tall, white clock tower dominated the campus and wide sidewalks seemed to wind and meander aimlessly in all directions. Lilly allowed her eyes to dart around thirstily, drinking in as much detail as her brain could hold, a soft breeze, white spotlights, green leaves, the smell of wisteria and lilac.

She was admiring an ivy wrapped doorway when she saw Max walking toward her.

"Hey Lilly, how's it going?" he asked.

He remembered her name, Lilly was surprised. "Good, just heading out." Lilly could feel the stares of the three girls watching with keen interest.

Emily jumped in linking her arm through Lilly's comfortably, "We're going to Clyde's for a drink if you'd like to join us."

Max looked at Emily, "Thanks, maybe later. A few of the guys on my floor were invited to a party."

Emily interjected, surprising Lilly and cutting her off. "Well, you have fun Max and maybe we'll see you around campus." Lilly was confused. *Did Emily know Max?* Before Lilly could ask, Emily was already steering her away.

Lilly made a small wave to Max before blindly following her new acquaintances to the bar. It was all so strange. The control Emily had assured her, their night, the conversation. Her dictatorship unquestioned by the other girls, even Max seemed to understand her word was final and it was law.

2. CLYDE'S

At Clyde's the strategy to pass back id's proved unnecessary. The girls simply pulled the heavy handle of a large oak door and walked in. They were early. The room was dimly lit and filled with a yellow haze that smelled like fried food and stale conversation. Aside from two professorial looking men at the end of the bar, the girls were the only customers. They seated themselves in a burgundy booth, sliding in two to a side. Porter and Emily across from Lilly and Celia. A sallow cheeked waitress with a dirty apron and blank expression took their drink orders.

As she walked away Porter cut to the chase, "How do you know Max?"

"Max? We waited for the elevator together," Lilly answered with confusion.

The girls looked intrigued but were not showing Lilly their hands. "He seems to like you," Emily asserted frankly.

"We just met," Lilly said defensively. Not liking how it felt to be questioned, Lilly switched to the offense and asked, "How do you know him?"

Celia and Porter looked to Emily, who looked directly at Lilly with a sharp flash of gold in her deep brown eyes and smiled, "Our paths cross from time to time."

The empty eyed waitress returned with their drinks, carelessly sloshing them onto the table as she put them down.

"What does that mean?" Lilly was interested. She was challenging Emily gently but could still feel the tension and anticipation radiating off of Celia

11

and Porter's bodies. Emily remained relaxed and calm and despite the spark in her eyes, she seemed to be enjoying this.

"I don't like to gossip," Emily confided with false modesty as she leaned in slightly, "but he tends to be a serial dater so we," she nodded to indicate the girls at the table, "like to keep our distance." Leaning back she added, "You're welcome to date whomever you want but in my opinion Max is not for you."

"Maybe the house party would have been fun?" Lilly tested Emily's mettle.

Emily sighed and explained as if she were talking to a five year old, "Lilly, a house party only benefits one person—the guy. He doesn't pay a cover charge for you, there is no thought or planning that goes into the evening, and it puts you in the awkward position of being with all of his friends and doing only what he wants to do."

"Ok," Lilly said dropping the issue. She didn't know why she cared how they knew him. It's not like she was going to date him. She wasn't going to date anyone. She came to Vanderbilt to get an education. Anything else was a distraction from her goals of getting a great job and getting the hell out of her mother's house.

"Furthermore, it's just stupid as a single freshman woman to attend a party alone with someone you just met, but I'm sure I don't have to explain that to you." Emily finished.

"No," Lilly agreed, disliking that it was her job to avoid assault rather than the responsibility of men not to assault her.

Emily switched gears, her tone bright and congratulatory. "I believe a toast is in order," she said as she raised her glass slightly, "as you're the Wilson Scholar."

Lilly nodded slowly, "I am." She was suspicious. How did Emily know that she was the Wilson Scholar? Lilly forced her face to remain expressionless and impassive.

Celia smiled encouragingly, "That's impressive."

"Thank you," Lilly smiled at Celia and waited to see where Emily was going. Lilly followed her logic: break the ice with a compliment, wade in with girl talk, and then strike the conversation you really wanted to have. Lilly admired Emily's strategy.

Emily added, "They only award one Wilson Scholarship a year, it's a prestigious accomplishment and a particularly elite group to join. Many former Wilson Scholars are leaders here in Nashville and around the world."

Lilly nodded and gave a bland smile. She replied with the canned response she had used any time someone brought up the prestige of her award, "It was an honor to be considered."

Emily put down her glass and crossed her arms. "You major in history of art and also mathematics but when I Googled you this summer all I found was computers and math. You're quite accomplished."

Lilly's answers were clipped. *How much did Emily already know about her?* "Thank you. I've worked very hard to become so." An idea popped into Lilly's head with neon brilliance, she was not Emily's roommate by accident. Lilly's heart pounded, but no one else at the table seemed to notice.

"I believe it." Emily stared expectantly at Lilly waiting for her to explain herself.

Lilly took a breath, trying to slow her racing heart, "Art history is an interest and a personal passion of mine. I excel in computers and mathematics but with Vanderbilt's history of art program, I thought I would take advantage of the opportunity to learn about something I don't know."

Porter was already bored and tapping on her phone screen with teal nails, her bracelets clinking together with disjointed notes.

Emily gave a satisfied smirk. "I respect that. I am pleased as punch to be your roommate."

Lilly smiled and nodded. She could tell Emily was excited. She kept readjusting her position in the booth as though news cameras might arrive any moment to document her personal victory to have Lilly has her roommate and her trophy.

Emily's eyes narrowed seriously, "The Wilson Scholarship requires a lot of work do you think you're up to the task?"

Lilly set her jaw but kept her voice light and even, "The scholarship requires I maintain a 3.7 GPA, complete a research project, and participate in campus life, which entails clubs and volunteerism. It's hardly a challenge, I would do all of that anyway," Lilly dared Emily to come at her again.

"You're competitive," Emily asserted leaning back, again satisfied with Lilly's answer and taking comfort in her words.

"When I have to be," Lilly said with an edge in her voice. She felt every pump of blood through her veins but Lilly would sooner die than let Emily know she threatened her.

Emily was unfazed and kept pushing. "The Scholarship covers room, board, and classes, right? You're still responsible for books, computer, travel expenses." Again, Emily was asking questions but seemed to already know all of the answers.

Lilly took a deep breath of yellow air, "You handled the roommate arrangements, didn't you?" Lilly fixed her roommate with a cold stare. She did not trust Emily and wanted to know who she was dealing with immediately.

"Yes, I did," Emily owned it with a prim purse of her lips. "I only surround myself with the best and most brilliant people. I knew I wanted you as my roommate, so I did everything in my power to make that happen and it worked." She smiled smugly, "Here we are together."

Lilly was genuinely blown away by Emily's audacity. Her blatant manipulation to get what she wanted was absurd. Emily had a total lack of remorse and Lilly couldn't decide if she was insulted or impressed.

"Does that bother you?" Emily asked coolly, folding her hands in front of herself.

"A bit, it's arrogant and manipulative, don't you think?"

Celia sat straight up upon hearing Lilly's comment and Porter looked up from her phone with sudden interest.

Emily remained composed, her face a placid pool, revealing nothing below its surface. "I prefer to look at it as smart planning. Some of the best business teams in the world started as college roommates, I just wanted to tip the odds in my favor. It could also totally work against me. We could easily hate one another and you could be my nemesis," Emily added confidently.

14

"You would be my nemesis, if anything," Lilly shot back.

There was a pause at the table as Lilly listened to her heart in her ears, thudding.

"Well played new girl," Porter said with a wry smile and raised her glass in salute. Their shared laughter broke the tension and Lilly allowed herself to relax slightly.

"Have you selected your scholarship project yet?" Emily asked in a more conversational tone.

"You have homework already?" Celia gaped.

"Wilson scholars are responsible for a project," Lilly explained gently to Celia, her heart settling to a normal, slower, rate. "I decide what I want to study and I'm assigned a faculty mentor to oversee my work." Then more authoritatively she said to Emily, "I'm launching a company before graduation."

"Have you started yet?" Emily asked with genuine interest.

Lilly spoke boldly, daring them to question her and hoping to startle Emily with her revelation, "I'm writing a program to track changes in an existing database for auditing and security use." It worked. Emily's eyes were wide.

"Was that English?" Porter asked stiffly.

"Porter, you are the worst," Celia joked.

As Lilly outlined her vision the bar began to fill up.

Celia noticed Lilly's wandering attention. "We're the life of the party: where we go, the party comes," she said with a conspiratorial smile. Lilly reciprocated the look warmly.

A team of eight young men came pouring through the doorway, immediately filling the bar with their laughter and the jovial conviviality of youth. The marigold room began to buzz with the cacophony of conversation. The girls at the table seemed to deliberately not take notice of their arrival, sitting a little straighter but never noticeably looking up. Lilly followed suit even as one boy in particular caught her attention. She allowed her eyes to linger a beat too long and he caught her. Their eyes met and Lilly felt a little blue firework bursting inside of her but she quickly looked away. Her hands tingled as she focused her eyes on the table and wondered, *Who was he?*

One of the men yelled, "Porter!"

Porter smiled and raised her glass as though toasting him and immediately returned her attention to the table. Shortly after ordering the boy appeared at the table with his eyes fixed on Porter. He cooed, "Porter, what are you drinking?" as he learned over the back of the booth to get closer to her in the corner.

"A G&T," she whispered with a smile.

"Of course you are," he said with a thick Southern drawl. There was a comfortable intensity between them. "I took the liberty of ordering you ladies another round." The same tired waitress appeared behind him with four fresh gin and tonics for the table and a tall beer for him.

"Stephen Calhoun, now aren't you just the sweetest. Thank you." Emily said smoothly, as the waitress distributed the drinks with a now familiar lack of interest.

Stephen Calhoun had a round face, untamed eyebrows, and crinkles in the outside corners of his muddy brown eyes. If Porter had had a nicer personality, Lilly would have said he was dating up.

"Anything for you, ladies," looking over at Lilly, Stephen asked, "Who is the new addition?" Lilly was surprised he noticed anyone other than Porter.

Emily announced, "This is Lilly Carter, my roommate."

Lilly liked how Emily spoke her name like a signature. It sounded polished and professional.

Stephen smiled warmly, a lopsided grin lighting up his whole face. "It is a pleasure to meet you, Ms. Carter—any friend of these fine women is a friend of mine."

Porter rolled her eyes as the guys at the other end of the bar hollered for Stephen to return.

"Now I'm going to go calm those gentlemen down. You ladies have a fine evening. I'll be back to talk more with you later, Porter," he said with another unabashed smile. Stephen grabbed his beer and walked back to the boisterous group.

"Who was that?" Lilly blurted out after he was out of earshot.

"That was Porter's future husband," Celia announced, matter-of-factly.

"Cecilia Mariweather Judd, you take that back this instant!" Porter demanded haughtily. Porter's face was stony as she turned to Lilly and explained firmly, "Stephen is a dear family friend whom I have known all my life." It was as though she were a politician parroting her talking points for the media. She repeated almost defiantly, "He is a family friend."

"Porter likes to pretend he's not the reason she came to school here," Emily teased, fanning the fire with comfortable ease.

"Stephen's your boyfriend?" Lilly asked. She was having a little more fun than she should teasing Porter. Now that the spotlight was on Porter she was warming up to the other girls and the experience.

"No. Stephen and I are not dating," Porter said, emphasizing the *not*. After a pause she begrudgingly added, "Stephen and I are too young to date each other right now. Naturally, we'll end up together but until then we're not exclusive."

"They'll be together soon enough," Celia confided nudging Lilly with her shoulder.

Porter continued, "We are waiting until I finish undergrad and Stephen is in law school. Then we'll date."

"You're just going to follow Stephen to whatever school he picks?" Lilly asked skeptically, not impressed with Porter's lack of ambition and feeling the cool confidence of gin.

"No," Porter bristled at the insinuation.

"What are you going to do while he's in law school?"

"I'm going to release a country music record," Porter stated as though it were totally obvious. She seemed irritated that she had to explain herself to Lilly.

"She has a phenomenal voice," Celia said sweetly.

Lilly nodded and sipped her drink. She allowed her attention to drift back to the brown haired boy who made her stomach lurch in a not wholly unpleasant way. As she tried to casually look for him, pretending her actions were not deliberate she caught his eye again. He winked at her but kept talking to whomever he was with, Lilly immediately felt warm all over.

Emily teased, "Aww, look at you, Lilly, all nervous because a guy winked at you."

Lilly fidgeted with her signet ring, her cheeks an embarrassed pink.

"He's just flirting with you," Emily taunted. She then turned, "Porter, do you know who that boy is with Stephen?"

"Which one?" Porter asked deliberately not turning around.

"The tall one in the blue polo shirt," Emily answered.

Porter waited a few seconds and then casually craned her neck to see the bar behind her. She turned back and nonchalantly gave her report, "I think that's Charlie Abbott; he's Stephen's year. He's from Colorado. I'm pretty sure he's the lacrosse team captain this year."

"He's cute," Celia chimed in with her consistent optimism.

Lilly took a nervous gulp of her drink praying the alcohol would calm her nerves.

"Are you ok?" Celia asked with concern, putting a cold and clammy hand on Lilly's wrist.

"I'm fine," Lilly answered.

"Oh Lilly, don't be nervous." Celia tried to comfort her with a supportive pat on the hand.

"He was winking at Emily," Lilly deflected.

"He most certainly was not winking at me. He is all yours," Emily said waving her hands in front of her chest as though fending off the thought physically.

"Bless your heart, you just don't like jocks," Celia said to Emily.

"Oh really?" Lilly said readjusting to face Emily.

"I like boys who are more academically inclined than Mr. Calhoun's friends. Not that I don't think Stephen is brilliant," Emily corrected herself. "His friends just aren't my style."

"Well, I think that's the nicest way I've ever heard you phrase that," Porter said with a roll of her honey brown eyes.

"What?" Emily asked incredulously leaning back against the booth.

"I think the last time you used the phrase 'stuttering morons,'" Porter arched a thick eyebrow.

"I would never! Porter Grace Cain, don't talk ugly," Emily scolded.

The girls all laughed at Emily's indignation.

"Porter likes jocks, Emily likes nerds—what kinds of guys do you like, Celia?" Lilly asked getting into the conversation.

"Oh, I'm not into guys," Celia explained with a warm smile that seemed to alight her face from within. "You see that brunette at the end of the bar?" Lilly looked over to see a petite girl leaning against the bar, twirling her long hair in her fingers, waiting for the bartender to notice her.

"Yes."

"That's my type," Celia shared.

"Oh," Lilly said, slightly surprised. As she took in this information Lilly felt more interested in this group. Maybe they were more open-minded than she had originally thought.

Porter followed their gaze disinterestedly and said, "She's pretty Celia, but that dress is uglier than homemade sin."

Emily looked over and agreed.

"But I'm off the market," Celia explained warmly as though she and Lilly were the only two people in the room. "My girlfriend, Claire, goes to culinary school in France. We've been together for two years."

Lilly liked feeling like she and Celia were alone together. Lilly let her guard down and probed what she hoped was her new friend gently, "That's a long time. Do you miss her?"

"She only left last week but yes, I do. It's a phenomenal opportunity for her but it means we have to be long distance. C'est la vie." Celia said with another soft silver smile.

"Do you cook too?" Lilly asked eager to keep the conversation with Celia going.

"No," Celia mused, "I'm far better at kissing than I ever was at cooking."

Lilly almost spit out her drink as she burst out laughing. She let the laughter wash over her and radiate through her cleansing the hard insecurity from her body.

"Enough trying to take the attention off of yourself, Lilly," Emily commanded. "That boy keeps looking over here. Why don't you go to the bar and pick up our next round?"

Lilly protested, "I don't even know him!" She looked around the table as Emily and Celia stared at her expectantly. Porter just rolled her eyes. "What if I get carded?"

"In that dress?" Emily looked her up and down skeptically for effect. "You'll be fine."

"You'll do great," Celia encouraged Lilly with a smile.

"Really?" she asked one more time, begging for a reprieve.

"Yes, please," Emily said brightly as Celia slid out of the booth for Lilly.

Lilly stood up. She suddenly felt awkward and uncomfortable. She didn't know how to act or how to walk—she felt like a phony. Standing at the bar, Lilly rocked from foot to foot. It wasn't long before she could feel someone standing next to her. She could smell his cologne, a woodsy spice that burned the back of her throat and made her want to cough.

"Excuse me," he said. She turned slowly but her eyes shot right up to his face as though she knew exactly who was there and where he would be, like they were old friends meeting in a familiar place, not strangers in a bar.

"Yes?" she said expectantly.

"Hi, I'm Charlie. I believe we have a mutual friend, Stephen Calhoun," his voice was deep and gravelly.

"Lilly Carter." She felt compelled to add, "I don't really know Stephen. I mean, we just met—I'm sure he's a great guy; I just don't really know him all that well." Nodding into the silence she rushed to include, "I know Porter. Well, I just met her too, but I know her a little better than Stephen." *Why am I still talking? Shut up, shut up, shut up!*

"Oh, okay." His eyes glittered with a sapphire smile as he looked down at her patiently.

The bartender leaned toward her, directing his left ear toward the sound of her voice.

Her mouth was dry as she choked out, "Four gin and tonics, please."

The bartender walked away, barely giving her a second look. Lilly had started to sweat with nervousness, she couldn't believe it was that easy. He didn't even ask for her ID. She exhaled with a smile as Charlie watched her. She squirmed, looking away uncomfortably.

Sensing her discomfort he said, "Sorry to have bothered you," and turned, but before he could step away, Emily appeared in his path.

"Hello, Charlie, I'm Emily, how are you doing tonight?"

"Fine and you?" He answered politely.

"I'm just peachy, thank you so much for asking. Would you help settle an argument? My friend Lilly and I were just having a discussion about lacrosse and she was saying that women's lacrosse was more challenging than men's because of the pocket on the net. Is that right?" She was blatantly lying, but Lilly followed Emily's lead.

Lilly added, "And the lack of padding! Women only play with mouth guards. Guys have a ton of padding and helmets. All we have is 'personal space.'"

"I guess," Charlie said and smiled. They were both relieved to have something to talk about. When the drinks came, Emily exited as smoothly as she had appeared, handing Lilly her drink and taking the other cocktails back to the table herself.

Lilly thought, *Maybe Emily would be a good friend to have around after all.*

"That's $35," the bartender said, wiping his hands on a white towel tucked into his front pocket.

"I'll get it," Charlie said stepping closer to her and to the bar.

"I've got it," she said solidly and snapped her debit card down on the bar. The bartender picked it up without comment. Charlie's mouth was agape with surprise. "So you're a year ahead of me?" Lilly asked, forcing the moment to a close.

Charlie smiled and slouched down so they could talk over the rising noise in the bar. "Two actually, I'm a junior."

"What's your major?" She was grilling him like Emily had done with her earlier.

"I'm pre-law. How about you?" He held a cold beer in his hand but kept his attention locked on her.

"History of Art and Mathematics."

"Wow. You don't mess around," he smiled jokingly.

"I like school," Lilly shared with a shrug, giving him a rare unguarded answer.

He nodded slowly with approval, "I do too." Charlie took a drink from his beer bottle. "So, what brings you to Nashville, Lilly Carter?" he asked looking into her eyes comfortably.

She was direct, "I wanted a big name school, but it had to be close enough to my family to get home if they needed me."

"So, you take care of everyone," Charlie said insightfully.

His accuracy startled Lilly. "Yeah, I guess I'm just the most organized," she deflected. Their conversation was drifting into precariously deep water and Lilly was not prepared to go there, especially with a stranger.

Seeming to sense her discomfort he said, "I'm organized to a fault. I don't like surprises."

Lilly continued, "I think that's really why I picked Vanderbilt. I just always wanted to be somewhere that wasn't chaotic and unpredictable."

It was Charlie's turn to nod with understanding.

Lilly kept going, "I wanted to go south. I felt like I could fit in here. It's more homey than the East Coast, I guess." Realizing she had revealed more personal information than she had intended, Lilly quickly threw out a distraction, "That and Vanderbilt had the best financial package."

"Did you get a scholarship?" He asked casually, letting her once again steer the conversation to lighter topics.

"Yeah," she looked over at Emily and added, "Actually, I got the Wilson Scholarship."

He nodded his approval. "You're that smart?"

"I guess," Lilly said with a laugh and took a quaff of her drink. *Was she bragging? It was true.* Her head was swimming with the alcohol, making the room shift and swell, like she was moving through mud.

"Those things are impossible to get, they didn't even give one out my year." Charlie looked at her with admiration.

Lilly gently placed her fingertips on the bar, attempting to steady her sloshing mind.

Noticing her distraction Charlie smoothly segued, "Now, my team is going to kill me if I stay over here much longer."

Lilly laughed at the gaggle of guys across the bar, gracelessly trying to distract his attention.

"And based on our all too brief conversation, may I have your number?" he asked seriously.

She obliged with a broad smile, "Yes, you may."

Once he had her number Lilly stumbled back to the table giddily.

"He asked for my number!" she blurted out before sitting.

"I'm so glad, Lil—that's really sweet." Emily said, before quickly changing the subject, "Are you ready to head home now?" Emily nodded to the scene unfolding in the bar, now packed with students. The room was swaying. The throbbing music made everything seem sparkly and impermanent. Emily added, "We're just ready to snuggle up in our beds."

"Yes, we can go whenever you're ready." Lilly looked at the other girls, their eyes were heavy lidded. *How long had she been talking to Charlie?*

When she got back to the room, Lilly delicately laid Porter's outfit over her desk chair and placed the shoes on the seat. She was still light-headed from the drinks but pulled out a box of supplies and set up her desk quietly anyway. After tidying up, Lilly crawled into her new and unfamiliar bed and quickly fell asleep too exhausted to wonder what might happen tomorrow.

3. ORIENTATION

Lilly woke up the following morning to golden sunlight streaming through the window. She looked around the strange room drowsily. Emily was already wide awake, make-up done, hair in place, looking fresh and revitalized as she sipped tea out of a Styrofoam cup. *How could she possibly make that look ladylike?* Lilly groggily padded to the sink and splashed cold water on her face. There was a lazy summer breeze wafting through the room, carrying the sounds of conversation from the quad below. Lilly felt stale but was satisfied that the room was organized. She noticed that Emily had already made her bed.

"You stayed up pretty late last night," Emily hinted.

"I'm sorry if I was loud." Lilly asked, "Did I wake you?"

"Not at all, I just noticed the room is spotless this morning."

"I like to know where my things are, it helps me stay organized." Lilly stretched her arms overhead and yawned, her arms dropped as she remembered something. "Although, I did forget to pack Tylenol, do you have any?"

"I do," Emily answered as she pulled a bottle out of her desk drawer. She asked with concern, "Were you over-served last night?"

It was the nicest way Lilly had ever heard someone ask if she was drunk. "Yeah, a bit over-served, I guess."

"Well, I am sorry. I should have kept an eye on how much they were giving you in those cocktails," Emily said, seeming to take a mental note.

"No, it's fine. I've never gone out drinking like that before." Lilly admitted as she popped the pills into her mouth and pulled her hair to the side with one hand, turned on the tap, and drank right from the faucet. She flipped her head up and swallowed the water and the pills together.

Emily's jaw dropped with a horrified expression, as if this simple action were a deliberate affront to her.

Lilly was oblivious to Emily's dismay and grabbed her towel and shower caddy. As she slipped on her flip flops, Emily recovered and said, "I didn't realize! Here we've gone and corrupted you! I forget that Celia can drink for days and you'd never know it. Porter and I never try to keep up; otherwise, we'd end up in the same boat as you this morning."

"I guess," Lilly shrugged and padded down the hall to the shower.

When Lilly got back to the room she was lost in thought. She absentmindedly threw on a clean white T-shirt and denim cutoffs. Sitting down on her bed she toweled her neck dry, her long red hair was still dripping. There was a knock on the door and Emily let in Celia and Porter; they both looked showered and fresh.

"Morning, gals," Celia called. "How are y'all doing this morning?"

Lilly said, "Thank you so much for guiding us home last night."

"Not to worry, lady, I spend enough time taking care of this one," Celia said rolling her eyes towards Porter.

"You do not," Porter pouted.

"You're just salty that I didn't let you stay and play with Stephen last night," Celia teased.

"Well, it wouldn't have killed you is all I'm saying," Porter crossed her arms and sat on the edge of Emily's bed. Then in a rather dramatic fashion she threw her arms into the air and collapsed backwards. She whined, "Girls, why is the sun so damn bright?"

"Porter's a lightweight," explained Emily authoritatively.

"I am not. Y'all just drink too much," Porter replied.

"Porter Grace, I am a lady who always holds her liquor," Emily said firmly.

"Always?" Celia said with a smirk.

"Well, maybe not always but there's no need to bring it up," Emily said haughtily. Celia and Porter laughed. Lilly couldn't help but smile.

"If you girls are done now, Lilly and I would like to go to breakfast." Emily asserted, linking her arm trough Lilly's. The thought of breakfast almost made Lilly sick. The Tylenol had helped her headache but she still felt queasy.

"Well, let's go, Miss Prim and Proper," Celia joked.

Emily walked out with her nose in the air, rolling her eyes at the other two girls for Lilly's benefit. Lilly followed Emily's lead with lackluster steps. She knew they could take Horton Avenue East to a trail before 18th Avenue South to get there but Emily, already familiar with the campus led them partially around the Horton Avenue cul-de-sac, where Lilly's family had dropped her off the day before, and cut across the Commons lawn or the lower quad, Lilly wasn't sure which.

"We're going to The Commons. My mother texted me, they're looking for us," Emily explained.

"The parents just stay through today?" Celia asked.

"Yes," Emily began confidently. "They have Parent Orientation which includes a campus tour and President's reception."

The Commons towered before them, a stately red brick building with giant windows overlooking a large green space. There was an enclosed patio with several green umbrellas covering tables and chairs that everyone seemed to be ignoring in deference to the air-conditioned building. Lilly gaped at the sheer beauty of the architecture as she realized this was where she would be eating almost every day. The fact seemed surreal.

"Hi Mama," Porter said to a heavyset yet polished woman walking out of the doors and toward them. The mothers were all well dressed, their manicured nails gleamed as they pecked over their daughters and exchanged pleasantries.

Emily's mother was the first to notice Lilly. "You know manners never go out of style, Emily Jane. Aren't you going to introduce us to your new friend?"

"Mama, this is my roommate, Lilly Rose Carter, Vanderbilt University's Wilson Scholar. She's from Cleveland and plans to study history of art and also mathematics," Emily announced as if she was giving a book report.

"Well, it's wonderful to meet you, Lilly," Emily's mother said warmly. "I hope our girls are taking good care of you."

"Yes ma'am, they are," Lilly answered trying to mimic their polite Southern courtesy.

Mrs. Parker nodded with approval, "Congratulations on the Wilson Scholarship. That is quiet an impressive accomplishment. We will expect great things from you."

"Yes ma'am," Lilly answered.

Mrs. Parker pulled an invisible piece of lint off of Emily's shoulder, "I'm so glad that you are going to be Emily's roommate. I know it was very important to Emily to be able to learn from you and spend time together."

Emily smiled like a Cheshire cat as her mother preened.

Lilly smiled back.

"What do you girls have planned for today?" Celia's mother asked warmly.

Emily answered promptly, "We have to finalize our schedules with our advisors and there are lectures this afternoon on campus safety, financial aid..." Emily turned to her mother and spoke conspiratorially, "But, we could skip those and join y'all at the President's reception."

Mrs. Parker's face grew firm, "You will do no such thing, Emily Jane. You attend your lectures and get to know your classmates," Mrs. Parker instructed. She then announced to the group, "Alright ladies, we need to get to the auditorium." Turning to Lilly she added more softly, "It was a pleasure to meet you, Lilly."

"Don't you girls get her into any trouble, you hear?" Celia's mom added for good measure.

"Yes ma'am," the girls said in unison.

Lilly noticed Emily's mother seemed to lead the other women the way Emily did their daughters. She said, "Have a nice time today girls. We'll have dinner together at eight o'clock. Lilly, you and your family are invited to join us."

"Thank you." Lilly replied, her voice tight.

"You're welcome dear. Alright ladies, let's head over to the auditorium," Emily's mother clucked. The mothers walked away, leaving behind an orange cloud of floral perfume. Lilly took one breath and felt ready to pass out.

The girls entered The Commons. "They knew we went out last night," Emily stated flatly, pulling the door to the building open releasing a cold rush of wind on their faces..

"Well, of course they did, there is nothing that gets by those women," Celia concurred.

"Your mothers all know each other?" Lilly asked incredulously.

"Of course they do," Emily answered, looking at Lilly like she was crazy.

Celia explained more softly, her voice a cool bubbling stream, "We've known each other our whole lives."

"Oh, I didn't know that," Lilly replied. Her heart sank a little as she considered the personal and emotional needs she expected to have as a college student. Financially, the scholarship provided for her room and board and all of her classes, it would not cover books and a computer but she had taken out a small loan to cover those expenses. But the girls had a huge advantage. They had people who cared and were invested in their success. Lilly wanted to do well but not having a support network behind her would make everything that much harder.

"Where did your parents go to school Lil?" Emily asked.

"They didn't," Lilly answered frankly.

"You're the first one in your family to go to college?" Celia said with genuine amazement.

"Yes," Lilly answered stiffly, she felt like a spectacle.

"Wow. That's a lot of pressure," Celia empathized.

"It's not so bad," Lilly lied.

"That's a big deal," Celia reiterated.

"Thanks," Lilly smiled. It was nice to have someone recognize what a huge accomplishment it was to go to college when no one had any interest in your future let alone your success.

Celia added quietly, just to Lilly, as they walked down the hallway, "Well, if you need anything, you know you can always talk to me."

Lilly smiled and nodded at Celia. It felt good to know someone who felt like a friend.

"Let's get some sausage gravy and biscuits. I'm starving, y'all," Porter whined.

Breakfast was a buffet in the student cafeteria. The room was a vast landscape of competing extremes; bright lights, dark coffee, cold drinks, hot food. The air was filled with a cacophony of smells and sounds that were like a punch in the face to Lilly's senses. New students milled around the space with grey plastic trays and thick white plates. The cafeteria would be a well-oiled machine next week but today it was chaos as the new students tried to find their places in the vast room.

The girls filled their trays and found an empty table in front of a bank of windows letting in the bright summer sunlight that reflected off of the water glasses. Lilly saw her mother sitting at a round table for ten by herself, reading a book. Melanie was both in the center of room and totally absent from the space. Lilly felt ashamed, Melanie was a mess. Her black and grey hair had frizzed in the humidity. Her blouse was stained and wrinkled. Lilly put down her tray, quickly ate half a bagel to settle her stomach, and walked over to where Melanie was sitting.

"Hey, Mom."

"Oh, hi, did you grab some breakfast?" Melanie asked absentmindedly, barely glancing up from her book.

"Yeah, I'm eating with my roommate over there." Lilly gestured vaguely to the other half of the bustling cafeteria. She didn't want her mother to know exactly who she was referencing in case she wanted to meet her, or what was more likely, Emily walked over to introduce herself.

Melanie nodded disinterestedly.

"My roommate's mom invited us to dinner tonight," Lilly continued. Melanie winced but made no comment. The deep creases at the corners of her hazel eyes twitched as she read.

Lilly exhaled audibly with irritation, "Are you going to the parents' lecture?"

"Yes," Melanie replied shortly. Her pencil thin eyebrows daring her daughter to question her.

"Ok, well the other parents have already left," Lilly did not even try to conceal her annoyance.

"I'll go when I'm done with breakfast," Melanie snipped. They both looked at the last bite of rye toast on Melanie's plate, a piece that she had clearly discarded.

Lilly rolled her eyes and continued, "Where's Sophia?"

Melanie returned her attention to her book, "She's swimming at the hotel."

Of course she was, Lilly thought to herself. Lilly would have been there with their mother, keeping her from embarrassing the family, and yet Sophia was at the pool. Lilly turned and walked away with red indignation.

She sat down at the table silently and finished her bagel, the Tylenol finally soothing the throbbing of bass in her ears. She hated that other mothers seemed to understand that doing things for your children was important and Melanie didn't care. Lilly's reality was totally different than the other kids, a fact that in that moment seemed profoundly insurmountable to her.

"Lil, my dear, is your mama going to this morning's lecture?" Emily asked with concern. *She missed nothing*

Lilly looked over to where her mother was still reading her book and spoke haltingly trying to keep her crimson rage from entering her voice, "I think she's heading over later."

Emily pressed, "Did you want to ask her to join us for breakfast?"

31

Lilly spoke with firm authority, "No. She's fine, she likes reading alone."

Emily dropped the issue but Lilly knew she was taking this in with the organized precision of a laser scanner. This would be catalogued and put away for future reference, whenever Emily needed it.

The day was a blur of frigid classrooms, new buildings, and uncomfortable desks. After their last lecture, Lilly walked back to the dorm with her new friends. Signs posted to tree trunks and on red brick walls promoted clubs, Greek life, and meeting times. Again, the sweet fragrance of wisteria seemed to swirl around her head. As Lilly walked she felt the magnitude of what could be her life here. The space was alive and vibrant and full of possibilities. There was so much she wanted to see and do and, this was a foundation she could build on. Lilly could feel the excitement in the air as she talked about her plans and goals for the coming year. When suddenly, she was looking at Porter's feet in midair.

"Stephen Calhoun, you put me down this instant!" Porter ordered from her inverted position.

"How y'all doing this lovely afternoon?" Stephen asked, flipping Porter right side up again with an impish grin.

"Excuse you! We *were* just fine," Porter exclaimed, "You better not have scuffed my Manolos, Stephen."

"We're doing just fine and how are y'all?" Emily responded, her teeth a white row of daisy's smiling easily up at Stephen.

A gravelly voice came from behind her, "Hey Lilly, how are you?"

"Oh, hi," Lilly said a bit startled. "I'm fine, Charlie, how are you doing?"

"I'm ok." He seemed taller in the daylight.

"What are you girls up to this evening?" Stephen asked wrapping an arm around Porter's shoulders confidently.

"We're going to dinner," Porter answered crisply, "with our mothers."

"Y'all are such good Southern women. It makes me proud just to look at you," Stephen said beaming over them like a farmer surveying his crops. "What about you Lilly? Are you joining these fine ladies?"

"No… I have to finish unpacking." She and Charlie shared a look and he smiled at her, a periwinkle explosion in her chest.

"Well that doesn't sound like much fun… does it Charlie?" Stephen said loudly as he nodded at Porter. She rolled her eyes and snuggled under his arm. She had apparently already forgiven him for scuffing her shoes.

"Not much fun at all." Charlie added, "Why don't you come out with us? We're heading to the lacrosse house, you can join us when you're done unpacking."

"Charlie Abbott, did I just hear you ask my roommate to go with you to the lacrosse house?" Emily gave Charlie a sassy, displeased look. "I'm sure you meant to ask her to dinner or something respectable," Emily directed the golden flash of challenge in her eyes.

"We could go to dinner?" he offered with a shrug.

Stephen put him in a headlock, "Lilly, you're going to have to excuse my friend here, he gets tongue tied when talking to a beautiful lady. He's from Colorado and doesn't know any better. What he meant to say was, 'Lilly, I'd like to request the pleasure of your company for dinner this evening. I realize it is late notice and we have only just met but I'd like to get to know you better and possibly take you on a personal tour of our fine University.'"

Lilly laughed as the boys roughhoused and exchanged friendly jabs.

Emily answered on Lilly's behalf, "That sounds delightful, although because it is such late notice, you'll have to give her until seven o'clock this evening to get ready for your date."

Charlie and Lilly just looked at each other and smiled sheepishly.

"Charlie will be at your dorm to pick you up promptly at seven o'clock this evening. He'll text you from the lobby when he arrives," Stephen responded with a punch to Charlie's ribcage. "Isn't that right Charles?"

Charlie grinned and punched Stephen back playfully, "That sounds great. I'll see you at seven, Lilly?"

She laughed, "That would be great. I'll see you then."

"I'm so glad we could have this conversation just the two of us," Charlie said rolling his steely blue eyes.

"It's much more intimate this way," Lilly joked. He held her gaze for an extra beat and she blushed, another tiny implosion making her heart soar.

The group then split directions, the guys walked right toward the lacrosse house West of campus as the women walked left past the East lawn and back to Crawford House.

As they entered the dorm Emily linked her arm through Lilly's. She said, "Just what would you do without me? We're going to have to be friends, just so I can make sure men treat you like a lady."

"Change the world, not the woman, Emily," Lilly replied firmly.

4. FIRST DATE

That evening Lilly got ready for her date with Charlie. She pulled on her favorite summer dress. The floral embroidery suddenly seemed faded and worn. Looking at Emily's cashmere sweater sets, crisp white button downs, and chic silk dresses Lilly felt underdressed and more than that, she felt deprived. She wasn't usually this insecure, but everywhere she looked she was confronted by Emily's considerable wealth.

Celia walked in and asked, "Lil, are you alright?" Her voice rippling through the room. "Want me do your hair and make-up before you go out?"

"Really?" No one had offered to do her hair before. Celia's question seemed to tap into a maternal void Lilly didn't even know existed inside herself.

"Sure. I'm like an underwire, I support you," Celia said with her eyebrows raised comically.

Lilly laughed, she wasn't going to say no. In what felt like minutes, Celia had pulled Lilly's hair into a quick up-do and freshened her face with the make-up Emily had left out on her desk.

"Thank you so much!" Lilly was impressed by the striking image she saw reflected in the mirror.

"You're welcome. Now let's go shake down Porter for some shoes." Celia said as she looked disapprovingly at Lilly's well worn flip flops. "You need to mix the high with the low," Celia explained delicately.

Turning away from the mirror, "What do you mean high with the low?" Lilly asked.

"Oh goodness," Celia was taken aback but explained patiently, "High fashion mixed with low fashion can create interest and dimension in your style."

"Oh," Lilly was still lost, it was like Celia was speaking Mandarin.

"Like your dress is bohemian and casual. If we match it with some shoes or a bag it should punch it up a bit so it enhances your look but still communicates your personal style."

"It sounds good," Lilly said with a shrug, adding, "but I don't think Porter will want to share her stuff again tonight."

Celia waved off the comment, "Oh, bless her heart, she needs to learn to share."

Lilly raised an eyebrow suspiciously, "You say, bless your heart, but it doesn't sound as nice as it sounds, you know?"

Celia laughed, gentle comforting waves beat upon the shores of Lilly's ears. "Bless your heart can mean anything. It's versatile and fluid, it's the southern woman's 'fuck you.' We like to say things with a little more elegance and grace down here."

Lilly liked that answer a lot. "Celia, may I ask you a question?"

"Sure, Lady, what is it?"

"What's the deal with Emily trying to ingratiate herself to me?"

Celia gave a knowing nod and exhaled. "Emily's just trying to get a jumpstart on life. Her mama told her this summer that they're grooming her to take over her company after business school and Emily takes that responsibility very seriously."

"What does her mom's company do?"

"Joan Parker PR. It's a big deal here in Nashville and they're big shoes to fill. Mrs. Parker doesn't just know everyone, she knows everyone who counts. Everyone adores her and wants to be like her. Mrs. Parker is an icon and a visionary in Nashville." More thoughtfully, Celia added, "I just think

Emily wants to make sure she does justice to that tradition."

Lilly's brow furrowed, "By using me?"

Celia bit her lip, "Not exactly, I think Emily just wants to surround herself with the best and most brilliant people." Celia smiled, "It's actually quite a compliment."

Lilly nodded but didn't say anymore. She had yet to determine if it felt like a compliment to her.

Emily and Porter came into the room, dressed for dinner. There was a commotion behind them, as the Southern mothers entered the cramped dorm room a flurry of greetings and glittering energy. There were now seven people crushed into a room designed for two.

"Hi y'all, we wanted to see what the dorm was like," Celia's mother announced, her hair wildly spiked in a daring silver pixie cut.

"Mama, don't judge," Celia scolded giving her mother a patronizing look.

"I know, I know." Her mother waved a hand dismissively. "I just wanted to see what y'all had signed up for here," her mother answered with a wry smile.

Lilly's mother arrived, but finding no available space in the room, stood awkwardly in the doorway. All at once a chorus of, 'Hello Mrs. Carters,' filled the room. Melanie responded cordially as the women introduced themselves and invited her to join them for dinner.

Melanie's decline was polite yet firm. Then she saw Lilly and asked incredulously, "Lil, are you going to dinner with them?"

In the excitement of getting ready for her date Lilly had totally forgotten that her mom and Sophia were still in town. Lilly's voice came out guilty and weak, "I'm not going to dinner with them. I have a date." Lilly wished the girls and their mothers would go before things became any more uncomfortable.

Emily's mother cut in, "Y'all are sure we can't convince you to join us for supper?"

"It's kind of you to ask but we're going to have to say no this time," Melanie answered politely. *She's really putting on a good show,* Lilly thought.

"Well, Ladies, we better get going if we're going to make our reservation," Mrs. Parker announced, reading the energy in the room expertly.

"Have a good night. Lil, I want to hear all about it when we get back." Emily said with a smile as they all filed out of the room.

After they had gone Melanie began, "I just stopped by to see if you wanted to order Chinese with Sophia and me."

"Oh, where's Sophia?" Lilly asked trying to break the tension.

Melanie spoke coldly, crossing her arms, "We couldn't find a place to park so she's sitting with the car so it doesn't get towed."

"Oh." Lilly felt intense guilt, her intestines twisted roughly with the sensation.

They were still standing there, awkwardly not talking, when Charlie knocked on the open door. Lilly felt her heart flip at the sight of him.

"Hey, Lilly, the girls let me in. They told me where I could find you." Turning immediately to Lilly's mother, he said, "Good evening, you must be Mrs. Carter, I'm Charlie Abbott. It's a pleasure to meet you." He stuck out his hand.

Melanie refused to uncross her arms and greet Charlie.

He seemed unsure of how to respond to Melanie's behavior but dropped his hand and smiled anyway, ignoring the slight. Lilly was relieved that he kept talking instead of giving Melanie the attention she wanted. "I haven't been inside this dorm since freshman year! It looks like they did a lot of work to improve it," Charlie said brightly looking around the room. "This is a great place to live. You really lucked out, I had to live on the other side of campus my freshman year, I was late to all of my classes." Charlie laughed comfortably.

Lilly smiled and asked, "Charlie, would you please give us a minute?"

"Sure thing, I'll just wait down the hall. Nice meeting you Mrs. Carter." He walked out.

Lilly waited a few seconds before talking, hoping he wouldn't hear her. "Mom, may I go out on a date with Charlie? He's really nice and I'd like to go," she asked in measured deliberate tones.

Melanie didn't respond. She stood obstinately in the center of the room. Her presence a severe granite obelisk obstructing all movement.

"If you really want, I can go back to the hotel with you and we can get Chinese," Lilly continued desperately, her voice hollow. Melanie seemed to absorb everything, Lilly's happiness, the noise in the room, it was all silently sucked into Melanie.

Still no answer.

"Mom, he's waiting for me so if you don't want me to go I need to go and tell him that."

Melanie looked at her daughter like she had slapped her, *finally a reaction of some kind.*

"What do you want me to do, Mom?" Lilly pleaded. She was almost wishing her mother would say 'no,' so she could be mad. Lilly hated feeling so vulnerable. She twisted the ring on her finger roughly.

A group of freshman walked past the open doorway. Their effervesce bubbling over in crystal laughter. Lilly wished she could join them, disappear into the orange evening light and never look back. But Melanie's rocky presence demanded her attention. Silent and still, she would not be ignored.

Melanie said, "Go on your date."

"What?" Lilly was startled by the answer.

"Go."

"Are you sure?" Lilly stammered.

Melanie repeated, uncrossing her arms and gesturing with a careless hand, "Go on your date. Just remember, your sister and I have to be back on the road tomorrow by two."

"Thanks Mom." Lilly hugged her mother. Melanie withstood the embrace with a rigid spine, her arms straight at her sides. "Do you want me to walk you out to the car?" Lilly asked brightly feeling joy slip back into the room.

"That would be nice, you haven't seen your sister all day," Melanie added sharply.

"I'll say hi," Lilly answered indulgently. "I just need to tell Charlie," she swiftly exited on light feet, barely able to contain her excitement.

Charlie looked relieved when Lilly met him at the end of the hall.

"I'm just going to walk my mom out and then I'll meet you in the lobby."

"Sure," Charlie agreed. "Mind if I share the elevator with you?"

"Not at all," Lilly was light as a bubble.

"I'll meet you in the elevator lobby," Charlie added.

"Ok, I'll go grab my mom." Lilly stepped quickly, trying not to run back to the room to collect her mother.

Once in the elevator lobby Charlie pressed the call button and they quietly waited for the elevator to come. Charlie rocked comfortably in his shoes. "Did you enjoy your day on campus Mrs. Carter?"

"It's Ms." Melanie corrected as the elevator dinged to announce its arrival.

Lilly bit her lips and sank her shoulders. Melanie was not going to make this an easy victory. Lilly made eye contact with Charlie nervously but he seemed unmoved by Melanie's rudeness.

"Excuse me, Ms. Carter," Charlie held the doors to the elevator open so the two women could enter first. He boarded after them and pressed the button for the first floor. They rode down in silence. When the elevator opened Charlie again held the doors and waited for them to exit before following.

"I'll just walk her to the car and I'll be back in a minute," Lilly instructed.

"Ok," Charlie nodded and walked back to the lobby of Crawford House. Lilly would not blame him if he left before she retuned. In fact, she might judge him if he stayed after witnessing her mother's behavior.

At the car, Lilly hugged Sophia. "You're not coming with us?" Sophia asked with confusion. The air, like tepid bath water swirled around them, the sky was a brilliant fuchsia.

"I have a date," Lilly said awkwardly. "I'm sorry I didn't get to see you today," she said sincerely to her sister.

Sophia shrugged, "No worries. You're ditching me anyway," she kidded.

"Sorry," Lilly said with a frown. Now that she had seen Sophia she was hesitant to go.

"Go on your date already. You can tell me about it tomorrow."

"Ok," Lilly hugged her. "I'll see you guys tomorrow at lunch." Speaking to her mother's back she said, "Bye Mom."

Melanie waved a hand without turning around.

Lilly walked into Crawford House. The lobby was a large atrium with brick walls, a wooden welcome desk, and a central station with entrances facing campus on the opposite wall. She found Charlie sitting in a fabric-covered chair staring at his phone.

"Ready to go?" she asked.

"Yes. Let's go." He pocketed his phone.

It was another warm night. Lilly silently admired the beauty of the campus, she was totally enamored with her new school. The smell of purple wisteria, the muggy Southern heat - Lilly was in love.

As they walked Charlie made polite conversation. "It was nice to meet your mom."

Lilly said, "Sorry about her, my mom's kind of..." she wasn't sure how to finish the sentence. Lilly shook her head. "She's just an asshole."

Charlie burst out laughing.

"What?" Lilly looked up at him quizzically.

"You're so candid," Charlie smiled, "I like it."

"Good," Lilly said frankly.

"So, is it just you and your mom?"

"And my sister, Sophia," Lilly added. Looking up at him trying to measure his reaction, "It's just the three of us."

"What happened to your dad?"

"Really? Do they have no boundaries where you come from?" She quipped, sliding easily into misdirection rather than showing vulnerability.

"Sorry," Charlie said sincerely.

Checking herself and attempting to be more open, she shared, "He's in Vermont. He does something with city administration, I don't really know. What about your family?"

"Mom, Dad, brother, me, we're not that interesting." He said, "This is my car," as he opened the door to a hunter green Jeep Wrangler for her. "The restaurant's only a couple miles away."

"Thank you," Lilly said as she sat down on the leather seat. The car was spotless. It still had that new car smell. She took a deep breath of the chemical cleanliness. Leaning back she rested her skull on the headrest as he made his way back around the car to the driver's seat. Charlie climbed inside, the car felt smaller with his large frame seated beside her.

"Tell me about where you grew up," Charlie suggested as he pulled out of the parking space.

"I grew up in Cleveland. It's in Ohio."

"I know where Cleveland is," he said, teasingly.

"Sorry, it's not a big town."

"I may look pretty but I'm not stupid." Charlie smiled, he was flirting with her.

She laughed.

"You know, I'm really smart," he assured her with a smile.

"You say that, but Margaret Thatcher would say, 'Being powerful is like being a lady...if you have to tell people you are, you aren't.'"

"Oh, wow, was that a political burn?" he asked, looking away from the road with a grin.

"It was," she laughed. Changing gears she asked, "How did you end up in Nashville?"

"My mom grew up in Nashville and we have a lot of extended family here. Stephen and I, we've known each other all our lives so he convinced me to apply."

"And you're pre-law?" She recalled from their conversation the night before.

"Yes," he said with a smile.

"Why pre-law?" Lilly asked with interest, trying to figure him out.

"I'm technically a history major. Law schools want you to know how to research and write and history seemed interesting," Charlie explained. "What about you, art and math, right?"

"Yeah, right now I'm an art history and mathematics major but I don't think that's where I'll stay. I need to make a living after I graduate and I don't know what kind of job I can get in art history," she said honestly.

"Why'd you register for it if you're already going to change it?" He asked seriously.

Lilly took a deep breath, trying to decide how honest she wanted to be with him. *She had nothing to lose and really.* "Art is my dream. It's what I'd study if I had all the money and all the time in the world." She laughed, "But since I don't have either of those, I will probably switch to computer science." She smiled sheepishly. *He'd find out sooner or later that she was poor, might as well get that out of the way now.*

"If you change majors to computer science, what would you want to do?" Charlie asked with sincerity.

"Hopefully, I'll graduate and have a job," Lilly said.

"That is the goal, isn't it?" Charlie asked rhetorically.

As they entered the restaurant Charlie explained, "This is the Hermitage Hotel's bar. I thought we'd get a drink first and then head over to City

House for dinner."

"Cool." Lilly looked around the paneled walnut walls. The room smelled of seared steak and mushrooms, Lilly's stomach rumbled.

Once seated, he ordered, "I'll have a Ciroc straight and she'll have a sweet tea. Is that ok?"

"That's perfect." Lilly sighed relieved she didn't have to explain that she was underage.

"So, you never really answered my question," he said.

"What question?"

"Your plan, if you switch to the computer science major, what do you want to do with it?"

"Well, I plan to graduate, possibly, with a Master's degree in five years. In the interim I plan to launch a company that I can either grow myself or sell for a profit. Then, I'll most likely head out to California to work at a tech start-up. What about you?"

He answered frankly, "Well, I graduate in two years. Then law school at Stanford," he rubbed his palms on his thighs and looked down for a brief moment, then looked up to catch her eyes. "At least that's the dream," he said with a shrug.

She nodded her approval.

Their drinks were served and the waiter disappeared.

He asked, "What kind of company are you starting?"

"A software company," Lilly answered. "Right now I'm building the software. I need to work on a project to keep my scholarship, so why not build a company?" Lilly said plainly as if most students did so.

"Well I wish you luck, that sounds awesome," Charlie smiled warmly at her.

"Thank you," she answered primly.

"Ready?" He asked, draining his glass.

She agreed quickly, taking a gulp of sugary tea, "Yes."

Leaving the bar they headed to the restaurant. It was all so smooth. Charlie held doors, put out his arm for her to take, and stood whenever she left or joined the table. It was as if they were in a well rehearsed play. No sooner did Lilly recognize that she had a need or a want than someone arrived to meet it. Lilly was impressed but kept her wonder to herself, she didn't want Charlie to know she was totally inexperienced.

At dinner he said, "We'll start with the oysters?" He looked to Lilly for confirmation.

She nodded her agreement.

After the waiter walked away, Charlie asked, "Do you mind if I order for you?"

"It's fine," she said, relieved to have the pressure off of her. Ordering was one less thing she had to manage as she tried to mimic the things the other women in the room were doing, crossing their legs at the ankle, sipping drinks, and smiling politely. They all seemed to have manicured nails and hair that held its shape even after they laughed. Lilly placed her hands in her lap and tried not to fidget with her ring.

Charlie continued, "I usually ask beforehand but we were talking and I forgot. I know, it's outdated, but if you met my mother, you'd understand."

Lilly was curious, "Are you close with your parents?"

"I'm close with my Dad," Charlie explained adjusting his napkin. "My mom can be a little much," he added with a grin.

"I know the feeling," Lilly agreed with comfortable disappointment.

"So, what did you do this summer?"

"I fixed computers. I write code and stuff like that," talking about things she understood was soothing to Lilly. She felt some of the tension in her spine release as she spoke, "What about you?"

"Well, mostly just played lacrosse. I'm team captain this year, which is cool."

"Was that part of why you chose Vanderbilt?" Lilly asked.

He spoke in an honest monotone, "I'm a legacy. I own the lacrosse team. I can do whatever I want and there really are no consequences."

"Oh!" His frankness startled her. She shifted uncomfortably in her seat. A waiter delivered food to the table next to theirs and a paunchy woman sent back a salad with too much dressing. His entitlement was repulsive. She tried to salvage the conversation and her opinion of him. "Do you get into a lot trouble?" Lilly raised a challenging eyebrow.

"I don't but I like having the option. It's kind of cool, to feel like you can do anything and get away with it."

Lilly nodded. It didn't sound very cool to her but she kept that opinion to herself.

The oysters came on a bed of ice. The waiter deposited them at the center of the table and quickly disappeared.

Charlie asked, "Have you had these before?"

"No." Her hands were still folded in her lap and she leaned in with her shoulders to inspect the dish.

"Ok, now some people will tell you that oysters are an aphrodisiac," he put up a hand to quell her invisible protest. "Don't think that just because we're alone you can take advantage of me."

Lilly laughed again, unleashing a loud cackle. The laugh was of shrill relief. At least he didn't take himself that seriously.

Charlie's face took on a stern look. "Ok, give me your hand." Lilly put her hand in Charlie's feeling the texture of his skin for the first time. She could feel the rough edges of his calluses from lacrosse. He grabbed an oyster by the shell and placed her fingers around the edges gently applying pressure to assure her grip. "Be careful, the edges can be sharp. Do you like hot? Like spicy?"

She shook her head, "No."

"Ok," Charlie cleared his throat, "we'll just put lemon on your first one." With surgical precision, Charlie loosened the flesh of the oyster from its icy shell with a fork. He then squeezed a fresh lemon over the oyster and Lilly's fingers letting the juice drip into the shell and down to Lilly's wrist, "You just tilt your head back and let the oyster slide into your mouth."

Lilly looked at him skeptically.

"Go ahead," he coaxed.

Lilly tipped her head back and felt the oyster slide into her waiting mouth. She took two quick bites, swallowed, and shook her head with a chill. "Slimy!"

Charlie then handed her his champagne flute. "Take a sip, the bubbles make it better." Lilly obeyed,, enjoying the mixture of flavors for the first time, the rich saltiness of the oyster, the cool freshness of the wine. It was heavenly. After drinking, she handed the glass back to Charlie, he reached across the table and wiped her chin where the lemon juice had dripped down her face with his thumb. "May I?" he asked softly, his breath a heady whisper.

Lilly was confused but answered, "Yes."

Charlie then stood up over the table, wrapped his hand around her neck and pulled her face to his and kissed her. The kiss surprised Lilly but she kissed him back enjoying the hard and passionate pressure of his lips on hers.

When their lips parted Charlie leaned back, and sat down, "I told you these things were dangerous."

Lilly was surprised to silence.

"Do you like them?" he asked referring to the oysters with a hand.

"They're good, salty," she agreed rubbing the back of her hand across her mouth, wiping away any residue of lemon juice and still feeling the coolness of her lips where his kiss had been.

They both laughed, he comfortably, she nervously. He reminded her of Emily, someone entitled doing everything in their power to get exactly what they wanted and getting it.

5. STRATEGY

The next morning Lilly awoke to the golden sunlight illuminating Emily primly reading at her desk. Emily looked up from her iPad as Lilly stretched.

"Good morning," Emily said with a sweet Southern lilt.

"Morning," Lilly growled with a raspy voice, still heavy with sleep.

Emily asked, "How was your date?"

"It was good," Lilly answered as she rubbed her eyes and came to life. "We went to the Oak Bar and then City House, it was really nice."

"Oh wow, The Oak Bar, that's a nice date." Emily sounded impressed, which satisfied Lilly. "He must be trying to impress you."

"Oh, yeah?" Lilly asked stretching her arms wide like angel's wings and yawning out loud.

"The Oak Bar is a Nashville institution, everybody who's anybody goes there," Emily explained. "Did you see anyone famous?"

"Not that I recognized," Lilly said, scratching her head and running her fingers through her long auburn hair, pulling out several tangles with her fingers.

"Think you'll go out again?"

"Maybe," Lilly answered feeling goose-bumps on her legs just thinking about seeing him again. She kicked off the covers quickly and walked to the sink to start brushing her teeth. She squeezed a pea sized dollop of generic grey-blue toothpaste onto her brush and went to work on her teeth as Emily talked.

"Why wouldn't you?" Emily asked. "Charlie Abbott is a great match. He's intelligent enough to keep up with you. He obviously wanted to impress you and from the looks of that smile, he did."

Lilly tried to stop grinning as she brushed her gums but failed, only to have white toothpaste and saliva dribble down her chin. She caught it with her opposite hand and went to the sink to wash up.

Emily sighed deeply at Lilly's lack of refinement and kept talking, "If you had a good time, why wouldn't you go out again?"

"He's nice," Lilly said as she wiped her mouth on her towel. She then ran her wet fingers through her hair again and tried not to imagine him pulling it as he kissed her. Coming back to reality she said, "But he has a lot of money," case closed.

Emily's eyebrows arched defensively.

"Not that that's a bad thing," Lilly clarified for Emily's benefit. "I just mean we probably won't have a lot in common."

"How do you know that?" Emily asked putting down the iPad on her desk and staring Lilly down with tiger's eyes.

Lilly sat down on her bed, "In my high school there were a lot of girls with money and some people, like me, who didn't have anything. It's really difficult to maintain relationships with people who are constantly outspending you."

"I don't know," Emily replied tilting her head slightly, "I think a lot has to do with who you are and if you get along. If you really like him and he likes you, you shouldn't let the fact that he has money stop you from being together. I happen to think you and Charlie are very well matched." Emily said confidently.

"Why is that?" Lilly asked skeptically.

"Your star is rising Lilly. You're the Wilson Scholar and a variety of opportunities are going to open up to you. But you don't know the first thing about decorum... or fashion." Emily looked Lilly up and down with an unimpressed gaze. "And Charlie can help you. His mama comes from a prominent Nashville family."

"Right." Lilly measured her words, trying not to sound defensive. "But I'm here because of my intelligence, not because I'm some pageant winner. And I plan to do more than just date a guy and pick up an Mrs."

Emily stood up, "I'm not saying you should only be together because you could help one another. I'm just saying that a little polish might go a long way."

Lilly remembered a conversation with her mother, "You think you're better than us," Melanie had shouted. She was drunk and everything relating to her was 'us' to Lilly's, 'them'. It had always been this way with her mother. Lilly didn't know how to respond, even now, *did she think that? Did Emily think that Lilly could be made better somehow? And what was better? Was it dating this boy who thought he could ask for anything and get it? How was that better than before? Better than her family, better than the tiny house she grew up in with its cracked linoleum floors? And better than what she had known just because it was different? Was different always better?*

"How would I help him?" Lilly asked interested in Emily's strategy. She did have to give Emily some credit she had manipulated her connections to get Lilly as her roommate. And based on what Emily had said before she wanted to be around Lilly to benefit from her success, if that was the case, she wouldn't want Lilly to fail or date someone who would distract her from her goals.

"Well, Charlie Abbott isn't all perfect." Emily added conspiratorially, moving to her own bed so she could whisper and still be heard. "His mama is Nashville royalty, all about appearances, but his Daddy's from Colorado. He has tons of money but doesn't care a bit about decorum." Emily shared with suggestive eyebrows.

Lilly asked defensively, "How do you know all this?"

"I do my research." Emily shrugged harmlessly and pursed her lips. "Anyway, Charlie would benefit from spending some time with you. A nice girlfriend would keep him grounded and it couldn't hurt for him to attend some events with you. He should be networking if he wants to go to law school here in Nashville." Emily raised one shoulder and suggested, "It could be good for the both of you."

Lilly rolled her eyes and shook her head from side to side, "It was just a date."

Emily changed her tone to a careless full volume, "See where it goes. He could surprise you."

Lilly rolled her eyes.

That afternoon, Melanie and Sophia picked Lilly up for lunch. The three of them drove to a pizza place near campus. There were weathered wooden picnic tables outside etched with the emblems, insults, and messages of students past. They ordered lemonade and sat in the shade of two overlapping faded navy blue umbrellas. Birdsong filling the cramped spaces between clouds of stuffy August air.

"So, do you like it so far?" Sophia asked, her toes dancing under the table inside her hand-me-down tennis shoes.

Lilly thought for a second and answered, "I guess. The people are nice." She was squinting at the bright sunlight as it peaked through a radiant silver cloud.

"When do your classes start?" Melanie asked toying with the red striped straw in her drink.

"Classes start on Monday," Lilly said with a sigh. Lilly was eager for her classes to begin. She wanted to know what she was up against and she wouldn't know that until she had a syllabus in hand and had met her professors.

"How many classes did you register for, high faluten college girl?" Melanie asked, swirling the ice in her drink with the plastic straw.

Lilly propped her elbows on the tabletop and gritted her teeth, willing herself to remain calm, she would not let her mother get to her. "I'm in five right now. Renaissance Art, Form and Composition, Statistics, French, and a Computer Science class I could probably teach."

"If you could teach it why are you taking it?" Sophia asked casually, taking a sip of her lemonade.

"I have to keep my scholarship and I don't know how hard Vanderbilt is going to be; I don't want to get in over my head," Lilly shrugged.

"You're not really challenging yourself," her mother observed.

Lilly hated when her mother sporadically showed up and tried to be a parent. Melanie was never consistent and the intrusive orders were always insulting. Lilly sat up straight and squared her shoulders, "It's the first semester. I'm in a competitive honors program and I have no idea what the course load will be like," Lilly said firmly, trying not to feel defensive.

"I just hope you're not limiting yourself," her mother added suggestively and then delicately took a sip of her drink.

Lilly hated that her mother knew exactly how to get under her skin. It infuriated her because Lilly would react angrily, unable to respond to a single insult without addressing the years of emotional warfare her mother had raged upon her. And Melanie would play innocent, like she hadn't done anything. Lilly spoke coldly, "I'm not limiting myself. I've never been to college before and I don't know what to expect. If I take all of my hardest classes now and I fail, I lose my scholarship. If I lose my scholarship I don't get a degree. If I don't get a degree I don't get a job. And if I don't get a job, I can't pay back my loans, and if that happens, all of this was a waste of time and my money."

"I'm paying for this too," Melanie said sharply looking up from her drink in a flash. "You fell ass backwards into the butter-tub, you better not mess this up."

Lilly spoke deliberately, her fingers knotted around each other in frustration. "The Wilson Scholarship—which I earned—covers my classes, room, and board but it does not pay for books or my computer. Signing my name to loan paperwork is not you paying for this. I'm the one who pays the loans back. I'm the one who goes to school and does all the work. I'm the one they will come after if I don't pay them back. So, no, you're not paying for this too."

Her mother looked like something had stung her, her mouth frozen in a stiff purple pout, but she didn't say anything more.

Lilly continued, "It's fine if you want to tell grandma and your friends that you paid for my education, I don't care. But don't sit in front of me and lie about how much you've sacrificed or done for me. I earned this. I'll pay for it. I'm doing it all on my own, just like everything else." Lilly was proud of her speech but she didn't dare smile. She tried to conceal her self-satisfaction and bit the inside of her cheek to keep from showing her pride.

"Pizza's here," Sophia said loudly, happy to change the subject as a waiter slid the pizza onto a metal riser positioned in the middle of the table.

The tension eased as they ate and had dissipated by the time Sophia and Melanie left. Lilly said goodbye to her family at the car, opting to walk back to campus alone. The car pulled away with its familiar shaky rattle, reminding Lilly of how grateful she was that the car was leaving without her in it. As the green Ford Taurus disappeared from sight Lilly felt a freeing calm spread through her body. She was excited for her new beginning and to be on her own—finally.

When Lilly got back to the room Emily was tapping loudly on her iPad.

"You know, that screen should recognize your tapping even if you do it a lot lighter," Lilly hinted.

"I know, but it's not doing what I want," Emily said with frustration.

"What's wrong with it?"

"I don't know! I hate these things!" Emily threw the iPad on the bed.

"Is it broken?"

"Probably, it keeps freezing," Emily complained.

"Do you want me to try to fix it?"

"Do you know how? Do you have one?" Emily asked hopefully.

"No, I don't have one, but I did a lot of work on these this summer. It was my job," Lilly added, her fingers already itching to play on Emily's iPad.

"You can look at it but all of my calendar entries are gone," Emily said, already resigned as she flipped open her laptop.

Lilly picked up the iPad from the bed and sat down, "What's happening?"

"It was working fine but all of my calendar entries just totally disappeared," Emily said with exasperation as she reapplied her lip gloss.

"Did you try deleting the mail profile and setting it up again?"

Emily's face registered confusion. "No."

"Ok, let me try that," Lilly's fingers moved deftly over the screen, closing tabs and windows, her face relaxed with complete calm and focus. Lilly waited patiently for the iPad to follow her commands, giving it time to reboot before she explained, "Ok, I reset it," Lilly handed the iPad back to Emily. "You just need to test it out. Try opening your email, check your schedule, and make sure it's working."

Emily toyed with the iPad, "It's not working," she deadpanned.

"Let me see it," Lilly said, grabbing the iPad from Emily's disappointed grasp. Lilly liked solving puzzles she would not be bested by a machine. "Tell me what's happening."

"The email starts to work and then stops. My contacts and calendar appointments are all syncing but after a minute they all just disappear," Emily said as she got up and started looking over Lilly's shoulder; she wasn't convinced Lilly knew what she was doing.

Lilly took no notice of Emily's hovering, she was already deep in thought. "Ok, I see what you're saying. I have your calendar open in month view and I can see the appointments syncing and then they do just disappear."

"That's what I said," Emily replied condescendingly.

Lilly lifted both of her hands up into the air. "But look, if I don't do anything, it starts doing the same thing over again. See, they're syncing again... and now they're gone."

"So, what is it doing?" Emily leaned back and crossed her arms.

Lilly started tapping again, "It doesn't seem to know what it is doing. But your email and contacts are fine now. It's just the Calendar that's freaking out. Do you mind if I go through your meeting requests?"

"It's fine," Emily said coolly. "I was just trying to update my calendar with my class schedule and appointments."

Lilly perused the sync log on Emily's iPad. "You have a lot of appointments." Lilly skimmed the list looking at the size of the appointment requests. "This might be it!"

"What?" Emily asked with interest, stepping forward.

"Your mom sent you a meeting request?" Lilly asked, slightly amused by the absurdity.

"We have conference calls to catch up. We're both extremely busy," Emily said defensively.

"Ok," it was Lilly's turn to roll her eyes. "Well, it looks like she sent this meeting request with a 40mb file attachment."

"So?" Emily said with annoyance.

Lilly took a deep breath, "That's really big. I think that's why your calendar can't process anything else. Is it ok if I cancel this meeting to see if it works?"

"Sure." Emily crossed her arms.

"Here you go," Lilly said, minutes later, handing the iPad back to Emily

"That's it?" Emily asked with skepticism.

"I think so," Lilly said calmly, she was confident she had fixed Emily's iPad but didn't want to seem cocky. "Play with it for a bit and let me know if you have the same problem." Lilly crossed the room and flopped onto her bed to check her phone.

"That's awesome," Emily said happily. "Thank you so much." She joyfully clicked through and found her iPad completely fixed.

"It's not a big deal." Lilly said, not even looking up from her own screen.

"Are you kidding me?" Emily was beaming.

"I don't mind." Lilly smiled up at Emily.

After a minute of silence, Emily asked, "Did you work in addition to all of the extra-curricular activities at school or just during the summer?"

"I work when I can, so weekends, holidays, whenever. I was on scholarship in high school too, so I needed to make my own income to pay for books, my uniforms, and fees for clubs and sports," Lilly said calmly as she rolled over onto her side.

"What do your parents do?" Emily asked, she seemed to be humbled by the realization that she had never needed to work.

"My mom's a secretary for a veterinarian, and my dad's not involved. What do your parents do?" Lilly asked.

Emily gave her usual canned answer but seemed to notice for the first time that it sounded pretentious, "My Daddy's a named partner at Cain, Parker, Rochester, and Willoughby. It's a law firm he founded here in Nashville. And my mama is an event planner; she handles all the major events that come to the city."

"Your Dad and Porter's founded a law firm together?" Lilly asked to confirm what she already thought she knew.

"Yes," Emily answered, she looked away slightly embarrassed.

"That's awesome." Lilly said with false brightness to ease the tension. She then looked down at her phone and ignored Emily.

Emily was unsure of what to say. The only things that came to mind were either an apology or an effort to show that she had worked hard to get where she was too, but that felt disingenuous. She looked down and re-sent a meeting invite, albeit a much smaller version, to her mother.

6. FALL SEMESTER, AUGUST 2009

Lilly was meticulously prepared for her first day of classes. Notebooks, pens, and her backpack were all ready for her departure. Even though it was only the first day Lilly felt the pressure to perform and prove herself to her professors and her peers, she wanted them to know that the Wilson Scholar was someone to watch, someone who was going to do great things.

As she walked across campus, dodging the other students hustling to class, Lilly stared up at the giant trees and was almost hypnotized in the end of summer heat. She wondered if she had ever seen so many shades of green. Some shades were vibrant and neon, others deep and heavy. The air smelled of flowers and cologne, it was familiar and warm. Over her shoulder she heard, "Lilly Carter," and immediately felt a chill run through her body. She slowly turned around and with a smile she said, "Hi, Charlie."

"Where are you headed?" He asked casually.

"The library."

"Homework already?" He asked with a bemused grin.

"Just getting the lay of the land," she was mortified. *I can't believe I just said 'lay' to him.*

"I'll join you." His hands were at his sides and a green backpack was slung over his shoulders

"Really?" She asked with some shock and then added, "I can find it. You know, I'm really smart." She repeated his line from their date with a teasing smirk.

Charlie spoke at full volume, "I know, you are highly intelligent and distractingly sexy."

Lilly swallowed hard and turned to conceal her embarrassment and walked into the library. Charlie followed silently. She marched purposefully through the cavernous building. Three lefts, a right, she moved as though on a mission.

"What are you looking for?" he asked after ten minutes of casually following her lead.

"The perfect study spot," she answered seriously.

"Ah, those are hard to find," he agreed with a knowing nod.

"You study?" she asked arching an eyebrow unsure of whether he was mocking her or not.

"I study all the time. I like the idea of impressing people with my intelligence."

"Because you're pretty?" She asked sarcastically.

"Aw, you think I'm pretty?" he teased nudging her with his bulky shoulder.

Lilly rolled her eyes, "No law school legacy?"

"Oh, yeah, I could do that too. But where's the fun in that?" Charlie laughed lightly.

"You like fun a lot," Lilly said her lips in a severe line.

"There's other things I like, too." He grabbed her hand and pulled her toward the stacks, weaving between the rows seamlessly.

"Where are we going?" she asked in an urgent whisper as she followed him.

"Shh," he said over his shoulder with a smile, continuing to move ahead.

They walked to a darkened corner where he dropped his backpack. He slowly took the shoulder straps of her blue backpack off of her shoulders, staring intensely into her eyes the entire time. All Lilly could do was breathe. He put her backpack on the floor quietly and gently ran his hands around her waist. She could feel his fingertips grazing the skin above her shorts, his hand tenderly creeping under the edge of her white T-shirt. He pulled her to his body firmly with the same rough urgency of their kiss the other night. He kissed her deliberately. Taking his time and lingering over each sweet action. She kissed him back. She wanted him, wanted this, and feared it might end too soon again so she greedily kissed him until he pulled away. They breathed heavily and then he reached for her again his fingers in her hair and the smell of his woodsy cologne making her lightheaded. After what simultaneously felt like forever and a minute, he stepped away, picked up her backpack and put it back on her shoulders. He then put his own backpack on, "Well, this isn't it," he said and walked away.

Lilly laughed and covered her face with her hands as she followed him out of the library. She could not believe this was happening. She was not the kind of girl who goes to the library to make out. *Well, apparently she was now.*

After parting ways with Charlie, Lilly made her way to the Academic Advising building. As a scholarship recipient she was required to meet with an advisor each semester to discuss her classes and review her progress. They spoke on the phone before Lilly even left home and her advisor had already recommended a new professor, Eilene Hendricks, as a potential mentor. Lilly was scheduled to meet with Professor Hendricks in her office. Lilly was eager to discuss her project and talk through some of the ideas she had percolating in the back of her mind.

She found Professor Hendricks in a cramped and darkened office on the first floor of the Information Technology building. The light from the window behind the desk shadowed its occupant in silhouette. "Hi, I'm Lilly Carter," she said, hesitantly entering.

A strong and cool voice greeted her, "Lilly Carter, the Wilson Scholar, at last we meet. Please sit down." Professor Hendricks turned from the box of books she had been unpacking and gestured to a wooden chair currently occupied with a stack of even more books, "You can just move those to the floor," she added, sitting down herself with a youthful bounce.

There were scraps of paper piled all over Professor Hendricks's office and hanging folders stacked on the floor. Empty shelves on the bookcase to Lilly's right held knickknacks that were waiting to be put into order, porcelain elephants, a set of wooden bookends, and a decorative box with a pink pressed flower framed on the lid. Several pictures and a course schedule were tacked to a bulletin board on the wall.

"Excuse the mess. I'm just moving in now," the professor explained. Eilene Hendricks had a voice that seemed to roll like cool water over rocks. She had short natural hair and eyes that expressed her excitement as much as her full red lips.

Lilly said, "Thank you for meeting with me Professor Hendricks," as she stacked the books from the chair onto the floor and sat down.

"You can call me Eilene, Lilly."

"Ok, Thank you, Eilene," it sounded awkward as she said it. "May I call you PH instead?" Lilly asked impulsively.

"Sure," Professor Hendricks laughed. "That would be fine." Her laugh was like music but Lilly was too anxious to notice.

She dove in quickly, "My advisor didn't have a lot of specific information on your background. What field of study is your forte?"

"You mean your Google search was not sufficient?" PH said with a wry smile.

"No. I asked my advisor about your credentials, published works, and research projects and she was not forthcoming. She said that you have a background in technology?" Lilly was concerned with whether PH would be able to help her or not. She was excited to have a mentor but wary of someone with no background in technology.

"No," PH answered nonchalantly, "Actually, my background in technology is limited."

Lilly let out a disappointed exhale.

"I teach basic programming and application development, but my primary focus is in the business side of technologies and start-ups." PH radiated comfortable confidence.

"Oh," Lilly was startled. This was either excellent planning on behalf of the university or a fortuitous turn of events. Lilly wanted to launch a company before she graduated, it was her goal, and PH could be the key to making that goal a reality.

PH spoke further in the same reassuring tone. "My strengths are on the business side of things. I don't deal with products, although I'm happy to learn what they do, my strong suit is in selling them to bigger companies, investors, whatever." PH waved her hand to signify any number of things.

Lilly nodded, her heart racing with excitement.

"Your academic advisor told me you're writing a program to track changes and errors in an existing database." PH announced, encouraging Lilly to speak.

"Yes," Lilly was impressed that the University shared this information so quickly. "Right now it's a web application. There are three pieces, the web browser, where the program actually runs, it will have client side validation which I did using Java. That's where the user interacts and enters their password."

PH nodded approvingly, "It's much easier to write with a Java Windows application than a native Windows application, good choice."

Lilly smiled to herself but tried not to reveal how much she liked hearing her work praised. She talked through her budding grin, her hands moving like anxious birds giving expression to her thoughts, "The second piece is a web server that validates the input and sends an update request to the server. It has an additional service side validation. The third piece is the database, so once the user passes the two first interfaces, then they gain access to the database. Once there, my plan is to script triggers to run that see modifications made and write that data into a log for audit purposes. Basically, the application is used to provide security and decrease breaches in data."

PH nodded, "Where did this idea come from?"

"My mom works in a veterinarian's office and every time she has to update someone's financial information she needs to document when she modified the information and why in an excel spreadsheet which is redundant and annoying so I thought this might be a helpful solution that any company could use."

PH's hands were steepled under her chin as her elbows rested on the arms of her chair. "What's your motivation?"

Lilly was prepared to explain herself. "I'm interested in developing a program that transforms the supervisory nature of data entry. Instead of users being forced to monitor or report issues with a database, the database would automatically track changes and eliminate the need for additional reporting."

PH nodded, "I understand the premise. What is your motivation?"

Lilly's face revealed her confusion, "Why am I doing this?"

"Yes. Why have you made this your project?" PH leaned back in her seat, delicately placing her hands in her lap.

Lilly shifted uncomfortably in her seat and spoke quickly, "I think it's a valuable tool. Businesses, universities, and governments all require employees to report and track their work. This would eliminate that requirement making business more efficient and effective. Businesses would then be able to reallocate that time, manpower, and resources to other areas."

"Yes, I agree. That would be a valuable tool." PH placed her elbows on the desktop and leaned forward, "Why is this your problem?"

"Excuse me?" Lilly was exasperated. *She had answered the same question three times. Why was this professor not getting it?*

PH began to speak philosophically, leaning to the right, "There's a reason we do things in life. Oftentimes it's because we're running toward or away from something. If you're going to build a business out of this solution you need to know what motivates you."

Lilly nodded obediently.

"Do you understand what a catalyst is?" PH asked as though the thought just occurred to her.

Lilly was insulted. "I know what a catalyst is, I just don't know what you're asking."

"It's a basic question," PH said in her cool tone that was starting to grate on Lilly's nerves. PH asked, "Is your goal to make money?"

Lilly shrugged and spoke defensively, "Sure, I'd like to make money, eventually."

"Why, eventually?" PH pointed with her right hand.

"Because I'm just starting to work on this project," Lilly said as if speaking to a moron, "It's not ready to launch."

"Once you have that money what do you want to do?" PH raised her eyebrows.

Lilly pulled an answer out of thin air, "I don't know... travel?"

PH took a deep breath, "There's no wrong answer, Lilly. I'd like for you think about what you want to accomplish and why you want to accomplish it. I can help you. But I need you to fully understand what will be expected of you and I need to know that you're willing to make that commitment."

"Ok," Lilly agreed.

"How about this? You'll think about your motivation and what you want to accomplish so that the next time we meet we have some real substance to discuss. And I will organize this office so that you don't have to walk around piles to get to your seat. Fair?"

"Fair," Lilly nodded.

"Ok, just call me or shoot me an email and we'll schedule our next meeting."

Lilly smiled, "Thank you." She left PH's office confused, she wasn't sure what Professor Hendricks expected of her. Lilly had so much she wanted to accomplish, *how was thinking about motivation going to help?*

7. COMPETITION

Lilly was laying on her bed reading when Celia poked her head in the door, "Hey."

"Hey," Lilly answered, looking up from her book.

"What are you doing?" Celia said as she walked into the room squinting at the shafts of late morning light that illuminated every dust particle as if it were a spotlight reflecting off of a glitter storm.

"Reading *The Little Prince* in French, I have to write a report by Wednesday," Lilly explained from her position on her stomach, legs slowly kicking the air.

Celia jutted out a hip as she stood next to the bed. "I need a manicure, come with me."

"Oh, I can't afford that. Thanks," Lilly answered. She was flattered that Celia had invited her somewhere alone. Still, there were some luxuries that were not for her.

"You need a pedicure. I'm buying." Celia said with a smile.

"Did Emily put you up to this?" Lilly asked with a knowing smirk. She had caught Emily cringing when she put on her flip flops a couple days before. Sure, she didn't have a pedicure but it was a little ridiculous to think about the amount of money Emily spent on her personal hygiene.

Celia gave her a bemused smile, "Emily did mention the need for an intervention but I talked her down to a mani-pedi date so it's either you come with me now or she attacks you in the dead of night with a pumice stone." Celia added half-jokingly.

Lilly laughed, "You don't need to do that." She held up her book with an apologetic expression, "I really need to read this anyway."

"This isn't a conversation. Grab your bag, let's go," Celia ordered.

"Fine," Lilly said with waning resistance and a smile as she picked up her purse. "When did you get so bossy?"

"Only when I have to be," Celia said, with a genuine smile, "and only with my friends."

The nail salon was in the middle of a strip mall near campus. The other customers were women who epitomized the vision Lilly had of Southern women before she moved to Nashville. Most ascribed to the belief that the, "higher the hair the closer to God." The air smelled heavily of nail polish remover and lavender bubble bath.

Celia wrote their names down on the sign in sheet and immediately collapsed next to Lilly on a cream faux leather couch and began complaining about Porter. "It's super annoying. She just plays the same three chords on that guitar over and over. I am not kidding, it is terrible." Celia stopped talking to pick out a polish color from the display on the coffee table in front of them adding, "Bless her heart."

Lilly smiled at her friend's phrase, pleased to feel in on the joke now. "You don't think she'll make it?" Lilly asked, surprised by Celia's honesty.

"Porter's determined to be a country star. She's been writing music since we were kids. She loves music, loves musicians, all of it. She could make it."

"Really?" Lilly raised an eyebrow, she was skeptical of that possibility.

Celia shared, "She released a Christmas album a few years ago and it sold pretty well. She didn't get a lot of popularity out of it but she did get some local interest and critical recognition, which is huge."

Lilly nodded, she didn't know Porter had released an album already. That was impressive. As she thought more about it Lilly felt like she was wasting her time getting her nails done while Porter was working. She needed to work harder if she was going to launch a company by graduation she needed to stop wasting time.

Celia kept talking, "People adore Porter, she always gets what she wants."

Changing gears, Lilly waded into a topic she wasn't sure Celia would be open to discussing, "Celia, can I ask you something about Emily?"

"Sure," Celia turned to look at her with concern, her translucent lashes and eyebrows flashing.

"Why is she so determined to make me over?" Lilly asked cautiously, measuring her words to assure her question didn't sound confrontational.

Celia exhaled, "Emily is meticulous in her planning and deliberate in all of her social interactions."

"So, she won't be friends with someone who can't do something for her?"

"Not necessarily," Celia looked up to the pockmarked grey ceiling as she thought. "Ok, I'm going to be honest with you," Celia sat up and made deliberate eye contact, "When Emily asked her parents to make a donation to Vanderbilt she made one request: that her roommate be the Wilson Scholar. By her estimations, the Wilson Scholar is guaranteed to make an impact on the school and in the world. Emily wanted to capitalize on what was sure to be a beneficial arrangement."

"How did she know it would be beneficial? What if I hated her?" Lilly suggested.

"I don't know what her backup plan was, I just know that she strives to surround herself with brilliant and creative people. She wants all of her friends to be smarter or better than she is, it's like that saying, 'if you're the smartest person in the room, you're in the wrong room.' Emily never wants to be in the wrong room."

Lilly had never heard that phrase, she thought about it seriously. As she was thinking, a nail tech with a surgical mask over the bottom half of his face called them back to the pedicure stations with a wave. At their seats, hot water was already bubbling in the pink foot baths. Lilly relaxed into the worn massage chair and closed her eyes letting the jets pummel her feet. Celia reached over and clicked on the massage setting on the chair which worked its way up Lilly's back and down again. As the masked nail technician began scrubbing her feet with soap and a blue pumice stone, Celia shifted to face Lilly, "What about you, lady, how's your project?"

"It's ok," Lilly said unconvincingly. "I met with my mentor and she wants me to tell her what my motivation is for the project."

"Sounds deep," Celia said empathetically.

"Yeah, I think she wants a five year plan but I don't know what to tell her. Five years ago I didn't think I'd be here," Lilly waved her arm to indicate Nashville, Vanderbilt, and where they were sitting.

"Really?" Celia was genuinely surprised. "I always knew I would go to Vanderbilt."

Lilly read the surprise on Celia's face as judgment and backpedaled, "I mean, I knew I'd be at college somewhere. I just didn't know where."

"Huh," Celia said thoughtfully, "I thought you were more like Emily, twelve steps ahead of the rest of us."

Lilly was insulted. "I wish," she said honestly. "I spend more time figuring it out as I go than I'd like, it's like my major…"

Celia looked up from watching the tech push back her cuticles, "What's your major again?"

"Well, I'm going for a double major in mathematics and history of art, right now." Lilly explained.

"What's your hesitation? Why, 'right now'?" Celia looked back to her toes.

"I declared History of Art as my major but I don't think I'll stay with it," Lilly said, showing her despondence. The nail technician applied lotion to her feet and calves, massaging them with strong fingers.

Celia was confused, "Why wouldn't you stay with it?"

"It's not practical. What sort of job can I get with a history of art degree?" Lilly posed. "I could write. Maybe become a professor," Lilly shrugged.

Celia listened as she handed her card to the masked nail technician and indicated that she would pay for both girls.

Lilly continued, "I should focus on computers. I know how they work. I know how to write code; I'm actually pretty good at it. I just don't love it.

Coding would be a job but not a dream for me, you know?"

"And art history is your dream?" Celia looked up from the receipt she had just signed with a loopy signature.

"I don't know if it's my dream, like my happily ever after, dream." Lilly confided. "It's something I'm interested in that I don't know a lot about." Lilly kept talking as she thought more, "I find art fascinating because I don't understand it."

"And even though art is your passion, you think you'll switch to computers?" Celia's voice was sad.

"Yeah, it's the practical decision," Lilly said, making the switch from an emotional place to a logical one.

"Coding?" Celia exhaled with an eyebrow arched.

"Yeah, I won a couple hackathons in high-school," Lilly admitted quietly.

"Good for you, Lil!" Celia smiled broadly and then as if the thought just occurred to her, "Why don't you just do both?"

Lilly thought on that for several minutes and then as if apologizing to Celia she said, "I could. That would make me a triple major in history of art, mathematics, and computer programming."

"I didn't think of that," Celia admitted. Then more optimistically she suggested, "You know Lil you should just do what makes you happy."

The trouble was Lilly wasn't sure what would make her happy. Her happiness had never been a consideration before, it felt strange to think about it now.

That evening Lilly was sitting at her desk plodding through her stats homework when Emily walked into the room. The warm quiet zone immediately took on Emily's high-strung energy, and jarred Lilly out of her focused reverie. "Hey, Lil, this is Julie Evans, a friend of mine from class. Her iPad is acting up and I told her about how quickly you fixed mine the other day and she was wondering if you could take a look at hers."

Lilly looked up slowly. Julie had shoulder length blonde hair, a weak chin, and was wearing a Lilly Pulitzer blouse that billowed like a tent around her tiny frame. Julie smiled nervously at Lilly and spoke with a heavy southern accent, "I'm such a moron with these things. Do you mind taking a look?" She held out the iPad to Lilly.

Lilly hesitated a beat and looked at Emily like she was crazy.

Julie retracted her arm and moved to leave. "Oh! Of course, I'm sorry, I know you're super busy with school so if you don't have time."

"She'll pay you," Emily said sassily as though Lilly should be jumping at the chance. Then to Lilly she added, "Nice pedicure."

Lilly rolled her eyes, she mumbled, "Fine."

"Julie, she'll do it," Emily said more loudly to catch Julie before she walked out the door. "She just gets dramatic if you don't ask nicely."

Lilly gave Emily a death stare but took the iPad and went to work. Twenty minutes and fifty dollars later, Julie's iPad was fixed and Lilly had a new revenue source.

Word of Lilly's skills travelled quickly, mostly helped along by Emily's shameless and constant marketing, and soon a steady stream of students began asking for her help. The money was good even though payments could be inconsistent. She had one student who paid her in rolls of quarters his mother had sent for laundry. She didn't mind, money was money, and Lilly was happy to start building up her savings account. Lilly quickly began to operate like a business, charging more for recovering files at two in the morning or destroying files that students did not want to share with the Genius Bar or the campus help desk. Not only was her business growing but Lilly grew more and more confident in her skills and herself. The negativity that seemed to constantly surround her at home melted away as more people recognized her talent and turned to her for guidance and advice. She had found her place in the campus community, she felt necessary and important, someone who contributed in the best possible way. Secretly, she was proud of herself.

Charlie lived off campus in the lacrosse house. It had all of the typical trappings of a frat residence, lawn chairs in the living room, empty beer cans piled in a mountain spilling over the trash can, and the mingling of smells that could only be described as sweat, vomit, and car air freshener. The main floor was surprisingly tidy with patched and used furniture that somehow withstood the abuse of a rotating team. Photos on the walls and in the hallways were of players in suits, bow ties, and navy blue blazers. The bedrooms were filthy. Collections of bottles littered any horizontal space with piles of clothes on the floor and team flags covering the walls. There were beds lofted and unmade futons below. Charlie's room was no exception, the bed was usually unmade and aside from the familiar scent of his cologne it had the stale smell of gym socks and old carpet.

"Want to watch a movie?" Lilly asked from her perch on the foot of Charlie's bed.

"The truth?" Charlie joked. 'The truth' had quickly become their shorthand for something intimate and just between them. Even in a crowd it was an agreed on a secret message to each other.

"The truth," Lilly laughed.

"Not really. Want to play catch?" He asked hopefully picking up his lacrosse stick and cradling it absentmindedly.

"Too cold."

"It's sixty-five degrees outside in October!" He said incredulously. "You're from Cleveland not Florida, you should be outside in this weather."

"Just because you're never cold," she started sassily.

"Correction: I am always hot. I am not, 'never cold'." He said authoritatively.

"Same thing," she said rolling her eyes.

"False. Always hot implies that my body temperature is in a naturally heightened state, leaving me impervious to the onslaught of cold weather in Colorado. Never cold implies that I never feel chilly, which I sometimes do when I eat ice cream." Charlie continued on his diatribe, "The only challenge my finely tuned body temperature also creates an unpleasant state of overheating here in the sweat box that is Tennessee."

"Gross," Lilly said with disdain.

"I can't help it if I am physically superior to all other skiers. My body temperature is my super strength," he announced, flexing his muscles for her amusement.

Lilly rolled her eyes, "Is that why you're wearing that crop top?"

"It's not a crop top," Charlie said with an insulted tone. Speaking proudly, he informed her, "This, is a lacrosse jersey. It is my favorite shirt and you should be thanking me for the fabulous view of my abs from the cheap seats." He pointed at her with his lacrosse stick.

Lilly laughed out loud. "You're an idiot," she said and pushed the netted end of the stick away from her face.

He smiled back at her.

"Alright, let's play a game," she said definitively sitting up straighter.

"I won," he announced promptly tackling Lilly back onto the bed and kissing her. Lilly relaxed underneath him.

She said, "I have to go study."

"Oh really," he rolled onto his side with a disappointed sigh.

"Yeah," she kissed his cheek and pulled her sweater back down.

Charlie lightly slapped her butt as she walked out of the room.

Campus was still green and summery Lilly was loving the warm October air and breathed deeply as she strolled back to Crawford House. Lilly felt like she was hitting her stride. Classes were going well, she had a job, sort of, and she felt like she was where she was meant to be. Things with Charlie were going well. She lived in a general state of euphoria. Her tough exterior seemed to melt away without the constant worrying about her mother. Lilly could relax and she found herself laughing more and getting to know her self, the defensive mask she had presented to the world drifted away. Lilly enjoyed the normalcy of Vanderbilt. She found herself thriving in the predictability of her days. The simple joy of having and keeping her own schedule without the added responsibility to care and supervise her mother was freeing.

Back at Crawford House, Emily sat at her desk and Celia splayed over the bed like a discarded magazine as they talked.

"Hey," Lilly said as she dropped her keys onto her desk. She tossed her bag on the floor, and flopped onto the bed. She gave a heaving sigh and said, "What were you two talking about?"

"We're going to New York over break with our moms," Emily said uncomfortably, looking in Lilly's direction but slightly past her face.

"That sounds fun," Lilly said, trying to continue sounding cheerful and not to feel the pangs of jealousy rippling in her body.

"You could come, if you want?" Celia added hopefully.

"No, I don't want to intrude," Lilly said, feeling her heart swelling into her throat. The words rushed out of her mouth over-excitedly masking her true emotions.

"You wouldn't be intruding," Emily followed politely.

"You know what, I'd like to go, but I have my scholarship project and I need to make some progress on that," Lilly explained.

"Are you sure?" Celia asked, sensing the tension in Lilly's voice.

"Yeah, you guys will have a great time. I'm sorry I won't be able to join," Lilly felt heavy. She was making light of it for their benefit.

"Ok, well we've got to get to class," Emily said as she grabbed her bag and moved to leave with Celia.

"I'll see you guys later," Lilly said weakly allowing all of the energy to seep out of her body.

Celia gave Lilly a warm smile as she left. Lilly was still paralyzed on the bed when Porter swung the door open minutes later.

"Hey, did I miss Emily and Celia?" she asked.

"Yeah, they just left," Lilly said scratchily.

"What's wrong with you?" Porter asked suspiciously.

"Nothing," Lilly lied.

Always to the point, Porter said, "Spill. I'm already late for class and I don't have time to drag it out of you."

"They're planning a trip to New York with their moms and I'm not going," Lilly shared.

"Thank God, I hate going to New York with those two," Porter sighed as she dropped her bag and collapsed across Emily's bed.

"What do you mean?" Lilly laughed in spite of herself.

"Oh, they're obnoxious. They both try to out-spend each other and neither of them really wear designer clothes."

Lilly laughed again. "They're always wearing designer clothes."

"If you mean their clothes come from *A designer*, not necessarily a good one."

Lilly looked skeptically at Porter.

"I'm not kidding. Look at the two of them; they look like they fell out of some East Coast catalogue. Don't get me wrong, I love them both to pieces, but they're not exactly high-end designer girls. All they're doing is wasting their money on pieces neither of them will ever wear. It's annoying," Porter finished.

Lilly smiled, feeling cheered, "Thanks."

"Seriously, you dodged a bullet there. I'm so glad I wasn't here. Now I can come up with an excuse."

"Nice," Lilly said with a weak laugh.

"Ok," Porter got up off of the bed and grabbed her bag. "I'm going to class. You ok?"

"Yeah, I'm fine. Thanks for the talk."

"No worries. Later."

Porter's unexpected generosity of spirit gave Lilly new hope. *Just because she couldn't afford to do everything the other girls did, it didn't mean that they couldn't be friends. Isn't that what Emily said anyway?*

That evening Melanie called unexpectedly. "Come home and visit, we miss you," she chirped into the phone.

Lilly was suspicious. She silently pursed her lips. Her mother never wanted to see her and most certainly didn't miss her.

"You could come for Thanksgiving," Melanie said with her usual annoyed and accusatory tone.

In a weird way the inflection of her voice did strike a chord in Lilly. She didn't have anywhere to go anyway. "I could try to come home," she said hesitantly.

"That would be wonderful. Sophia and I miss you around here," Melanie added, sugar-coating her offer.

Lilly was skeptical of her mother's intentions but there was something in hearing her mother ask to see her that touched Lilly. It reached the hard little rock deep inside her gut that wanted to be loved, wanted a mother who remembered birthdays, and the way you like your eggs. Mom's like Emily's who sent care packages for no reason and took you on trips to New York just to go shopping. Lilly wanted that so much that she said, "Sure. I could rent a car and drive in for a long weekend."

"Great, I'll get a turkey we'll have some stuffing and mashed potatoes." Melanie sounded bright and happy.

Must be a new guy, Lilly thought to herself. "That sounds great, Mom. I can't wait to see you."

"I love you," Melanie sang into the phone.

"Love you too," Lilly said as she hung up with an unfamiliar lightness in her chest.

8. TURKEY DAY EVE

Everyone was meeting at the bar before heading home for the Thanksgiving weekend. For Lilly it was only her second time going out and she was actually looking forward to cutting loose before making the long drive home. She was in her dorm room organizing her notebooks from the past semester on the bookshelf above her desk. She had Pandora on and was dancing around the room as she worked. Celia knocked on the open door and laughed as she caught Lilly mid-twirl. Lilly's face reflected her surprise at being caught dancing but she quickly grabbed Celia's hand and pulled her into the room with a ballroom spin. When the song was done and the girls were breathless from dancing, Lilly walked to her computer to turn down the music. "What's up?" she asked.

"I was just returning this book I borrowed from Emily," Celia explained.

"She's still in her last final," Lilly shared. "You can just leave it on her desk. Oh," remembering something Lilly asked, "what are you wearing out tonight?"

Celia placed the book gently on Emily's desk and turned to face Lilly, "Actually, I'm leaving early."

"What do you mean you're leaving early?"

"My flight departs at five. Mama bumped up our departure so we could have some quality time together before Emily and her mom join us."

"But we were supposed to go out tonight," Lilly whined.

"You're going to have a great time and Charlie's going," Celia hinted.

"No, he has a lacrosse scrimmage," Lilly pouted.

"Are you sure? Porter said he and Stephen were coming," Celia said with a quizzical look.

"I don't think so," Lilly said grabbing her phone to check if Charlie had sent her any updates. Nothing from anyone, Lilly felt deflated.

"You're going to have a great time," Celia insisted as she re-tied a green silk bow in her hair. "If y'all need anything just holler at me." With that, Celia hugged Lilly and left.

Lilly spent the rest of the day coding furiously on her laptop. She had had a breakthrough the week before and was racing to build while her ideas were still fresh. It wasn't until Emily sprayed her with perfume and pushed her out the door that Lilly even looked up.

The bar was packed with students. A band played on stage as patrons jostled to get a drink and shouted to be heard over the music. The lead singer whipped her hair around and jumped from the front of the stage to the top of a speaker. Lilly admired her fearlessness. It was a great night to be out in Nashville and Lilly was happy to be a part of it. She was smiling to herself and started moving to the music.

Josh, a boy from Lilly's statistics class, gently touched her elbow to get her attention. She could barely hear him over the commotion.

She was leaning in to hear Josh more clearly when she saw Porter and Charlie step out of a darkened doorway. Porter was adjusting her shirt and smoothing her lipstick as Charlie pushed his hair into place and waited for Porter to lead the way out.

What were they doing in there together? In that brief moment, it was as though someone had sucked all of the air out of the bar. The room clicked to a stop and Lilly felt a silent moment of clarity. Charlie said he had scrimmages and wasn't going to be around. Yet, he was here and kissing Porter. Lilly turned over this new information in her mind slowly like a rock found in the woods, exploring it's smooth surfaces and jagged edges. He had betrayed her trust entirely. It was sad and for some reason inexplicably funny. She opened up to no one, trusted no one. She had let him in and he kissed her friend. She had clutched the rock too tightly and a sharp edge cut into her skin. The savage rawness was a familiar feeling, disappointment

76

and profound hurt. If Lilly was truthful with herself she could admit that this was the only possible outcome—she had known nothing but disappointment in her life. To think Charlie was different was laughable. She had been hopeful and idealistic—*how stupid of her.* The cut bled profusely but if she wrapped it tightly it could be stopped and concealed. If she filled herself with enough anger, there wouldn't be any room left to feel the hurt. Neither Porter nor Charlie saw Lilly as they walked to the back of the bar and out of her line of sight. With a rush of noise and a strange sucking sound as though all the wax in her ears had been removed. Lilly came back to the noise of the bar, the commotion, flashing lights, and crashing music.

Josh was still talking, totally oblivious to the scene Lilly had just witnessed, "Can I buy you a drink?" he asked.

"Yes," Lilly answered seriously, her face taking on a determined glare.

"What would you like?" Josh asked.

"A double of Jack."

"What?"

"Jack Daniels, and make it a double please," she said clearly into his left ear, her hair brushing against his face.

Josh looked at Lilly like she was crazy but he approved of her selection. He ordered two doubles of Jack and paid. Lilly smiled as they both lifted their shot glasses and clinked them together. They threw back their shots after which Josh took a deep swig of beer from the bottle in his hand. He then passed his beer bottle to Lilly for a chaser.

"Did you just do a shot?" Emily asked from behind Lilly.

"Double," Lilly answered handing Josh's beer bottle back.

Emily looked at Josh accusingly. "Did you say, 'hi,' to our friends yet?" she asked Lilly protectively.

"No. Not yet. Josh, this is my roommate Emily. Emily, this is Josh. He's in my stats class."

"Hi Josh." Emily gave Josh a fake smile, and turned to Lilly, "Excuse us, we need to go say 'hello,' to our friends." Emily pulled Lilly's arm as she started walking.

"Thanks for the drink, Josh," Lilly called as Emily dragged her away.

"What are you doing drinking shots? I left you alone for ten minutes," Emily scolded.

"It's fine," Lilly said with annoyance. She didn't need Emily's mothering now.

"You're going to regret that decision," Emily warned.

"Bet you I don't," Lilly mumbled under her breath.

The room was dim as Emily and Lilly walked to the back of the bar where their friends were congregated in a circle. Charlie leaned down to kiss Lilly's cheek as she joined the group. Lilly said, "Bless your heart," and roughly shoved his arms away. He looked confused but let it go.

"Surprise," he said with a broad smile.

She just glared at him, "I thought you had a scrimmage?" She said as an accusation.

"It was cancelled, fields were too wet to play."

Not believing a word of what he said, she replied, "I'm sure," sarcastically.

Charlie tried to ask what was wrong with a look, but Lilly tossed her hair over her shoulder and looked away. He gave up after a couple attempts and went back to his conversation with Stephen. Lilly stood next to Stephen, on the opposite side, and watched Porter and Charlie for clues as to what had happened. She felt stupid and betrayed. As she kept drinking, Lilly got angrier but still didn't say anything.

Max joined the group and wrapped his arm around Lilly's shoulders. In addition to being the first person she had met on campus, he was Stephen and Charlie's friend from lacrosse. As she stood fuming under the weight of Max's arm the band leader yelled out to the crowd, "Y'all need to help me. There is a fabulous musician in our midst and she has yet to come up on stage. Can y'all look around for my dear friend, Porter Cain?"

The room turned to find Porter as Emily yelled, "She's right here, Deb!"

Porter smiled and rolled her eyes. She waved to Deb as if the bar's attention was the last thing she wanted. It was clearly a play for even more attention but Lilly seemed to be the only one who recognized Porter's showmanship.

"Y'all chant with me now! Porter! Porter!" Deb was clapping her hands together on stage getting the beat going with Porter's name. The drummer chimed in with a down beat.

Stephen laughed and graciously twirled Porter and positioned her to walk to the stage. Everyone's eyes were on her and the crowd parted as she walked. Porter was pulled onto the stage where Deb handed her the microphone. "Thanks, y'all." Porter smiled. "What am I singing?" The band quickly picked up the beat. As if she had practiced with them hundreds of times, and maybe she had, Lilly didn't know, Porter patted her left hand on her thigh and just started belting out a song.

It was then that Lilly realized her friends weren't just being nice, Porter was talented. She had a beautiful voice and she seemed to own the stage. Porter danced across the stage, her blue Luccese boots flashing in the lights. The crowd's eyes were fixed on her, except for Lilly who watched Charlie intently. Charlie caught her staring at him and gave her a warm smile. Before Lilly could respond, Emily grabbed her arm and pulled her out onto the floor to dance.

On the dance floor Lilly ran into Josh again. He asked if she wanted to come with him to a party Lilly said, "Yes." Lilly then pulled Emily aside and told her, "I'm going to a party with Josh. I'll see you back at the room."

"Are you sure? Is everything alright?" Emily couldn't tell if Lilly was enjoying herself or if something was wrong.

"Yeah, he's a nice kid. I'll see you at home later," Lilly answered flippantly.

With a lost expression on her face, Emily hugged Lilly and said, "Ok, text me if you need me."

"Sure," Lilly said unconvincingly and followed Josh.

Lilly gave Charlie a fake smile as she marched out with Josh and his group of friends. Once again Charlie looked confused but watched her walk away. She set her jaw and kept her eyes fixed on the door. She would not give him the satisfaction of seeing her fall apart. He'd have to watch her confidently walk away.

The party was a crowd of people Lilly didn't recognize and she immediately regretted coming. They were on the second floor of a duplex that had obviously been student housing for many years. The paint was cracked and chipping off of the walls. The bannisters and woodwork were dented and gouged. Students milled through the cramped rooms, smoking on the porch, everyone was yelling to be heard over the thumping music. Lilly wanted to leave but realized that she was going to be sick. She found a restroom and fell to the floor. Lilly felt someone come in behind her and pull her hair back and hold it for her.

The disembodied male voice asked, "Are you ok?"

"Yeah, I just had too much to drink," Lilly sputtered. Lilly was embarrassed that now some stranger was holding her hair, she felt so alone. *Wasn't this what college friends were for? To be there when you made bad decisions? Great friends,* she thought to herself sarcastically.

"Who are you here with?" He asked, "Do you want me to go get your friends?"

"They're not here. I came with some guy from class." she admitted, "I don't even know whose house this is."

"It's my house."

Oh God, Lilly thought, totally embarrassed. She got sick again. Face still in the bowl, she muttered, "Thank you so much, I'm sorry."

"It's ok," he confessed, "My night wasn't that great anyway."

She took a deep breath, "I'm sorry I'm ruining your break party."

"Actually," he said, "it's a birthday party."

"Whose birthday is it?" she asked.

"Mine," he admitted with a laugh.

"Oh-my-gosh. It's your birthday and you're holding my hair. I'm so sorry." Lilly finally looked up at the stranger and recognized him. Lilly was pretty sure they had a class together, though at the moment she couldn't remember which one.

"Thanks," he laughed, "for coming to the party."

"I'm so sorry. Happy Birthday," Lilly was completely mortified.

Again he confided, "I'd rather do this than make small talk out there. If it's alright with you, I'll just hide out in here until you feel better."

"Thank you..." Lilly let her voice trail off, she didn't know his name.

"It's Drew," he filled in for her with a smile.

"Hi, Drew. I'm Lilly Carter," she said with a laugh and added, "I hate small talk too. I never know what to say."

Drew and Lilly had an immediate and comfortable intimacy. He flushed the toilet and handed her a clean wash cloth from a linen closet behind the door. As she wiped her face, he dumped the cup he had been holding and rinsed it. He then filled the cup with cold water and handed it to Lilly so she could rinse out her mouth.

"Why'd you drink so much tonight?" He asked, sitting on the lip of the tub behind her, propping his elbows on his knees.

"I caught my boyfriend kissing my friend."

"Oh, wow," he said. "Did you have a fight?"

"No. They don't know that I saw them," Lilly scratched her head and pulled her own hair up off of her neck.

"What are you going to do about it?"

"I don't know." Lilly leaned back, relaxing against the cool tub next to Drew's legs. They sat in silence for a moment.

"That sucks," he finally said.

"Yeah, it does." Lilly replied saltily as she waited for the room to stop spinning. After another long pause she said, "I think I'm going to head home."

"Why don't you let me walk you back?"

"You shouldn't leave your own birthday party. I can make it on my own."

Lilly stood up ready to march herself home, thinking the cold air would help her sober up.

"I'd feel better if you let me walk you back."

"Ok, but my overprotective roommate will be there so be ready to explain who you are to her."

"Ok, I can handle that. Let me help you walk." Drew escorted, or rather carried, Lilly back to the dorm. She was glad to have the support, physical and otherwise, especially after feeling so abandoned by her friends. As they got closer to the dorm he said, "Look, they're going to want you to sign me in if I take you all the way up to your room."

"That's fine," she mumbled.

"Ok," Drew said closing his mouth and raising his eyebrows as they walked up to the desk.

As Lilly signed Drew politely made conversation with the desk clerk. A little further on, Drew pretended not to notice as Lilly threw up again into a small trashcan on the floor. They made it to Lilly's door. Emily was still out.

"I'm so sorry, I ruined your birthday," Lilly said as Drew used her key to unlock the door.

"I'm sorry your guy cheated on you."

"Yeah, he's a jerk," Lilly said with a laugh, trying to downplay the devastating pain she felt and reignite her anger.

"He really is, because you're a great girl."

"Thanks." Lilly was leaning on the doorjamb trying to keep her eyes open.

Drew said, "Look, I could give you some line about how great it was to meet you but you're drunk and probably won't remember this anyway, so I'm just going to tell you the truth. I noticed you on the first day of class and I tried to work up the confidence to come talk to you all semester and I never did. Then you showed up at my party, on my birthday, and even though you're a mess and clearly going through some stuff, I just want you to know that I think you're beautiful and if you gave me a chance I would never treat you like that. If you remember this at all and are even remotely interested, I hope you come find me after break. I'd like to see you again."

"Ok," Lilly smiled and put her hand up for a high five. Drew laughed and slapped her palm lightly.

"May I have your number?"

"Sure," Drew handed his phone to Lilly and she slowly typed it in.

He immediately called her, "So you have my number too," he explained.

"Thanks."

"You just puked so I'm not going to kiss you but under any other circumstance I would so... good night." Drew smiled and waved a little bit as he walked away. He got halfway down the hall when he turned around and said, "You should really go inside and go to bed."

"I am," Lilly said and walked inside closing the door with a gentle click.

9. THANKSGIVING

The next morning Lilly woke up with a massive hangover and rushed to the car rental place. She had reserved the last economy car on the lot with money from a school loan. Lilly figured that by working over Christmas break she could make up the cost of the car and still buy her books, albeit late for the semester. As she settled into the driver's seat she took a deep breath of dry spruce air freshener.

Her mind wandered as the miles flew. Lilly couldn't help but think the dark thing that she had suspected all along, Charlie should be with a rich girl. Emily had convinced her to try dating him even though they were so different but deep in the back of her mind Lilly still held on to her belief that they were doomed from the start. Lilly couldn't wrap her mind around what had happened. Charlie had completely broken her trust. All she wanted to do was call Celia and talk it out, but Celia was in New York with her mom. There was no way Lilly could call her, she'd just have to push it out of her mind and wait. Lilly tightened her grip on the steering wheel, cranked up the radio and drove on.

Finally home, Lilly pulled her bag out of the trunk and smiled to herself. She was excited to be home. Maybe Maybe Melanie had some sort of 'come to Jesus' moment where she realized she wanted to be a good person, a good mother. Lilly's heart swelled with the thought. She couldn't wait to get inside even though every instinct in her body was on high alert. When Lilly walked through the door her mother and sister were fighting but she hugged them both anyway and smiled because even the fighting was familiar, she was home.

It wasn't until Lilly was talking to Sophia alone later that night that she learned how bad things had gotten at home. They were watching TV together in the living room. Sophia was draped over the couch like a wet noodle and Lilly was curled up in the rust colored lazy boy in the corner.

"What happened to your jeans?" Lilly casually asked Sophia.

"This hole or this one?" Sophia asked pointing to two tears in her pants.

"Either of them, why are you wearing pants with holes in them?" Lilly looked at her sister like she was crazy, not recognizing that three months ago she was wearing torn clothing regularly. Emily had made a deeper impression on Lilly than she realized.

"I'm wearing them because we're poor," Sophia said defensively. "The hole at the knee I tore at a football game and Mom put this hole here when she shoved me."

"Shoved you?" Lilly was confused.

"Yeah, we were fighting and she told me I looked like a slut and then pushed me over the bed."

Lilly was horrified. She sat up and leaned in, "How does that even happen?"

"I don't know. She was trying to hit me while I was down and I kicked her and then she cried and left me alone."

Lilly's eyebrows knit together. "Where did you kick her?"

"In the stomach and in the leg."

Lilly was shocked by the revelation and by Sophia's cavalier attitude about it.

Sophia rolled her eyes, "She acted like she was dying and kept limping around the house for a week to make me feel guilty. She'd even shudder when I walked by as if I'd kick her again. You missed a real show."

"What were you fighting about?"

"I don't know," Sophia shrugged. "She was drunk. What do we always fight about?"

Lilly stiffly processed this information. She wanted to restart the conversation, she had so many questions but she wasn't sure what to say.

"Are you ok?"

"Fine," Sophia got up and left the room, effectively ending the conversation.

Lilly moved to follow but before she could stand her phone buzzed, Charlie was texting her. "Hey, Lil."

"Hey," she wrote back.

"You didn't say goodbye before you left. :("

Lilly didn't answer.

"Are you mad at me?" he quickly followed.

"No. Why would I be mad at you?" She asked. She was setting him up, waiting to see what he'd say.

"No reason. You just seemed angry at the bar..."

She didn't wait for him to finish his thought, "Nope, I'm fine."

"Is your break going well?"

So, you're kissing one girl and texting another? Classy, Lilly thought to herself. She typed, "I guess."

He sent back, "?"

"It's ok. What are you doing?"

Charlie kept texting but Lilly stopped responding. He wasn't who she thought he was and the giddy butterflies she usually felt when he texted were gone. Now she just felt sick.

Despite her promises of an idyllic family visit, Melanie drank too much wine at dinner and was snoring in the recliner by eight. Sophia had a date with her boyfriend and disappeared. There was an acrid smell in the house that reminded Lilly of an armpit, she wondered if anyone was doing laundry. She had already checked the fridge but there was nothing inside except for an outdated brick of Velveeta and various dressings and sauces. Lilly coded in her room. Looking at her screen the room faded away, the sound of her mother's snores silenced, and all she saw were green numbers and letters and the black background. Solid things that made sense and frustrated but could never disappoint her.

Lilly's phone buzzed again as she changed into her pajamas and expecting Charlie she ignored it. As she crawled into bed she looked again to see a text from an unknown number. "Hey Lilly, it's Drew. I hope you got home safe and are feeling better."

"Thanks Drew. Feeling much better. Sorry again for ruining your party."

"Thanks for giving me an excuse to leave. :)"

Nice, she thought to herself and laughed. She typed, "My pleasure."

Lilly fell asleep with a smile on her face and the thought that something fresh and new was starting.

Lilly awoke to Melanie yelling. "Get up! Get up! Lilly, where are your keys?"

Lilly's eyes weren't even open as she answered, "In my purse. Why?"

"Time to get going!" Melanie announced loudly.

"Where are you going?" Lilly rolled over, "I can move the car."

Her mother was already opening Lilly's purse.

"What are you doing?" Lilly sat upright adrenaline rushing through her body. "I'll move the car," she repeated.

Her mother smiled condescendingly at Lilly and walked out of the room with the keys in hand. Melanie was fully dressed and Lilly could smell the heavy waft of her perfume.

Lilly jumped out of bed. "Mom, give me the keys back."

Her mother ignored her and shoved some papers into a tired looking briefcase.

"Mom, you're not on the rental agreement. You can't take the car," Lilly reasoned in her bare feet and pajamas as Melanie moved rapidly from room to room.

Sophia came out into the kitchen in her ripped jeans and a Bart Simpson T-shirt. She had a backpack on her shoulder.

"Why is she stealing my car?" Lilly asked desperately.

"Oh, you didn't know?" Sophia asked with vague surprise.

Nothing was making sense to Lilly. "What?"

"Her car got repossessed," Sophia explained shifting her weight. "She said you were coming home so she could go to some conference."

"What? Mom is that true?" Lilly felt so stupid. *This was why she asked me to come home, why she said she missed me.* Lilly's stomach turned. Her face drained and she twisted her ring anxiously.

Melanie kept moving and talking to no one in particular, "Time to go. Get dressed, we're leaving in ten minutes!"

"It's Thanksgiving," Lilly said desperately, "Nothing's open!"

Sophia rolled her eyes and looked sadly at her older sister who had so quickly forgotten what life at home was like, an unpredictable cyclone of emotional, mental, and physical torture.

"I'm leaving in eight minutes," Melanie sang out in her off-tone warble.

Lilly's mind was racing. The only way to get the keys back would be to physically take them from her mother and Lilly did not want to do that. She didn't want to fight anyone. Her mother had used her, lied to her, and was going to steal her car. If Melanie got drunk and wrecked it, Lilly would be responsible for the damages. Melanie had two DUI's, she couldn't rent a car for herself, *that's why she called me.* Lilly barely had enough money to rent the car, she was under 21 and the rates were astronomical but she had shrugged them off because her mom had said she missed her. *What an idiot.* Lilly almost screamed with anger at her own stupidity.

Melanie walked back into the kitchen and sloshed coffee into a travel mug.

"Where are we going?" Lilly begged.

"On an adventure," her mother said maniacally in the same cold voice Lilly remembered from her childhood. A rush of memories flooded Lilly's brain, the nights she and Sophia got to 'camp out' at her mother's office or play on the jungle gym at church until ten at night because her mother was busy 'working.' Melanie sipping from her 'water bottle' as her daughters begged for her attention. Lilly came back to herself and the chaos that was again her life, Melanie was carrying a suitcase to the car.

"Where are we going? I have to be back at school on Monday." Lilly tried to sound firm, even as she felt more and more powerless.

"Hurry up," her mother called.

Sophia sat down at the kitchen table to tie her tennis shoes.

"Where are we going?" Lilly asked Sophia.

Sophia didn't look up. "I don't know, some conference."

"What are *we* going to do?" Lilly asked.

Sophia shrugged and walked out the garage door to the car.

With an exasperated sigh Lilly hustled to her room. She threw on a pair of jeans and a bra. She stuffed her computer into her backpack and carried it out to the car. Melanie had the engine idling and was sitting in the driver's seat.

"Mom! You can't drive the car," Lilly shouted through the passenger window. "I don't have insurance for multiple drivers. I'm the only one legally allowed to drive the car." Lilly wasn't sure if that was true but she thought that maybe if she used official terms her mother might hand over the keys.

"Gotta go!" Melanie started backing down the driveway leaving Lilly to step out of the way of the rolling vehicle.

"Mom! It's her car! Why do you have to be such a bitch?" Sophia yelled from the backseat.

Melanie stopped the car with a jerk and sat there silently as Lilly walked down the driveway and got in, throwing her backpack on the floor. She hated her mother with her whole body. "Where are we going?" Lilly demanded.

"On an adventure," Melanie said with a strained voice as she turned on the radio and cranked up the volume so she could avoid further questioning.

Lilly couldn't even speak she was so livid. As Melanie drove, Lilly wondered why she hadn't just stayed home and reported the car stolen. She wished she had thought of that earlier. They drove for two hours and eventually pulled into a bleak hotel parking lot somewhere near the Michigan border.

A cold wind swirled through the car as Melanie got out taking the keys and her purse with her. The sky was cold and grey. It had looked like rain all morning but the clouds had yet to break, filling the air with an ominous stillness. Lilly readjusted in her seat pulling the sleeves of her sweatshirt down so she could warm her hands inside of them.

"Why didn't you tell me the car was repossessed?" Lilly asked in a monotone, looking out the window.

Sophia shrugged, "I thought you knew."

Lilly turned on her sister in the backseat, "How could I possibly know that, Sophia?"

Sophia was defensive, "I don't know. I thought that was why you were coming home."

"No," Lilly spoke with vehement anger. "She told me she missed me and I should come visit."

"She's such a bitch," Sophia said as she exhaled.

"She really is," Lilly agreed shaking her head into her hands as she doubled over her knees. Her speaking muffled by her position, she said, "This is insane. She stole my car, lied to me, and essentially kidnapped us."

Melanie came back outside still wearing the residue of the persona she had worn for the desk clerk's benefit. "Here's the room key." She handed the card to Sophia. "I have to go to a meeting, we're in room 135."

"Is there a pool?" Sophia asked indifferently, accustomed to situations like this.

"I don't think so, you'll have to ask. I have to go. Love you," Melanie sang.

"Mom, the keys," Lilly said in monotone.

Melanie walked inside without responding.

"It's Thanksgiving," Lilly said exchanging an angry stare with Sophia. "There's no fucking conference." Lilly spat the words out.

Sophia shrugged, pulling her bag out of the backseat, "Then why are we here?"

Lilly exhaled in disgust.

"What?" Sophia asked staring at her older sister in the parking lot.

Lilly shook her head from side to side slowly, "Because it's convenient for whatever guy she's fucking."

"UGH!!" Sophia yelled up to the sky, "I hate her!"

They trudged to room 135, both girls stewing in their resentment. Once inside they discarded their belongings and collapsed onto the beds.

"What do we do?" Sophia asked Lilly from her position sprawled across the bed near the window.

"There's nothing we can do," Lilly answered frankly. She was sitting on the edge of the other bed. She hadn't taken her shoes off and was staring down at her hands uselessly. Looking up she gave Sophia a wry smile and cleared her throat, "She told me she missed me and that we were going to have a family Thanksgiving."

Sophia gave her big sister a pained look.

"It's why I came home," Lilly bit her lip and snorted air out of her nose disgusted with her own naivete.

Sophia sat up and crossed her legs beneath her, "It's not your fault, Lils."

Lilly rolled her eyes and scratched her head, pulling her fingers through her hair to the ends. "I'm just an idiot."

"No, you're not. You wanted a normal mom," Sophia said, immediately understanding what Lilly was saying with sisterly intimacy.

Lilly gave her a weak smile, relieved she didn't have to explain any more. "Is that so bad?"

"It's not," Sophia said. "It's just not our reality." Sophia spoke firmly, "That's not her and it will never be her."

"I know," Lilly agreed, looking back down at her hands as she played with them aimlessly.

Sophia frowned. "I'm glad you came home."

Lilly looked up and smiled, her shoulders dropping, "I'm glad I get to see you."

Sophia smiled and shrugged her shoulders.

Lilly clenched her fists and hit the mattress, "I just hate her so much. She used me and she doesn't care." Lilly counted off on her fingers, "She stole my car, she lied to me, and what makes me sick to my stomach is that she thinks that I'm the bitch for not happily going along with this like it's normal."

"It's not normal." Sophia added, "It will never be normal."

"Right?" Lilly spat, "She thinks my role in this world is to just be of use to her for whatever she wants."

Sophia tucked her hair behind her ears with both hands. "That's all anyone is good for to her. We don't matter, we're not people, we're here to be used and if you turn it around on her she's outraged," Sophia said with cold brutality.

"Why does this have to be how we live? It's not fair."

"It isn't fair but we'll get out. We'll get the fuck away from her and never treat our kids or anyone else like this," Sophia declared.

The girls went to bed before Melanie returned. Lilly could hear Sophia's rhythmic breaths going in and out. The cars buzzing past on the turnpike, the occasional shuffling of another guest walking down the hall, the other lonely souls who had nowhere else to be on Thanksgiving. Lilly did not sleep, she was waiting.

Melanie stumbled into the room late that night. She was drunk and clumsily fell over as she attempted to make her way around the room. When she finally passed out, Lilly crawled out of the bed she was sharing with Sophia, found Melanie's purse and stole back the keys to the rental car. She could feel her heart beating in her ears as she crept back to bed. Sophia rolled over and looked at Lilly as she lay down.

"We leave in the morning," Lilly whispered. Sophia went back to sleep.

Melanie woke up early the next morning, showered and dressed. Lilly could feel her heart racing, the thud of it inside her chest. She was terrified and yet anticipating the moment when her mother would realize that the keys were gone. Lilly felt like a caged animal, ready to break free as soon as there was an opening. Her breathing was shallow, the air was dry and she could feel it filling her lungs. *What would Melanie say? What would she say back?* Lilly couldn't even imagine it. Lilly got up and began re-packing her bag even though her hands were trembling. She brushed her teeth and was about to shower. She had the keys in hand, attempting to hide them in her grasp so Melanie couldn't steal them back while Lilly bathed. Lilly was about to step into the bathroom and lock the door behind her when her mother looked up at her and glowered. Melanie's nostrils were flared, her already too thin eyebrows raised.

"Where are the keys?" she said coldly.

"They're not yours, they're mine. I rented the car and I'm leaving," Lilly's voice was calm and emotionless.

"Give me the keys Lillian Rose," Melanie said savagely.

Lilly stood up straighter, "No. I'm not giving you the keys. You don't get to manipulate me into coming home, steal my car, and kidnap Sophia and me. This trip is done. You are not forcing us to stay here," Lilly continued in monotone.

Melanie's voice came out shrilly, "Give me the keys."

"No." Lilly added generously, "If you want to come with us thats fine, but we're leaving."

It was then that Melanie slapped her eldest daughter across the face. Lilly's head turned and she saw Sophia sitting up in bed watching the scene, afraid to move. Lilly was too stunned to react, images of her childhood flashed before her eyes, her mother yelling, her body covered in bruises from Melanie's rough reprimands. Lilly felt like that little girl again, terrified and unsure of what this mother monster might do next.

As Lilly stood frozen Melanie pried her fingers open, digging her nails roughly into Lilly's skin the cold metal of the key stabbing into Lilly's palm as Melanie physically pried the keys from her daughter's grasp. Lilly watched it happen, as though from above, in the scene and yet absent from it. Melanie put the keys into her purse and left the room. Lilly looked helplessly at Sophia who rolled over and went back to sleep. Lilly would never be able to protect her sister, she couldn't even protect herself.

After Melanie left, Lilly took a shower, the hot water stinging the gouges Melanie had left in her palm. Lilly cried silently, a balled up heap on the tub floor, and prayed for an escape.

Melanie returned at lunch bearing cold pizza and a smile as if nothing had happened. The girls were sullen and silent but greedily ate their first meal in twenty-four hours.

"Let's get going," Melanie said after the girls had eaten. Lilly and Sophia quietly carried their bags to the car. As Lilly walked to the passenger side her mother tossed her the keys, her hand still throbbing stabbed fresh as the cold keys landed.

"You can drive," Melanie said lightly as she walked around the car to the passenger seat.

Lilly was confused but said nothing. She had been sufficiently beaten down. Lilly started the car, turned on the heat, and turned off the classical radio station her mother had been blaring. She entered their home address into the GPS. Before they left the parking lot Melanie was asleep, her chardonnay breath filling the car with heady fumes. Lilly had to crack her window to diffuse the smell.

Every mile home and every mile back to Tennessee Lilly vowed to never fall for her mother's lies again. The little rock in her chest froze with all of hatred and disgust Lilly felt for her mother. She could almost feel the rock in her fist, hard, cold, and angry.

10. NASHVILLE WINTER

Back at Vanderbilt Lilly called her advisor promptly to change her major from History of Art to Computer Science. She registered for six classes in the spring semester, one more than a typical packed schedule of five. She added a practicum in application development with PH, and couldn't wait to get started. She was ready to cut ties with her mother and take the steps that would cut Melanie and her chaos out her life forever.

In her room, Emily was already blasting Christmas Carols and dancing as she hung up her clothes.

"Oh, hi," she yelled over the sound when Lilly walked into the room. "Don't you just love Christmas?"

"Emily, Thanksgiving *just* ended."

Dismissing Lilly's hint with a wave of her hand Emily replied, "I love Christmas!" She grabbed a canister of fake snow off of her desk, stepped up onto the heat register, and began spraying the windows with white dust.

"Oh Lord," Celia announced dramatically, entering the room with Porter, "We're too late. It's already started."

"Merry Christmas y'all," Emily called out over the music as she continued spraying.

"Hey Lil. How was your Thanksgiving?" Celia asked, turning down the speakers on Emily's desk.

Lilly plastered an empty smile on her face, not allowing herself to think about the cheap motel, no food to eat, and the lies her mother told. All of it was blocked out, even as she unintentionally rubbed the sore scabs on her hand. "It was great. How about you? How was New York?"

"I think I've convinced my parents to let me go to Paris this spring. They might ask me to stay and help out at the store though," Celia's voice trailed off.

"You'll find a way around that," Porter said conspiratorially.

Celia immediately smiled, "True story!" She laughed with Porter as they high-fived lightly.

"I didn't know your parents had a store," Lilly said.

"Oh, yeah, my parents have a furniture and design shop here in Nashville." Celia said as she sat on Emily's bed.

"Really? That's awesome." Lilly was blown away, that was so cool.

"Momma's an interior decorator and Daddy's a master carpenter. They've had their business since I was five," Celia explained.

"Lulu and Jack are the best," Emily affirmed as she stepped off of the window ledge.

Celia smiled at the compliment.

"They designed our entire house," Emily continued, "anybody who's anybody in Nashville shops at Lulu and Jack."

Celia said, "They're always working. My parents don't come from money like these two." Celia nodded to Emily and Porter.

"Lulu's the reason half of my wardrobe is monogrammed," Emily stated, ignoring the jab.

"If it isn't monogrammed, is it even really yours?" Celia asked teasingly.

"It's not like you don't have money," Porter said directly to Celia.

"Well, too much of a good thing, is a good thing," Celia replied with a smirk trying to deflect.

"Right," Porter stuck to her guns, "but you're making it sound like Emily's and my families don't work as hard as yours," Porter defended.

"I really don't think they do," Celia admitted calmly from the bed.

"Well, bless your heart, I don't think that's the case," Porter said defiantly.

"Bless your heart," Celia answered back standing up, "My parents work all the time to provide for our family. Investing isn't working, Porter."

"My parents don't just invest! You know very well that my Daddy runs that law firm and they don't pay my mother for singing at church. That is a service she provides to our faith community for free. Don't tell me that's not working," Porter yelled.

"It isn't!" Celia yelled back.

Emily stepped in, "Y'all need to calm down and stop talking ugly. It's Christmas and I will not have it."

Both Celia and Porter acquiesced but silently glared at one another.

Emily moved the conversation forward and said to Porter, "My dear, how is your momma? Will you tell her I'm so sorry I didn't come say hello when I dropped you off but I had to take Stephen and Reagan home too?" Reagan was a friend of theirs from high school Lilly had heard them talk about before. She went to school out of state but apparently saw the girls over breaks.

"She understood," Porter replied.

"You know I sent Reagan a birthday gift in October and can you believe that bitch didn't send a thank you note?" Emily said. It was the angriest tone Lilly had ever heard her use.

"Oh, Em, I'm sure she didn't mean it," Celia cooed.

"It was rude," Emily added with a stern look.

"She's dumb as dirt but she's a sweet girl, I'm sure it's just an oversight." Porter said.

Emily pursed her lips, unconvinced.

Porter continued conspiratorially, "Can we discuss her 'ombre' hair style?"

"I know," Celia agreed.

"Doesn't she know we're from the South?" Emily asked. "Put a baseball hat on and get yourself to the salon."

Lilly chuckled to herself at Emily's Southern rules of etiquette. Emily diffused the situation flawlessly. Lilly was impressed. She did enjoy being Emily's roommate, moments like these reminded her why. Lilly listened to the girls' gossip as she folded laundry and debated whether she really needed to buy notebooks for all of her classes or if she could reuse a couple from last semester to save money. When she had first moved in she had found the girls constant chatter overbearing and annoying. Now the white noise was a comfortable and homey sound she had missed.

There was a knock on the open door and Charlie walked in, "Good evening, ladies."

"Hey Charlie," they replied in unison.

Lilly stood silently, staring at the stack of white T-shirts she had just placed in her drawer, refusing acknowledge him.

"Want to grab some dinner, Lil?" he asked.

"What?" Lilly looked to Porter to gauge her reaction; she was staring down at her manicure.

"Do you want to go to dinner?" Charlie asked again.

"Don't you want to go to dinner with Porter?" Lilly attempted to clarify finally looking him in the eye.

"I already ate," Porter said indifferently.

Charlie laughed, "No, I asked you."

"But I thought," Lilly was totally unsure of how she should finish the sentence.

"What?" Porter asked looking up.

Charlie was staring blankly at Lilly. Emily and Celia had stopped gossiping and were waiting to hear what Lilly would say next.

"I thought you two were hooking up," Lilly said slowly, uncomfortable with the room's attention.

"What?" Porter cackled.

Emily and Celia exchanged shocked stares.

"I saw you guys before break, at the bar," Lilly continued, "you were coming out of the coat room."

Lilly gestured with her hands, "I don't know. You were tucking in your shirt. She was fixing her lip-stick."

"We had coats on Lilly. We took them off and went to meet you. How tacky do you think I am?" Porter said defensively.

"Is that why you were so weird over break?" Charlie asked with a smirk.

Lilly shifted her weight uncomfortably from foot to foot. "Well, I didn't know. I thought you two were together."

"No offense Charlie, but no," Porter said with disdain.

Charlie laughed, "Thanks, Porter."

"I'm sorry," Lilly apologized, looking around the room wide eyed and embarrassed.

"You really have a wild imagination," Porter said to Lilly.

"I guess," Lilly said looking to Emily and Celia for some sort of support. They were both avoiding eye contact. Lilly was mortified. She looked down at her hands, they were sore from how tightly she had been wringing them and the cuts from Melanie's fingernails were still tender and healing.

"Well now that that's settled," Charlie moved on, unfazed. "Do you want to go to dinner?"

Lilly exhaled, "Yeah, that would be nice." As they stepped out into the cool night air Lilly blurted out, "I am so sorry, Charlie."

"Its fine, Lil," he laughed.

"I just thought..." she started.

"Please, don't worry about it," he smiled, putting his hand on her shoulder.

"I didn't mean that 'bless your heart' that night at the bar either," Lilly confessed.

"Oh, that's what you said." Charlie added with a nod, "I couldn't hear you over the band."

"I thought you kissed her... and then you were kissing me."

"Yeah, no," Charlie said with a laugh.

"I know, but I saw you two and it looked to me like you had just hooked up. I guess I was just jealous and overreacted."

"Jealous?" Charlie said with a raised eyebrow.

Lilly took a deep breath, "I am so embarrassed."

"What were you jealous about?" Charlie teased.

Lilly covered her face with her hands. "Do I have to say it?"

"I don't know why were you jealous, Lilly?" Charlie laughed, tucking a piece of red hair behind her ear.

"The truth?" she asked weakly, looking up at him with pleading eyes.

"The truth," he answered with a warm smile, as if he already knew what she was about to say.

"I like you," she admitted out loud.

Then Charlie said, "Lil, I really missed you over break. I'm crazy about you."

Lilly blushed. "I'm crazy about you too, Charlie."

"There's no one else I'm interested in at all." Charlie said and pulled her into his arms. "And if it's alright with you, I'd like to just date you."

"I could get used to that," she grinned. Lilly had never been rewarded for letting her guard down around another person, it was liberating. Especially after the violation of trust she had felt over Thanksgiving.

"Good."

She smiled right before he kissed her. His lips were cold as she comfortably leaned into his embrace. Lilly could feel elation fluttering all through her body. She melted into his arms and savored the feeling of his lips on hers.

Later that night in her dorm room Lilly began working through the backlog of requests. Kids from the floor had texted, messaged, and emailed her with computer issues. Lilly got to work installing printers, recovering documents, and deleting incriminating photos or videos people did not want found.

Soon, money was rolling in and Lilly methodically saved at least half of every payment. The smaller amounts she saved in entirety. The half of the money she allowed herself to spend was used for two things. One half went to paying down her loans. The other half went to incidentals like books, clothes, and school supplies.

On her drive back to school Lilly decided that she was ready to talk to PH again about her project. Lilly wore her usual uniform, a white T-shirt tucked it into dark washed skinny jeans and black motorcycle boots to their meeting. She marched to PH's office with a confident stride and rapped on the door frame with her knuckles.

"Ah, Miss. Carter, come in. It's been a while," PH said from behind her desk. PH returned her attention to the glow of her screen. "Give me a minute. I'm just wrapping up this email."

Lilly sat down in a wooden chair across the desk from Professor Hendricks. As promised, books were on shelves and diplomas hung in ornate frames on the walls. Enya played lightly in the background and the room smelled like lavender incense. There was a framed print on the wall that caught Lilly's attention. It read, "The intuitive mind is a sacred gift and the rational mind is a faithful servant. We have created a society that honors the servant and has forgotten the gift. - Albert Einstein" Lilly took a moment to consider those words; they seemed to touch on something personal for her. Lilly always prided herself on being rational and logical. She wondered to herself, *Was that a working-class ideology? Were her values of logic and rational thought just carried over from a family of blue collar workers? As someone who values time keeping and timeliness because their time was always kept by someone else - a boss or manager with all powerful authority over a paycheck.* Lilly sat stunned and silent. She had come to PH's office ready to explain her love of symmetry and the order that coding provides but that quote told her that that was not what PH was looking for, she wanted innovation and intuition. *Did she ever remember how to think intuitively? To dream? To imagine?*

"Did you think about my question?" PH caught Lilly off guard, she had been so lost in her own thoughts she didn't realize that PH had finished typing and was looking directly at her.

"Yes," Lilly shifted in her seat uncomfortably.

"Good. And what did you conclude? What is your motivation?" PH folded her long elegant fingers patiently in front of herself.

Lilly decided to be honest. *What did she have to lose?* "I came here today to talk to you about symmetry and my love for order and organization. I was going to tell you why I like coding and that as someone who is self-taught I have phenomenal capabilities," she modestly added, "though they may be somewhat lacking in structure. I didn't realize until I sat down here and read your wall," Lilly gestured to the quote with her hand, "exactly what you were asking."

PH exhaled slowly and smoothly, "Would you like an extension?" PH betrayed no emotion.

"No. I think I can answer your question without more time."

"Ok." PH nodded for Lilly to proceed.

"At home, it's just my mom, my sister, and me. My mom drinks and she takes whatever's bothering her out on us. I'm not motivated to build something that makes business easier, like I said last time. I'm motivated to get my sister out of that house and to make sure neither of us have to go back there ever again."

PH nodded. She waited a few moments before speaking, allowing Lilly's words to come to rest in the space. Eventually, she said, "Right now your motivation is to escape or run away from one place to another." PH put up a hand, "Not, that I don't think that is valid or important, but now I want you to think about where you're going."

Lilly nodded and swallowed. Her heart was racing. It had taken all of her courage to say those words out loud. To own her fear of returning home, to tell someone else about her background and her family's embarrassing secrets.

"We can run from lots of things: responsibilities, troubles, our families." PH took a deep breath. "In the end it doesn't matter because we always carry those things with us." PH placed a soft hand on her chest, indicating her heart, "And it's important not just to know where you're coming from but where you want to end up. I could tell you to keep coding, push your project forward, all of that, but if you're not working toward what you really want it's a waste of your time and mine. So," PH sat up straighter, "Now, I need you to think about where you're going. How is this project going to take you there?"

Lilly nodded, she felt relieved and also exhausted.

PH saw the strain on Lilly's face and said, "This is hard work Lilly. Take your time and get back to me. I don't want to dissuade you from working on your project. I'm presuming that because you are already an overachiever that you're continuing to build this project as you ponder the larger questions."

"Yes. I'm still working on it," Lilly shared. "I'm not sure where it's going next but I've had a couple recent breakthroughs."

"Good. Take advantage of those and keep pushing. Where are you in your development?"

"Most of the triggers are scripted. I've written them as generically as possible, so it's applicable to a larger pool. I'm thinking we could use the University's IT help desk as a target database. I would just need University approval to access it."

"I'll take care of that piece. And then you're ready to beta test?"

"If you can get me access to the University's database, I can be ready to test. Creating it on the server should be quick and easy. I would just need to determine what logic needs to be applied and a way for users to supply data that makes sense to them. I may also consider a separate database for the modification table so that it doesn't compromise the security of the University's proprietary data." Lilly sighed, "It's still going to take a lot of work."

PH nodded, "It sounds like you're working hard and I would encourage you to keep it up. Think on where you're headed and we'll get together before finals to discuss your next steps."

"Thank you PH." Lilly moved to stand.

"One other thing," PH spoke strongly and clearly. "Don't say, 'I'm thinking we,' when you mean, 'I know I can.' It's not a personal criticism, it's something we, as women, are taught to do all our lives. We're raised to be team players not braggers. It is appropriate for you to take credit for your ideas and your work."

Lilly nodded sheepishly and smiled. She gave PH a relieved look, "Ok, I will. Thank you."

"My pleasure Lilly, keep up the good work."

Lilly left PH's office feeling confident and strong. She just had to figure out where she wanted to go in life and how she was going to get there.

11. WORKING

The next day Lilly spent the morning in the library working alone. She relished the solitude and productivity that came when she hid herself away and could focus on her work. She took her laptop to lunch with her and worked dutifully on her project, getting it ready to test on the University's servers. If PH could get her access, Lilly wanted to be ready the minute they got approval. She was feeling pretty productive when she walked into her stats class late that afternoon and saw Drew. She sat next to him in the back of the room, instead of taking her usual spot in the front of the lecture hall.

"Hey, how's it going?" he asked as she sat down.

"Good." She smiled up at him while pulling her laptop out of her bag to take notes.

"I take it you remember what I said?"

"Most of it," Lilly smiled.

"Damn! I was hoping you would forget that," he joked easily.

Lilly laughed.

"Did you have a nice break?" he asked.

"Yeah, it was fine. Too short, four days isn't long enough to really relax." Lilly glossed over the drama that was her trip home, she didn't know him.

"I hear you. Break up with the guy?" Drew asked leaning in with his face uplifted hopefully.

"No," Lilly smiled and rolled her eyes.

"Well, it was worth a shot," Drew said relaxing back into his seat and leaning away from her. "Now, could you scoot over? I was saving this seat for her," he nodded to a girl walking into the lecture hall.

"Oh, I'm sorry. I thought..." Lilly could feel her face flushing with embarrassment.

Drew grabbed Lilly's arm as she reached to pick up her bag and move. "Carter, I'm kidding. I have no idea who that girl is," he laughed as the girl made her way to a seat up front.

Lilly laughed with relief. "Jerk," she said and lightly punched him in the arm. Class began and Lilly dutifully paid attention.

After class Lilly was still typing notes rapidly as Drew stood up and stretched. "Want to grab dinner?" he asked comfortably.

Lilly was surprised by the invite and accepted before even thinking, "Sure." As they left the classroom Drew held the door for her. "Thanks," she smiled and asked awkwardly, "So, what are you majoring in?"

"I double major in graphics and design."

"Oh, that's awesome," Lilly said encouragingly.

"It's cool. I work in the IT department on campus. I do a lot of the artwork for faculty presentations."

"That's cool," Lilly said, impressed.

"It's a lot of charts and graphs but they let me play with logos sometimes and that's fun."

"It's nice they let you try new things."

Drew nodded, and held the door to the cafeteria for her. They quickly snaked through the crowds of students waiting in lines for their meals. Lilly ordered a turkey wrap, chips, and a bottle of water. After swiping her ID to pay, she found Drew in the dining room already eating.

Lilly pulled out a metal chair with a loud scrape and sat across from him. She carefully placed a napkin on her lap. Drew was already plowing through his burger.

"You said you're working in the IT department on campus?" Lilly asked her curiosity peaked.

"Yeah, five days a week," he said before taking another giant bite of his burger.

"How did you get that?" She asked as she methodically un-wrapped her sandwich and opened her bag of salt and vinegar chips, savoring the sting of the first crunch.

"Applied," Drew shrugged and shoved a catsup covered fry in his mouth. "Are you looking for a job?"

"Yeah," Lilly admitted. *It would be ideal for her project if she was already working in the IT department.*

"Cool, yeah, just apply online. They just had a spot open up, you could get it before Christmas break and then start when you get back."

"That would be perfect." Lilly could hardly believe her good luck. This was turning out to be a great dinner.

"So your boyfriend said he didn't kiss your friend and you just believe him?" Drew asked as he took a chip from Lilly's plate and popped it into his mouth. Lilly was startled by his familiarity.

"I thought they were kissing but they weren't," Lilly replied, defensively.

"Because he said so," Drew added.

"No, they both said they were just taking their coats off. I thought it looked weird but I was wrong."

"And you believe them?" Drew asked skeptically.

"Right," she said. "Why would he say he was interested in only me if he didn't mean it?"

"So you wouldn't suspect he was kissing your friend." Drew stated the obvious.

"I don't think so," Lilly said curtly.

"Oh, well, of course. If you don't believe it then that obviously makes it true," Drew said throwing his hands into the air dramatically.

She replied, "Of course, I'm glad you see things my way."

"You are ridiculous and delusional, Carter. It must be nice in that imaginary world."

"It is nice. You should try being optimistic sometime," Lilly suggested.

"Yeah, that's not for me. I'll stay in the real world, thanks."

"Your loss," she teased. "Where are you from?"

"New York."

"How did you end up here?" Lilly was genuinely interested.

"I'm from upstate, I wanted to go to school somewhere warmer but I needed a big name and SMU didn't want me." Drew was comfortably frank.

"You're from Ohio?"

"Yeah," Lilly was confused, "How did you know that?"

"First day of class," Drew said leading her down a path, gesturing with a fry in hand.

She didn't get it.

He continued to guide her, "We had to tell the class something they didn't know about us and our name."

"Oh, right," Lilly remembered but she couldn't remember what Drew had said.

"Do you remember what I said?" He asked popping the fry into his mouth.

"I'm sorry, I don't," Lilly felt guilty.

"I said I was from New York," Drew answered, looking at her as if to question if she had a brain in her head.

Lilly cracked out a laugh, he got her. "Right," she nodded, "smart."

"That's why I sit in the back of the room," he tapped the side of his head with a greasy finger.

Drew was brazen and funny. It was unnerving to be called out, but in a way Lilly found it refreshing. After months of being surrounded by soft southern pleasantries, Drew was like a cold bucket of water, uncomfortable but invigorating.

Based on Drew's recommendation, Lilly had filled out an online application and called the campus IT department. She interviewed and got the job. She had thought they would wait until spring semester but the IT department was short staffed and they asked her to start before the holiday break. By the end of the week, Lilly was updating and organizing the online databases of student created research four nights a week.

Lilly could see her breath as she hiked slowly up the steps to the building that housed PH's office. Lilly was dreading this meeting. She was concerned that her work wasn't where it needed to be and she didn't want to let PH down.

Lilly knocked lightly on the wooden door frame to PH's office.

PH didn't even say hello, "Are you ready to start beta testing?"

Lilly took a deep breath, "I'll need some more time. Coordinating with the campus servers is taking longer than I expected."

PH considered Lilly's words thoughtfully and then asked, "How long until it's on the servers?"

Lilly shrugged, "A week, if the IT department does the work on their end. They haven't been very helpful." Building the site wasn't as difficult as working with the IT department. No one wanted to help her and many of the full time staff just ignored her and her emails. It may have been due to the upcoming holiday break but to Lilly it felt deliberate and as if they were dismissing her and her work as unimportant.

"Ok," PH looked satisfied. "Early December is fine. You're using my 100 class as beta testers. You're ready to present the concept to the class and provide a one page write-up with instructions on what you would like them to do, how they log-in, and anything else you'd like them to know?"

Lilly typed this information into her phone. "Yes, I'll be ready for them on Wednesday."

"How's the rest of the project coming along," PH asked the top of Lilly's head.

"Slowly," Lilly admitted, looking up.

"What's the hold-up?" PH crossed her arms and looked at Lilly quizzically analyzing her form from across the room.

"I've been busy with school and work, and... other things."

PH dipped her head suggestively, "Social life?"

"Not really, I haven't been spending much time on my social life," Lilly confessed not wanting PH to think she did not take her work or her education seriously.

"You need a social life," PH stated as a fact.

Lilly was taken aback.

PH leaned forward and rested her forearms on her desk as she gestured with her hands, "I'm not saying you give up your work or focus all of your energies on friends and romance but you need those things to be happy, as a human being. You're a smart girl. But you trend towards introversion, unless you're talking about your work or about theories in general. You get uncomfortable when things get too personal."

Lilly shifted in her seat. She was surprised by how much PH had observed.

"I think it's good for you and your project if you can break out of your shell and develop your emotional intelligence as much as you have your intellectual side."

"I guess," Lilly was unsure of how to respond.

"It will be hard for you." PH leaned forward to make her point, "But these are important skills that you're here to develop. The purpose of college is not just to learn in the classroom. You learn from your peers, your experiences, the city, you can be inspired every day, and all of it will make your work better, your life better, the world better."

Lilly nodded.

PH leaned back and crossed her arms, "What?"

"Thank you for saying that. I thought you were going to yell at me."

"Not at all, I respect you as a person Lilly. I'm not going to yell at you unless you need it and you don't need to be yelled at now. You need to learn how to build healthy bonds with other people. That is just as much a part of your education as the rest of your work at school. I would like to encourage you to polish your work and, when you're ready, I'd like to schedule a meeting with you and a potential investor."

Lilly was silent, wide-eyed, and stunned. She didn't move a muscle.

PH leaned back slightly as she spoke, ignoring Lilly's rigid state, "My boss has a contact here in Nashville that she would like me to introduce you to personally. I don't have a lot of information but it should give you a chance to practice your business etiquette and negotiation skills."

Lilly was ecstatic. "You're serious?"

"Completely. But you'll need to pick up the pace."

"I'm on it."

Lilly quickly found tons of work to do. She was figuring out how to make all of the pieces work together. She was putting in long hours in the IT department too. She was able to use her paid time to work on her project and focus even more time on her beta testing. Lilly was hard at work at a coffee shop on campus making sure her project was ready to go live. Lilly savored the new book smell that greeted her every time she opened the door at Grinders. It was a little busier than the library but usually a cozy place to talk or get some work done.

She was wearing cuffed dark-washed jeans, a thick sweater, and flat brown lace up oxfords. Her hair was up in a messy bun with her long auburn bangs parted in the middle framing her face as she hunched over the computer in a deep leather chair. Her face was awash in the glow of her screen as she tapped her foot and coded to Blondie playing through her ear-buds. She happily e-mailed the IT department so they could get the software on the server before her presentation to PH's 100 class Wednesday.

A shadow appeared over her small table. "Lilly?" Someone was standing next to her.

Lilly pulled out her ear buds and looked up, "Oh! Hi, Drew." she said, mildly surprised to see him. He was wearing a fitted grey T-shirt tucked into a studded belt and dark washed jeans that were cuffed, like Lilly's. His boots were worn and rough looking.

He gestured to the seat across from her, "Mind if I join you?"

Lilly was embarrassed she had totally blanked on her manners. "Oh! Yes, sit down," she said with a nervous smile. "How are you?"

"I'm good. What are you working on?" Drew asked, gesturing toward her open laptop.

"Oh," Lilly snapped the top down on her laptop. "I'm coding," she explained.

Drew nodded slowly, "For a class?"

"No," Lilly laughed lightly, "It's a project I'm working on with one of my professors," Lilly tucked some stray strands of hair behind her ear.

"Tell me about it," Drew pressed as he leaned back comfortably in his leather chair.

"Seriously?" Lilly asked with eyebrows raised. No one ever wanted to hear about what she was working on. PH liked updates but even those conversations had to be kept short. Lilly could always tell when she had talked too long because the other person would have this glazed and half-baked expression on their face.

"Yeah, I'm interested," Drew smiled at her and leaned forward, his elbows propped on his knees, as he looked at her expectantly.

"Ok," Lilly exhaled and smiled, she'd give him a shot and see how long it took before his beautiful and rugged face turned into a slack jawed mask as she spoke. She gestured with her right hand to the computer, "So, I'm writing code for a new software product. Today I'm designing user interfaces."

"What does that mean?" Drew laughed.

"Ok," Lilly readjusted herself in the seat folding her hands on the table and sitting up straighter. He wasn't bored yet she'd talk a little longer this time. "So coding is actually super creative and you have to develop interfaces that make sense for your end users." She placed a hand on her collar bone referring to herself, "As an engineer I need to make sure that my software serves the entire population that will be utilizing the software in implementation." She loosely gestured with the same hand, "So, I don't have to go back later and re-engineer or fix it. It's super important that software products provide cultural adoption." She started using both hands fluidly as she spoke, hitting her stride, "So, that means that you have a tool or a piece of software that people actually want to use. It needs to be intuitive and easy to navigate, there's actually a lot that goes into it."

Drew was still watching her with interest. "So how do you make sure that it's easy to navigate or is adopted by the culture?" he asked seriously.

Lilly was impressed. He hung on longer than most. "Basically, you need a diverse group of individuals to perform preventative oversight. They essentially test and use the software as you go along and tell you what's right or what doesn't make any sense to them."

"Cool," Drew said with a slow nod.

Lilly squirmed with the compliment, "Yeah, I think so." She liked talking about her work.

"So, who are your testers?"

"Actually, my advisor has been super helpful and I'm using one of her classes as guinea pigs," Lilly laughed as she divulged this detail.

"And the guinea pigs are alright with this?" he joked with skeptical eyebrows.

"They're fine," Lilly said with a dismissive wave of her hand and a laugh.

"So, you said your friends don't want to hear all about this?" Drew asked dropping his scruffy chin.

"Right?" she laughed. Adding sarcastically, "Coding is so cool I can't believe they're not interested."

"Oh, you shouldn't do that," he said with startling intensity.

"Do what?" she nervously tucked her hair behind her ear where it promptly fell forward again.

His eyes were warm as he implored gently, "Don't belittle your work. What you're doing is amazing."

She stared into his eyes for longer than she had intended. She finally whispered, "Ok," holding his gaze.

He added, "You look really stunning when you talk about your work. You should do it more often."

Just then a girl with a burgundy pout and a chestnut brown bob walked into the coffee shop. Seeing Drew and Lilly she quickly marched over. She smiled aggressively, "Hey, Drew."

Drew leaned back as he acknowledged the unwelcome interruption. "Hey, Nicole," he said confidently. He held out a hand to indicate Lilly, "This is my friend, Lilly."

"Hi," Lilly greeted Nicole with a polite nod and smile. The ripples from the gaze she had shared with Max were still washing over her.

The girl shifted her weight to her back foot and cocked her head with attitude. "I'm Drew's girlfriend," Nicole clarified with a sassy bob.

"Hi," Lilly said again more uncomfortably. Lilly looked to Drew for some explanation and he rolled his eyes while Nicole stared Lilly down.

"You're friends with Porter Cain," Nicole continued as she rudely pointed at Lilly.

"Yep," Lilly said and nodded slowly. She now knew where the conversation would go so she leaned back and just let Nicole run with it. Porter was performing more and more and she was quickly becoming a campus celebrity. Unfortunately, that meant that people like Nicole felt the need to tell her what they really thought of Porter's talent.

"She's going to be like super famous," Nicole stated confidently.

"I guess," Lilly said with disinterest. She hated when conversations started this way.

"I've heard her on the radio. Drew, haven't we heard her on the radio?" Nicole continued in a perky voice.

"Yeah, I guess so," Drew said. He looked to Lilly and asked with laughter in his eyes, "Lilly, you're friends with her?" He was enjoying this too much.

"Yes," Lilly started to speak but Nicole cut her off.

"Porter started here this year and has been writing music all her life. Her mother's some huge gospel singer." Nicole took a quick breath and prattled on, "Porter Cain's in my philosophy class. She is so beautiful in real life. Don't you think she's beautiful?" Nicole asked Lilly actually suspending her monologue for Lilly's answer.

"Yes, Porter's really pretty."

"I don't think pretty is enough, she's stunning and truly beautiful," Nicole corrected.

Lilly sat quietly as Nicole continued raving about how amazing Porter was. After listening as long as she could without gagging Lilly said, "I'll see you around, Drew," and stood up to leave.

Nicole answered, "It was awesome meeting you, Lilly." Seeming to completely forget the evil eye she had given Lilly when she walked in, "We should get together and do a double date sometime," Nicole said eagerly and loud enough for the whole coffee shop to hear.

"Sorry, Lilly," Drew said with a poorly concealed laugh from his seat.

Lilly walked out of the coffee shop carrying her computer and supplies in her backpack. She took a deep breath once she was safely outside, relieved to be away from Nicole and surprised by the intimate interaction with Drew.

Lilly asked Drew on their way out of work a few days later, "Did you know they have a Whiskey Drinker's Society? Stephen just bought Charlie a membership as a Christmas gift."

Drew didn't even look at her, "I'm sure there are societies for all sorts of drunks."

Lilly laughed.

"People like to make up societies. Losers need groups. They make themselves feel better by calling it a society." Drew said with his usual cavalier tone.

"You're terrible," she laughed.

"You say that," Drew looked intensely into her eyes, "but you don't mean it."

He took her breath away, Lilly could feel her heart racing and her lungs constricted. He was right.

He leaned toward her as though he might kiss her but she quickly tucked her hair behind her ear and cleared her throat as she looked away. Their stats class would be over after their final and Lilly thought that would be a good thing. Spending time with Drew was becoming less of a guilty pleasure and more of a bad habit. She needed to break the cycle. The challenge was that Lilly liked spending time with Drew. He was comfortable to be around and where she sometimes felt out of place or like she needed to impress Charlie, she felt the exact opposite with Drew. She never dressed a certain way because she was going to see him and she certainly didn't waste time trying to ingratiate herself to his friends. Still she could sense that their relationship was drifting into a grey area and she wanted to avoid that, which she did the same way she had always avoided difficult situations, by focusing on her work.

12. FIRST SEMESTER FINALS

Finals week was blustery and cold. That Monday Emily came back from her Public Relations Strategy final with a flyer in hand announcing a floor meeting they were required to attend, it was in twenty minutes. Lilly used the time to finish reading an article and write out responses to the five questions her French professor had assigned.

Emily and Lilly walked to the meeting room and sat in the back talking. The room was large and beige with chairs arranged conference style. The metal chairs quickly filled with exhausted students, most looked angry to be pulled away from their last minute cramming for an unscheduled meeting with no stated purpose. Several students were reading materials or quizzing themselves on flashcards as they waited for the meeting to start.

The RA for their floor stood up in front of a long conference table and called the meeting to order. She babbled about regular topics like not burning popcorn, they caused the fire alarms to go off and the building had to be evacuated—every time. Then she gave a vague introduction to a middle aged man with sweat stains on his oxford and a beer belly.

He slowly stood up to speak. "Good afternoon y'all, I'm Information Technology Department Manager Don Inglesbury." He had a twang and a swagger in his gait as he paced the front of the room.

Lilly sat up straighter and paid attention. She worked in the IT department, but she had never seen him before.

"Our office is responsible for the maintenance and connectivity not only to the internet, but also to our university library system and databases." He pushed his glasses up further on his nose by the bridge.

A couple students nodded their understanding.

He took a deep breath and continued in a slow march, "Now, we don't know any of you as well as we know many of the other students on campus and that is something I'm here to talk to you about."

"I'm bored," Emily whispered.

"Shhh," Lilly hissed. She could feel her stomach tightening.

"Your floor is something of an anomaly on campus, whether y'all know it or not."

Lilly bit her bottom lip a little harder than she had intended and drew blood. "Fuck," she whispered to herself as she sucked her lip and the coppery flavor of her own blood flooded into her mouth.

Emily gave her a disapproving glare.

Don kept talking, "Our offices have not received a single call from your floor since September." Don surveyed the room with an angry gaze. "This is unheard of and dare I say impossible." He hiked up his pants with a swift hitch, "We're wondering if all of y'all are either not doing your assignments or if y'all have someone on the floor who is performing this maintenance for you."

The other students began to murmur and talk amongst themselves. Lilly was spinning the signet ring on her finger.

"What do you mean?" A thick boy wearing a Nirvana T-shirt asked loudly.

"Y'all should have regular maintenance issues," Don waved his arms to show his exasperation, "like losing connectivity to the internet, document sharing questions, finding lost files, system update questions, there's usually something happening with your computers that you want to call IT about."

"So nobody's called you?" The boy loudly interjected again.

"Exactly," Don smiled but it made him look more scary than happy.

The room started talking more audibly this time.

Don shouted to be heard over the hub-bub. "Now, I want to make clear, you're not in trouble. You're not going to be getting anyone else in trouble. We'd just like to speak to whoever it is you go to when y'all have problems with your technology."

"We take our stuff to Lilly," Julie Evans, the first person Emily had brought to Lilly to fix her computer, explained. *Damn it, Julie! Shut up!* Lilly thought to herself.

"Who's Lilly?" Don asked scanning the room like a laser beam.

The room turned to look at the back of the room. Emily looked at Lilly sharply. Lilly stood up slowly and half raised her hand, "I'm Lilly." It was mortifying to be called out in front of the entire floor.

"Thank you, Lilly. I'd like to talk to you after your meeting is over," he said from across the room.

Lilly said, "Sure," and sat down quickly. She immediately thought about her scholarship and was certain that she was going be expelled.

Don waddled back to his seat where he took a kerchief out of his pocket and mopped his sweaty brow.

The RA quickly wrapped up the meeting with a reminder not to leave food in their rooms over break. The meeting disbursed quickly as the other students rushed to get back to their studies. Lilly stayed seated waiting for the room to clear out. Julie Evans gave her an apologetic shrug as she left but Lilly turned away from her stiffly.

Emily asked, "Do you want me to stay?"

"No. I'll be fine," Lilly said, hoping that it would be true.

Emily got up, giving Lilly half a smile and a quiet, "Good luck," before she left.

Once the room had cleared Lilly slowly walked to the front of the room.

"Hi Lilly, I'm Department Manager Ingelsbury," he reached a chubby hand out for a shake.

Lilly gave his hand a firm shake, "Lilly Carter," she replied professionally.

"You're the one that's been fixing all of the tech issues on the floor?" Don raised an eyebrow in doubt, "Just you and no one else?"

"Is that a problem? I was just trying to help," she explained seriously.

Don raised his voice an octave to a sickly sweet pitch, "You're sure it's not your boyfriend you're covering for—he's not going to get into trouble if you tell me."

Lilly looked at Don like he was the stupidest person on the planet.

Don dropped his saccharine tone in response to Lilly's glare. "I just ask because some of these problems are fairly complex and someone would probably need a lot of help to do this kind of work. It's really technical stuff and hard to do so I'm pretty sure it's a guy or a couple guys fixing things around here."

Lilly squared her shoulders and her jaw, "Actually none of it has been particularly difficult. Maybe the technicians you're used to working with are just unqualified."

"That may be," Don said slowly, nodding his head but not seeming to believe her.

"It's just me Don, what's the problem?" *you sexist asshole,* she thought.

"Not really a problem…we just need to document all of the issues that come up across campus. It's what determines our staffing levels, our funding, and all that official stuff. If you're fixing things we don't have record of what went wrong or of what was done to repair it." Don put his hand up as if to stop her from jumping in. "And it's great that you're helping your friends now, but you're going to move to a new dorm next year. And we're not going to have the funding or the appropriate staff to address the needs of our students next year because the numbers will be artificially decreased, because of you. Do you see what I mean?" he asked.

"You want me to stop helping people?" Lilly answered confidently even though her heart was pounding loud and fast. "Am I in trouble?"

"No, you're not in trouble, but we would like you to forward any issues that the other students bring to you to our offices. I have some business cards you can pass out to the kids," he said handing her a handful of bent and worn business cards from his thick sweaty palm.

"Ok," she said eager to get out of the room and away from him.

"Thanks for coming forward." Don added with another menacing smile, "I would have hated to have to track you down."

"Right," Lilly turned on her heel. She could feel his eyes boring into her back as she walked away.

She quickly walked back to her room. Her heart was racing.

Emily looked up from her color coded flashcards when Lilly entered the room. She asked, "What did he want?"

Lilly threw Don's business cards in the trash. "They don't want me fixing computers anymore. He wants me to give people his business cards instead."

"That's stupid," Emily said leaning back in her desk chair. "Are you going to do it?"

"Probably, I don't want to lose my scholarship." Lilly collapsed backwards onto her bed and covered her eyes with her arms.

"If you can fix something faster than they can, why would we want to call them?"

"He's worried they're going to lose funding or staff because I'm helping people and it messes with the numbers." Lilly rolled her eyes to the ceiling.

"Well, the good thing is you don't have to fix people's computers anymore," Emily said, trying to sound optimistic.

Lilly threw her arms down to her sides on the bed. "Yeah, but that means I don't make any more money when people need something fixed."

"True. But you have that job on campus now. I'm surprised he didn't just ask you at work," Emily added.

"I don't know him. I think he's in administration or something. I'll talk to Drew about it, he might know who this guy is," Lilly decided.

Lilly spent the rest of the day in the library trying to catch up on her coding, she had devoted so much attention to finals that she didn't have time to follow up on the comments and suggestions PH's 100 class submitted to help her improve her project. PH sent several notes with the beta tester comments, suggesting how to apply their requests to make the site more user friendly, which helped Lilly to understand and visualize what PH wanted. Lilly liked how quickly she was able to work through the changes with PH's comments.

By Wednesday of finals week Lilly was exhausted. She had two tests to go and had just left a hellacious Renaissance Art final. Her phone rang as she trudged back to the dorm.

"Hey," she smiled to herself as she spoke to Charlie, an icy wind blowing her hair behind her.

"Hey, Lil, how are you?" Charlie asked.

"I'm good my Renaissance Art final kicked my ass. I'm on my way back to the room, I think I'm going to take a nap. I'm totally fried. What's up?"

"Nothing, I'll meet you there," he sounded weird.

"Ok," she said, not sure of how to read his tone. She hung up and shoved the phone and her hands deep into her pockets.

When she got back to the room there was a bouquet of wildflowers, wrapped in brown paper resting across her desk. She quickly dropped her bag and walked over to smell the flowers. They were beautiful. As Lilly picked them up she found a jewelry box underneath the blooms. She gently lifted the box and ran her fingers over its textured surface.

"Do you like it?" Charlie asked from the open door.

"I didn't open it yet," she admitted, stunned.

"Well, go ahead. Open it," he said encouragingly.

Lilly opened the box gently as if it were Pandora's. The box was black, heavy cardboard. It looked severe with a black ribbon and silver lettering. Lilly slid off the ribbon and flipped the box around in her hands trying to figure out how it opened. When she finally tilted the lid back and up it revealed a silver David Yurman bracelet. The light glinted off of the metal and a large square cut blue topaz stone. It was made of two bands of etched metal that looked like the tension rods of a bridge. Lilly did not think it was pretty at all, but it looked expensive. "Oh my gosh, Charlie!" her voice came out high pitched and shrill.

"Do you like it?" He asked again as he walked to her from the doorway in two quick steps.

"Of course, I like it. It's gorgeous!" She lied as she stared at the bracelet.

"I thought you could use a little something for Christmas," he said proudly, bending his knees deeply so he could make eye contact with her.

"It's not Christmas yet," she mumbled.

"I know, but I thought it might be nice to have during finals, a little something to keep your spirits up," Charlie lit up the room with his smile.

"Charlie, this is too much," Lilly said as she broke her gaze with the bracelet and smiled weakly at him.

"You don't want it?" he teased gently.

"I can't accept this," Lilly was shocked and flattered but it wasn't right.

"Why not? It'll look great on you," Charlie said. "Here, let's see it on your wrist."

"I can't take the bracelet, Charlie," Lilly continued to protest as Charlie took the box from her hands and pulled the bracelet out.

"Sure you can," he said as he wrapped the bracelet around her wrist and fastened the clasp.

"Oh! Sparkly," Emily announced as she walked into the room.

"I'm not keeping it," Lilly said firmly. Her hands were trembling and she felt cold. The bracelet was heavy on her wrist, it felt like a shackle.

"Just beautiful," Emily said. "Good job, Charlie."

"I do my best," he smiled. "I'm glad it meets your standards, Emily."

"Charlie, I love it, but I can't keep it," Lilly said again, imploring Charlie with her eyes to understand.

"Look what Charlie gave Lilly," Emily announced as she grabbed Lilly's arm and held it up for Celia and Porter to see from the doorway as they followed her inside.

"Oh, pretty," Celia confirmed happily.

"Very nice," Porter said approvingly. "David Yurman?"

"Yes," Emily confirmed.

"I'm not keeping it," Lilly announced to the room her voice and resolve getting weaker by the second.

"Why not?" Celia asked sweetly. Her face looked serious as she saw Lilly's white lipped expression.

"Don't you like it?" Charlie asked again, hurt in his voice.

"No, I love it. It's just too much," Lilly said, wishing they were still alone.

"Don't be rude, Lilly." Porter ordered, "It's a gift, say thank you."

Lilly looked up at Charlie's face and at the girls standing all around them, "Thank you," she said, cowing to peer pressure.

"You're welcome," Charlie said with a smile as he put his hand on the small of her back and kissed her.

"Alright, we'll give y'all some privacy," Emily said waiving her arms and averting her gaze.

"No need Emily," Charlie said, pulling back. "Lilly's taking a nap and I need to study." He kissed her again. Leaning back at the hips he said, "I'll see you later."

"Ok," she exhaled smiling up at him.

He squeezed her hands before he walked out of the room.

"We're going to the library," Emily announced as she shoved some books and notebooks into her satchel.

"Awesome bracelet," Celia said quietly to Lilly as she followed the other girls out the door.

"Thanks." Alone again, Lilly quietly looked down at her wrist, terrified of what she had gotten herself into with no idea how she would ever get out of this. She felt cornered and didn't know what to do next.

When Lilly sat down to take her stats final the next morning wearing the bracelet, Drew just rolled his eyes.

"Don't ask," she said, furious she had let Porter shame her into accepting the gift.

Lilly flew through the exam. She wanted to get out of the room and away from Drew before he could comment on Charlie's gift but she had to wait to ask him about Don.

She waited outside the door to the auditorium scrolling through her phone and anxiously stressing about her last final, French. She needed to go study more, she danced impatiently in the hallway. Finally, Drew walked out of the classroom laughing and chatting casually with the professor. They shook hands and Drew turned to her.

"What's up Carter?"

"I might be in trouble," she led cryptically.

"I like it." He gave her a mischievous grin, "How can I help?"

Lilly tucked her hair behind her ear, "Do you know Don Inglesbury? He works in the IT Department."

"I don't know him," Drew answered. "He does the oversight of the help desk."

"Ok, well we had a floor meeting because he wanted to find out who does the IT maintenance on the floor. I... um... I..." Lilly did not like how what she was about to say would sound.

"What?" Drew laughed, he seemed to enjoy watching Lilly squirm.

Lilly exhaled audibly and decided to just rip the band-aid off. "I've been earning money on the side by fixing computers for the kids on my floor."

Drew laughed, "You sound like someone beat that out of you."

"I hate this," she said angrily.

"So, what? You made some money off of the rich kids and got caught. Now they want you to stop?"

Lilly exhaled again, this was thoroughly unpleasant. If she didn't get caught she never would have spoken of this. She felt common and guilty. "Yes," she said through gritted teeth.

Drew spoke nonchalantly, "He's just trying to cover his ass."

"I guess," Lilly answered, unconvinced.

"Look, you needed money and you found a way to do it. It's nothing to be ashamed of," Drew shook his head from side to side.

Lilly stared at the ground.

Drew stepped forward and lightly touched her arm, "Carter, it's not a big deal. He just wants to keep his job and his funding, let him."

"Ugh," Lilly said with dramatic disgust and an exaggerated head roll.

"You're not going to win this," Drew said seriously. "So, you stop fixing computers, it's finals anyway you'll be home for a month and then when you come back it's totally forgotten. The kids on your floor call IT, you have extra time to do whatever you do, and Don's happy."

"Yeah," Lilly pursed her lips and stared off into the distance.

"I know you like being perfect but that's not life."

Lilly nodded and begrudgingly said, "I know."

"Don't get all bent out of shape," Drew wrapped his arm around her shoulders and started ushering her down the hall.

"I'm not," she said.

Drew looked down at her, "You're salty as hell."

"Yes," Lilly said with a laugh and a smile, "I am."

"Let it go, Carter."

13. CHRISTMAS BREAK

Lilly worried about not making enough money to cover her expenses but tried to block it out of her mind as she worked. Sitting in the cold back room of The Computer Repair Shop on Madison Lilly thought about the different worlds that she and Charlie inhabited. He was vacationing in Rome with his family over the holiday while she worked as many hours as possible back in Cleveland. She pictured the bracelet safely hidden in her bag, untouched and unopened since she shoved it there before leaving school. She couldn't keep the bracelet in good conscience. *And really, did he know her at all if he thought that it was an appropriate gift? They had only known each other for a few months.* She needed to focus her full attention on school anyway. Her project was really coming together, there was potential for her to build something real. Lilly took a deep breath, it smelled like ink cartridges and chemicals, she had to break up with him.

Christmas was typical. Lilly and Sophia exchanged gifts privately. Sophia gave Lilly a Liz Claiborne duvet covered in pink and green rosettes for her dorm room. Lilly gave Sophia a new pair of seven jeans she had found on sale that didn't have any holes in them. Melanie told the girls that her gifts were their education and winter coats and they should be grateful. Lilly tried to be gracious even though Melanie never bought her a coat and Lilly was paying for school herself.

In her mother's presence Lilly fought a constant battle to keep her composure and keep herself from yelling but after another evening where Melanie lamented to Lilly's grandmother over dinner about how she didn't have money for rent or the heat because of how much she was spending on Lilly's education, Lilly snapped.

127

They were in the dining room of the rented house Melanie and Sophia shared on a quiet cul-de-sac in the West Park neighborhood of Cleveland. Their neighbors were mostly retirees and city workers required to live within the city limits but unwilling to move downtown. The room was modest but cozy. The table, buffet, and china cabinet were all relics purchased at garage sales and clearly bearing the watermarks of basement floodings and the scars of careless use. The meal was basic, spaghetti, frozen meatballs, and canned sauce, but it was the best that Sophia and Lilly could put together.

Lilly had vigilantly watched the oven to assure that the garlic bread did not burn, as was Melanie's tradition. Lilly had grown accustomed to the meals at school that neither required the use of a fire extinguisher nor had to be pitched based on the percentage of burnt sections to frozen. Though everything had been done to assure the meal's success, the hum of conversation was interrupted as Lilly put down her fork with an angry click. Unable to restrain herself for another moment, Lilly firmly stated, "That is a lie, Mom."

Melanie spoke evenly, "Excuse me?"

Lilly's voice was tired, "You're not spending anything on me. Stop lying to Grandma about where your money goes."

Lilly's grandmother sat perfectly still, her stoic midwestern face a shield of ice. The look conveyed her disapproval succinctly. She was watching the conversation unfold. Her pencil thin eyebrows arched up toward her halo of white curls. Grandma was a religious zealot who believed anything good was earned through hard work, anything except whatever Melanie wanted. Melanie was the eldest of three children and her mother's favorite. When anyone else had a complaint, Lilly's grandmother attributed it to their lack of prayer or a willingness to work hard. When Melanie complained, Grandma patiently opened her checkbook and asked, "How much?" Melanie could do no wrong in her mother's eyes and by proxy Lilly and Sophia were ungrateful, god-less, girls with no respect for authority and their saint of a mother.

"It's like I was saying," Melanie spoke directly to her mother, "kids these days are so ungrateful."

Grandma gave a firm nod, willing to support Melanie but not to enter into a verbal assault on her granddaughter.

Lilly felt the sting of shame and disapproval it burned and she swiftly launched a full attack, "I'm not ungrateful. I have a scholarship, which I earned. It's a full ride. You literally spend nothing on me except when I'm home on break. I am grateful that you let me stay here and that you let me eat, but outside of that you don't pay for anything I do."

"And where do you get your clothes?" Melanie asked condescendingly rolling her eyes expressively to her mother.

Grandma's fork was poised midair, waiting for the answer. She only allowed her eyes to move between Lilly and Melanie.

"I buy them myself. I have a job and I pay my own cell phone bill, I have since I was sixteen." Lilly's voice was controlled, she theorized that the second she raised her voice in an argument that was the moment she lost her credibility. Also, it annoyed the crap out of Melanie who loved to get a rise out of other people.

"And where do you think my money goes? I provide this home for you and your sister, I pay all the bills," Melanie started her familiar tirade as her mother stared disapprovingly at Lilly.

"I imagine you spent it on booze for yourself," Lilly said frankly. She added, "You didn't even put together this dinner, Sophia bought the groceries, I cooked, you just showed up half drunk after it was all done," Lilly said confidently daring her grandmother to doubt her.

Melanie took a generous gulp of merlot. "Who was supposed to pick up your grandmother?"

"You can pick up Grandma," Lilly acknowledged, "but don't pretend that you had anything to do with this meal or keeping this house running because you do the minimum and you're just asking Grandma for more money so you can spend it on yourself."

Melanie still hadn't raised her voice. "If you're so miserable here, why don't you leave?"

Lilly couldn't speak. Her mother should spend Christmas alone she was a horrible and miserable person. But Lilly froze, all the truths were there on the tip of her tongue and yet she couldn't say them out loud. She didn't want to hurt Melanie, she just wanted her to stop lying and manipulating other people. Lilly silently picked up her plate, walked to the kitchen, and began doing dishes.

After the meal was over, Lilly's Grandmother came into the kitchen carrying her plate and cutlery and placed it on the counter. Lilly looked up from her task hoping for some sort of support.

Her grandmother folded her hands in front of herself and spoke firmly, "You've always favored your father's side, ever since you were a baby."

Before the sting of the insult could fully rest Lilly had her comeback ready. Setting her jaw Lilly said, "She's robbing you blind."

"That may be so," Grandma acknowledged, "but she's your mother."

This was the first time Lilly had ever heard her Grandmother acknowledge that she knew she was being used. Lilly was shocked. "You know?" She asked, flush with amazement.

"I don't know what you're talking about," Grandma clipped. "You're dripping water all over the floor."

Lilly turned to see where her elbow was dripping water and when she looked back her grandmother was gone. It was strange to realize that her grandmother knew she was being used and didn't seem to care. Lilly tried to make sense of it but the only answer that seemed to fit was that her grandmother was lonely and Melanie might lie and take money from her but she called every day. Lilly surmised it was a trade-off. Her grandmother would have to give her money and in return Melanie would always call her to complain about the imaginary injustices of the world. When she thought about it, Lilly actually pitied her grandmother who seemed to think that the only thing she had to offer the world, or a friend, was her money. Then again, Grandma had raised Melanie and taught her to be this person maybe she saw nothing wrong with this arrangement.

The next day Lilly was coding on her bed, wrapped in her new pink floral duvet, when Sophia walked into her room.

"So, how do you like it?" Sophia asked.

Lilly looked up from the screen, "What? The duvet? I love it." She snuggled into the plush comforter.

"No, school."

"School? Yeah, it's fine."

"Is it a lot different than being here?" Sophia asked wistfully.

"It is. It's nice." Lilly didn't know how to tell Sophia that it was heaven. Lilly couldn't tell her sister how wonderful it was because Sophia still had to stay home, she still had to live with Melanie's erratic mood swings and drunken binges.

"That's a good thing," Sophia nodded as she looked out of the window at the snow falling.

"We have to keep working. I hate it here," Sophia said seriously, walking out without another word.

Lilly spent the rest of the night coding furiously. She wanted something better, something more. Melanie was poison and the more time Lilly spent with her the worse she felt. Lilly wouldn't come back home again, her rage fueled her work but Lilly did not like how consumed she was by her fury. Living like this, with lies, financial insecurity, and mental imbalance was all too stressful. Melanie was not worth it.

At the end of break Lilly repacked her bag and finally pulled out the bracelet. As she looked down at the twisted metal there was a knock on her bedroom door. Lilly closed the box and shoved it back to the bottom of her bag.

"Hey," Sophia said as she poked her head into the room.

"You can come in," Lilly said relaxing and pulling the jewelry box back out.

"What are you doing?" Sophia asked curiously.

"Packing."

Sophia jutted her chin toward Lilly's lap, "What's in the box?"

"Close the door," Lilly instructed.

"Oh!" Sophia smiled brightly, "Is it a present for me?" She swiftly stepped into the room and closed the door behind herself.

"No. It was a gift from Charlie, I'm not keeping it," Lilly said as she turned the open box to face Sophia.

"Holy shit, Lil," Sophia gasped crossing the room in a bound.

"I know," Lilly said seriously.

Sophia's eyes were huge, "Is it real?"

"I think so," Lilly admitted.

Sophia shoved her sister's shoulder roughly. "And you've just had that thing sitting in your bag?"

"What am I supposed to do with it?" Lilly lifted her hands and shoulders emphatically.

"What is it for?" Sophia leaned back with suspicion, trying to read her older sister's face.

"Christmas."

Sophia took a breath and gave Lilly a judgmental look, "Eew, are you sleeping with him?"

"That is none of your business," Lilly snapped the box closed, shoving it deep into her bag. "And no," she added tersely, "I'm not sleeping with him, yet."

"Gross! He wants to," Sophia teased with a smile.

"He's just trying to impress me," Lilly said quietly.

"Maybe he has a tiny weenie," Sophia whispered.

Lilly burst out laughing.

"Seriously, oh-my-gosh, that's what it's for," Sophia hypothesized with a laugh.

Lilly gasped for air. "Stop it!"

"That's probably why you got a bracelet. He's thinking, 'Don't be disappointed in my tiny weenie, I'll give you jewelry.'"

Both girls laughed hysterically. One of them snorted which sent them both into more fits of laughter.

"I have to give it back," Lilly finally said, out of breath and wiping tears from her eyes.

"Yeah, you do," Sophia confirmed. "That's just too much. It's super nice but totally inappropriate."

"Right? That's what I thought but these girls at school were like, 'Oh it's so pretty. Say thank you' and I got all intimidated and didn't just tell him to take it back."

"They were all there when he gave it to you?" Sophia asked, with a look of disapproval.

Lilly shook her head, "They just showed up as he was giving it to me and I didn't want to shoot him down in front of them."

Sophia rolled her eyes, "Yeah, you're a real saint for taking that obscenely expensive bracelet so he wouldn't feel bad," she said sarcastically.

"Shut up. I know. I did the wrong thing. I'm giving it back."

"Good," Sophia affirmed with a solid nod. "Are you ready to go?"

"Yeah," Lilly agreed, zipping her suitcase shut.

Sophia drove Lilly to the airport. She had borrowed a car from a friend for the trip.

"Have a safe flight," Sophia said, acting tough as she hugged her big sister goodbye.

"I'll miss you best buddy," Lilly said.

"Aww, I am your best buddy," Sophia replied happily.

"You are," Lilly said and hugged her sister more fiercely.

14. SPRING SEMESTER

Campus was quiet when Lilly got back to Vanderbilt. The winter was less aggressive in Nashville, and it made Lilly optimistic for spring and all of the new beginnings possible in the New Year. Emily wouldn't be back until the following morning and Lilly had the room to herself. The new floral bedspread Sophia bought her for Christmas looked beautiful. She was lying on the bed reading when the door was suddenly kicked in. The crash startled Lilly and it took her a moment to process. A tangled mess of arms, legs, and flying clothes followed.

"What the hell?" Lilly blurted out.

"Oh, hi," a girl with black curls said as a skinny blonde boy with several tattoos kissed her neck and shoulders. "This is Trevor. I'm Amy, your new roommate."

Trevor came up for air and said, "Nice to meet you." Lilly barely had time to respond before he was back to pulling Amy's hair and kissing her face.

"Excuse you!" Lilly said, "I already have a roommate." She wasn't sure who she was talking to as it was clear that neither of them were listening. "Seriously, you're going to have to leave." Lilly was making her voice louder in hopes of distracting them.

The girl held up a piece of university letterhead. Lilly snatched it out of her hand. "You're in 212, your room is 214," Lilly announced with a self-satisfied tone.

The girl snorted and the boy laughed. "Our bad," he said as they quickly grabbed what they had thrown and walked out, still tangling their fingers together. They proceeded to bang on the door to 214.

Lilly heard the door open and immediately pitied her neighbor, Jessica, a mild-mannered girl from Phoenix. She barely had time to say hello before Lilly heard them push her aside and, based on the noise, find the bed.

Rather than listen to the remainder of the interlude next door, Lilly decided to go for a walk. She grabbed her bag and locked the door. The door to 214 was still open and Lilly glared her disapproval through it, in case anyone was looking.

Outside the brisk air felt refreshing, it was peaceful and serene on campus. Lilly thought more about her project. Essentially, she was automating Don Inglesbury's job. After his menacing comments last semester Lilly refocused the program to address the issues he brought up. He would no longer be able to tell another student not to help someone else because 'the school needs to track it.' If it worked, the system would constantly monitor activity providing real-time data based on the specifications outlined. She thought to herself, *The software should also allow for requested alarms to notify management if activity was significantly lower or higher in specified areas.* Lilly headed back to the dorm to write that down.

She gingerly opened the door to her room. When she walked in she saw Amy and Trevor, smoking. Not only was Emily's bed a mess of clothes and tangled bodies, they were wrapped up in Lilly's duvet!

"How the hell did you get in here?" Lilly demanded shoving the door wide open.

"Shhh," Amy said in a mocking whisper to Trevor behind navy blue fingernails.

"No, this is not ok!" Lilly yelled, ripping the comforter off of them in a rainbow of pinks and greens flying through the air in an angry arc. "This is mine, it is not yours."

The intruders looked at Lilly like her hair was on fire.

Lilly yelled, "Get the hell out of my room before I report you to campus security!"

Amy and Trevor looked at each other and started laughing.

Lilly could feel the blood rushing to her face. "I am not kidding, get the hell out!"

Trevor grabbed his pants and pulled his T-shirt on, "You don't need to get so worked up," he said. Leaning into her personal space, he added, "it was just a little fun, and your blanket is so cozy."

"You're disgusting," Lilly said flatly. "Get out!"

"Is everything ok in here?" It was Charlie. Lilly had never been more relieved to see him. Leaning in the doorway he was a gentle giant but in that moment he was her giant, "What's going on Lil?"

"Dude, your girl is going crazy," Trevor said, combing his fingers through the greasy blonde tangles atop his head.

"Hold on. His girl? His girl? Is that what you just said?" That was it; there was no calm and collected Lilly anymore. She snapped, "How dare you insinuate that I belong to him in any way. I am my own person and I stand by what I said, whether he does, or any man does, means nothing. Do you hear me you insignificant perv? Nothing." She stepped into his personal space spiting fire and hot breath into his face, "So why don't you take your tacky ripped jeans and your Wal-mart T-shirt and go home to the trailer. Nobody wants you here and while you're at it take this whore with you!" Lilly then turned to Amy. "This is not your room. Who the hell do you think you are breaking in here? I am calling campus security and having you both removed, if not arrested, for trespassing."

Lilly was hot and out of breath, she could tell people were staring and she didn't care. The rage filled her so completely that her body trembled with its force. *This drama was unacceptable and Lilly would not stand for anyone trying to ruin the sanctuary she had created. She spent all of her energy working to get out, to get away from people like this, people like her mother. They were not going to bring that shit into her life again. Her life would be normal, damn-it!*

Trevor ducked past Charlie who said nothing but secured the area with his presence alone.

Amy had her arms wrapped over her tanned topless breasts, flattening them to her chest like pancakes, as she said, "Could you close the freaking door so I can get dressed?"

"No," Lilly said with annoyance, she owed Amy nothing. "Leave my room now! This is ridiculous. You do not get to behave this way and you certainly don't get to treat me or my things with disrespect."

Amy quickly put on her shirt. She said, "Bitch," under her breath as she picked up her bra and left.

Lilly agreed with her, "That's right, I am a bitch. Get out now," Lilly said with a menacing smile. She then grabbed the paper with Amy's name and address; they had left it on Lilly's desk. She marched out the door and into the hallway. Charlie stepped behind her silently. She slammed and locked the door and marched across the icy quad to Residence Life in silence.

The Residence Life building was located across the quad from Lilly's dorm. It had a modern and clean sign out front but the interior was tired with worn carpeting and utilitarian looking desks piled high with folders and paperwork. The outdated furniture was torn at the edges and ready to move on to its next life at the bottom of a trash heap.

The RA on duty was named Casey. She was a slender girl with mousy brown hair and a high pitched child-like voice. Casey sat behind a messy desk as she said, "It was most likely an accident, if you could try to be a little understanding of her situation as a new student."

Lilly shifted her weight. "So you're not going to do anything?"

Casey's answer was meek and faltering, "Even if we did move Ms. Matthews, we couldn't do it for at least another month. It's the first day back from the holiday break and we don't know which students will be returning."

"So you're saying, she gets to stay and there is nothing you can do about it?" Lilly crossed her arms.

"We might be able to move her later in the semester," Casey scrolled through something on her computer screen, "just not immediately."

"How soon can you get her out?" Lilly demanded.

"We'd have to hold a hearing with the Residence Life board. Also, there is no smoking in the dorm rooms. If any of the materials in the room are found to have burn marks or require cleaning because of the smoke, you will be fined."

Lilly slapped her arms down to her sides in exasperation. "I wasn't the one smoking in the room!"

Casey parroted a policy she had clearly memorized. "Students are responsible for all of the University issued furniture in the room."

Lilly gestured wildly with her arms, "Fine. That's great. She breaks into my room with an unauthorized guest and she gets a hearing while I pay for it. That seems fair," Lilly said sarcastically and marched out of the office in a huff.

Lilly hiked across the quad still angry and frustrated. It was one of those bright grey days in winter where it almost hurts to look through the cold clear air. The clouds seemed to beam down on them, reflecting off of their clothes, making everything look neon.

"Do you want to talk?" Charlie asked.

Lilly was exasperated. She answered firmly, "Nope."

"Did you have a nice break?" he inquired, trying to break the tension.

Lilly's voice was clipped and she spoke sarcastically, "It was great."

"Did you do anything fun?"

Lilly stopped marching and turned to face him. "No, Charlie, I didn't do anything fun. I worked. That's what people like me do, we don't go on vacations, we work."

A few minutes later Charlie tried again. "Want to get something to eat?"

"Fine," Lilly said trying to take a deep breath and feeling guilty for snapping at him. This was not a side of herself she wanted him to see. She was furious at Amy, at Residence Life, and at herself for freaking out and yet she couldn't stop. The flood gates were open and everything she didn't say to her mother was coming out. Like a waterfall, she just couldn't hold anything back anymore. "Don't look at me like that." she snapped, "The only person I am more irritated with than that girl right now is you." She knew she had gone too far but it was too late and she couldn't dam her feelings anymore.

"What did I do?" He was shocked.

"I don't know Charlie, what did you do? Who gives someone they've known for four months a bracelet?"

"You're mad that I got you a present?" He looked amazed.

"A bracelet worth hundreds of dollars," Lilly gestured wildly with her hands.

"You don't like it?"

"It is not a matter of not liking it. It's a matter of cost. You don't even know me," she hissed.

"Seriously, if you're mad about that girl breaking into your room, fine, but don't take it out on me." They were both walking quickly and talking loudly.

Lilly's eyes were fiery, "I'm mad at her for breaking into my room. I'm mad at you for being totally out of touch with reality. Why would you give me something like that? I can't possibly reciprocate that kind of gift. Unless you're expecting some other type of reciprocation in which case, you are totally out of line."

Charlie put a hand up in front of Lilly and she slowed to a stop. He took her forearms in his hands, looked into Lilly's eyes, and said calmly, "If you don't want it, you could have just told me. I'll take it back."

"Good. Take it back, I don't want it." Lilly pulled the bracelet out of her bag and thrust it at him.

He carefully placed the bracelet into his pocket. He asked, "Are you breaking up with me?"

Lilly tried to muster some of the angry confidence she had just had in Residence Life. It was as if all the energy had drained away from her body. Her answer was sad and slow, "Yeah, I think that's what that means. I can't be with someone like you."

"What does that mean?" Charlie asked with a crushed look.

"It means," Lilly sighed aloud and looked up at the naked tree branches above them, "I can't afford to be with you."

"I see," Charlie looked down at his shoes.

Uncomfortable with the silence Lilly asked quickly, "You know what I felt when I thought you had hooked up with Porter?"

"What?" he asked meekly.

"I was relieved, Charlie, because you belong with someone like Porter. You should be with someone who has money, someone who can do the stuff you like. You just bought a $500 bracelet and gave it away. I don't think anyone in my family has ever bought anything that expensive."

Charlie nodded and looked around the quad aimlessly, "So you don't like me because I have money?"

"I do like you," Lilly admitted, her voice catching in her throat. "I like you so much, but I can't just take bracelets and flowers and act like it's totally normal."

"It is normal, Lilly," Charlie said firmly.

She shook her head and wiped the cold tears forming in her eyes, "Maybe where you come from."

"And you're just going to end us?" He looked into her eyes as if willing her to change her mind.

"I have to," she said. "What are we going to do, date until you want to go on vacation and I can't come? Or you want to pay for everything like I'm some sort of leech? I won't do that." Tears were quickly rolling down her face, "I got here on my own, I can pay my own way. I don't need some guy to take care of me."

Charlie kicked the ground. "I don't want to take care of you. I thought it would make you happy. I didn't realize you'd hate me for it."

"I don't hate you but that gift had nothing to do with me. I don't even wear bracelets."

With a sudden spurt of uncharacteristic emotion he demanded, "Then why did you take it?"

"Because you wanted me to," she gestured with a limp wave of her arm, "and the girls were all there, I don't know. It was a bad decision on my part. I'm sorry I took it to begin with," she shook her head quickly, as if still convincing herself. "I shouldn't have. I'm not mad at you. I'm just sorry, I can't be that girl."

"You are the girl I want to be with," Charlie said trying to look her in the eye but she kept shifting her gaze, refusing to look at him.

"No, I'm not." She shook her head stubbornly, "You want to be with a girl who wears silver bracelets and goes to Europe. You don't want to be with someone like me."

Charlie grabbed her shoulders and pulled her in for a hug, "You know, I really like you Lil."

"I really like you too," Lilly said with a lump in her throat as she wrapped her arms around his warm waist.

After several minutes of silence, he kissed her forehead and walked away.

Lilly stared straight ahead refusing to watch him walk away. When she was sure he was gone and she felt frozen through, Lilly walked back to her room. Once there, Lilly took her duvet down to the laundry room cursing Amy with every step.

The following day Lilly woke up late and went to breakfast in the dining hall. She ate alone and walked back to the dorm. She spent the day coding and organizing her bag for the first day of class.

That afternoon, Amy appeared in Lilly's doorway.

"How's my favorite neighbor?" she asked in a condescending tone.

"I'm fine," Lilly said coldly. "How are you, Amy?"

"Just great," Amy paused for effect, "Campus security stopped by while you were at breakfast. "

"What did they want?" Lilly tried to sound calm so Amy wouldn't know how much she was getting to her.

"They wanted to make sure you knew that this was a non-smoking dorm and if they find any burns or damage to the room or the furniture they'll be forced to charge you a fine."

"I don't smoke." It was Lilly's turn to pause for effect, "Don't you mean campus security stopped by to see you?" Lilly could feel her jaw tightening.

Amy smiled brightly. "I told them they got the names wrong." She was clearly proud of herself. "It looks like your parents will be getting a letter regarding your unseemly behavior." Amy smiled again with self-satisfaction and crossed her arms. "Good luck explaining your terrible behavior to your family."

"You're despicable," Lilly said standing up.

"Aww you don't mean that," Amy sneered. "You're just jealous you didn't think of it first."

"I'm just sorry that you think lying will work. I don't even know how you got into this school you're clearly not very bright." With that Lilly slapped the door shut in her face.

Lilly was fuming but there was nothing she could do. Amy was making every effort to get under her skin and it was working, which only made Lilly madder. Lilly was aggressively cleaning the room, when Emily got back.

"I can't believe she did that," Emily said after Lilly told her about her exchange with Amy. "Will your parents be upset? Will they believe it?"

"Oh," Lilly said with a start, she hadn't even considered or cared what Melanie would think, probably because to Melanie that sort of parenting was uninteresting and if she said anything it would be a snide remark made in public to shame Lilly. "No, I don't think my mom cares. If anything, she'll trash talk about me to my grandmother but she doesn't care about what I do."

Emily looked deeply concerned and empathetic.

Seeing the pity on Emily's face Lilly quickly shifted the conversation, she didn't need Emily's sympathy, "My concern is just my scholarship and my academic standing. That girl is clearly a pathological liar," Lilly said. "What do I do, Em? Do I try to talk to campus security or are they just going to think I'm nuts?"

Sensing Lilly's discomfort with revealing more about her family life, Emily did not press her further. She responded with typical grace, "Lil, all you can do is take a deep breath and remember, 'You can't expect crazy to act right.'"

"What does that mean?" Lilly asked.

"It means she's not right in the head so expecting her to make sense or trying to understand where she's coming from is never going to work. You've just got to let it go, go with God. She's messed up, bless her heart, and there's nothing you can do about it so it's best to just live and let live."

"Right," Lilly sighed with exasperation, "but she's going out of her way to make my life difficult."

"The best you can do is avoid her; she's poison and you don't want to be around poison, Lil."

"You're right," Lilly admitted.

Emily perked up, "Good, now let's not think about her anymore."

"Alright," Lilly laughed, "I won't think about it."

15. GOAL SETTING

It was two weeks into the spring semester and Lilly had just delivered a recap of her beta-test results to PH. The software still had bugs that she would need to fix but overall Lilly felt it was a success. She had used the holiday break and her free time without Charlie to focus on her scholarship project and she really felt good about her work. There was room to improve, but that was good, it meant she could keep working to make it better. Lilly impatiently tapped her boots on the floor. PH was looking at her hands playing with them, dancing them over her desk top, teasing them over her keyboard and then pulling them back together again. Finally, she clapped, startling Lilly.

PH spoke in her usual confident voice, "I agree with your synopsis that there's room to grow."

Lilly nodded, pleased with that answer.

But PH kept talking, "I disagree with your interpretation that it went well." PH hovered her hand over Lilly's documents and reports, "This was a disaster. The program is clumsy. It is not intuitive."

Lilly's eyes bulged she didn't think it was that bad.

PH looked into the middle distance, bringing three fingers together as if grasping an idea out of thin air. "But I think was bothers me most is that it's not pretty." PH looked Lilly in the eye, "It's not elegant. The functionality is course and clumsy." She held her hands up in two gentle fists and looked to the sky as if begging the gods for an indulgence. "I want art. I want symmetry. I want beautiful colors, and clean lines, and to not have to think so hard just to use it," PH looked at Lilly with disappointment, placing a hand on her chest.

Lilly returned her gaze with a cold stare.

"It should be effortless on my part and it's not," PH took her hand off of her chest gesturing, "It's like work. It's as if I asked you for flowers and you brought me dandelions and baby's breath." PH flipped the papers on her desk with her fingers. "It's all garbage, it's filler. It's almost worse than if you just brought me nothing at all because now you have not just disappointed me you've given me something that annoys me." PH's brow was wrinkled with frustration.

Lilly was blown away and crestfallen. She had expected constructive criticism, not to be torn apart.

PH read the defeat on Lilly's face. She leaned back and spoke more conversationally, "I realize this is difficult to hear but you should try being a user on this thing, it's miserable."

After taking a deep breath Lilly composed herself and said, "I see. Thank you for the constructive criticism."

"Lilly, you think I'm being hard on you but I know you're capable of more and I firmly believe that you can do better if I push you." PH implored Lilly to understand with her eyes.

Lilly answered coldly, "I will see what I can do to improve. Thank you for your time." With that Lilly stood and hoisting her backpack onto her shoulders walked out.

PH let Lilly leave without another word.

Once outside, Lilly stormed across campus cursing her mentor.

"Lil, wait up!" Celia shouted, jogging to catch up.

"Oh, hey," Lilly said as she waited for Celia.

"Where are you going in such a hurry?" Celia asked out of breath.

Lilly answered, "Nowhere."

"Are you alright?" Celia's eyes were wide with concern.

"I'm fine." Lilly added angrily, "My advisor is just an asshole."

Celia frowned, "Want to grab a hot chocolate with me and talk about it?"

Lilly shrugged her shoulders underneath the straps of her backpack, "Sure."

The girls walked to a cozy cafe near campus. The acidic smell of hot coffee seemed to permeate the air. Lilly could already feel her blood pressure dropping. After the girls had their drinks in hand they sat down in the cushy leather chairs at a small table.

Celia asked, "What did PH say?"

Lilly spoke tersely, "She said my project was garbage. That it was clumsy and it just annoyed her. It was worse than doing nothing."

"Oh wow." Celia's eyebrows shot up in dismay. Her hands were clasped daintily around her hot beverage. "That's a hard no, alright."

"She's such a bitch. She doesn't do any of the work. She just sits at her desk and critiques everything I do. She couldn't do what I do. She has no idea how much time and effort went into that project." Lilly threw herself backwards into the seat cushion, "She's a no-name advisor at a college in Nashville - if she were any good at what she does she'd be in Silicon Valley advising actual tech startups, not college kids on their scholarship projects." Lilly shook her head, "I can't believe I ever listened to her."

Celia crossed her ankles and leaned in, "Why was she being so mean to you?"

"I don't know." Lilly crossed her arms, "What does it matter?"

"Well, there's a chance she wanted your work to be better," Celia suggested gently.

Lilly glared at her friend angrily.

Celia shrugged, with patient disregard of Lilly's expression, "Maybe you don't want to hear it yet, but she might be trying to help you."

Lilly gestured with a firm right hand, "I worked my ass of on that beta, Celia, and she called it garbage."

146

"Maybe it's not that its garbage it's just that she thinks you can do better," Celia offered softly.

"Maybe," Lilly admitted begrudgingly, looking around the shop and refusing to make eye contact.

"Don't cry about it," Celia sat up straight. "Think like Elizabeth Taylor, 'Pour yourself a drink, put on some lipstick, and pull yourself together.'"

Lilly guffawed indulgently.

"It works for me," Celia said with a wry smile.

Lilly smirked and took a sip from her cup.

Now that she had broken the tension Celia asked, "What else did she say?"

Lilly took a drink and softened slightly, "She said it was ugly and the colors weren't pretty."

"Ok, you can update design." Celia encouraged, "Is that hard?"

Lilly took a deep breath. "Not if you know what you're doing. But I don't know the first thing about design. I'm focusing on user experience not what colors to use," Lilly said caustically.

Celia gave her a disapproving look.

Lilly begrudgingly admitted, "I guess I did focus really hard on making it work the way I thought it should and not a lot of time thinking about how other people might see it."

"There," Celia nodded and tried not to smile too brightly, "that's something you can change or at least work on to make it better."

"I guess," Lilly stared off into space but she couldn't stop her mind from trying to find a solution.

Celia watched her friend thinking, she could see the wheels spinning.

Several minutes later, Lilly announced, "Celia, I need your help," she spoke clearly with an idea in mind.

Celia readjusted in her seat, excited to hear what Lilly had to say. "What is it?"

"Will you test the beta and tell me what you think, honestly?"

"Sure. I'd be happy to do it. Can you send me the link? I have my iPad in my bag I can test it right now." Celia reached down and pulled her iPad out of her bag.

Lilly quickly sent Celia the link and waited anxiously as she clicked across the table. Lilly tried to distract herself with her phone but found she was just staring at Celia as she worked. Aside from a few sighs and nods Celia gave Lilly nothing to go on and it was torturing Lilly to no end.

After ten minutes, Celia looked up and took a sip from her cup.

"What do you think?" Lilly asked anxiously.

Celia took a deep breath and spoke apologetically, "I see where your advisor is coming from, it's not very good."

Lilly's heart sank. A part of her was hoping that Celia would tell her that PH was an idiot, and that the program was great.

Celia saw Lilly's disappointment but couldn't lie to her friend. "It's just not fun or pretty. It's really confusing."

Lilly's face stretched as she heard even more criticism of her work. She tried to hear it graciously but she was tempted to grab Celia's iPad and snap it on her knee.

Celia read Lilly's face and rolled her eyes. "Don't be so dramatic, Lil. You should be taking notes. This is important stuff you can use to make your project better."

Lilly knew Celia was right. She slowly pulled out a notebook and a pen and listened as Celia rattled off suggestions, comments, and ideas. She needed a logo, a home page, and a link on every page to get back to the home screen, two or three signature colors max, matching fonts and not Times New Roman, a header, all of the pages needed the same or similar layouts. An hour later Lilly didn't think there was anything left for Celia to critique or anything on the site that she didn't want to change.

"Are you ok?" Celia asked when she was done.

Lilly's hand was cramping from writing so much so quickly and her hot chocolate was cold but she had a solid direction to follow. "I'm fine. I asked you to look at it," Lilly said with a dejected sigh.

Celia cringed, "You're not mad?"

Lilly looked at her friend's worried face and gave her a weak smile. "It's going to be a lot of work but thank you for your help." Lilly did not feel assaulted like she had with PH. She felt like she had a list of concrete issues she could fix, ideas to improve. She wasn't thrilled to have so much more work to do but it was better than just hating PH like she had been earlier. Lilly regretted insulting PH, she didn't take criticism well.

Celia finished her drink and placed the cup on the table firmly. "The only thing you'll need to do now is find someone to design the site and help you make it pretty."

"Yeah," Lilly said, contemplatively.

Celia shrugged her shoulders, "Any ideas?"

"I know someone who can help." Lilly didn't say his name out loud but she was thinking of Drew. She quickly texted Drew asking him to meet her for dinner.

Lilly wore a teal hand-me-down cardigan from Emily over her usual uniform of a white T-shirt and jeans. She had a soup and sandwich, which she ate as she waited for Drew to arrive.

Drew strolled in late as usual. Lilly gave him an expectant look, waiting for him to explain his tardiness. After a couple minutes of silence, Drew started, "So, you wanted to talk?"

Lilly decided that it would be faster to just cut to the chase. She leaned in, "I invited you here to ask for your help."

"What's up?" He leaned forward to meet her gaze.

"I need a graphic designer to help with my scholarship project."

"Are you allowed to ask for help?" he asked with eyebrows raised.

The thought had never occurred to her. Her face registered this fact.

"I'm just messing with you, rule breaker," Drew said teasingly, referring to the trouble she got into at the end of last semester for repairing other student's computers and making money off of the enterprise.

Undeterred, she leaned in again, "So, can you help me?"

Drew shrugged carelessly, "Sure thing, Carter. What do you need?"

"I need a logo and a whole list of other things. The design element is totally lost on me. I can make the site function, I can't make it pretty." Saying it out loud, the thought occurred to Lilly that that was true of herself and her relationships. She could make it work but it wasn't going to be pretty. Remembering where she was she quickly dismissed the thought. "Could you do it?"

"I'll take a look at it and let you know what I think," Drew said flippantly.

"Ok," Lilly pulled out her phone. "I'm sending you the link."

"Awesome. I'll get back to you later tonight?" he moved to stand.

"That would be amazing," Lilly said happily.

"Alright, you already ate?"

"Yes," Lilly looked down at her empty tray.

"I'm going to go get some dinner. I'll see you later, Carter," Drew said as he stood.

"Thanks, Drew," Lilly said with appreciation. She went to stand-up too but Porter was walking right for her table. As Drew walked toward the food stations Porter brushed past him.

"Hey," Porter said as she sat down, slamming her tray.

"What's up?" Lilly asked somewhat confused.

"Emily told me where to find you," Porter explained, reading Lilly's expression.

"Why are you looking for *me*?"

Porter took a deep breath, ignoring her food, she said, "You've been working on your scholarship project for five months straight?" Porter's eyes were wide as she looked to Lilly to confirm her statement.

"I guess," Lilly admitted.

"How do you do that?" Porter spoke firmly and seriously.

Lilly just looked at her.

"I am dedicating summer break to writing my next album. What do you do to stay focused and not get distracted?"

"I don't know," Lilly confessed, haltingly giving Porter an uncomfortable expression.

Porter searched Lilly's face for information trying to read her. "Do you turn off your phone? Do you meditate? Do you get into a zone? What happens when you do your best work?" Porter looked at Lilly intensely which only made Lilly recoil.

"I don't know that I do anything differently," Lilly started.

Porter cut her off, "Did breaking up with Charlie help? Ending things and cutting all ties." Porter struck like there was blood in the water.

"No," Lilly shook her head firmly. "I broke up with Charlie... for... other reasons," she recovered. "Anyway, I don't like going out, and to be honest PH told me I needed to spend more of my energy on making friends which only seemed to make me want to stay home more," Lilly confessed.

Porter was unimpressed. "You just didn't want to do anything but work?"

"Yeah," Lilly felt more certain now. "That was it really. I wanted to work and everything just seemed to be shifting in my favor to make it happen."

Porter looked at her like she was crazy.

Lilly read her face. "I know that sounds weird but in a strange way it's like the universe conspires to help you attain whatever it is that you really want." Lilly came back to herself, "Do I sound spacey?" she asked deepening her voice.

"Yes. You sound," Porter thought for a moment and said, "spacey."

Lilly shrugged, "Sorry if that's no help."

"No," Porter considered thoughtfully, "It's exactly what I thought."

Lilly was startled, "Really?"

Porter gestured with her hands smoothly, "Yeah, the answer isn't in you. The answer is in me."

Lilly did not remember saying that at all but went with it.

"If I want to write an album, I just need to do it," Porter picked up a fry and ate it.

Lilly nodded.

"Thanks for the advice," Porter said with an impressed tone.

"Yeah, sure," Lilly crossed her arms over her chest, it was getting colder. She could see snow falling outside the windows.

"Is your project done?" Porter looked intrigued.

"Not even close," Lilly confessed.

Porter nodded and took a bite of her wrap. She then looked around the cafeteria silently as she chewed.

Lilly wasn't sure what to do. Porter didn't ask her another question she just people watched and ate. Squirming in the silence, Lilly volunteered, "We just finished beta testing and it's a mess. I'm having a graphic designer help me completely re-work the site."

Porter arched an eyebrow, "Who?"

"Drew, I work with him in the IT department," Lilly said, frankly.

Porter nodded and finished her meal. She grabbed her tray, stood up, and said, "You'll fix it."

"What?"

"Your site, there's no way PH's going to let you get away with not finishing it." Porter added, "You'll be fine."

Lilly wasn't sure what to say.

"I'll see you later," Porter said before Lilly could recover. She wasn't sure what just happened. *Did Porter predict what she was going to do or just tell her to do it?* Lilly was confused.

When she opened the door to her room Emily was doing her make-up in the mirror and Celia was laying on Emily's bed, reading a magazine.

"Hey Lil," Emily said as she lined her eyes in the mirror.

"Oh, hey," Celia said sitting up. "How was your meeting with the graphic designer?"

"Oh, it was good." Lilly threw her bag down. "He said he'll do it."

"That's awesome," Celia said happily. "Did you give him my color recommendations?"

"I did," Lilly smiled.

"You picked the colors for her project?" Emily asked from the mirror.

"Yeah," Celia answered innocuously from the bed.

"Why didn't you ask me?" Emily turned to face Lilly.

"I don't know, Celia offered," Lilly admitted sitting on her bed tucking her right leg beneath her.

"I live with you," Emily said jealously as though that were some sort of justification.

"Sorry," Lilly shrugged. "Do you want to look at it when the graphic designer's done?"

"No," Emily turned back to her own face in the mirror.

Celia and Lilly exchanged a look.

Trying to change the subject, Lilly asked, "Where are you going?"

"I'm meeting a friend for drinks," Emily said as she watched herself apply mascara.

Lilly looked to Celia for more information but Celia avoided Lilly's gaze which made Lilly suspicious. "Anyone I know?"

Emily finished applying her lipstick and turned to face Lilly. She looked strikingly beautiful. "I'm meeting Max for drinks at Clyde's tonight."

"Oh," Lilly tried to keep the emotion out of her voice. "Is this your first date?"

"It's not a date," Emily clarified, despite the fact that she was clearly trying to impress Max. "Well, I need to get going. I'll see you girls later," Emily said as she walked out the door, leaving Lilly staring with her mouth wide open.

As the door closed Lilly immediately turned to Celia, "How long has that been going on?"

"No idea."

Lilly shrugged, "I had a weird conversation with Porter tonight."

"What did she say?" Celia asked with a chuckle.

"I don't know if she was telling me that I should fix the beta or if she was saying that I would. It was really strange."

"I'd just ignore her she's in some weird head space. She'll be fine in a few weeks." Celia yawned. "Ok, I'm going to bed."

"Yeah, good night" Lilly nodded.

Celia yawned again. She got up and stretched. "I'll see you later." Celia left and closed the door with a click behind her.

Lilly thought about Emily and Max as she brushed her teeth. *She did not see that coming.*

16. MAKING NICE OR NOT

Lilly woke up the next morning to find Emily serenely reading gossip blogs on her iPad.

"Good morning," she said sweetly as Lilly opened her eyes. "I got you a coffee on my way home from the gym."

"You've already been to the gym?" Lilly asked groggily. She got up and grabbed the coffee off of her desk and took a sip; extra cream, two sugars, just the way she liked it. She smiled, the perks of having a perfectionist for a roommate.

"Three miles, it's nothing to brag about," Emily confided.

"It's three more miles than I ran today." Lilly said as she placed the coffee back down and grabbed her towel and shower caddy heading down the hall to the showers.

When Lilly got back to the room Celia and Emily were happily chatting. Celia had moved the stack of laundry that had piled up on Lilly's desk chair to the hamper. She had also organized Lilly's desk.

"I'm sorry," Celia said referring to Lilly's now meticulous desk, "I couldn't help myself. I hope you don't mind?"

"Not at all, you can clean my room any time," Lilly joked. She wasn't used to someone else cleaning up after her, it was nice.

"What's going on with you and Charlie Abbott?" Emily pressed.

"Nothing," Lilly dismissed her question.

"It's just weird that y'all were all about each other last semester, he gave you that bracelet, and now you act like you don't even know each other. I don't think I've seen you say two words to Charlie since Christmas."

"We weren't 'all about each other,'" Lilly said defensively.

Emily prodded, "Are you kidding me? You talked to Charlie every day and when you weren't talking to Charlie, you were talking about Charlie. You were obsessed."

"I was not obsessed," Lilly said a little too loudly.

"Maybe obsessed is a strong word," Celia said trying to ease the tension. "We just thought y'all were the cutest couple and we're trying to understand what happened between you two."

"Nothing happened," Lilly lied. "I guess we just don't have that much in common."

Emily said cautiously, "I just wanted to make sure that everything was alright between y'all because we're attending an auction this weekend and I invited him."

Lilly was confused, "What auction?"

Emily perked up, dancing like an excited puppy, and waving her hands for emphasis, "There's a local private collector, who wants to remain unnamed, that is looking to auction some of the works he's accumulated."

Lilly eyed Emily suspiciously as Celia gave a supportive smile.

Emily confided, "According to my mother it's a collection of," Emily's eyes rolled back in her head ecstatically, "music memorabilia, original works, there's photos of Lorretta Lynn in the studio, signed sheet music from Dolly Parton, they're supposedly all coffee stained and incredible."

Lilly's good humor returned as she watched Emily geek-out.

"Anyway, my mother had a brilliant idea to not only invite other collectors to bid but to have us come and encourage people to buy. So not only do we get to go to this fabulous party for free, but we also get to see these exclusive pieces, even before the museums get their hands on them!" Emily was giddy.

"And they're hosting it at Third and Lindsley," Celia said with excitement.

"What's Third and Lindsley?" Lilly was clueless.

"Only the best live music venue in Nashville," Emily explained authoritatively. "You would never guess by looking at it but it is where true country fans go to hear the best music and musicians perform. You're going to love it."

"Isn't this so cool?" Celia asked rhetorically.

"That's amazing," Lilly said with uncertain eyes.

Taking a more serious approach Emily asked, "You and Charlie will be fine though? Right?"

"Sure," Lilly said. It had been weeks since they broke up, or rather, since she broke up with him. "That sounds like a lot of fun." She was lying.

Lilly went to work that morning with a sense of dread. She didn't want to see Charlie, she wasn't ready. And work was frustrating her. It turned out that Drew was right. Don Inglesbury was just a mid-level manager overly intense about keeping his job. Unfortunately, Lilly had to work with Don to do her job. He begrudgingly assisted her but every interaction she had with him made her hate him more.

Lilly was working late that evening when Don stopped by on his way out of the office.

"You need to calm down with the long hours," Don said with a chuckle, his belly rocking up and down with each word like a hiccup.

Lilly swiveled around in her chair. Trying not to grimace, she said with forced brightness, "I noticed there's an easier way for us to set up the servers, if you're interested I can show you what I found." Lilly moved to turn back to her computer screen to show him her work.

Don stepped into her cubicle and put a thick sausage finger in her face, "Stop trying to do all this fancy shit. You're just a cog in the machine. You're infantry it's not your job to tell us if the bridge is out, it's your job to march." Dropping his fleshy hand down to his side, he added in a sickly sweet tone, "you see what I'm sayin', darlin'?"

Lilly's voice caught in her throat as she looked up at the larger man who was surprisingly red in the face.

Spittle flew from him lips, "You're not paid to think, you're paid to work."

Lilly frowned and nodded slowly. Then she looked him square in the eye and said, "It's a good thing you don't waste any time thinking then, isn't it?"

Don glared at her but turned on his heel, and walked out in a huff.

Lilly sighed and collapsed back into her chair. Her heart was racing. She laughed out loud at her own audacity, she couldn't believe she had the presence of mind to put him in his place, she had wanted to do that ever since his speech last semester.

The auction at Third and Lindsley was nothing like Lilly expected. It looked and smelled like an old Mexican restaurant in a strip mall. Track lighting illuminated the works throughout the long and narrow room. Guests strolled through the gallery with plastic cups and black paper napkins in hand. The air smelled vaguely of turpentine and bacon from the appetizers. Lilly made a point to laugh politely and smile graciously but even so, her attention was fixed on Charlie.

"How's it going, Coach?" Stephen asked as Lilly stood off to the side watching the congregation around Charlie.

"It's good," Lilly said heavily.

"He looks miserable," Stephen said referring to Charlie who was still laughing with a few friends.

Lilly was startled by Stephen's intuition. She didn't bother lying instead she spoke honestly in a sad tone, "He looks happy."

"Oh that?" Stephen brushed away her comment with a wave of his hand. "No. That's all for your benefit," he explained.

"You think so?" Lilly asked skeptically.

"Oh definitely, look at you, Coach. You look amazing he's an idiot for not being over here talking to you right now."

"Thanks, Stephen," Lilly said as he wrapped a reassuring arm around her shoulders.

"He won't tell me what he did." Stephen continued, "But I was sad to hear you two weren't together anymore."

Lilly sighed guiltily, her shoulders slumping under Stephen's arm. *He didn't even tell his best friend it was all her fault.*

Max broke away from the gaggle of older women he had been entertaining and joined them. "Now which of these fine pieces should we buy?" he asked her.

Lilly answered with a relieved laugh at the absurdity of his comment, "I can't afford anything."

"Oh Lil, don't be silly. We're not buying anything but let's pretend, shall we dahhhling," he said with a mock classy tone.

"Oh, yes, of course," Lilly said mirroring his voice. "Do, let's pick out something for the summer home."

"Yes, I'd like to get the Picasso off the mantle. It's been there for far too long."

They both laughed.

"What are you three talking about?" Porter asked walking up to the group in a stunning neon pink dress with stacks of gold bracelets on both wrists.

"We're picking out pieces for the summer home up in Kennebunkport. Do be a dear and help us," Max said in his rich tone.

"You're ridiculous," Porter laughed, casually lacing her fingers through Stephen's. She then looked up as a thought occurred to her, "Lil, Emily's looking for you."

"Ok, thanks," Lilly ducked out from under Stephen's other arm and walked to where she had last seen Emily. As she wandered around the gallery trying to find her, Charlie walked up to her with two cocktails.

"Jack and coke?" he offered one to her.

"Thanks," she said. Lilly squeezed the lime that had been resting on the rim into the drink, avoiding eye contact until she was ready to face him.

They tapped glasses, "Cheers." She glanced up but looked away quickly.

"So, were you just going to ignore me forever?" Charlie started.

Lilly spoke with confidence, "That was the plan," and took a sip of the drink from its clear plastic tumbler looking across the room at nothing in particular.

"And that's non-negotiable?" He tilted his head to look into her eyes.

Lilly returned her gaze to the red brick walls, "Tonight it is," she coughed out quickly.

"Solid. And the plan for tomorrow night?" he asked undeterred.

"It looks like more of the same," Lilly's heart was racing. She wanted to kiss him. She wanted him to kiss her. This dress, this hair, it was all for him and she wanted to tell him that. She missed him. Her inner monologue was screaming and all she could do was pretend to be calm and at ease.

"Well, I'll just have to keep trying," he said with a wink and walked away.

She tilted her head back to look up at the tall ceilings.

Then as if propelled by something stronger than herself she placed her drink on an empty table, grabbed his hand, and pulled him into the industrial stairwell. He turned and in a startlingly fluid motion his lips were on hers, her hands were tangled in his hair, and they both breathlessly kissed one another. This could have lasted for hours if not for the other attendees trying to come in and go out past them on the narrow walkway.

Lilly stepped back out of breath and wiped the smeared lipstick off of her face. His lips were colored to match hers. The cold air coming in from the open door at the foot of the stairs felt refreshing on Lilly's skin, she was sweating. He leaned against the bannister, watching her.

"It's not that I don't want to be with you," she finally said.

"Then why won't you?" he asked seriously.

"Because you're too perfect, you'll never understand where I come from, the fucked up mess that I am," she tried desperately to explain.

Charlie stood tall and cradled her face in his hand, "You're right,"

She looked up at him in shock. It was one thing for her to admit her weakness it was totally different to have him confirm its validity. It was like a sucker punch in the gut, it took her breath away.

"I'm never going to know if you don't let me in," he added. He then kissed her forehead, adjusted his tie, and went back inside.

17. A NEW PROJECT

In mid-February, Emily burst into the room with a panicked look on her face. "Lil, I need a huge favor," she said with a desperate look.

Lilly was doing her homework for her practicum course with PH on the bed. Her hair a wiry pouf of jumbled crimps and curls surrounding her face in a warm red halo. "What do you need?"

Emily pulled out a desk chair and sat down to face Lilly on the bed. "Ok, my mama is doing the PR to support the Nashville ballet's summer program and they're doing an online fundraiser to coordinate with the ball they're hosting at the end of the campaign."

"Ok," Lilly looked at her roommate with confusion, so far there was no question.

Emily took a breath. "Well, the company they hired to build the site totally dropped the ball. Mama's freaking out but," Emily bit her bottom lip and finally blurted out, "I told her you might be able to help."

"How am I going to help?" Lilly scratched her head and ran her fingers through her messy hair, pulling out the tangles by hand.

Emily folded her hands in front of her body like a prayer and held them at heart's center, "Could you build the fundraising site? I know you're super busy with school and your project and its late notice."

Lilly's face dropped. *Typical,* Emily had a habit of volunteering Lilly to help people without asking her first. This was just like her computer repair business last semester, Lilly rolled her eyes and asked, "When do they need it?"

"The ball is in two weeks."

"Emily," Lilly tried to explain practically, "that's not a small project."

Emily begged, "I know but it's for a good cause and I'm sure the PR firm would compensate you for all of your work."

Lilly asked, "How much?"

Emily dropped her voice an octave, "Mama said they're willing to go up to $10 grand."

Lilly could feel her heart rate quickening and the fresh air that came with the thought of that kind of money. It was astronomical to her. Ten thousand dollars was huge. Of course she'd do it. She had to do it. Lilly tried not to betray her total elation to Emily. "Ok, but only for the full ten thousand, and," Lilly composed herself and sat up, "I'll have to talk to your mom to find out what they want and how much time it's going to take to build."

Emily hugged her hard. She quickly let go and started flitting about the room rapidly, "I'll get her on the phone right now."

Lilly silently tried to figure out if this was real as Emily handed Lilly her iPhone and Lilly spoke with Mrs. Parker. Rather, Mrs. Parker spoke and Lilly listened. When Mrs. Parker was done insulting the company that left them in the lurch, Lilly asked some pointed questions regarding the site. "How do you envision the site working?"

"Fortunately, they did build out the piece that allows the site to securely accept credit cards and financial pledges."

Lilly nodded firmly, that was good news. "Ok. What other functionality did you want from the site?"

"We want it to collect names and addresses so that we can send thank you notes and information about the upcoming season to contributors," Mrs. Parker said, calming down. "We want it to thank them on the screen first but later we'd like to send more personal notes after the event."

"Of course," Lilly started, "Does the site look good?"

"It looks unprofessional. We gave them all of the graphics, it's all done, they just never put them onto the site," Mrs. Parker sounded frustrated again.

Using a soothing tone Lilly said, "Mrs. Parker, if you just need the address fields, a thank you screen, and the format polished I may be able to help you."

Mrs. Parker sighed, "Thank you Lilly."

"It's my pleasure Mrs. Parker. If there's anything else you think of later, please feel free to text or call me," Lilly added.

"I just sent you screen shots of what we want to help you get started," Mrs. Parker said with a relieved tone. "I hope you don't mind, I had Emily text me your email address."

"Not a problem, thank you," Lilly smiled looking over at Emily's guilty face. As soon as she hung up Lilly did a happy dance, she was back in business. She could make money doing what she was good at and no one could stop her. After she finished her personal victory dance and Emily stopped laughing, she went to work building the fundraising page.

There was a lot of back and forth but Lilly was patient and diligently listened to all of Mrs. Parker's instructions and requests as she worked quickly to build the site. It reminded her of Melanie making outrageous demands, except Mrs. Parker wasn't drunk and these were problems Lilly could do something about. After a long week of work Lilly had successfully constructed a test site.

Lilly emailed Mrs. Parker, "I added a button; the administrator can use it to pull up an overview of the site usage. If you're ok with that then, I'll just add the list for pulling down who donated."

Mrs. Parker emailed back almost instantaneously, "This is magnificent, Lilly. Thank you so much. The button is great and the tracking is exactly what we needed. I am just going to say right now, you are my favorite, don't tell my daughter."

Lilly laughed out loud and typed back, "Here's an image of the Admin page. I'll have Steve from the ballet set it up on the staging site so that you and the other leads can mess with it. What I'll need to happen before this thing goes into production is for you to just go through it. We can set up multiple tests to just poke it until it dies. Or doesn't. We're just looking for behavior that doesn't line up with what we expect to happen, or stuff you want changed. Once that's done I'll push it to Steve and he can release it to go live. Then you can have both the ball and the online fundraising operational simultaneously."

An email flashed back, "I hope you realize that you and Emily will have to attend the event as my special guests now. :)"

Lilly rolled her eyes.

The day of the ballet fundraiser was warmer than it had been in months. It had been a long and frigid February. It was supposed to get cold again the following week but the day was gorgeous with sunshine, blue skies, and the promise of spring.

Lilly got back to the dorm and found a slick grey box on her bed. "What's this?" She asked as she threw her bag on the floor.

"You should open it and find out," Emily said with a knowing smile.

Lilly was uncertain. She walked to the bed and gently lifted the solid lid off of the garment box. White tissue paper was snuggly wrapped around something bright red. "Em, what is this?" Lilly was nervous, her breaths shallow and short.

Emily was watching her. With hands clasped in excitement she beamed, "My mama sent a little thank you present."

"Are you kidding me?" Lilly ripped away the tissue paper. "She already paid me to build the site."

Emily shook her head, "She wanted you to know how much she appreciated your help."

Lilly looked down at a strapless satin classic red A-line gown. She gasped out loud and put her hand to her mouth as she gaped at the beautiful dress.

Emily giggled with excitement.

When Lilly could finally speak she coughed out, "Oh-my-gosh!"

"Do you like it?" Emily asked, hopefully.

"Emily it's beautiful!" Lilly pulled the dress out of the box and held it up to her body smiling at her reflection in the mirror above the sink. "It's amazing! Did you pick this out?"

"I had nothing to do with it. I just told her your size." Emily crossed her arms around her body watching Lilly joyfully dancing around the room, carrying the dress with her.

Lilly laid the dress on the bed to take it all in, "I don't have words!" she sighed happily.

Emily chided, "Well, go shower we've got to get you ready. You're already an hour behind," she added, unable to resist the jab at her roommate.

Lilly was giddy and excited as she showered. Earlier that day she was not looking forward to the ball. Now she was breathless with delight.

Back in the room, Celia was waiting with a blow dryer, hot curling iron, and a stack of bobby pins. Lilly clutched her towel with her fist as she put down her shower caddy and hugged Celia hard, "Is this real?" she whispered.

"All real," Celia smiled. "Ok," she guided Lilly to her desk chair, "let's get you ready."

Lilly laughed as Celia brushed and dried her hair.

Emily was at her desk, generously coating her lashes in mascara with a thick black wand.

After her hair and make-up were done Lilly tenderly lifted the dress off of her bed and stepped into the classic red gown. The moment Celia zipped the dress up was of supreme happiness for Lilly. Mrs. Parker wasn't her mother but it felt so much like something a good mother would do, know you had a big event and do something special to commemorate it, just to let you know she was thinking of you and proud of you. Lilly wasn't sure if she was happier because she got to wear such a phenomenal dress or if it was because she felt loved and supported by Mrs. Parker in a way she never had by her own mother.

Mr. Parker was the only one in the car when it arrived. He explained as the girls got into the backseat, carefully tucking their skirts inside. "Your mother's been at the hotel all day. Her dress is in the trunk, the pretty people are getting her ready there."

Lilly asked Emily with a whisper in the backseat, "Pretty people?"

Emily rolled her eyes and spoke at full volume, "Dad calls the make-up artist and hair stylist, pretty people."

"Well isn't that what they do?" Mr. Parker said gruffly from the front seat.

"Yes, Daddy, they make us pretty," Emily agreed, doting on her father.

Lilly and Emily giggled in the backseat. The trip took minutes which made Lilly wonder why they didn't walk but she didn't have long to think about it before valets were opening their doors and they were walking past two giant stone lions as they entered the Loews Hotel lobby. There were ornate crystal sconces, huge chandeliers dripping in glass and sparkling in the light. The girls carried their dress skirts in their hands as they hiked up the sweeping white marble staircase. Uniformed wait staff wandered through the crowds offering hors d'oeuvres and champagne. It was even better than Lilly had imagined.

"Are you girls alright on your own?" Mr. Parker asked as they reached the top of the staircase.

"Yes, Daddy," Emily answered obediently, dropping her hem to the floor. Lilly followed suit.

"Alright, I'm going to go find your mother so she can come out and run this thing." Mr. Parker wove through the crowd, carrying a garment bag over his arm.

Lilly and Emily wandered around the room looking at the auction items on display; signed shoes from recent performances and photographs from previous shows. There were ballerinas weaving through the crowd, chatting with guests. They stood out obviously with their poise, posture, and delicate movements. Everything they did seemed elegant. They girls only saw glimpses of Mrs. Parker for the first half of the evening. She was flitting from group to group, laughing with guests and ballerinas, and discretely directing staff. Lilly was impressed by how flawlessly the night progressed. When Mrs. Parker finally had a moment for the girls she rushed to hug Emily and Lilly.

"Are you girls having fun? Everyone is talking about how stunning you look and wondering who you are," Mrs. Parker placed a hand gently on Lilly's arm, "I told them you're actresses from New York."

"Mama," Emily rolled her eyes.

Mrs. Parker gave her daughter a discerning look. "You know I'm kidding Emily Jane," looking at Lilly she deadpanned, "they all know you're my sister." She laughed rapturously. She was truly a woman in her element.

Lilly laughed and snorted as Emily rolled her eyes at her mother. After she caught her breath Lilly gushed, "Thank you so much for the dress, Mrs. Parker."

Mrs. Parker beamed, "I'm so glad you like it. It looks stunning on you."

"Thank you. You didn't need to get me something so extravagant," Lilly added, looking down at the fiery red gown, in awe.

"Lilly, you're the reason we were able to pull this off. I am truly grateful." Mrs. Parker pulled Lilly in for another hug, the jewels on her bracelet dug into Lilly's skin. "Come with me." Mrs. Parker took Lilly by the wrist and brought her to the podium where earlier in the evening the ballet company had stood and waved their thanks to the attendees.

Mrs. Parker clicked on the microphone and pulled it down to her mouth. "Ladies and gentlemen, Nashville ballet lovers here and away, thank you so much for joining us this evening. I am Joan Parker of Joan Parker PR." She paused for applause and added, "We have a fabulous and exciting announcement to make."

The room hushed.

Mrs. Parker continued in a clear and strong voice, "As many of you know fundraising is a journey with many exciting twists and turns, not unlike ballet, it requires grace and composure under pressure."

There was a murmur of agreement from the crowd.

Mrs. Parker went on, "As some of you may know, earlier this month we were not sure we would be able to pull off this spectacular event and the online fundraising piece in time for tonight."

Concerned glances were shared among the guests and nods of understanding passed among the members of the ballet administration.

Mrs. Parker paused to assure she had the room's undivided attention before continuing, "Fortunately, both have proven to be a huge success." She beamed, "And our reports show that we have not only reached our fundraising goal..." she paused for dramatic effect, letting the room wait for her announcement a second longer, she looked as if she was savoring the suspense, "but if donations keep coming in at the same rate, we're on schedule to double our budget for the summer season."

Wild applause filled the room. Lilly beamed and clapped loudly. The room was full of smiles and congratulations. Guests raised their glasses and cheered. After the ruckus quieted, Mrs. Parker continued, "I'd like to make one additional introduction and let you get back to this fabulous evening. To my right is a young woman who saved the day," Mrs. Parker lifted an arm, gesturing to Lilly "She's the reason we were able to see our vision come to fruition. Miss. Lillian Carter, Vanderbilt University's Wilson Scholar, thank you for all you've done to help. Our ballet and our city thank you for your efforts and your contributions."

Lilly was stunned as the room erupted in a fresh chorus of applause and cheers. She folded her hands in front of herself and smiled. She squeezed her hands so tightly that she felt the indent of her signet ring stabbing into her finger as she stood, frozen. Lilly let the praise wash over her as she tried to smile politely through her stage fright.

Even with a ball room of people looking up at her Lilly could feel a burning sensation like someone specifically was watching her. It wasn't until she allowed her eyes to scan the room that she saw Charlie, beaming up at her. His smile illuminated his face and his eyes seemed to sparkle with a fresh blue intensity. Her face reddened as she realized that it was pride, he was proud of her. After Mrs. Parker was finished, Lilly tried unsuccessfully, to find Charlie. Various patrons and attendees stopped to thank her and share their congratulations. She was mid-turn when she found herself face to face with a handsome man in a well fitted tuxedo.

"Max!" Lilly said with a startled jolt. She could feel his brown eyes sweeping over her like a blanket. He looked handsome in a tuxedo, his dark hair slicked back, and clean shaven.

"Hi, Lilly," he said with a smile. "Congratulations." He leaned in and kissed her cheek.

"Thank you so much," she said graciously in the Emily voice she had been using all night. She then switched to her own comfortable tone and asked, "What are you doing here?"

Max laughed easily and smiled down at her. "I'm accompanying my mother.

My dad's out of town on business and she hates coming to these things alone."

Lilly nodded. "Where's your mother now?"

"Talking to a professor from school, I think. Not mine," he added with a conspiratorial smile.

Emily joined them, "What are you two smiling about?" she asked casually. "Hi, Max, how are you this evening?"

"I'm well, Emily, thank you for asking. How are you?" Max sounded so formal. It rekindled Lilly's interest in the nature of their relationship.

"I'm well, thank you," Emily said with a cozy southern lilt.

"Your mother did a wonderful job this evening," he spoke sincerely gesturing with his head to the elaborate and magnificent room.

"Thank you so much, she loves these events, and the Nashville ballet has always held a special place in her heart." Emily leaned toward Max intimately, "My grandmother was a ballerina and Mama hoped I might be one too," Emily shared. She then pointed a toe out from the hem of her ball gown and added, with a self-depreciating smile, "but I have two left feet."

"I'm sure you're a beautiful dancer," Max replied politely.

"I hope you're not asking me prove it," Emily flirted.

Lilly was not sure what was happening.

"Oh, Lilly, I forgot, Charlie was looking for you," Emily said carelessly with a laugh.

Lilly was shocked, Emily was usually so discreet.

Max nodded respectfully. "If you ladies will excuse me, I promised my mother a champagne cocktail."

"Of course," Emily answered as Max stepped away.

Lilly fought to say something but found her tongue heavy and slow.

"I'm going to go check-in on Daddy," Emily said innocently and walked away.

Lilly exhaled audibly as she wandered through the crowd. She felt a gentle tap on her shoulder, it was Charlie. He handed her a cocktail in a traditional champagne glass, it was garnished with a sprig of green rosemary.

"Thank you," she smiled. "What is it?" she asked as she took the drink out of his hands by the stem.

"It's pink," he smirked. "A champagne cocktail, I think."

"Fair enough," Lilly replied as they clinked glasses gently and each took a sip.

"What are you doing here?" Lilly asked happily, pleased that Charlie saw her in the dress and was there for Mrs. Parker's announcement.

"Porter's singing. Stephen and I tagged along so we could see what all the fuss was about."

Lilly nodded, of course Porter was singing. Emily hadn't mentioned that earlier but Lilly had to admit she hadn't asked.

Charlie asked over his glass, "Are you having fun?"

"It's nice," Lilly confessed, surprised that she was honestly enjoying herself. "Are you having a good time?" she hinted, wondering if he had bought a date but knowing it wasn't her place to ask.

"I am now," he looked into her eyes suggestively.

Lilly looked away quickly, not daring to meet his gaze, "I'm sure there are a number of girls vying for your attention tonight," Lilly teased, still feeling the sting of his comment at the art gallery.

"There's only one girl I'm interested in," Charlie said as he looked down at her with intensity.

Lilly smiled politely and swept her eyes around the room trying to avoid eye contact.

Charlie read her distance and offered, "How is your project coming along?"

"It's good," she rocked on her feet. "We're finished beta testing. Now I have to prepare to present my findings. PH also set up a meeting with a potential investor." She took another sip of her drink.

"That's great," Charlie said with a congratulatory note.

"Thanks," she smiled, finishing her drink she said, "I'm going to keep moving. I've got to..." her voice trailed off.

"No, you should," he stepped back to allow her to pass. "I need to go find Stephen anyway."

In her haste to make her exit Lilly almost ran into PH. "Oh-my-gosh! Hi, PH," Lilly said comfortably. Remembering herself and where she was she quickly returned to her Emily-esque tone, "I mean, Professor Hendricks. I didn't know you would be here." She quickly handed her empty champagne glass to a passing waiter.

"Good evening, Lilly," PH said with a broad smile that seemed to shine a spotlight on her face.

"I'm so happy to see you," Lilly spoke happily, relieved to find someone that she knew in the sea of strangers. It was so weird and exciting to see PH out of her office and away from school.

PH seemed amused by Lilly's enthusiasm, "I was not expecting to see any of my students here tonight." PH took a graceful sip of her drink, "You built the fundraising site?"

"I did," Lilly admitted with a suspicious tone.

PH nodded her approval. "Good. I'm glad you're using your intelligence and strengths for noble purpose."

Lilly blushed. She hadn't thought about it that way before.

"I suppose this will delay your work on your project," PH said with a wry smile.

"Oh, I..." Lilly faltered.

"I'm only teasing, Lilly." PH touched her upper arm in a gentle and reassuring gesture. "It's impressive and a wonderful feat. You should celebrate and enjoy the evening."

"Thanks," Lilly was relieved that PH was only joking.

PH spoke seriously and in a hushed tone, "They compensated you for your work?"

"Yes," Lilly nodded down quickly, afraid she might be implicating herself but feeling compelled to answer honestly anyway.

PH raised her eyebrows to emphasize her point, "A freelance contractor would expect to make anywhere from ten to 20 thousand dollars on a project like this and with such short notice," PH referred to Mrs. Parker's speech.

Lilly nodded.

As it occurred to PH she quickly added, "It's none of my business as your advisor, but as someone who is older and has some experience, did they compensate you appropriately?"

"Yes, the low end," Lilly admitted.

PH smiled softening her features, "Well done. You did a wonderful job, Lilly."

Lilly smiled with relief, "Thank you."

"You know, you had me worried at our last meeting. I didn't know if you really heard me. You seemed distant and not really confident that I was giving you good advice. But this," PH gestured with her arm to the entire room, "is beyond what I had hoped and imagined. I'm truly blown away by your work Lilly."

"Thank you so much, PH," Lilly wanted to hug her advisor but held back out of respect. Then remembering something she added, "PH, I had an interesting conversation with Don Inglesbury in the IT department."

Glasses clinked and a nearby conversation erupted in laughter, PH's brow furrowed, "Yes?"

"He got in my face and basically told me to stop trying at work. He called me a cog in a machine."

"Where was this?"

"At my desk in the IT department."

PH looked furious. "Lilly, that's bullshit."

Lilly was shocked she had never heard PH swear.

"I'm going to speak to the head of the IT department about Don."

A moment ago Lilly had worried that she might be in trouble, she was glad to be on the other side of PH's ire, "Thank you."

"He's wrong, Lilly." PH said firmly. "I just want you to know that what he said is completely inappropriate. Do not take what he said to heart."

Lilly nodded, "I won't."

PH took a deep breath, "You will find, in life, that there are people who do not want you to succeed, for whatever reason. Your job is to ignore them and keep working. You cannot be concerned with the smallness of others when you are focused on attaining your own goals. Let his comments encourage your growth, do not allow them to stunt your progress."

"I'll keep working," Lilly affirmed.

PH searched Lilly's face and finding what she was looking for nodded affirmatively. "Good. I'm pleased to see you giving back and shining." PH placed a delicate hand on Lilly's shoulder, "I'm proud you."

Lilly felt a leap in her chest of victory and personal satisfaction, she said, "Thank you, PH."

As PH walked away Lilly saw Porter moving toward the stage, her sequined gold gown gave her an ethereal glow in the ballroom. Lilly quietly made her way down the stairs holding up the hem of her dress. Lilly was in a transcendent place, it had been a perfect evening. Outside, she walked across campus and back to her dorm alone, feeling more happy and confidant than she ever had in her life. It was her nineteenth birthday and the best birthday she could remember.

18. BOUNCE BACK

The next week Emily insisted all of the girls go to the lacrosse scrimmage to support Charlie and Stephen. Lilly tried to plead that she had work to do but Emily would not hear it.

"You have been sitting in this room for weeks, it is time to get out and have some fun," Emily ordered.

Lilly rolled her eyes.

"Seriously, get up," Emily grabbed Lilly's arms and pulled her up from her seat at her desk.

"I'm not done yet," Lilly whined but didn't put up a real fight.

"Go, take a shower!"

"I'm clean," Lilly said unconvincingly.

"It's been three days since your last shower, that's disgusting, go bathe," Emily said firmly with a finger pointed toward the hall.

"It's not that long," Lilly said defensively.

"I counted, three days, no shower, and don't think I didn't notice you fake showering at the sink on Tuesday. A washcloth with water is not the same as soap and a shower," Emily said sternly.

Lilly smiled, "How long have you been practicing that line?"

"Three days!" Emily said with exasperation.

Lilly laughed and rolled her eyes, grabbing her shower caddy and towel she walked to the door and opened it.

Emily yelled after her with disdain, "And no more sweatpants!"

Lilly rolled her eyes as she walked down the hall.

It was a beautiful day. Lilly hadn't spent a lot of time outside, mostly just between classes, and on her walks to and from the library. It was nice. She did feel better now but she wouldn't tell Emily.

They found seats at the top of the metal bleachers and watched the scrimmage below. Once Lilly spotted Charlie, her eyes stayed on him. He was in his element. Lilly watched him running down the field cradling the ball rhythmically rotating his shoulders in sync with his stride. The entire game was like a slow motion tease and Lilly tried to keep her composure as she followed his every move with thirsty anticipation. He clearly loved what he was doing and his teammates obviously respected him. Lilly groaned.

"What's the matter with you?" Emily asked tartly.

"Nothing," Lilly lied.

Celia and Porter made their way down the row to sit with them.

"Hey! Look who's out!" Celia teased.

"Hi-i-i," Lilly said laughingly.

Celia sat down comfortably next to Lilly. "Did you see the ass on Charlie?"

"What?" Lilly laughed.

"I don't know Lil," Celia said with a teasing voice. "I could switch teams for some of that."

"Shut up," Lilly said with a laugh as she leaned into Celia with her hip and shoulder.

"It's a shame, y'all don't go out anymore," Emily added suggestively.

"Is he seeing anybody?" Porter asked from the end of the bench.

Lilly clenched her jaw, trying not to show any emotion.

"He was seeing that Autumn girl, I think," Emily said without confidence.

"Her name's Summer," Celia corrected her.

Lilly shot Celia a death stare, *she knew Charlie was seeing someone else and did not tell her?*

"Oh," Emily rolled her eyes, "Autumn, Summer, whatever. They're not real names," she added definitively.

Porter laughed.

Celia waited for the other girls to be distracted and then asked Lilly quietly, "Are you ok?"

"Fine," Lilly said quickly with attitude and stared down at the field.

Celia gave her a disapproving look.

A couple minutes later Lilly hissed, "You knew he was seeing someone else and you didn't tell me?"

Porter and Emily made eye contact as they both eavesdropped.

"You said you didn't want to talk about Charlie," Celia said calmly under her breath.

Lilly was so frustrated that she yelled at full volume, "Yeah! Not about stupid stuff, but tell me if he's dating someone!"

The people in the row in front of them turned around to see who was talking. Lilly clamped her mouth shut.

Celia waited a minute to respond and then turned to Lilly so they were looking at one another. "He dated someone," she whispered with a sassy face.

"I know that now," Lilly whispered back. "Who is she?"

Celia looked around at the people sitting around them. The game was getting exciting and everyone seemed to be watching the lacrosse players sprint from one end of the field to the other. Seeing no one she considered interested in their conversation, other than Porter and Emily, Celia spoke a little more audibly, "She's on the volleyball team. They went out a few times, I don't think it went anywhere." Celia shrugged, "He's single now."

"Oh," Lilly was disappointed. She knew she had ignored his calls and messages but she didn't really think he'd move on.

"I didn't think you cared," Celia added.

"He's my ex, of course I care," Lilly hissed.

"You broke up with him," Celia reminded her at a whisper.

Lilly said closer to full volume, "So, what?"

Emily turned and gave them both a disapproving look. "Y'all this is not the place for private conversations," she rolled her eyes towards the row in front of them that had grown suspiciously quiet.

"Fine," Lilly said with an exhale.

"Good," Celia added sassily.

After the scrimmage the girls made their way through the crowd, Stephen and Charlie jogged over to the bleachers to meet them. Stephen promptly wrapped Porter in a sweaty hug.

"Eww! Stephen!" Porter yelled but pulled his shirt towards her when he moved away and gave him a kiss.

Turning her attention away from Stephen and Porter's public display of affection, Celia said, "Charlie, you were awesome!"

"Oh, thanks. It was the rest of the guys, they do a great job. Thank you so much for coming," he beamed. He was sweaty and needed a shave. Lilly stood silently thinking about nothing but tearing his clothes off.

"This was so much fun," Emily chimed in brightly.

"Y'all look great out there," Porter said as she rubbed Stephen's shoulders.

"We were screaming so much, I thought Lilly was going to lose her voice,"

Emily added making eye contact with Lilly and smiling with an overly confident look in her eye.

"It was a great game," Lilly choked out trying to cover Emily's comment with a justification that had nothing to do with Charlie.

The group started moving toward the parking lot.

Charlie waited for the rest of the group to walk ahead. He gently held Lilly's wrist so she would hang back with him. After the group was several yards ahead he said, "I miss you."

Her heart was racing. The skin of her wrist was on fire where his hand had been. She looked up at him, nervously, "I miss you too... I just don't think it's a good idea."

"So, this isn't a 'we can move on' moment?" Charlie asked quietly.

"What do you mean?" She asked more hopefully than she had intended.

"Well," he looked around the stadium and out to the parking lot, "I've missed you and thought that maybe we could go out sometime?" He looked down at her with the full impact of his gaze unwavering.

"Oh," Lilly was startled. She had not expected him to be so honest. "We should..." she motioned to the group walking ahead of them and started to walk away.

"Look, I just want to know when we can be friends again," Charlie said as they walked towards the others.

"Not yet," Lilly said nervously as they rejoined the group.

After the lacrosse game Lilly spent the next week holed up in the library, becoming even more of a recluse than she had been already that semester.

Celia found Lilly in a small glass room in the back of the library. The door was closed and Lilly was surrounded by a fortress of books and only looked up when the doorknob jangled as Celia entered the room and closed it behind herself.

"You can't stay mad at me forever, you know," Celia informed her as she casually sat down across the table from Lilly and started dismantling Lilly's barricade of books.

"I'm using those," Lilly said with annoyance.

"You're done and you know it," Celia said firmly.

Lilly sat back and crossed her arms.

"You're still mad that I didn't tell you Charlie dated someone?" Celia said as she organized Lilly's chaos.

"You're supposed to be my friend."

"And I'm not now?" Celia asked sarcastically.

"Why would you keep that from me?"

Celia stopped moving books and looked Lilly dead in the eye. "What would you have done with that information?"

The question caught Lilly off guard and she didn't have a response.

Celia put down what she was holding, "If you can honestly tell me that you would have done anything but get angry and just stay in your room then I'll apologize."

Lilly said nothing. She hated when Celia was right.

Celia looked at Lilly, "From where I'm sitting, the only thing I saved you from was four weeks of being angry about something you were going to do nothing to change." Celia took a breath, "So, I did, I let you work and I didn't say anything and Emily didn't say anything either, because we weren't helping you."

"You think you helped me?" Lilly gave a sarcastic laugh rolling her eyes to the ceiling.

"Maybe you don't think so but you worked for weeks and you never asked if he had moved on, you never wanted to talk about him," Celia reminded her tapping her foot as she spoke.

Lilly's lips were a thin line of anger.

Celia put her hands up in surrender. "You're mad now and that's fine but you're going to need to get over it and forgive me."

Lilly rolled her eyes.

"I brought notes on your project," Celia said coldly.

"Oh, thank you," Lilly said begrudgingly.

Celia sat down, "Can we talk about that?"

Lilly's mood broke, "Yes."

"Good," Celia jumped right in, "because I think it's much better than the last version but you still need to fix some things."

"Sorry for overreacting," Lilly said apologetically before getting started.

"I know," Celia said knowingly as she reached into her bag and pulled out an organized stack of papers with coordinating folders and paperclips in bright colors. "Shall we get to work?"

Lilly leaned in and nodded.

19. A NEW SOLUTION

Lilly had a meeting with PH in early April to review her progress and deliver an outline of her final scholarship presentation for the year. The meeting with PH was strenuous. Lilly was on edge the entire time, waiting in the wooden desk chair on the other side of PH's desk. She showed PH the recommendations Celia had given her and the design work Drew had already completed. When PH finally opened her mouth to give her verdict, Lilly held her breath.

PH looked down her nose to review the list in her hands, "It looks like you added all of the changes suggested by your beta testers. The refreshed graphics look much better. And I'm pleased with the modifications you made to enhance functionality."

Lilly couldn't help but smile so hard her cheeks hurt.

PH smiled warmly. "It looks really great. On another note, I was reading through your latest assignment for practicum this weekend and your solutions were really interesting."

"Were they wrong?" Lilly shifted her weight, already preparing her argument for how she could fix the assignment and get it to PH later that day.

"No, it was all right," PH paused. "It was just different than I had envisioned." PH gestured with her free hand. "Obviously, when I write an assignment I have a solution in mind and try to give my students enough information to lead you all down the same logic path."

"Right," Lilly's brow furrowed deeply, "do I need to fix my answers?"

"No, your answers are great. They're actually really creative and exciting." PH waited a moment and then said, "None of my other students looked at these problems in the same way you did and I found it really interesting to follow your process."

"Oh," delightfully surprised, Lilly added, "thank you."

Professor Hendricks continued, "I'd really like to talk more about your thought process because I think that you're on to something that we should look into further."

"Oh, ok." Lilly ran her fingers through her red hair and nodded.

"If you don't mind sharing your interpretations with me, I think we might be able to coax something out of them."

"Sure, what do you mean?"

PH spoke with her hands, "I think your solutions might work in a new way. I think you're on the path to developing a new approach to coding."

Lilly looked startled but PH was looking ahead and missed it.

"What you've written shows creativity and a simple solution to some really complex problems. If you crystalize the process, you could be on track to building something great." She smiled and reframed her statement. "I'm not being clear and I'm sorry. I'm excited about your work, Lilly. I think what you're working on could be the next big thing in applications and software development."

Lilly crossed her arms, "For the class?"

"No," Professor Hendricks said making deliberate eye contact with Lilly and gesturing broadly with her hands, "for the industry, the world, everybody."

Lilly paused. She was quietly thinking about what Professor Hendricks was saying, trying to process it all before speaking.

"I don't want to add to your already substantial list of responsibilities," PH shifted in her seat, "but I think with some more focus and attention, this project could be the difference between you working for a great company and running a great company.

Lilly nodded her agreement, "I'd like that."

PH sighed, "I'm sensing some hesitation. What is it?"

"I just," Lilly looked down at her shoes, "I guess I wanted to be great or at least do well in art."

PH nodded, "Your first major? History of art?"

"Yeah, I wanted to do something creative and I haven't even had the opportunity to try. Maybe I'd never be a painter or an artist but my work would be creative." Lilly frowned and twisted her signet ring self-consciously. "I just wanted to try."

PH exhaled, "Lilly, you're right, in this field you're never going to have a piece of art that you can hang on the wall or a piece of music that people can hear and you can say, 'I wrote that' or 'that's mine.'" But, regardless of that fact, this," PH gestured to Lilly's test results and programming work for PH's practicum course, "this is still art. It is *your* art. You are still making a valuable contribution. Because of your work, people's lives will be easier, will be better. It may not be traditional but what I see in your work and your solutions is beauty and elegance totally unlike anything else I've seen before. Lilly you are an artist."

Wet tears were tracing paths down Lilly's cheeks.

"With time and dedication, your work will continue to improve. And even though it is not exactly what you had in mind, it is what you're good at and if you want to apply yourself to making a difference in the art world, this may be how you do it."

Lilly grinned through her tears. She sniffed and rubbed her face with her sleeve, "I do work pretty hard on this for it not to be my art." She laughed at herself.

"Exactly. You wouldn't put this much time and dedication into this work if it were not important."

Lilly sighed and agreed, "It is important."

"Good," PH nodded. "Shall we start by meeting twice a week? I'm free Mondays and Wednesdays, will that work for you?"

Lilly nodded her head quickly, "Yes, I can do that." She wiped her cheeks dry with her palms. "I will call you from home after finals."

"Excellent," PH smiled. "Then that's where we'll start. With regard to your Wilson Scholarship project, I'd like you to get ready to present."

Lilly exhaled hard.

PH leaned back into her chair, "If possible, for you and your family, I'd like for you to come back to Nashville this summer to present your project to the investor I mentioned earlier this year."

Lilly looked strained, she was sure she would have to use the money she had saved from fixing computers and building the ballet's fundraising page to afford the trip.

PH smiled again, "I don't know what this company is looking for specifically so I'm not sure if your project would be a good fit. I don't want to get your hopes up, but I mentioned that this might be a possibility and it seems that the investor is interested in meeting with you to discuss your work."

Lilly could feel the blood coursing through her veins. She wanted to jump up and yell with happiness but she kept her body still in her seat.

PH spoke with cool confidence, "You'll need to polish your presentation for an outside audience."

"I will." Lilly nodded seriously.

"I'm confident you will," PH said firmly, "otherwise I wouldn't have arranged this meeting."

"Thank you so much Professor Hendricks," Lilly said with a breathy exhale.

"My pleasure," PH said in measured tones. "It's going to be a lot of work and I want all of the changes you have listed here," she held up the sheet of modifications Lilly had given her, "active and ready to use."

Lilly nodded obediently but couldn't keep the grin off of her face. "Ok, I will. It will be ready and professional."

"Good," PH gave a satisfactory nod. "We'll start our meetings next week.

If you have questions or need anything we'll talk then. I want you to be aware that my intent is to be silent in this meeting and let you take the lead."

Lilly nodded.

"And Lilly," PH added, "you really are an artist."

"Thank you PH," Lilly smiled. Lilly flew out of PH's office. She skipped on her way back to the dorm and didn't care who saw her. Lilly was so ecstatic she could scream.

Lilly was on her phone, texting Sophia the good news and waiting for the elevator, when a text from Charlie popped up.

"Date this week?"

She smiled to herself and texted, "K. After finals B4 summer break."

"Deal."

20. FRESHMAN YEAR ENDS

Finals week went by in a rush. Lilly barely had time to study, let alone pack up her room to move home. Emily had responsibly been packing a box a night for the past week.

"I'm leaving packing tape and a sharpie here for you," Emily instructed as she finished writing a label on her last box to go home. Mr. and Mrs. Parker were picking up Emily and all of her belongings after her last final that morning.

Lilly stood up and hugged her roommate. "Thank you so much for everything this year. I couldn't have done this without you."

Emily gave Lilly a tight squeeze. "Don't forget I need your rooming deposit so we can live together next year."

"You're sure you want to live in the dorms again? Celia was saying that she and Porter are going to get an apartment off campus…" Lilly led.

"You need to stay on campus for your scholarship and I am not breaking in a new roommate," Emily said firmly. "Write me the check right now so you don't forget."

"Ok," Lilly turned and pulled her checkbook out of her desk drawer. "We send in the money together and that enters us into a lottery?" Lilly hadn't had time to review the process with finals and her presentation work taking up so much time.

"Yes," Emily explained patiently, "we submit our money and they put us into a lottery. I've already ranked our top three dorm choices. Once we get the building they randomly select the room."

"Right," Lilly ripped the check out with a loud tear and handed it to Emily.

"I'll drop this off on my way home today."

"Thank you so much," Lilly said again.

"And don't forget to book the flights I sent you for the fourth of July."

"I won't," Lilly assured her.

"Are you sure you don't want me to pack up some of your stuff before I go?" Emily suggested.

"No," Lilly shook her head. "I'll do it tomorrow. Sophia's coming to pick me up and we can handle it."

"Ok," Emily gave Lilly one more hug and left to take her last final of freshman year.

Lilly's final was later in the day and she crammed in as much studying as she could before taking her test. Before she left to go home for the summer, Lilly met Charlie for a date. He took her to an upscale burger place with exposed ductwork and cowhide seating. They sat in a dark booth in the back. After dinner Lilly took her white linen napkin off of her lap and placed it on the tabletop gently. When she looked up she said, "Thank you, Charlie."

"I missed you, Lil," Charlie said honestly.

Lilly felt the familiar tug at her heartstrings, it was easy to belittle what she felt for Charlie in her mind, it was a lot harder to look into his eyes and say it, so instead she confessed, "I missed you too, Charlie."

Charlie grabbed her hands and pulled her slowly up to stand.

"Hey," he said.

She answered with a yawn, "Hey." With finals done she was starting to feel the familiar exhaustion that came from exerting herself mentally. The meal gave her a warm drowsy sensation through her body.

"Let's get back together."

She was wide awake now, "What?"

"Lil, there's no one else I'd rather be with than you."

Lilly took a step back and looked at him directly, "Charlie."

"Is that a yes?" he asked.

"Charlie… you can't buy me stuff like that bracelet. It's too much."

He leaned forward and wrapped her in a bear hug. "No more gifts," he agreed.

"I like you," she confessed. "Just take it down a notch, ok?"

"Ok. I'll try but I'm still going to do nice things for you."

"Nice is good, just don't go overboard," she said from where her head was resting on his chest.

"So we're dating?" Charlie whispered into her hair.

"Yes, we're dating," she finally agreed. He kissed her softly.

They rode back to campus in silence, both of them afraid to break the spell cast by this unexpected turn of events.

Walking her back to the dorm he asked, "May I see you again?"

Lilly smiled up at him, "I'll see you in the fall."

Seemingly on impulse he pulled her into his arms and kissed her. Months of pent up sexual frustration seemed to burst on their lips as they clung to one another in the blue night. Lilly felt herself being pulled in to Charlie's gravitational force and she stopped fighting the urge to follow. She felt the moment in all its glorious and conflicting intensity. His hands in her hair, his breath on her neck, it all felt deliriously magical. She felt like she was where she fit and yet nowhere near where she belonged.

Her heart raced as he kissed her, pulling away only to dive deeper. His fingers guided her hips towards his as he traced the skin on her lower back with passionate longing. Lilly pulled back and held his face in her hands, she stared into his bright blue eyes for a lingering second as she made her decision, weaving her fingers through his she took him up to her room.

They awoke to bright sunlight and the sound of other students moving out of the dorms. She gave a heaving sigh, "Why didn't we do that before?" She laughed out loud.

Charlie wrapped her in a bear hug. He sighed heavily, "I just want you to know that was not my plan."

Lilly giggled, "Me either."

Charlie bowed his head and bumped his forehead against hers deliberately. She pressed back feeling for the first time, the comfortable intimacy of lovers. She breathed softly and stretched.

Charlie rolled over, pulling on underwear and his pants. He walked barefoot and topless to the sink to splash water on his face. Lilly watched him with amazement. He was beautiful. She blinked remembering flashes of the night before and watching the muscles in his back ripple as he bent over.

She put on her bra and pulled the sheet with her as she went to the wardrobe to find something to wear.

"Hey," he said walking to her and pulling her into his bare chest. She took a deep breath of him and rested her head on his torso. She committed the moment to memory, the sunlight, his head resting on hers, the smell of his body, the fabulous exhaustion she felt. She savored the feeling of that morning.

Her phone rang, echoing in the half empty room, shattering the peace of the moment. It was Sophia. Lilly gave Charlie an apologetic look, her sister was coming to help her move out.

"Hey Soph," Lilly said tucking a piece of hair behind her ear and sitting on Emily's bare mattress, still wrapped in her top sheet.

"Hey, I'm parking. You need to come let me into the dorm."

"Ok!" Lilly said brightly. "I'll meet you in the lobby."

"I know where it is," Sophia said confidently. "I'll call you if I get lost."

"Ok. Bye." Lilly hung up and looked up to see Charlie pulling last night's shirt back over his head, she was sad to see his abs go.

He sat on her bed and pulled on his shoes, "Moving out?"

"Yeah, my sister is parking," Lilly said with disappointment.

Charlie stood up and looked around the room. "Want help?"

"You don't have to help," she answered automatically.

"I want to, if you'll let me?" he said with a bold smile.

She smiled back and shook her head, "Ok."

Lilly quickly brushed her teeth, dressed, and ran downstairs to meet Sophia. She hugged her sister hard when she saw her, "I missed you."

"I missed you too," Sophia agreed, returning Lilly's embrace.

On the elevator ride up to the room Lilly did all the talking, "Charlie's going to help us move."

"Ok," Sophia gave her a nonchalant shrug.

"He just offered to help this morning," Lilly gushed. She wanted to spill her guts, to tell someone she had slept with Charlie Abbott but she fought the urge to say any more.

"Cool," Sophia said as she followed her sister off of the elevator and down the hall to her room.

When the girls entered the room it was empty. It was like someone had punched Lilly in the chest. The sun was still shining the bed was still a mess, only Charlie was gone.

The shock registered on her face and Sophia haltingly asked, "Was he supposed to be here now?"

Lilly didn't answer, she was dumbfounded. She didn't have words. He was gone. She couldn't hide the shock on her face as Sophia softly touched her sister's arm in sympathy. Lilly looked at the unmade bed, her sheets on the floor, everything reminded her of him and their night together.

"Lil?" Sophia was unsure of how to comfort her sister.

Charlie walked in carrying a stack of cardboard boxes. "Hi, I'm Charlie. You must be Sophia," he said warmly as he leaned the flat boxes against the wall and put a hand out to shake Sophia's.

Sophia looked brightly at Lilly to show how impressed she was, "Nice to meet you," Sophia said with a smile.

Lilly was beside herself. He was there. He didn't leave. She stayed in a state of shock as he got to work packing up her room, joking with her sister, and carrying box after box to the bin he had procured from the building for her move.

He came back into the room to find Lilly still staring in wonderment, "Are you alright?"

"I'm fine," she said hugging him tightly.

When they were done Lilly returned Emily's and her room keys to the RA on duty and met Charlie and Sophia at the car. They were laughing together as Lilly approached.

"Nice meeting you, Charlie," Sophia said as Lilly joined them. "Thanks for all the help."

"My pleasure," he smiled warmly at her.

Sophia then got into the car and began adjusting the radio and the air conditioning so she wouldn't interrupt their goodbye.

Lilly stepped into Charlie's arms and he kissed her deeply. He pulled back with a smirk and asked, "May I call you?"

"Yeah," she said adding, "I'd like that."

"Good," he kissed her one last time before opening the passenger side door. She sat down and buckled her seatbelt. Looking over her he added, "Great meeting you, Sophia."

"You too," Sophia smiled as she put the car in gear and Charlie slammed the door closed.

"So that's bracelet guy?" Sophia asked with a smirk.

"Yeah," Lilly answered dreamily, "that's Charlie."

"Does he have a tiny weenie?" Sophia was fighting a losing battle to keep a straight face.

Lilly was shocked by her sister's intuition, "Stop it!"

"Why can't you stop smiling?" Sophia teased, looking away from the road to smirk at her sister.

"I can stop smiling," Lilly tried forcing her lips and cheeks to relax and failed. "Well, I can't stop now!"

"Sure you can't," they both laughed as Lilly tried to frown, which only seemed to add to her inability to stop smiling.

Lilly took a deep breath, and turned her head to face her sister, "How's home?"

Sophia shrugged, "We're ok. School's good but easy. They elected me editor of the yearbook for next year."

"That's awesome Soph, congratulations!" Lilly smiled broadly.

"Thank you." Sophia added more quietly, "I'm interning at the clinic this summer."

Lilly's eyes bulged the Cleveland Clinic was one of the premier hospitals in the country. Lilly was astounded and proud. "That's amazing. Soph, that is so incredible."

"It'll be good," Sophia nodded in agreement. "Anything that gets me out of there as fast as possible."

Lilly's voice took on a serious note, "I'm working on it, Soph."

"I know you are," Sophia glanced over her shoulder with a soft smile, "but I still need to do it myself."

21. HOME

The following morning Lilly sat down at the dining room table. Familiar sounds were coming from the kitchen, the chaos of her mother cooking, Sophia's laugh. Lilly watched her mother carry in the meal on chipped and worn serving dishes, wearing her threadbare apron covered in stains from meals made long before this one. Melanie brought out canned cinnamon rolls, burnt again, and slathered in icing.

"How were your exams?" Melanie asked as they each cut the bottoms off of their burnt rolls.

"Good," Lilly said, licking her fingers, coated in sugary icing.

"Do you really think this is a good use of your time?" Melanie deadpanned, taking a small bite of her cinnamon roll.

Lilly cocked her head to the side and raised her chin, "College? Yes, yes I do." She answered firmly.

"Money's tight right now I'm going to need you to start contributing."

"Ok," Lilly said slowly and evenly. "What does that mean?"

"You're going to need to start pulling your weight and paying rent," Melanie said with a sigh.

Lilly pursed her lips, "You just figured this out?"

Melanie gave her a salty look.

Lilly took a deep breath, "It would have been helpful for you to tell me this before I came home so I could make the proper arrangements."

Melanie rolled her eyes, "You're working at the computer shop, you can afford to pay rent and clean up after yourself."

Lilly bit her bottom lip, too stubborn to complain about the situation further, "Sure, how much would you like for rent?"

"$300 a month seems fair," Melanie answered daring her daughter to protest.

Lilly calculated the three months and held her breath, "Fine. But I will expect that money to go directly to your rent for this house. If you are visibly drunk or belligerent I will promptly move out and you will never see me again."

Melanie laughed in Lilly's face, "Sure thing kiddo," she replied sarcastically, clearly proud of herself for extorting nearly $1,000.00 from her daughter, "whatever you say." With that she walked out of the room leaving her dirty dishes on the table, clearly expecting Lilly to clean up after her.

Throughout the early summer, Lilly worked, methodically saving every dollar. Conference calls with PH kept her busy with her project. She spent her days in the back room of the computer repair shop and most nights refining her presentation for her investor meeting. Late at night, after they both got home from their respective jobs, she and Sophia would sit outside watching the stars from the broken concrete of their driveway.

It was on one of these seemingly endless summer nights that their peace was shattered by Melanie slamming open the screen door, "What are you doing?" she slurred from the porch.

"Nothing," Sophia and Lilly said in unison.

"You're always doing nothing, both of you!" She shouted from the doorway.

The girls sat silently waiting. Sometimes she would just go inside.

"You don't care that I'm in here all by myself. You sit out here every night. Why did you even come home?" she spat at Lilly, getting louder.

"Let's go in," Lilly mumbled to Sophia, hoping the neighbors didn't hear Melanie yelling. To her mother Lilly said, "We're coming, Mom."

"You never want to spend time with me. You think you're better than me," Melanie added sulkily. She wasn't going to give up this fight as easily as Lilly had hoped.

"We don't think we're better than you," Sophia said as she squeezed past their mother and through the narrow doorway into the house.

"The hell you don't," Melanie shouted, moving quickly and shoving Sophia into the wall, breathing heavily in her face. She used her larger frame to trap Sophia between the door frame and the wall. "You think you're going to leave me but you're never going to leave. You're not smart like Lilly, you never were."

"Let go of her," Lilly yelled.

"You're not better than me, you're just like me," Melanie said with spittle flying out of her mouth and onto Sophia's flushed cheek.

"Let go or I will hit you," Sophia said savagely as she struggled to free herself from her mother's grasp.

Melanie held her ground, "You'd never hit me. I'm your mother."

Sophia used the wall as leverage and pushed herself towards Melanie, throwing the larger woman off balance and onto the floor.

"Don't you touch me again! Do you understand me, you drunk bitch?" Sophia was now standing over Melanie, animatedly pointing her finger. "I am leaving you, just like everyone does because you're nothing!" Melanie seemed to give an involuntary shudder at the words as she lay sprawled on the floor.

"Sophia, stop!" Lilly ordered, seeing her mother reduced to a simpering pile of defenseless flesh she felt responsible to protect her from further attack but Sophia was not finished making her point.

Sophia turned to Lilly with a crazed look and yelled, "You're not here. You don't know what I deal with, she does this all the time and I'm done." Turning aggressively towards her mother, "Do you hear me Melanie? I'm done." Sophia turned on her heel and walked out of the room.

Melanie seemed to shrivel into a ball on the floor as the sound of Sophia's retreating footsteps pounded down the hallway stopping only for the crash of her bedroom door slamming behind her.

"Mom, go to bed," Lilly instructed angrily.

"Why does everyone want to leave me?" Melanie sobbed from the floor.

"I'm done," Lilly said, more to herself than anyone, as she stepped forward to hoist up her mother.

"You're never coming back," Melanie continued to whine as Lilly grappled with her rubbery frame.

"I'm here, Mom, I'm here," Lilly said with annoyance as she helped her mother to stand. She was too drunk. There was no use in trying to reason with her at this point.

"But you'll leave me. Sophia's going to leave me," she wailed.

"I have to leave, I'm in college, but I'll come back," Lilly attempted to pacify her mother as she navigated their way down the hallway, turning on lights, keeping Melanie supported and her feet moving in the right direction.

"If you're so smart, why do you need college? Sounds pretty stupid to me," she slurred, drunk logic once again taking over.

"You mentioned that before." Lilly said seriously, unimpressed by Melanie's sloppy attempts to manipulate her despite her drunken state.

"Sophia's not smart like you. She'll never leave me," she said as she lay down in bed. "Sophia loves me, not like you."

Her words were mumbled, but still clear. Unexpectedly, the the statement stabbed into Lilly like a hot iron, piercing straight through her chest. Before Lilly could respond, Melanie had passed out. Lilly sat down on the edge of the bed as Melanie's meaty shoulder rose and then fell with each rhythmic breath. Lilly stared down at her hands. "You drunk bitch," she whispered.

22. JULY 4, 2010

Lilly flew to Nashville to meet with the investor PH recommended the week of the Fourth of July. She walked out of the airport into the muggy Tennessee heat, dragging her bag behind her. Grateful to see Emily parked curbside in a silver BMW convertible. Upon seeing Lilly, Emily quickly jumped out to hug her and throw her bag in the trunk. Gingerly stepping into the pristine vehicle, Lilly could already feel her sweaty thighs sticking to the leather as she pulled the door closed behind her. Emily screeched away from the curb with a jolt.

Emily's natural blonde highlights glinted in a polished ponytail that streamed behind her like a banner. It was too loud to talk with the top down so Lilly silently watched the scenery roll by, grateful to be back in Nashville and away from her family. Emily zipped past a sign that read *Belle Meade Country Club*. They were quickly surrounded by huge trees, tennis courts, and golf carts. The bright blue sky peaked through a canopy of lush trees and sculpted shrubs. A green fortress opened before the car with birds singing softly, the sun shining above, and the smell of roses.

"Ready to grab some lunch?" Emily asked as she pulled into the valet line.

"Yes," Lilly said, remembering that she hadn't eaten since her breakfast of peanut butter and jelly on toast. It had to be about two in the afternoon and she was starving.

Coming to a stop Emily said, "Here," and popped the trunk, "grab your suit and we'll head to the pool after we eat."

Lilly didn't say anything as she dug through her bag, gracelessly yanking her suit from a tangle of underwear and pajamas and shoving it into her purse. Emily then led the way to a quiet patio surrounded by bright purple hydrangeas and leafy green trees. There was a breeze sweeping through the air and a water fountain made calming hollow sounds as the girls sat down on smooth wooden chairs. A waiter took their orders with crisp proficiency and promptly delivered their sweet teas.

After taking a sip Emily said with a smile, "I'm so glad that you're here. I thought this afternoon we'd just hang out by the pool so we can relax and you can tell me all about what you're doing in Cleveland," Emily said brightly. "Tonight we're meeting Porter, Stephen, Celia, and Claire for dinner at Husk. Claire says it's amazing so I'm super excited. Thursday we're going to my parents' lake house. We're going to go boating and water skiing."

"I've never been water skiing," Lilly interrupted.

"It's super easy. Don't worry, we'll teach you." Before Emily could finish the same waiter delivered their salads and disappeared.

"Thank you so much for planning all of this," Lilly gushed as she prepared to dig into lunch.

"It's nothing, Lil, I'm just glad that you could come out and see us," Emily smiled genuinely.

As the girls ate, Lilly looked up, "Don't forget, next Wednesday I'll need a ride downtown to meet with Professor Hendricks."

"Oh, that's right, are you ready to present your project?" Emily's fork hovered above her meal as she leaned in for the details.

"I'm super nervous," Lilly admitted. "It just feels like finals never ended. I talk to PH two maybe three times a week and I've been working non-stop." Lilly stuffed a heaping forkful of chicken Cesar salad in her mouth.

Emily leaned back again and relaxed into the chair, "It is a lot of pressure. Did you want me to come with you?"

"Yes," Lilly admitted between bites. "Would you mind?"

"Not at all, it'll be fun!" Emily smiled satisfactorily to herself.

When the waiter brought the check, Lilly smiled. "I'll get it," she confidently reached for the bill.

"Oh, Lil, you can't pay for that here." Emily looked embarrassed.

"Nonsense, you're letting me stay with you and your family and I'm going to pay for lunch. I want to help." Lilly beamed proudly, she had waited for this moment.

"That's wonderful, Lil. It's really sweet of you." Emily gently explained, "But this is a private club and you're here as my guest. They don't even take money. My family has a membership so they're just going to add it to our monthly statement."

Lilly was confused and embarrassed; it registered on her face.

Emily reached across the table and softly took the bill out of Lilly's hands. She smiled politely as she said, "It's not a big deal. It's just that when we eat here it is always on the member, but thank you so much for offering."

Lilly put her hands in her lap and felt stupid for not knowing that she couldn't pay for lunch at the club. It seemed like whenever she got too comfortable this wealthy world found a way to remind her of her place. It was exasperating.

Emily signed the note, "Ready to go?"

Lilly nodded obediently and stood.

Back in the locker rooms the girls changed into swimsuits. Lilly had an old floral print bikini that seemed worn and tattered next to Emily's bright blue Ralph Lauren two-piece that showed off her figure beautifully. Lilly self-consciously tugged at the fabric of her suit, hoping if she pulled one more time it might miraculously stretch and cover her chest with a little more fabric. As they walked out to the pool carrying the scratchy white club towels over their shoulders, Lilly strategically pulled the rough towel over her breasts and held it there to make it seem that was the way it had fallen and pretended to be unaware of how it was resting.

Outside the sun was aggressively scorching everything it touched. The girls chose two forrest green lounge chairs by the pool. Emily lay down with one knee propped up looking like a magazine spread. Lilly lay down on her stomach trying to conceal her exposed cleavage and the fact that she had left her shades in the car. Emily kicked one leg over the other, wiggling her toes playfully.

Lilly was already starting to fall asleep on the lounge chair. The stress of traveling and her embarrassment at lunch seemed to all melt away. The sun was baking her skin and warming all of the stress out of her body. Lilly's eyelids heavily drooped as she surrendered to sleep and slipped into a blissful dream.

That evening the girls met their friends for dinner. Husk looked like an old Southern home. The red brick exterior poked up behind a toothy white picket fence. Inside, the room was large and bright purple with shimmery olive green drapes, and blue watercolor paintings filling all of the wall space that was not already taken up by gigantic windows. The aroma of shrimp and grits wafted from a table nearby. Lilly's stomach grumbled in anticipation. Emily led the way to the table where their friends stood up to greet them.

Celia hugged Lilly happily and introduced Claire, "This is the love of my life, Claire Davenport. I'd like to introduce Lillian Rose Carter, my dear friend from school."

Lilly smiled and warmly greeted Claire, "I am so pleased to finally meet you."

"Hello," Claire smiled politely as she clasped Lilly's hand. Claire was just as slim as Celia, with a dark chestnut bob, muddy green eyes, and thick eyebrows. She wore black cigarette pants, a long white oxford, and red ballet flats. Her pout was painted in a dark classic red and she smelled like a woman should smell, like mystery and classy hotel rooms... she made Lilly intensely aware of the fact that she smelled like strawberry body wash.

After a brief introduction Lilly moved around the table greeting the rest of her friends. Stephen clapped her in a bear hug and picked her up, "How you doing, Coach?"

"I'm great," she smiled as she tried to keep her light dress from fluttering too high in the back.

"Stephen, you're going to crush her," Porter said, snipping at him comfortably

Stephen gently planted Lilly back on her espadrilles.

"Hey, Porter," Lilly said brightly.

"You look nice," Porter replied without her usual air of condescension.

"Thank you," Lilly said happily. The simple act of Porter not insulting her brightened Lilly's mood.

Lilly smelled Max's potent cologne before she saw him. The oppressive musk filled her nostrils and seemed to make her lightheaded as he said, "Damn, Carter," smoothly looking her body up and down.

Stephen interjected, "Maxwell, do you not see this woman is confident, brilliant, and possessing so much more than just a pleasing figure."

"I see all of that," Max said appreciatively.

"Max, I really don't need you," Lilly said sharply.

"I know," Max answered dreamily taking a deep breath. He sighed, "That's what makes it so much better."

Lilly could not help but laugh, "You are absurd," she said with a grin.

"Absolutely," he agreed, "may I?" He pulled out her seat.

"Thank you," Lilly said with a forgiving smile.

As they placed their drink orders Lilly shifted in her seat, grateful that she had selected a light dress that evening as the room got hotter. The server returned and Lilly took a generous gulp of her sweet tea, trying to cool down. Conversation had turned to family stories and Lilly listened happily to her friends regaling each other with their personal histories.

Emily shared, "My mama and Daddy have the best marriage. Daddy tells mama exactly what to do," pausing for effect she added, "and mama ignores him."

The group burst out laughing. Lilly crossed her legs under the table as Max caught her eye and raised his glass in salute. She took a generous gulp of sweet tea, wishing it was something harder.

"What about you, Yankee girl, any good family stories to tell?" Emily asked. The table turned its attention to Lilly.

"Yours are all so good, I can't think of one," Lilly said and took another long drink. Lilly could think of absolutely nothing in her family history that would be appropriate or amusing to this crowd.

Stephen quickly stepped in to fill the lull and the conversation kept flowing as they all laughed and talked through the night. The boys were on their third cocktail when Max casually draped his arm around Lilly's shoulders as he talked.

She looked at him jokingly, "Seriously?"

"Can't blame a man for trying," Max said as he lifted his arm.

After the dinner plates were collected, Emily dragged Lilly to the ladies room with her. Lilly checked her make-up in the soft light as Emily washed her hands.

"What's going on with Max?" Emily asked suspiciously.

"He's just being Max." Lilly said, frowning at her reflection and making eye contact with Emily in the mirror

"Ok, well it's up to you how you want to handle it, but you don't want people talking," Emily warned.

Lilly turned abruptly to face her friend. "What would they say?"

"Just that Max and you seem to be really friendly this evening," Emily suggested.

Lilly could feel shame stabbing through her body. With Porter she expected to be on edge, with Emily, it caught her off guard.

"Emily, nothing is happening between Max and me. However, it's Max's job to keep his hands to himself and my job to tell him if I'm uncomfortable. He is a friend and if he wants to show his affection in a way that I am comfortable with, it is completely acceptable. What other people say is not my problem and frankly none of their or your business."

"I just wanted you to be careful so people don't talk," Emily said defensively.

"People are always going to talk Emily, but that's their problem, not mine," Lilly said firmly with confidence. "I'm not going to stop enjoying my evening because of how someone else might interpret it." Lilly glared into Emily's eyes with the same intensity she had used the first night they met.

"You're right, I'm sorry," Emily said backing down.

"I am right. It's not my job to change how I behave to accommodate anyone else."

Emily bit her lip and said nothing.

Lilly kept going, not willing to stop her momentum, "If anyone has a problem with how I comport myself they can talk to me directly."

"That's fair," Emily agreed.

"And while we're on the subject of other people's business, what's going on with *you* and Max?"

"What?" Now it was Emily's turn to be caught off guard.

"You two were spending a lot of time together at the end of the school year, why aren't you sitting next to him?" Lilly crossed her arms and stared at Emily expectantly.

Emily took a deep breath and reached for a brown crunchy towel to dry her hands, "I told you Lilly, Max and I are just friends."

Lilly looked at her skeptically.

Emily rolled her eyes with annoyance, "Fine. You speak a word of this and I will tell everyone you are a liar." Emily looked Lilly in the eye severely.

Lilly's eyes widened with intrigue. She had never seen Emily so intense.

Emily surveyed the rest of the bathroom, assuring that no one was listening. Once satisfied that no one was present she turned on all of the faucets and spoke quickly and quietly to Lilly. "Max and I have a purely physical relationship."

Lilly's face clearly registered her shock. This was the most delicious thing she had ever heard. She eagerly awaited more details.

Emily looked at her squarely, taking in Lilly's clear amusement at her expense. She inhaled deeply, "I planned to stop once we got to college but," she looked around the room avoiding eye-contact, "that has proven difficult."

Lilly's mouth dropped open. She could not believe she couldn't tell anyone this news. This was the best gossip she had heard all year. "How long has this been going on?" she asked with a smirk, reveling in Emily's embarrassment.

"Too long," Emily said firmly.

"How did you not tell me this? I had no idea," Lilly added in disbelief.

Emily rolled her eyes as if to convey that she could keep anything from Lilly if she wanted. Exhaling she said, "I prefer to keep my affairs discreet."

Of course she called them affairs. Lilly fought the urge to roll her eyes. "So, are you dating?"

Emily looked at her firmly and pulled a paper towel using it as a barrier as she went to work turning off the faucets by hand. "No. Are we done?" she asked impatiently.

"Not even close," Lilly chided with a smirk. "I'll drop it for now."

"Are we ok?" Emily asked sincerely once the last faucet was off.

Remembering her anger, Lilly asked, "Is that all you had to say to me?"

"Yes, I didn't mean..." Emily clearly wasn't sure where to take the sentence next.

Lilly shook her head as if to clear it, her long curls flew over her shoulders. "It's fine. Yes, we're ok. Are you good?"

"I'm good. I'm sorry." Emily did not seem to like apologizing, but handled the situation with typical grace.

Lilly turned back to the mirror and smeared on fresh lip-gloss. "It's forgiven, it's forgotten," she said calmly with poised polish. The girl who had trudged into Emily's dorm room last August had transformed into a self-possessed and confident young woman.

"I adore you," Emily beamed at her.

"And I you!" Lilly announced as she linked her arm through Emily's, pushed the door open, and marched back to the table.

Back at the table their bills had been left. Lilly casually picked up Emily's and her own and placed her card on top.

Emily discretely asked, "Are you sure?"

Lilly smiled calmly and nodded. This dinner had been the most expensive she had ever eaten but she was determined to show her gratitude to Emily.

Emily smiled satisfactorily, "Thank you."

"Thank you," Lilly answered with a smile.

On the ride home Lilly and Emily giggled and talked the entire time. The evening seemed to be a revelation to them both as the dynamic in their relationship had transformed. For the first time Emily spoke to Lilly as an equal and Lilly responded in kind.

That night, Lilly slept soundly in the guest bed in Emily's family home and awoke to the sound of the horses outside. Lilly stretched out on the deliciously soft and buttery sheets. The house was quiet. Lilly wrapped herself in a robe that was laid out over the footboard of the bed as if someone knew she might need it. She wandered out to the patio in her bare feet. Lilly held onto the wrought iron guardrail as she looked over the pastures and the lake. A cool morning mist hovered over the fields and the water. There was a knock at the door. Lilly quickly ran across the room, her bare feet lightly dancing over the thick carpet.

"Good morning Lilly," Mrs. Parker announced. She was in jeans and a floral button down. Her shoulder length brown hair was pulled into a low ponytail.

"Good morning," Lilly stepped out of the way as Mrs. Parker carried in a wicker serving tray.

"How did you sleep, dear?"

"Wonderfully," Lilly said, still in a sleepy euphoria.

"Good, I'm so glad," Mrs. Parker said as she carried the tray to the patio table and set it down softly. She then turned and joined Lilly next to the bed. "This was my bed when I was a little girl and I've never had a bad night in it."

Lilly smiled and nodded, "It's beautiful."

"I love it," Mrs. Parker ran her hand over the footboard. She then pulled Lilly in for a hug. "How's my favorite computer genius?"

"I'm great Mrs. Parker," Lilly smiled returning the embrace happily and letting herself relax into a mother's arms.

"Good." Mrs. Parker stepped back and held Lilly's hands in hers as she spoke, "Did you have a nice flight?"

"It was alright," Lilly answered basking in the motherly attention Mrs. Parker radiated.

"The ballet has already starting planning their fundraiser for next year. We may need your talents again," she said with a bright smile.

"I'd be happy to help Mrs. Parker. It was a lot of fun working with you," Lilly could feel the warmth shining from Mrs. Parker's smile. It was incredible to have that sort of love and attention just beamed upon her, Lilly did not want the moment to end.

"Good. I'm glad you had a good time, I did too," Mrs. Parker squeezed Lilly's hands in hers and let go.

"Your home is amazing Mrs. Parker. Thank you so much for having me."

"Oh, in a southern woman's home there is always room for improvement. It's our pleasure to have you, Lilly." Mrs. Parker's smile did not fade.

"Oh good, breakfast," Emily walked into the room and out to the patio as her mother smiled.

"Enjoy your breakfast girls," With that Mrs. Parker walked out with a wave.

Emily and Lilly ate breakfast together on the porch filling their mouths and their stomachs with fresh eggs, bacon, hot biscuits, and honey. Lilly watched the steam rise from her breakfast, she breathed deeply. "Do we need to get packing to get on the road?" She asked absentmindedly as she bit into a hot buttery biscuit.

Emily finished drinking her orange juice and gently placed the empty glass on the tabletop with a soft click. "I packed this morning when I got up and you just need to throw your bag in the car, right?"

"I think so," Lilly licked a biscuit crumb off of her lip and arched her eyebrows, "everyone's meeting over here?"

"No, we just meet up there. I said noon, so you have time to shower and get ready," Emily smiled. She took a breath, "Lil, I want to talk to you about last night."

"Ok," Lilly took a careful sip of her tea.

Emily folded her hands in her lap primly. "I'm glad you yelled at me."

"What?" Lilly laughed uncomfortably. "I didn't yell at you."

Emily gave an acknowledging nod, "I was wrong last night and it needed to be said."

Lilly nodded with a slight frown.

"When you came to Vanderbilt," Emily gently placed her hands on the edge of the table, "you had a chip on your shoulder. You were ready to fight Porter, me, anybody who got in your way, and you lost that this past semester." As if sensing Lilly's negative response she added, "And I love you just as you are. I just want to make sure you don't lose that edge completely, like last night. It was wonderful to see that fire in your eyes again."

Lilly thought for a moment. When she opened her mouth she spoke thoughtfully and slowly, "I'm not as combative, I'll agree to that. But I still have an edge, Emily."

"You say that, but I don't see it. I get that you're happy with your project and at school but I worry that you'll get complacent."

"I'm still challenging myself and growing if that's what you're saying," Lilly said defensively.

Emily took a deep breath, "It's hard to balance creativity and happiness. To be creative you almost need to live in chaos - Porter lives in a state of perpetual upheaval, so I've seen it, I get it. But with you it seems like you need the opposite. You seek out calm and routine and structure."

"I do," Lilly nodded in agreement.

"But you broke up with Charlie and, to be honest, I would think it flipped your world around, at least from my perspective, it did." Emily looked to Lilly for some clarity.

Lilly was honest, "I broke up with Charlie because we're not from the same place, economically." Emily went to speak but Lilly put up a hand silencing her. "I know you don't agree with me. I didn't want to worry about expensive jewelry or if we each paid our fair share. I've actually been talking a lot with Charlie this summer because I don't want that to be a sticking point in our relationship going forward. You're right, I need stability and serenity to work and to be happy."

Emily bit her tongue.

Lilly continued calmly, "And honestly, I still don't know if we can make it work but I know he's willing to try and I know I am too."

Emily's face was covering in shock, "You're back with Charlie?"

"I am," Lilly corrected herself, "We are," with a confident smile.

"That's wonderful!" Emily gushed.

Lilly went back to Emily's other point, "Emily, chaos may work for Porter, but I need something different. You have to understand that not being unpredictable, or insane, or an alcoholic is a wildly unlikely outcome for me. Normalcy, routine, and the things that I seek out to balance my life are really the most radical things I can do. I was raised by wolves and the fact that I'm here, where I am now, it is a total miracle. Even I'm not really sure how it happened."

"I only know what you've shared about your family, which isn't much, but if you've found peace ad serenity and it helps you then I'm glad."

"Thank you."

Emily replied with a worried tone, "You've just got this negotiation with your advisor and I looked into this company and I do not feel good about you doing business with them."

"Ok. I won't." Lilly answered with a wry smile.

"I'm serious," Emily said firmly.

"I know Em," Lilly reached across the table and held Emily's hand in hers. "And that's why I have you, to help me." Lilly squeezed Emily's hand and let go. "Because I don't know a damn thing about what I'm doing, I need advice and I need help."

Emily gave Lilly a smile, "I'll do my best, I promise. Just please don't sign anything."

"Oh, absolutely not. This meeting is an opportunity for me to practice my negotiation skills. This is not a sign forms or make final decisions meeting. It is preliminary and it was set up by PH's boss, so it's probably just a charity meeting anyway." Then changing gears, Lilly said, "Now, may I go get ready?"

"Yes," Emily laughed. "Let's go."

The ride to the lake house was quick. Lilly had imagined a quaint cottage on a lake with peaceful trees clustered around it. She should have known better than to expect something small of Emily's second home. The house was a sprawling structure with green shutters and a matching boathouse out back. There was a long dock out to the water with jet skis and a speedboat parked and waiting.

Lilly trailed behind Emily to the main living area. It was bright and airy with a wall of French doors leading to a patio with a pool and a view of the water. There were dark wood floors covered in a blue striped carpet. A fireplace and a pair of couches clustered around a large wooden coffee table. Beyond the fireplace Lilly could see into a bright kitchen and a dining area wrapped in windows looking out over the water. Blue and green vases perched on the shelves of built-ins flanking either side of the fireplace and a pelican statue posed jauntily by the hearth.

"You're staying in the crow's nest," Emily called from the kitchen as Lilly lingered over the view.

Lilly asked absentmindedly, "Where?"

"It's just at the top of the stairs off the entryway," Emily explained as she moved quickly through the house. "Here, I'll show you your room," Emily said, leading the way through the house.

The crow's nest was a quiet room at the top of the stairs with two full beds and its own bathroom. There was a lantern hanging over a bright blue ottoman in the middle of the space.

"Emily, it's adorable, but," Lilly began.

Emily cut her off, "Why don't you go get your bags from the car? I'm going to open some wine."

Lilly marched downstairs to the car, slightly irritated. She pulled her bag out of the backseat as Max pulled in quickly, his red mustang convertible kicking up dust as he skidded to a stop.

"Hey," Lilly said as she threw the bag over her shoulder.

"Hey Lil, how's it going?" He jumped out of the car and slammed the door.

"Good," she replied. "I didn't know you were coming."

"What? And miss your first water skiing lesson?" Max said as he leaned in and kissed her cheek. He then wrapped his arms around her in a hug. She was entangled in his arms when the next car pulled in and beeped hello.

"Hey, y'all," Porter called out from the passenger seat of Stephen's Land Rover.

Max stepped back, letting Lilly go as Porter, Stephen, and Charlie got out of the truck.

"Charlie! What are you doing here?" Lilly started eagerly moving towards him.

"Coming to see you," he said as he sauntered over to greet her with a quick kiss. His dark hair had just been cut and his blue eyes seemed to glow like sapphires under his dark eyebrows. His skin was fresh and soft with defined ridges on either side of his mouth.

"Max," Charlie greeted his friend with a firm handshake.

"Hi," Lilly said intimately staring up at Charlie with unabashed adoration. Charlie turned and kissed her again taking her bag out of her hand. He was holding her hand as he walked inside, she skipped beside him giddily. "Where to?" he asked as he ducked under the doorway.

"Up to the right," Lilly instructed, finally understanding why Emily had placed them in their own little haven.

Charlie made quick work of the stairs, taking them two at a time. Upstairs alone he asked suggestively, "Are we staying up here or going back down?"

"Emily just opened a bottle of wine, so we really should join the party," Lilly said guiltily.

"Ok, don't want to be late," Charlie put down her bag and surveyed the room.

It was then that Lilly ran to him and jumped into his arms wrapping her legs around his torso and her arms around his neck. She kissed him passionately, running her fingers through his hair and tugging it gently as she tenderly bit his bottom lip. He kissed her back with the same passion and held her up with his hands planted firmly on her bottom.

An hour later Lilly and Charlie rejoined the group in the airy kitchen where ceiling fans hummed overhead as the group talked and ate lunch.

Before Lilly could sit down, Celia seamlessly strolled toward her and grabbed her forearm, guiding her outside the door and onto the porch away from the group.

"Lilly Carter," Celia said with an accusatory tone, once the door closed behind them, "Did you and Charlie sleep together?" Celia raised her eyebrows suggestively.

Lilly bit her lips together but couldn't help from smiling. She had waited so long to tell someone other than Sophia.

"You slut," Celia slapped her arm lightly with the joke. She asked with excitement, "For the first time just now?"

"No," Lilly admitted.

Celia's mouth dropped. "You've been sleeping with Charlie and you didn't tell me?"

"I didn't tell anyone," Lilly said discreetly.

"When did it happen?"

Lilly was excited to finally spill. "After finals, before we went home for the summer, Charlie and I went out on a date." Lilly stopped to smile broadly.

"It was ok?" Celia asked with a motherly tone.

"Yeah, he was amazing." Lilly rocked from side to side, thinking about it again made her giddy.

"Good, and did you?" Celia gave Lilly another suggestive look.

"Celia, I saw fireworks," Lilly confided with wide eyes.

"Good Lord," Celia looked to where Charlie was standing in the kitchen with approval.

"Have you and Claire?" Lilly asked.

Celia looked at Lilly like she was crazy, "Oh God yes, I'm a Christian, not a saint."

Lilly laughed out loud.

"So, are you two back together?" Celia asked with a raised eyebrow.

"Yeah, we are," Lilly looked to where she could see Charlie through the window, laughing and talking with Stephen. "It's really great," she said slowly and happily.

"I can't believe you didn't tell me," Celia lightly shoved Lilly again.

"I'm sorry. I wanted to tell you in person," Lilly beamed.

"What about last night?" Celia demanded her hands on her hips.

"Well, everyone was there," Lilly shrugged, "and this worked out anyway." Lilly smiled at her friend.

"Oh, Lil, I'm so happy for y'all," Celia smiled and gave her a big hug.

"Thank you," Lilly grinned.

"We need to celebrate. Let's get you a drink," Celia instructed, shoving her cup into Lilly's hand.

Back in the kitchen Lilly clumsily spilled the drink down the front of her outfit. Celia quickly pulled out the club soda.

"Oh, forget it," Emily said with a wave of her hand and grabbed Lilly taking her back to her room to change. Emily loaned Lilly a beautiful pink floral print dress. As she waltzed down the hallway to the great room, Porter marched out and into the hallway. She quickly sized Lilly up.

"Are you just going to spend the next three years borrowing our clothes and pretending to be rich, Lilly?"

"What?" Lilly said, a lump lodged itself in her throat.

"That is Emily's dress?"

"Yes, she said I could borrow it," Lilly said defensively.

Porter continued, "Are you just going to pretend to be someone you're not?"

"I'm not pretending to be anyone," Lilly stated, with confidence.

"If you're not pretending, why are you still playing dress-up in all of our clothes?" Porter was ruthless.

"Porter!" Stephen yelled from the other room. "Get your gorgeous ass in here!"

"Stephen Calhoun, don't you speak to me that way. So help me God, I will end you," Porter commanded firmly as she marched to the living room leaving Lilly stunned and insulted.

Lilly walked into Claire and Celia's room and sat on the bed sullenly. Celia was sorting through a huge tackle box of jewelry.

"Hey, Lady, I'll be ready in a minute," Celia lied without looking up.

Lilly already knew the jewelry process was one of Celia's rituals and one that could take an hour if you let her. Lilly silently mulled over what Porter had said.

"Lil, what are you thinking?" Celia glanced up from her search and into Lilly's eyes through her reflection in the mirror.

"Nothing," Lilly lied unconvincingly. "I just talked to Porter."

"Oh God, what did she say?" Celia asked her eyes empathetic and concerned.

Still reeling from Porter's audacity, Lilly spoke in a shrill shocked voice, "She asked if I'm just going to pretend I'm rich."

Celia exhaled aloud and walked to Lilly's side. Rolling her eyes she said, "That girl could start an argument in an empty house." Pausing she added, "Let me tell you something, Porter Grace Cain is just a spoiled brat. She's just threatened by you."

"I don't think that's it, Celia. She doesn't seem threatened at all."

"Alright," Celia conceded. "Maybe she's not threatened. But she picks on you because she knows she can get away with it. You just need to stand up to her, Lil, and I promise she'll knock it off." Celia waited a beat while she pulled the hair away from Lilly's face, "Do you want me to talk to her?"

"No," Lilly said feeling soothed, "I'll take care of it."

"Good," Celia smiled and took Lilly's hand, dragging her back to the party.

Later that evening the group watched the sun set over the lake. The night was cool and sweet. Crickets chirped as the day dwindled in a golden explosion of light that bounced off of the water and the wine glasses. It was unbelievably beautiful and Lilly caught herself smiling as she looked out at the peaceful tranquility of the night. The boards of the dock creaked under foot as they toasted the end of the day.

Charlie went inside to grab a sweater for Lilly and Stephen came over to talk.

"Having fun?" He asked casually.

"I am, this is so beautiful," she answered wistfully.

"It is something," Stephen said finishing his drink. "You seemed upset earlier."

"Yeah," not wanting to complain to Stephen about Porter. She asked, "Why has Max been all over me the last two nights?"

"It's just Max," Stephen was unfazed. "You know he flirts."

"I know it's dumb but I wanted Charlie to say something."

Stephen twirled the ice in his tumbler casually, "Why?"

"I don't know," she shrugged, trying to downplay her comment. "I guess I want to feel protected or taken care of or something."

Stephen nodded slowly and looked down at her, "You know, Gloria Steinem would say, 'A pedestal is as much a prison as any small, confined space.'"

Lilly gave Stephen a surprised look. "Did you just quote Gloria Steinem to me? Who are you Stephen Calhoun?" Lilly laughed.

"I am many things, Lilly Carter, much like yourself." Stephen put his empty glass down on the weathered wooden railing and looked at her seriously, "But if you don't know already you need to understand Charlie's not going to get into a fight over something stupid."

"I don't want him to get in a fight, but a little support would be nice." She looked out over the water.

"It's not his style. Anyway, I didn't think the damsel in distress thing was your style." Stephen cocked an eyebrow in her direction.

"It's not. It would just be nice to know that Charlie had my back," she added defensively, feeling judged by Stephen.

Stephen squeezed her shoulder softly, "He has your back Lil, but he's not going to fight your battles for you."

"I don't want someone to fight my battles for me. But supporting me would be nice." Lilly was regretting ever bringing this up to Stephen.

"Not going to happen," he replied firmly.

"What's not going to happen?" Charlie asked as he came back and held up the sweater for Lilly to slip her arms into.

"You're not going to pick a fight in Lilly's honor," Stephen explained openly.

"Nope, not going to happen," Charlie confirmed as he pulled her hair out of the collar of the cardigan, his fingers briefly dancing over the skin on her neck giving her goose-bumps.

Pleased he reacted so calmly to her insecurities Lilly asked, "Why not?"

"Because it's stupid," Charlie answered frankly.

"What's stupid?" Max asked as he joined the group and wrapped his arm around Lilly's shoulders.

"Max, back off," Lilly snapped, pushing his arm off of her.

"Sorry, Lil," Max stepped back he was holding his hands up in front of himself as in surrender.

"See, you're fully capable," Charlie announced with pride.

"That's not the point," she stated with frustration.

Charlie smiled.

Lilly stopped talking, they weren't listening to her anyway.

Later that evening Lilly and Charlie quietly snuck away to the crow's nest. Once upstairs Lilly stood in front of Charlie, silently staring into his eyes in the dim light from a single bedside lamp. She smiled.

"There she is," he said as he bent down and kissed her nose.

"There who is?" She wrapped her arms around his waist.

Charlie squeezed her a little tighter, "My beautiful girl."

"I've been here all night," she answered defensively.

"You were, but you were salty after Stephen hung you out to dry," he smiled.

She laughed and put her hands on his shoulders, "He did hang me out to dry! I just wondered why you didn't get upset with Max," Lilly asked sensitively, remembering how angry she felt seeing Charlie and Porter together and not understanding why he didn't respond in the same way.

Charlie cradled her in his arms swaying back and forth rhythmically, "I don't say anything because it doesn't matter. You can handle him and any

217

situation you're put into Lilly Carter. You're magnificent."

23. CONFRONTATION

The following morning Porter and Lilly were in the kitchen silently going about their routines. It was already muggy and hot outside and the girls were comfortable in pajama shorts and tank tops. Lilly was sitting at the table eating a bowl of cereal as Porter stood at the counter cutting up strawberries. She had slipped on the dock the night before, her ankle was tightly wrapped in an ace bandage and she carried all her weight on the opposite side.

"Morning, y'all," Emily chirped brightly as she came in from her run, the screen door slammed behind her, startling them all.

"Morning," Porter and Lilly mumbled.

"Are the boys up yet?" Emily asked.

"Hiking," Lilly replied between bites.

"Fishing," Porter followed.

Emily took a strawberry from the bowl Porter had on the counter and took a loud bite, "What's the matter with you two?"

"I'm fine," Porter said as she took her bowl of berries and a glass of juice outside onto the porch, letting the screen door slam behind her as she limped to the table.

Lilly said, "Nothing," and looked out the windows over the lake.

"Liar," Emily asserted with a raised eyebrow. Emily sat down across the table, "Lilly Rose, I'm your roommate, I know you. What's wrong?"

Lilly pondered this point thoughtfully and then turned her attention away from the view out the window and looked into Emily's eyes, "To be honest, other than Porter being totally obnoxious this entire trip, I am still a little miffed that Charlie's never going to stand up for me."

Emily was confused. "What do you mean?"

"He's never going to fight for me," Lilly said with a shrug, putting her spoon down in her empty bowl.

Emily looked perplexed, "Who does he need to fight for you? Why do you want him to fight?"

"I don't want him to fight," Lilly was avoiding looking Emily in the eye. "I just want him to be on my side."

"Lil, Charlie's on your side," Emily defended.

"I guess," Lilly started with an unconvincing tone.

"Oh my Lord," Porter said as she hobbled back through the screen door. "You are so annoying!"

"What did I do?" Lilly asked with surprise.

Porter waved her hands as dramatically as possible while still balancing on one leg. "Do you even hear yourself? You are insufferable." Porter counted off on her fingers, "The guy buys you jewelry, flies across the country to surprise you, and all he gets is to put up with your whiney, self-obsessed..."

"Porter!" Emily interrupted her.

"No, Emily. She's obnoxious and selfish," Porter continued. "And she's mad at him for nothing." Pausing for effect, "She's just using him."

"I am not using Charlie," Lilly said shrilly as she stood up to defend herself.

"Aren't you?" Porter asked condescendingly.

Lilly spoke clearly, "Porter, believe it or not, I'm not with Charlie because of his money. If anything, I am with him in spite of his money. Charlie is very good to me, I know that. I appreciate that. I just want him to stand up for me sometimes." Lilly's face was red and her hands were clenched around the top of her chair.

"When you got to Vanderbilt you didn't even want us around. Why is it Charlie's job to hold your hand now?"

"Maybe I wouldn't feel like I needed to defend myself if you wouldn't attack me all the time," Lilly's voice rose an octave. *Stephen must have told Porter about her comments last night.* Lilly exhaled slowly, trying to calm herself down.

"I don't attack you." Porter crossed her arms in front of herself.

Lilly pointed at Porter, "Right now, you are attacking me right now Porter. I wasn't even talking to you, I was talking with Emily, and you just marched in yelling. I know I don't have money, Porter."

"Lil," Emily said with concern.

Lilly cleared her throat and composed herself, resting her hands on the seat-back gently. She said, "What I don't understand is why it is so important to you to put me in my place and constantly point out that I don't belong."

There was an extended silence.

Porter skip-hopped to the island and leaned on it heavily, "I am not against you, I'm for Charlie."

Lilly was ready to blow up again when Emily interjected with a hand up toward both girls, "I'm going to step in right here because this is going to get ugly. Porter, you're mad because you don't really trust Lilly's intentions with Charlie. Is that fair?"

"Yes, that's fair," Porter agreed, gently folding her hands on the marble countertop.

"And Lil, you feel like you need Charlie to defend you because you feel like an outsider and somewhat threatened by Porter and the rest of us?" Emily suggested.

"Yes," Lilly said crossing her arms over herself and shifting her weight.

Emily looked back and forth between her two friends. "It sounds to me like y'all need to spend some time getting to know one another."

Both Lilly and Porter refused to look at one another.

Emily rolled her eyes, "Y'all need to look at each other, and you both need to grow up."

After a hesitant pause Porter said, "I could do that." Her sudden change in tone caught Lilly off guard.

"Yeah, me too," Lilly found herself agreeing.

Emily took a deep breath, "Good." She paused a moment and then began instructing them, "To begin, Porter could you share what's bothering you?"

"Well, she broke up with Charlie for no reason last year and now all of a sudden they're back together?" Porter raised a skeptical eyebrow.

"We made up!" Lilly yelled, "And we've been together for two months, it's not all of a sudden!"

Porter scoffed.

Emily stepped between them, equidistant from both, "Alright y'all, enough. Porter if they want to be together that's their business. I know you and Stephen are worried about Charlie but he's a big boy and he made his decision. Y'all can't change it." Emily took a breath.

Porter changed her tone, "She just seems to have made herself comfortable as a part of our group."

"Why is that such a problem?" Lilly asked defensively.

Porter glared at Emily who glared right back. Finally, Porter said, "I guess I was just jealous of all of the attention you were getting."

"Me?" Lilly asked in disbelief, her crossed arms dropped to her sides.

Emily continued gently, "What about you, Lil?"

Lilly chose her words carefully. "I guess I've been defensive because I was intimidated by you," she confessed, offering up her own olive branch.

"I'm not intimidating," Porter said firmly.

"Seriously, you terrify me," Lilly said with a laugh.

"Why?" Porter asked cracking a smile and rolling her eyes in amusement.

"Because you know what you want. You have life all figured out and I'm working really hard to get there but I always seem to be behind."

"You'll get there," Porter added encouragingly.

"Yeah, eventually," Lilly said with resignation.

"You'll get there, Lil," Porter spoke firmly making Lilly think that she believed in her more than she believed in herself.

Lilly smiled.

"I'm sorry for being so hard on you," Porter said sincerely.

"I'm sorry for being defensive." Lilly looked up at Porter from across the room.

Porter nodded.

"I'd like it if we could be friends," Lilly said slowly.

Porter nodded, "I'd like that, too."

The girls smiled at each other.

"Y'all can hug now," Emily suggested, pushing Lilly forward.

The girls met in the middle of the room where they hugged each other awkwardly.

The rest of the week was a steady stream of activity culminating with Lilly's meeting with PH and the investor. Lilly had prepared for the meeting but was still nervous.

Located in a repurposed shipping container, the restaurant, 404 looked like an upscale Chipotle. Lilly wore a summer dress and carried her laptop in a bag, slung over her shoulder. Shifting her weight from foot to foot, Lilly nervously scanned the room for PH.

PH stood and walked over to meet Lilly and Emily. She smiled as she took Lilly's arm in hers and quickly whispered, "My boss knows this guy and they're old friends. I'm pretty sure you're going to hate him but we need to be polite."

"Got it," Lilly smiled as they exchanged greetings and she introduced Emily.

PH guided them back to the table where she introduced Mark Sands. He was tall with a head of messy grey hair that was thinning on top. He shook Lilly's hand with a two pump jerk and promptly forgot her name. He spent the remainder of the meeting calling her, 'Darlin'." He didn't even acknowledge Emily, who pursed her lips and folded her hands, completely unimpressed.

Throughout the meal Mark talked about his company and his thoughts. Lilly listened for PH's benefit but said nothing, not that Mark offered her the opportunity. Emily followed Lilly's lead and silently observed clearly taking mental notes to never offer to attend a meeting like this again. As Mark rambled on she blatantly pulled out her phone, a rude and totally out of character move for Emily, but Lilly appreciated the silent commentary. When she heard her phone buzz she smiled. Emily was texting her at the table. Lilly fought the urge to read her phone but smiled at Emily to say, 'thanks for staying, I know he's a tool.' When the meal was done and Mark finally had to leave for another appointment he stood, shook Lilly's hand again, and said, "Thank you for your time Miss. Carter. It was very nice getting to know you. I'll be in touch with you shortly to plan our next steps together."

Lilly had all meal to carefully plan her next words. Initially, she had been crushed and totally demoralized by his lack of interest in her project. She had expected Mark Sands to at least want to hear about her work and felt totally deflated when she found he was more interested in hearing himself speak. However, as the meal dragged on, rather than feeling deflated or sorry for herself, she became insulted and angry. She was not going to allow him walk all over her. When she spoke it was calm and deliberate. "Mr. Sands, I appreciate your time as well. I don't think that will be necessary."

"Excuse me?" His face flushed with indignation.

Lilly wasn't sure where her voice was coming from but she spoke directly and looked him in the eye. "Mr. Sands, since we sat down, I have literally said nothing. You have not asked me about my project, my plans, you didn't even ask me my thoughts on the weather. I have no desire to work with you now or ever." She flushed with relief at having spoken her mind honestly, she felt vindicated.

Mark Sands threw his napkin down on the table. "You should learn to respect your elders."

"I listened to you for an hour. I'm done." Lilly stood up, pulled her unopened bag back onto her shoulder, threw two twenties on the table and walked out of the restaurant with Emily following behind, her mouth agape.

In the car Lilly collapsed onto the hot leather and waited for Emily to get the air conditioning blowing.

Lilly spoke first, "What a dick!"

Emily followed, "Right?"

"PH is going to kill me," Lilly said under her breath.

"She's coming now," Emily announced nervously as she rolled down Lilly's window.

PH marched out to the car authoritatively her summer dress billowing in the wind detracted nothing from her imposing steps. "I'm not going to smile so it looks like I'm yelling at you," PH said firmly through the window. "Don't smile."

Lilly and Emily fought the urge, their eyes large as they listened to PH.

PH placed a hand on the window ledge, "He's a jackass and he's throwing a tantrum. I told him I'd come talk to you. I will tell him I could not sway your opinion." She gave Lilly a meaningful look.

Lilly smiled quickly but forced her cheeks to return to neutral. "Thank you," Lilly shook her head seriously. "I can't work with someone like that. I don't care how much money he or his company has, I won't do it."

PH nodded, "I totally understand and actually, that is a wonderful thing to know and recognize. Pay attention here Lilly this should guide your path, it is very important to fully understand what you are and are not willing to do for money." She took a breath, "Ok. I have to go back in there. Thank you both for listening as long as you did, I can tell my boss we put forth a reasonable effort."

Lilly felt comfortable adding, "I don't know why your boss is friends with him."

"I don't know either. We all make mistakes." PH shrugged, "We'll keep our calls next week, Lilly."

Lilly nodded her agreement, "Yes."

"It was nice meeting you, Emily." PH added.

"Nice meeting you, too," Emily smiled.

PH turned on her heel and walked inside. Lilly and Emily said nothing as they pulled away from the restaurant. Once they were safely down the road Emily said, "Your advisor is awesome!"

"I know," Lilly agreed. "She's pretty bad-ass."

On the way home from the airport in Cleveland, Lilly stole a glance at her mother in the passenger seat. Melanie was pickled in cheap boxed wine and exceptionally hungover from the night before. Her frizzy hair was pulled back into a stiff, matronly bun. Her clothes were ill-fitting and frumpy— "great finds," Melanie would call them—from the local re-sale shop. The shirt was short-sleeved denim with flowers embroidered over the left breast and an inscription that read, 'Friends are like flowers, pick yourself a bouquet!' She wore it over pleated green shorts that pinched at the waist like a rubber band around an orange. Her jowls sagged and sweat glistened above her pencil thin eyebrows. Lilly wondered how she had ever emerged from this person. She looked at Sophia, expertly maneuvering through traffic in her Ohio State t-shirt and cut off denim shorts, at least there was one person Lilly could relate to at home. She had been on the ground for less than an hour and already felt prepared to return to Nashville and never look back.

Melanie fanned herself dramatically. The sweat on her back seeping through her blouse left dark spots on the back of her shirt like map points in a navigation app. Her legs made a sticky smacking sound when she lifted them off of the faux leather cushion. Melanie sighed dramatically, blowing air out of her mouth over her face. The girls ignored her. So Melanie made even louder sighs to garner their attention and sympathy. Her daughters said nothing for several minutes, exchanging knowing glances and eye rolls in the rearview mirror.

"Mom," Sophia finally said in measured tones, "Are you hot?"

"I'm fine," Melanie answered lifting her arms and fanning her face even though there was a robust breeze charging through the car.

Lilly stared out the window but listened intently to the exchange in the front seat.

Sophia spoke logically, "If you're hot, all you have to say is, 'I'm hot. Could you please turn on the air conditioning?'"

"No, you're the driver and the driver makes the rules," Melanie answered.

Sophia rolled her eyes, her patience fading, "That's stupid, Mom. If you're hot just ask to have the air conditioning turned on."

"Nope. Driver makes the rules," Melanie insisted as she pushed out her bottom lip and blew air onto her own face.

Sophia pressed, "So if a driver tells you to get out of the car, what happens?"

"Then I would have to get out of the car."

"That's just stupid. What if the driver said you couldn't take your shoes?"

"Then I'd have to walk barefoot."

Sophia took her eyes off of the road to give her mother a condescending scowl, "Seriously?"

"Yes."

"Fine." Sophia pulled off of the highway sharply, the wheels kicking up gravel and dust as the car swung wide around a curve.

"Soph," Lilly said from the backseat.

"Nope. I want to test this theory," Sophia said firmly to her sister.

Lilly rolled her eyes and looked back out the window.

"So if the driver tells you to get out of the car, you'd just get out of the car?" Sophia asked animatedly, like a happy cat toying with its dinner before devouring it.

Melanie nodded obediently with her hands folded primly on her green lap.

"Sophia," Lilly said again, exasperated with her sister.

"No, it's a stupid game. All she has to do is ask for air conditioning. She's an adult," Sophia said angrily as she pulled onto a side road. Coming to a stop, Sophia commanded her mother, "Ok, get out."

"Mom, just ask to have the air turned on," Lilly said with annoyance.

"Driver's rules," Melanie answered obediently.

Lilly's voice rose with anger at the stupidity of this conversation. She barked, "Mom, that isn't a thing. If you want air on ask for it, don't fan yourself and try to manipulate Sophia into doing what you want. You can ask. You have a voice."

Melanie got out of the car.

"No shoes, driver's rules," Sophia said before Melanie could close the door behind herself.

Melanie removed her shoes, wincing at the rocky road under her now bare feet. She went to grab her purse.

"Nope. No purse, driver's rules," Sophia said hammering her point even further.

Melanie left the purse and closed the door.

"Mom, get back in the car," Lilly said out the window. Then, cocking her head to the left, "Sophia, stop it, just turn on the air conditioning."

"No," Sophia answered with irritation. "She can ask for air conditioning. She doesn't have to do any of this. She's just being an asshole so we cater to her and let her manipulate us into doing whatever she wants." Sophia pulled away leaving their mother on the side of the road.

"Sophia, go back," Lilly said furiously, looking frantically ahead and then back to their mother, abandoned in the dusty July heat.

Sophia stared straight through the windshield as she answered angrily, "She's doing all of this to herself. She just made up 'driver's rules' and refused to simply ask for what she wanted. She should sit on the side of the road."

Lilly flung her head back onto the seat cushion and stared up at the sagging ceiling of the car. She was so frustrated, she just wanted to leave all of this and both of them behind. She tried speaking logically, "Could you please stop wasting time and pick her up? The longer you do this the longer we have to be in the car with her!"

"She's being stupid," Sophia said sulkily.

Lilly looked back at her mother getting smaller in the distance. "You could have just turned on the air conditioning. Why did you need to do this? What point have you proven?"

"She needs to act like an adult."

Lilly grabbed the back of the headrest of the passenger seat and pulled herself forward so she was leaning over the console in the front seat. "Do you really think this exercise is going to get her to act like an adult? Do you think this will help? Do you honestly think she's going to get back in the car and say, 'gee, I was being an idiot, could you please turn on the air conditioning Sophia?' She's not right mentally. There is something broken in her. She's not all there. Who gets out of a car in the middle of nowhere instead of asking to have the air conditioning turned on? There's something wrong with her mentally. You can't treat her like a normal person because she's not normal, Sophia."

Sophia glanced at her older sister. "No. I'm not going to be manipulated into doing what she wants."

"Fine," Lilly snapped. "Do what I want, go back and pick her up."

Sophia begrudgingly turned the car around on a dusty berm. The girls drove silently and pulled up next to their mother who was standing on the side of the road where they had left her, crying.

"Mom, get in the car," Lilly said through the window, a tired sound in her voice.

Melanie shook her head, refusing to look up, her bun pointing to the sky.

"Oh my God! Driver's rules, get in the God damn car!" Sophia ordered with a yell.

Melanie scurried in and cried silently as she cowered next to Sophia.

"Driver's rules, buckle up," Sophia spat.

Melanie buckled up obediently.

"Soph, please turn on the air conditioning," Lilly requested as though demonstrating appropriate behavior to a child.

Sophia rolled up the windows and complied. They drove the rest of the way home in silence.

Later that evening Melanie appeared in Lilly's room, looking haggard and broken. "Hey mom."

"So you see what I have to deal with," Melanie started.

Lilly inhaled deeply steeling herself for whatever spin her mother would put on the day's events.

"She's cruel, your sister," Melanie bit her bottom lip as though trying to fight off tears. "She left me for dead on the side of the road today and I think we both know she wouldn't have come back if you weren't there too."

Lilly looked her mother in the eye, "Can you blame her?" she asked sincerely.

Melanie straightened with the direct question, "I guess you agree with her."

"I don't agree with leaving people on the side of the road but you were behaving like a child," Lilly replied frankly.

"If she were considerate she would have turned the air conditioning on."

"You didn't ask her to turn on the air, you mimed it. It is not her job or anyone's job to read your interpretive dances. You can ask to have the air turned on," Lilly said, unable to keep the condesending tone out of her voice.

"Well, I guess I'll have to remember that the next time one of you needs

230

something," Melanie snipped back.

"Like what?" Lilly couldn't resist asking the loaded question.

"Like the next time you need a place to stay in the summer maybe I should make you ask."

"I do ask," Lilly said firmly. "I also pay rent."

"Well, maybe next time you need a place to stay we won't have any room," Melanie said sweetly.

Lilly nodded. It was her mother's high hand, the only thing she still had that she could hold over Lilly's head. Lilly considered her response for a moment. This was the turning point, she could allow her mother to continue to use her power to keep her in her place and silently be cowed as she had in the past or she could stand up to her mother and jeopardize her future living arrangements. Sophia shouldn't have left their mother on the side of the road but asking to be spoken to rather than manipulated was not an unreasonable request. Her mother could be bluffing but in the event that she was not Lilly should take her threat seriously. Was she ready to cut this bond? Finally she answered, "Well, I hope it doesn't come to that but if that is the case then I will simply have to find alternate arrangements. As you have already cashed my check for August, I'm going to stay here until I return to school this fall. But going forward I will seek lodging elsewhere in the summer. Thank you for letting me stay here as long as you have already."

Melanie was stunned. She gaped at her eldest daughter, "See that you do," she spat as she marched out of the room her head held high.

Lilly breathed deeply, her heart was still racing.

24. SOPHOMORE YEAR

In a blink the summer was over and Lilly was back on a plane headed for Nashville. This time she was returning to school and her friends but more than that, she was leaving her mother's home forever. As her flight descended into the Nashville Airport she felt like a different person. Lilly had learned more about herself and who she wanted to be that summer. She was standing on her own. She was no longer beholden to her mother. She knew she could never return home after this, it was terrifying but incredibly liberating.

She couldn't help but think about how much life had changed over the last year. When she started college, she never could have imagined she'd shoot down her first investor. Lilly was proud of how she handled Mark Sands. Before their meeting she would have been happy that someone, anyone, was interested in her work. She knew now to be more discriminating in her selection process. Lilly smiled to herself in the dim cabin lights. In a few days she'd be starting her second year of college. She closed her eyes and rested her head on the seat-back. Life was good, she exhaled.

Sophomore move-in was much smoother and less stressful than Lilly's first year. She knew where she was going and she had only packed clothes and necessities in a single suitcase on wheels. That and her backpack were it for the year—Lilly didn't count her massive purse. She was living in a new dorm on campus with Emily. She pressed the elevator button for the twelfth floor, rolling up she hoped she had brought enough supplies. Emily's email and several subsequent calls had all been clear, bring only items that touch your body daily. Initially, Lilly had been suspicious and even though she did stash some extra snacks in her luggage she trusted Emily and was sure their dorm room would be fine.

The stainless steel elevator doors clanked open to reveal a clean grey wall with grey metal doors in both directions, it looked like a hotel hallway with large metal numbers on each door. The hallways dead-ended on either side into floor to ceiling windows with views of the lush green campus. Lilly checked her phone again and re-read the address as she stepped off the elevator. She walked toward the sunlight and found room 1212 at the end of the hallway, the door nearest the window. The ground looked far away from so high up.

Lilly turned the handle and the heavy grey door with its smooth silver numbers swung open easily. It revealed a hallway that led to a wall of windows at the back of the apartment. The floors were tiled and the wheels of Lilly's suitcase clicked over the grout lines as she dragged it behind her. Lilly quickly passed two doorways on her left darkened bedrooms with small beds and large windows. Two doorways on her right revealed a coat closet and a spacious bathroom with double sinks. As she entered the common area she found an open galley kitchen, a large dining room table, as well as a gas fireplace in the living room. What drew Lilly's attention was the view, that dwarfed the space, of the campus and the city of Nashville beyond. Lilly dropped her bags by the couch and stared out.

"Pretty amazing, isn't it?" Emily's voice came from behind her.

"Hey," Lilly's eyes were still wide with disbelief as she turned to greet Emily. The girls hugged, "This is amazing Emily, how did you?"

Emily waved off Lilly's question before she could finish. "They just picked us early in the lottery and I thought you'd like this room the best, too."

"But we got to pick the building. How did we get the penthouse apartment?"

"Just the luck of the draw," Emily said with a smile.

Lilly knew it had to be more than luck but she diplomatically dropped the issue as she explored the rest of the apartment. Emily did not disappoint; dishes in the cupboard, soap by the sink, and sheets on the beds. Lilly was amazed.

"I hope you don't mind," Emily started, "I already picked my room."

"That's fine," Lilly said with a laugh, still amazed by her good fortune.

"You're closer to the hallway and the door but we're the last door on the top floor, I don't think we'll get many uninvited guests."

"This is great," Lilly exhaled. Both bedrooms had huge windowed walls and closets with full length mirrors on the doors. Emily's room was the same Lilly Pulitzer- Hawaiian punch explosion of colors and monograms from last year. There were desks in each room and bedside tables with lamps. Lilly smiled to herself, *this was going to be a good year.*

Classes started on a muggy August day. Lilly was excited for her first face-to-face meeting of the year with Professor Hendricks. After the failed meeting with Mark Sands over the summer Lilly felt closer to PH and her project work showed the productivity of her enthusiasm. PH's campus office still smelled warmly like vanilla and cocoa butter lotion. Lilly had forgotten how PH left the air around her smelling sweet, she took a deep breath. PH looked refreshingly the same. Her hair hung past her shoulders in thick black coils. She wore a peach summer sweater with her sleeves pushed up above her elbows over oatmeal dress pants and snakeskin ballet flats. She wore thick gold hoops in her ears and no make-up.

"Welcome back, Lilly," PH said, relaxing into her chair and crossing her legs.

Lilly started the conversation quickly, "I know where I want to go."

PH took a moment to figure out what Lilly was talking about, casually taking a sip of hot coffee from a blue Vanderbilt mug, "Your motivation?"

"Right," Lilly plowed ahead. "I think I've got it."

PH smiled knowingly at Lilly's excitement and put down her cup to listen in earnest. "Good, tell me."

Lilly spoke clearly and calmly, placing her hands in her lap. "My motivation is for a better life. I don't want to go back to where I came from, ever."

PH nodded steepling her fingers under her chin. She curiously asked, "Do you think that's enough?"

Lilly spoke with passion, "Yes, because I want it so much. I'm prepared to do everything it takes. I want a better life and this is how I'm going to get it. I have worked too long and too hard to go back to where I started."

"That is some strong motivation," PH agreed with a serious nod.

Lilly sat taller in her seat feeling proud of herself.

"But it's not a destination," PH said calmly, folding her hands in her lap.

"Excuse me?" Lilly's bliss came to an abrupt halt.

PH continued, "You're still talking about where you've come from not where you're going."

Lilly thought for a moment. "But isn't 'not there' a destination? I don't know where life will take me," she justified.

PH nodded patiently and explained, "Having a real palpable goal is important. What sets successful leaders apart is that they come from a place of strength, not a place of fear."

Lilly nodded, slightly distraught.

"Let's try thinking about the question in another way. What is success to you? What does success look like? What does it smell, taste, feel like? How will you know when you've obtained success?"

Lilly leaned forward, "Ok."

PH used large sweeping motions with her hands, "When you say, 'not there,' do you mean not your mother's house? Or Cleveland? Or Ohio? Or the United States? Are you a success if your company is a small tech start up that gives back to the community? Or does it not matter how big you are as long as you're making lots of money?" PH brought her gestures down to scale and spoke calmly, "My job is to help you get where you want to go and for me to do that I need to know where you're headed because the advice I give you for one path may be the complete opposite for another."

"I see what you mean."

"Don't beat yourself up about not getting it right away. It's hard to come from a challenging background. To have someone ask you questions that flip your perspective can be really jarring. Many people don't get to a place where they can think beyond the here and now until much later in life. But you have a brilliant mind and it's a gift. You owe it to yourself to think about five, ten years down the road and who you want to be. What you want to be doing. All of those big picture things."

"Ok."

"It's hard because it's worth it. I promise you that." PH said, picking up her cup again and taking a sip.

Lilly smiled. "I get it, it makes sense. I don't know exactly where I want to be right now but I'll get there." Lilly said confidently.

"I know you will," PH leaned forward, "which is why I think you're ready for the next step."

Lilly arched her eyebrow a curious smile creeping across her face.

PH spoke with a gleam in her eye. "After our disaster of a meeting with Mark Sands this summer I got to thinking about your project and where you could go next."

Lilly listened with eager anticipation.

PH spoke with her hands, "I have an idea that I think will sound more intimidating than it really is but I want to assure you that I know you're ready for this."

Lilly's eyes were wide and her heart was racing. *What did PH want her to do now?*

"It's time to pitch you project to a group of angel investors," PH paused and let Lilly process her statement.

"I just don't think it's ready," Lilly said quickly with a shake of her head.

"Lilly, you've done all the work. The interface is beautiful and it works!"

"There are still things I need to fix. How do we even know if they're going to like it?"

"You don't know if they're going to like it. That doesn't mean you don't try, it means you pitch. If they don't want it, they'll tell you what it needs to be better. If they do want it, you get funding to do what you love," Professor Hendricks explained.

Lilly shook her head and leaned back, "But I'm not a sales person. I don't know what to say…"

PH used a soothing tone, "You don't have to be a sales person or change who you are to sell this program. You just need to try. If it fails," PH shrugged, "so what? You're a college kid with an idea, you can make it better and come back next time more prepared."

Lilly still looked unconvinced.

Professor Hendricks continued gesturing smoothly with her hands, "Lilly, you are in a great position. You have an idea. If it works and the investors like it you have some real momentum. If it doesn't work and they hate it you got free feedback on your project. It's a win-win but you can't do all this work and never show it to anyone."

"I guess." Shifting her gaze up to PH's face, Lilly revealed her insecurity, "But what if it fails?"

PH leaned forward and spoke in her most reassuring voice, "Lilly, I know you're scared and this is a big decision but putting yourself out there is not as scary as it seems. You know I would never push you into a situation that makes you uncomfortable. I will push you out of your comfort zone."

Lilly nodded.

"This is just a tryout, nothing is set in stone."

"Ok," Lilly said with a deep breath. "When is the angel investor event?"

"It's in a month," PH answered tilting her head to the side, intrigued by Lilly's possible change of opinion.

"Let's book it," Lilly answered firmly feeling a fluttery lightness in her chest.

"You're sure?" PH tried to read Lilly's expression.

"Yes," Lilly nodded firmly. "I'm not ready, but I'm never going to be ready."

PH looked at her quizzically.

"If you believe in me and this project enough to suggest an investor then I think it's time I do too."

PH nodded slowly, convinced Lilly was on board, "I'll reserve a booth," she said with a smile.

"Thank you," Lilly said looking her advisor in the eye, "for believing in me and this project."

PH smiled warmly, "It is my pleasure, Lilly. I'll send you the registration information and after you read it over we'll discuss what to bring and how you want to present."

"Great," Lilly beamed. She left PH's office in a jubilant and contemplative mood. *Where did she want to end up?* She had never really thought of the future as being on her terms before. It was exhilarating to feel like she was moving forward with her project and with her life.

She wanted to ask Drew to graphically design some promotional pieces for the angel investor event. She decided to call him right away while the adrenaline from her decision was still strong.

Drew picked up on the second ring, "Hey, Carter, what's up?"

"Hey." Lilly hadn't expected him to answer, "How's it going?"

"Good," he answered. "How are you?"

"I'm alright," she hesitated before diving in. "I need your help."

"Sure, what's up?"

"I'm going to this investor event and need signs. Is there any way you could design a poster and some handouts for me?"

Drew was unfazed, "Sure. I can print them at work. They never lock up the giant printer. When do you want them?"

"In a month, is that enough time?" Lilly asked.

Drew's voice had its usual carefree sway, "Sure, that's more than enough time."

Lilly backtracked, "Are you sure? You don't have to, if you're going to be busy."

"No big deal, Carter. I'll take care of it. You want me to drop them in

Professor Hendricks' office? She's still your mentor, right?"

"Yeah, that would be awesome. Thank you Drew." Lilly was startled by his memory.

"You're welcome. You'll email me the specs?"

"Yes. Of course," Lilly stammered. "I'll send you what I want and you can make it pretty."

"Sweet, done, I'll call you if I have any questions."

"Ok, thanks."

"No worries, later." He hung up.

She stared at the phone in her hands for a few seconds in wonderment. Talking to Drew was so easy, as if he implicitly understood her.

25. BUILDING

Lilly spent the following two weeks thinking about her conversation with PH and frantically revising her project. She had yet to come up with her motivation. She had lots of ideas, but no one thing stood out to her as the path that was meant for her.

Campus was hot and everything seemed to drag. The muggy heat seeming to bore into the air-conditioned rooms of the dorm. Lilly decided to visit Celia in her new apartment. Celia and Porter were living off-campus, the building was just a short walk away on a quiet tree lined street.

"It's beautiful," Lilly said as she wandered around the spacious rooms, her steps echoing off of the hardwoods into the vast space.

Celia beamed, "I love it. It was a gift from my mama."

Lilly choked, "The whole apartment?"

"Yes. She's so good to me," Celia said with a smile.

"Wow," was all Lilly could say as she breathlessly walked from room to room.

"I still have to decorate. Mama sent those from the shop," Celia pointed to two industrial looking lamps waiting for a table on the window seat.

"They're gorgeous." Lilly tried to conceal her jealousy. She hated the feeling of envy that was welling up in her chest.

Celia gestured to the empty living area, "The furniture is all coming, my mom and I picked out some really amazing pieces. It's all Celia with tiny touches from Lulu and Jack," she smiled.

"That's incredible," Lilly said supportively. "I can't wait to see what furniture you've picked out."

"It's going to be stunning," Celia shared.

"So, do you think you'll take over Lulu and Jack when your parents retire?" Lilly asked as she opened the door to a built-in wooden cabinet with leaded glass doors.

"I don't think so," Celia said, hopping up onto the marble island to sit and talk. "I'm going to law school after we graduate."

"Still law school? But you're so creative," Lilly nudged.

Celia kicked her legs from her marble perch. "I am creative, but I'm not good at designing for other people. I'm too organized. In design you're constantly adding and changing. I would pick out a piece once and be done and that's no way to run a business," she explained. "I can still have fun at home with design but it's not my life. You know?"

"It's just too bad that you won't get to play and design as much. I didn't think you were so keen to go into law."

Celia leaned back, "You didn't?"

"I just mean," Lilly looked around the lavish apartment, "if I had unlimited resources, I would probably want to do something creative and fun, not just something to make money. You know?" She shrugged.

"Lil, my parents worked so that I would have the freedom to make this choice," Celia explained. Lilly could hear the hurt in her voice.

She paused for a moment realizing how offensive her comment sounded. Her mind was racing but her mouth was frozen. Finally she sputtered, "I'm sorry, Celia. I shouldn't have said that," stumbling over her words, "I just meant that you have a gift."

"Lil, everything we have my parents made. They built it out of nothing." Celia added reproachfully, "We're not old money like Emily and Porter."

"Is that why you and Porter were arguing last semester?" Lilly asked, making the connection.

Celia rolled her eyes and smirked. "Porter thinks her parents worked hard for all they have and she has no idea what my parents have done. It drives me nuts some times. Bless her heart, she just has no concept for what my family has been through to make Lulu and Jack possible," Celia confided.

Lilly looked up from her hands to Celia's face sheepishly, "I guess I just didn't realize that your family had accomplished so much in such a short time."

"We work hard and I'm going to school so that my parents won't have to work forever," Celia said seriously.

"That's really admirable Celia."

"It's just what you do for people who have always taken care of you. It's really selfish if you think about it. I'm only hoping that I can return some of what they've given me. Don't you want to do that for your mama?"

Lilly snorted, "Not really. My mom's not like that. I mean she paid bills and made sure we didn't starve. She drinks," Lilly finally admitted out loud.

"Lilly, I didn't know." Celia face showed shock and concern.

Lilly shook her head, "It's not a big deal." She smiled to comfort her friend who was obviously distressed by this revelation, "We just don't have the same relationship."

"What happened to your daddy?" Celia caught herself, "If you don't mind me asking."

Lilly played with her ring and spoke in a higher pitch, masking her emotions, even from herself, "He liked drinking too. We haven't seen him since Sophia was a baby."

"Wow," Celia said quietly, "I'm so sorry Lilly."

"Don't be," Lilly smiled bravely, "I'm fine. I got here on my own and I'll get to wherever I'm going on my own."

"You are a success story. Just like Lulu and Jack," Celia said supportively, hopping down off of the counter to hug Lilly.

"Thanks." Not wanting to talk anymore, Lilly made up a weak excuse about studying and quickly left. She was anxious to get outside and breathe. The air was still thick with humidity but Lilly was relieved to be by herself. It wasn't fair to judge Celia because she had money and Lilly felt guilty about how she had approached that conversation. She wondered if Celia would judge her too, about her drunk mother.

Walking back to the dorm and lost in thought, Lilly was next to Drew before she even noticed him walking toward her.

"Hey, Carter, what are you doing in my neighborhood?" He looked pleased to see her.

"Hey, you live here?" She looked around the landscaped yards in surprise.

"I rent," he said with a smile, adding, "Obviously. Are you living off campus this year?"

"No," Lilly pointed behind herself with her thumb, "I was just visiting a friend. She just bought a place a few blocks back."

"Of course she did," Drew said condescendingly.

"What?"

Drew rolled his eyes, "Nothing. So you'll be here for high tea and charity events?" he teased.

"Maybe," Lilly replied dryly.

Drew asked casually, "Still with the boyfriend?"

"Yes," Lilly said suspiciously.

Drew watched her squirm, "Lacrosse team, right?"

"Yes."

"I saw him playing the other day."

"Yeah, that was him," Lilly shared, waiting for one of Drew's uncharitable comments.

Drew delivered his punch-line, "He looks like an asshole."

Lilly laughed, "That's part of the attraction."

"If he's so great, why are you flirting with me?" Drew asked with confidence.

"I wasn't flirting with you," Lilly said with indignation.

He pursed his lips. "You want me to ask you out."

"I didn't say that." Lilly shook her head slowly.

"Just because you didn't say it, doesn't mean you don't want it." Drew looked at her suggestively.

Lilly snapped her lips closed. She couldn't think of a response. She was starting to sweat and not just because of the end of summer heat.

Basking in the tension, Drew asked, "Where are you going?"

"It's two in the afternoon. We live in Nashville, I'm on my way to a honky tonk to get drunk," she joked trying too hard to play cool when she was really flustered.

Drew laughed, "That sounds like an excellent idea. Let's do it."

Lilly laughed again nervously.

"Do you want to drop your back pack off at my place before we go?" Apparently he thought this was an earnest idea.

"Oh, you're serious?" She waffled, shifting foot to foot.

He looked at her like she was nuts, "You're not?"

"I was just kidding," Lilly backtracked. "I have a lot of work to do... homework. And weren't you going to design some signs for me?"

"There's always work to do Lilly. You can always re-take a class; you can never re-live a party. Let's go to a honky tonk." Drew wrapped an arm around her shoulders and guided her ahead.

"Ok, let's go to a honky tonk," she agreed without enthusiasm. *She should have said no*, she knew it but she didn't want to admit that he had embarrassed her with his comment about her flirting.

Lilly and Drew got into bars without IDs, under the guise of going to lunch. They danced, sang, and generally embarrassed themselves. They were at Acme, the room was surprisingly busy for a weekday afternoon. The floor was sticky with spilt beer and grime. Lilly was half-drunk and swaying to the music.

Drew leaned in and asked sincerely, "You are the most beautiful woman here. Why are you dancing with me?"

Lilly laughed out loud, "Because I can."

Drew shook his head and began doing a particularly wild dance when he knocked a beer out of another patron's hand. The two started shouting and pushing one another.

Lilly acted on instinct. "Hey! Hey! Hey! We're leaving," Lilly announced with hands up as a circling group of bouncers quickly moved through the crowd towards Drew.

"You better get the fuck out of here!" the other guy shouted as his group of friends pulled him back.

Lilly positioned herself between him and Drew. "We need to go, now," she said firmly to Drew looking him square in the eye.

"Good thing your girl is here otherwise I would beat your ass!" the other guy shouted again.

Drew threw a punch over Lilly's shoulder and connected with the other guy's face. In one fluid motion a bouncer with a chin strap and a barrel chest physically picked Lilly up from behind and moved her out of the way. The other bouncers seemed to appear from all directions, dragging Drew and the other patron to opposite entrances of the bar.

"Wait here," the bouncer instructed Lilly and moved to assist his coworkers. Lilly stood stock still, waiting for him to return. The music kept blaring and people returned their attention to their own conversations and drinks after watching the commotion. Several minutes later the bouncer came back, "You're going to need to get your friend out of here."

She nodded. "Thanks."

They had taken Drew out the back and into the alley. Lilly walked outside unharmed but shaken up. She trembled as she stepped into the drizzling rain. The water felt good on her skin. She just wanted to go home.

Drew was swearing and yelling at the remaining two bouncers standing at the door like Corinthian columns. They just watched as he ranted. Lilly felt the rush of adrenaline dissipating. She waited for him to pull himself together enough to stumble to a cab. Drew was out of control.

"I'll walk you home," Drew slurred when they got out of the taxi at his building.

"You're not walking me home," Lilly answered over her shoulder as she paid the driver. "It's too late for you to walk home alone."

"Then you have to stay. If I'm not walking you home, you're not going," Drew commanded drunkenly.

"Fine, I'll sleep on your couch," she agreed, giving in to drunk logic. She was done with this night and with him.

"Ok," he said, stumbling to his door.

They entered a side door to an older duplex and walked up the four short flights of creaky, carpeted steps. The hallway smelled musty, like old garbage. They entered the second floor apartment through the kitchen. The room was dark and Drew didn't turn on any lights as he stumbled through the space. Lilly checked the time on the stove clock it was one in the morning. *How did it get so late?*

Drew wandered down a darkened hallway to the right mumbling about a blanket. Lilly quietly scanned the apartment. Moonlight beamed brightly through several windows lining the wall to her left. There was a stack of dirty dishes in the sink and an overflowing trash bin on the floor. She walked into the dining room and found a ping pong table littered with Solo cups. The living room housed a bean bag chair on the floor in front of a large television with a gaming console and video game boxes piled on the floor. There were two air conditioning units on full blast. Lilly felt goose-bumps on her arms she rubbed them with her hands trying to warm up.

Drew walked back in with a stack of blankets and threw them onto the futon. Seeing her rubbing her arms he asked, "Do you want a sweatshirt?" He was speaking at full volume.

She whispered back, "Yeah, it's cold."

"I like it that way," he smiled in the dark. "Sorry the place is trashed. I cleaned up the bathroom, so at least the seat's down." Drew laughed to himself.

"Thanks," she smiled.

"My roommate's already in bed so you'll be fine to sleep out here." Then remembering he said, "I'll get you that sweatshirt, do you want some pants too?"

"Yes," she grinned, "thanks."

Drew nodded, "No problem." He quickly returned with everything Lilly needed.

She changed in the bathroom and quietly tip-toed back to the futon. She was adjusting the blankets and trying to get situated when Drew came back out.

"Carter, we need to talk," he said sitting down on the coffee table.

"What's up?" she asked, propping herself up on an elbow.

"I know you like bracelet guy," he said.

"Charlie?" she suggested, wondering what was coming next.

"Yeah, bracelet guy," he was still drunk. "I don't want you to freak out or think that we can't be friends anymore."

"Drew," Lilly started but he kept talking over her.

He rambled quickly, "Because we can be friends and you don't have to say anything if you don't want to but I like you."

Lilly's slowly closed her mouth and stopped protesting.

"I'm not in love with you or anything but I like spending time with you. Because today," Drew sighed aloud, "today was crap, and then I saw you and it was awesome. You're so much fun, Carter. I just want you to know that I'm here if you ever think..." The words tapered off as he spoke in intoxicated stream-of-conscious. "I don't know."

"Ok," Lilly said as she lay back down and closed her eyes to go to sleep.

After a minute Drew said, "You can't just be quiet. You can't do that to a person. I told you how I feel and now it's your turn."

Lilly sighed deeply, eyes closed like a coward. "Drew, I don't know what to say. I really like you."

Drew dropped his head into his hands, "It's because of the fight?"

Lilly sat up and looked him in the eye, "It didn't help. The fighting is stupid and I hate it. We had fun today and maybe if I weren't dating Charlie, things would be different but I am dating Charlie."

Drew nodded and looked down at his feet.

She offered. "I just want to be friends and I don't want to mess that up."

"I got it." Drew scratched his head and stared in the opposite direction.

"I'm sorry," Lilly said remorsefully, not sure why she was apologizing when he was the one propositioning her. She never should have gone out with him today. She just wanted to leave.

When he looked back he sounded tired, "What about the flirting? Was that just a game?"

Lilly sighed aloud. "I shouldn't have done that," she bit her lip. "I like that you like me. But it isn't fair to you and I'm sorry. I'm sorry, Drew."

"No, not at all, I'm an idiot. I'm going to bed," Drew said as he put his hands on his knees and stood.

"Goodnight." She lay down quietly.

"Goodnight, Carter."

After Drew went back to bed Lilly lay awake on the couch until daybreak. At dawn, she changed back into her clothes and snuck out of Drew's apartment. The air was cool as she walked towards campus. The grass was still wet from the rain the night before and larger puddles were quickly drying on the sidewalk giving the air an earthy smell. As she walked across campus she ran into Emily leaving the gym.

"Hey!" Emily was startled to see Lilly. "Where have you been? What are you doing up so early?"

"Long story," Lilly sighed. It wasn't until they matched their strides that Lilly realized she had been speed walking home from Drew's house.

Emily shook her head from side to side, "Charlie let you spend the night and didn't offer to walk you home?"

"Spend the night?" Lilly was confused.

Emily leaned back to give Lilly a discerning stare, "You didn't sleep in your room. I thought you were with Charlie."

Lilly exhaled, *there was no way to make this story sound good.* She opened the door to their building for Emily and followed her inside. "After I left Celia's I ran into Drew and we went out. We drank too much and I ended up staying there. I slept on the couch."

"And you didn't kiss him?" Emily said with disbelief, pushing the elevator call button, the doors opened immediately.

"No!" Lilly shook her head quickly, "Not at all!"

Emily watched Lilly's face sharply with a raised eyebrow.

"What?" Lilly asked incredulously as she boarded the elevator and pushed the button for the twelfth floor.

"That look! Don't you lie to me Lilly Carter I am not friends with dishonest people."

"I'm not lying. He just," Lilly gestured with her hands, "He just told me he likes me and I shot him down."

Emily pursed her lips. "You were leading him on."

Lilly spoke angrily. "I spent the day with someone I thought was a friend, those are two very different things."

Emily sighed with exasperation and looked up at the ceiling. "Lilly, what is your five-year plan?"

Lilly was totally lost, "My what?"

Emily looked at her seriously, "You're letting things fall apart, and I'm wondering why."

"What have I let fall apart?" Lilly looked at Emily with confusion as the girls walked off of the elevator and to their apartment.

Emily was clearly just getting started, "You insulted Celia yesterday. You're running around with some boy drinking all day. I just want to know if this is it. Did you meet your goals and now you're just going to quit and go home to Cleveland? Because if that's your strategy," Emily threatened, "I can always find a new roommate." Emily unlocked the door and marched into the apartment, leaving Lilly reeling in the hallway.

Lilly was stunned to silence. She didn't know what to say. Emily had never spoken to her like this before.

"Put on some tennis shoes," Emily instructed when Lilly walked inside.

Lilly looked at Emily like she was crazy. "What?"

"Put on your running shoes. We're going for a run."

"But I don't," Lilly started.

"Now!" Emily was furious. Her anger startled Lilly and she followed orders silently.

Once outside Emily said, "Follow my pace." The girls started jogging. It was almost October and several trees on campus had burst into radiant autumnal colors. There were a few brown leaves on the ground that Emily seemed to strategically target and crunch under her feet as she ran. Emily spoke evenly, "I know you don't have it easy. I know you come from a more challenging background. I don't know the details and that's your business." Looking over at Lilly she added, "Hold your arms up higher, it will help you breathe more deeply."

Lilly lifted her arms and carried them by her bust like Emily. Her gym shorts that were already uncomfortably shifting north with each step.

Emily relaxed into her stride. "Look, I get that you worked hard to get here and college is hard. But that doesn't mean you get to give up. You keep working even when it sucks, even when you want to quit. It's like running. I hate running but I do it and it feels good and I'm healthier and better for it. You have to keep running. You have to keep pushing because if you don't, they win."

Lilly gasped, already winded, "Who's they?"

"All the people who said you couldn't make it. You have to keep moving forward, keep getting better, leaner, faster, because you've got competition." Emily thought for a second and then spoke as if answering a rhetorical question, "Sure, now you're the Wilson Scholar at Vanderbilt but there are a million other kids at thousands of other schools all around the world working harder and smarter than you." Emily looked over at Lilly again, "Don't drag your feet."

"I can't run anymore," Lilly said starting to slow down. Her head was pounding with a hangover she hadn't even begun to nurse.

"Nope, we're not done." Emily grabbed Lilly's hand and pulled her back to the same pace, matching their strides. "You don't have to do it all alone. You have me, you have PH, and your mind. Lilly you're so fucking brilliant, it pisses me off." Refocusing her point, Emily said, "You're not allowed to waste your potential. I'm not giving up on you. You're better than this, Lilly Carter. Even if you don't believe in yourself, I do, so you can't give up. I won't let you." Emily barked, "Sprint!"

Lilly felt her feet pounding into the cement. Her body begged her to stop but she kept pushing to keep up with Emily. She was angry and tired and frustrated beyond words. She chased Emily down and when they finally stopped Lilly gasped for air and doubled over, hanging her head between her knees.

Emily asked as she breathed deeply, "What are you doing, Lilly?"

"I don't know," Lilly gasped, taking a breath between each word. Lilly propped her hands on her hips, "I don't know what comes next. PH wants me to figure out what I want to do with my life and I don't know! I got to Vanderbilt because I wanted a better life. I just followed a path; after eighth grade, high school; after high school, college. I don't know what to do next. No one I know has ever made it this far. There are too many options I don't know what to do anymore. Because I don't know the answers and that terrifies me because it means I could end up back where I came from and all of this will be a waste."

Emily nodded, "Ok, let's keep moving. Jog with me."

"Fine," Lilly gritted her teeth and matched her stride to Emily's slower pace. After the break it felt good to pick up speed again. The cool air was refreshing as Lilly took deeper and deeper breaths. Her muscle memory from lacrosse kicking in now that she was warmed up.

"Why didn't you come to me?" Emily demanded.

"Em, I should be able to figure out my life." Lilly clipped with self-righteous indignation.

Emily ran comfortably. "It doesn't make you stupid if you can't figure out what you want to do next. It's stupid that you didn't ask for help."

"Fine, you're right," Lilly said between breaths. "I need to walk, my head is pounding."

"Fine," Emily relented. "We can stretch."

The girls walked off the path into a green patch of grass and began stretching. Emily said, "Can we talk about your future?"

"Fine," Lilly agreed.

Emily spoke with casual confidence, "You don't like crowds or a lot of people in one place so a huge multi-national corporation is not for you. And a small business won't be big enough to feed your ambition. You need a mid-sized company that is growing, to start. You're building this software program, do you want to keep it or do you want to sell it?"

Lilly thought as she reached her hands to the ground. "I don't know."

Emily stretched her arms across her body. "If I told you that you have to sell it, would you freak out?"

"Probably not," Lilly stood straight and shrugged.

"Ok, you don't need to keep it then," Emily answered for her. "The investor route is a good one. You just don't want to work with anyone like that guy we met with this summer."

"Ugh, never." Lilly shook her head quickly.

Emily thought for a minute, "Do you care where you live? Do you need a support network?" Emily raised her eyes suggestively to imply the Lilly would definitely need a support network.

"I don't care where I go," Lilly said ignoring Emily's expression, "with enough money I can fly to my support network."

Emily looked annoyed, "Seriously? After the conversation we just had about your lack of direction?" Emily answered her own question, "You need a support network Lilly. You don't have that at home and you need to learn to use the one you have here. I'm not saying you have to stay in Nashville forever but for the next five years, you probably should," Emily asserted.

"And you guys are all just going to stay here and support me?" Lilly asked sarcastically.

"Not just you." Emily explained, "This is the home of country music so of course, Porter's going to stay. Celia's going to go to law school and her connections are all in town. My mother's company is here and I'll need to start working my way up there while I'm in business school. It makes sense for us and it makes sense for you."

Lilly could smell the booze radiating off of her body and rather than think more about her future, Lilly returned to an old and comfortable pattern. She turned her anger on Emily and put her on the defensive, "While we're talking about our five year plans, what the hell are you doing with Max?"

"We're not talking about me," Emily said sharply, knowing exactly what Lilly was trying to do and not letting her off the hook. Emily folded her hands in front of herself politely. "But to conclude our original conversation, you know what you want, go for it. I'll always be there for you Lil." Emily hugged her awkwardly, as though the situation called for it, not that she genuinely wanted to give her friend a hug. "Also, I'm sure I don't need to tell you that accomplishments will not make you happy or feel fulfilled. You need to find that in yourself, it's a choice you make."

Lilly knew that but didn't say anything.

"I need to finish this run though." Emily smiled as she took off in the direction they had just come from.

Lilly said, "Thanks," to the sound of Emily's retreating footfalls.

26. REVELATIONS

Back in the dorm Lilly threw her shoes on the floor roughly. She took some Advil, drank a bottle of water and took a long hot shower and thought about what Emily said. Now she felt that she needed to work even harder at school and on her project. It was all so overwhelming. Be a friend, get your homework done, deliver your project, compete with the rest of the world. She couldn't enjoy or be good at anything because she was constantly chasing whatever came next. She was busy all the time and yet she never felt as if she got anything done. It was exhausting.

Celia knocked on the front door, "Good, you're here," she chirped as Lilly answered the door in her towel.

"I have to get dressed. I have a class."

"I'll walk you." Celia walked to the living room to wait.

Lilly toweled herself off and dressed quickly throwing her hair up into a soggy top-knot. She grabbed her own bag walked out with Celia, locking the door behind her.

Celia asked, "What have you been up to lady?"

Lilly tucked her hands into the shoulder straps of her backpack. "Emily and I went for a run."

"Oh, what did you do?" Celia chided gently as she pushed the call button for the elevator.

Lilly frowned cataloging Emily's complaints with a bored voice. "I was rude to you yesterday, I'm not working hard enough, I need to utilize my support network, I know what I want to do, I'm just not saying it, and I spent the night at Drew's place."

Celia's eyebrows shot up.

Lilly exhaled, "He told me he has feelings for me and I laid on the futon all night feeling guilty about it."

Celia frowned, "Why?"

"Because," actually trying to name it now, Lilly didn't know why she felt guilty and her face reflected her internal conflict.

Celia shook her head, "You don't need to feel guilty just because he has feelings for you."

"You're right," Lilly agreed. "Why should I feel bad about that?"

Celia smiled sincerely as they stepped into the elevator.

The silver elevator doors clanked shut. "I need to work harder. I'm just so tired of always having to work so hard," Lilly took a deep breath and leaned back into the wall.

Celia nodded. "It'll make you stronger."

"I hope so," Lilly confided.

After class, Lilly walked back to the dorm in a fog. Once there, she pulled out her phone and called Sophia to talk. She needed her sister. Lilly took a deep breath and dialed. The phone rang once.

"Oh good, you heard," Sophia said with a sigh as she answered the phone.

"Heard what?" Lilly's eyes darted around the dorm room looking for what could possibly be wrong. "Mom's fine. We're fine," Sophia said with a voice tired beyond her seventeen years. "Dad died."

It was so far removed from what Lilly feared that she almost laughed. Forcing the sides of her mouth down Lilly asked, "What happened?"

"Drunk driving, he hit a tree or two trees, I think." Sophia paused a moment and took a deep breath. "I think he drove through the first tree but it was small and then he hit the second one and snapped his neck. He died on impact."

Lilly didn't want to know the next answer but she had to ask, "Was anyone else in the car?"

"No, thank God."

Thank God, Lilly agreed in her mind, a wave of relief washing over her as Sophia continued, "He was alone and he didn't hit anybody else."

"Good." Lilly clarified, "I mean not good... But good that no one was in the car. Are you ok?"

"I'm fine," Sophia sounded lost.

"This is so weird," Lilly finally said after a prolonged silence.

"Yeah, I don't know what to feel. I mean I'm sad, because we should be sad, right? But it's also kind of like when someone famous dies, you feel bad for their family but not really yourself."

"Yeah," Lilly nodded with agreement. "I mean, he was our dad... I guess, but it's not like we knew him so how could we possibly miss someone we didn't really know?"

"Exactly. Mom's all worked up," Sophia shared.

"Why?" Lilly asked with skepticism.

"It's mom, she could care less, but it's an opportunity to get attention so she's acting like it's some personal tragedy."

"Have they even spoken since we were babies?" Lilly asked.

"Probably not, but she's been on the phone all day with grandma acting like they were best friends. And then when she gets off the phone and I ask how she's doing she looks at me like I'm crazy. 'I didn't know your father,' is what she said to me."

Lilly laughed out loud, "Of course, that guy you married and had two children with, total stranger. Glad she's approaching this healthily." Lilly rolled her eyes.

"You didn't expect her to do it any differently, did you?"

"No, I guess not," Lilly confessed.

"You should call her." Sophia added, "It might be nice…"

Lilly's sighed, " You're right. I'll call her. I love you, Soph."

"I love you too, Lils."

Lilly hung up and quickly called her mother. She paced the room as she waited for Melanie to answer. Lilly was conflicted. She wanted to do the nice thing but she wasn't sure if she could stand her mother's dramatic and self aggrandized grief. Melanie picked up.

"Hello," Melanie's voice was ragged and hoarse.

"Hey Mom, how are you?" Lilly forced herself to sound sincere.

There was a long silent pause as the women just breathed. Finally, Melanie spoke, "What do you want?"

Lilly was taken back, "To see if you're ok." Lilly snapped.

"Like you give a shit," Melanie laughed with disgust.

"That's why I called," Lilly answered, trying to keep the irritation out of her voice and failing.

"Look, college girl, you don't need us anymore. Why don't you just leave us the fuck alone?" Melanie replied.

"Are you sure?" Lilly answered calmly as she felt her stomach flip again. She leaned back into the desk chair and raised her face to the ceiling.

"You couldn't wait to leave us, just like him, so why don't you live your life and leave us out of it." Melanie sounded cold, like she was reading a script. "Grandma's calling, I've got to go." Melanie hung up.

Lilly was trembling. Her hands felt like ice and her head was so heavy. She closed her eyes, placed her fingers to her lips and took a breath, trying to stop the world from spinning even more out of control. It was no good. She bent over and threw up into the trash bin. When she was empty, she gagged again and walked to the sink. She rinsed her mouth with cold water and spit. As she came up, she caught sight of her face in the mirror, her eyes were red-rimmed and bloodshot. She pulled her towel off of its hook in the bathroom, carried it to her room, and blanketed it over her pillow. She then lay down and closed her eyes waiting for sleep to take her.

The following afternoon Lilly put together a care package for Sophia, she didn't know how to sign the card so she just wrote, "I love you." After she dropped the small cardboard box off at the post office, Lilly called Sophia to check in on her. Sophia picked up on the second ring.

"Hey Lils," Sophia already sounded better.

Lilly exhaled in relief. "Hey Soph, how are you doing?"

"I'm alright."

"You sound good," Lilly said with relief.

"Yeah," Sophia exhaled as she spoke. "I just needed to wrap my head around it, you know."

"Yeah," Lilly nodded, even though her sister couldn't see her.

"How are you doing?"

"I'm ok." Lilly shrugged, "It's not like I knew him." Feeling her emotions rising, Lilly added, "Also, I'm pretty sure Mom disowned me yesterday."

"What?"

"Yeah," Lilly said, somewhat disheartened. "She thinks I'm just like him, I wanted to leave and so I should just live my life and leave her out of it."

Sophia gave a short laugh, "Lucky."

Lilly smiled, "Yeah." Lilly laughed too and then added sarcastically, "It's just so hard, I'm really going to miss her. She's such a good mom."

"Yeah," Sophia agreed, "the loss is really yours."

Lilly smiled to herself, she loved her sister and felt better already.

"What else is going on with you? You were upset when you called yesterday. Did you want to talk about something?" Sophia said with sisterly intimacy.

"Oh," Lilly's voice was bright with the new topic. "My professor wants me to present my project at an investor's event."

Sophia was biting her nails on the other end, "Really? What does that mean?"

"I don't know exactly," Lilly confessed. "I put together a presentation and some posters and then I spend a day just pitching to anyone who stops by our booth. They invite all of these people with a lot of money and if someone likes the project they could invest, so I could be paid for my work."

"Wow, Lil, that's huge."

"Yeah," Lilly agreed with breathy excitement. "It could be really great."

"It sounds like it." Sophia smiled.

Lilly laughed. "What about you, how are your college applications going?"

"I got my early acceptance letter to Ohio State."

Lilly's mouth dropped, "Congratulations! Sophia that is huge! I am so proud of you."

"Thank you," Sophia said graciously.

"Are you just completely thrilled?" Lilly asked animatedly.

"Yeah, I am, I cannot wait to go," Sophia said honestly.

"What did Mom say?"

"She said something about all of the work it took for me to get there. I'm sure she thinks I got in because of her," Lilly could hear the sarcasm in her sister's voice.

"Whatever, you're amazing and that's why they want you. I am so proud of you!"

"Thank you," Sophia beamed.

"Hey, Soph, I'm at my building, can I call you back when I get upstairs? I'm going to lose you in the elevator."

Sophia hesitated, "No, I've got to get to work. I'll talk to you later though. Congratulations on your investor meeting."

"Thank you! Congratulations on Ohio State! I love you."

"I love you too, Lils. And don't worry about Mom, she's just a bitch."

"I know," Lilly agreed, "it still hurts though."

"I know, but she's not worth it. She's just worked up because Dad's dead."

Lilly nodded, "I don't know, if I will call back this time."

Sophia agreed, "You shouldn't. She's just playing games. You don't owe her anything."

"You're right," Lilly agreed with a sigh of resignation.

"I'm always right," Sophia chided. "I love you. I'll talk to you later."

"Deal. I love you too." Lilly hung up with a smile on her face. She would not allow her mother to hold her back anymore.

27. INVESTORS

The building that housed the Angel Investor event was cold and cavernous, an airplane hanger turned into an event center. It seemed to stretch out forever in all directions. It was filled with people milling slowly from booth to booth. The list of companies and individuals seeking sponsorship filled fifteen pages of a program. Some had videos and interactive games. Others just had a person sitting in a folding chair with some printed materials. There was a crowd gathered around a particularly flashy booth that played loud music all day and rotated a microphone between a cast of peppy students, hired for the event. Lilly felt like a tiny fish in an ocean. By nature, Lilly was not outgoing so the effort to talk all day was exhausting. Professor Hendricks was on hand to provide support but Lilly did all the heavy lifting, explaining the product and what financial backing she would require to continue to grow.

As the event was coming to a close, Lilly's face was tired from smiling. She and PH sat down in folding chairs behind a table in the booth. The day was long and they were both worn out. They still beamed at every passer-by but most moved quickly to the flashy booth down the aisle.

"Well, I'd say this was a success for your first show," PH said as she stretched and flexed her muscular calves.

Lilly nodded, "At least we know to rent a sound machine next time."

"I'm in, anything that might help," PH said with a shrug.

As they chatted an older gentleman approached, "Good afternoon, Ladies."

"Hi Mr. Vetter," Lilly grinned as she stood up again. Earlier in the day he had patiently listened to Lilly's pitch even though she was fairly certain he was not interested in investing. Lilly was happy to see him again.

"I told you I'd come back," he said with a grin. He wore a navy blue suit and a crisp white shirt with a cornflower blue tie. His face was friendly with a sweet smile that looked like he had just told a joke and they were both in on the punch-line.

"I'm glad you did," Lilly answered. "Did you have some more questions?"

"Actually, Ms. Carter, I spoke with my daughter, she'll be along shortly, and we'd like to discuss your needs further."

"Excuse me?" Lilly said in disbelief.

PH stepped to Lilly's side with a concerned look.

"Miranda and I would like to discuss an investment in your company," he said again.

Lilly just stared at Mr. Vetter, waiting for him to make sense.

"Hi," a breathless woman with thick auburn hair approached. "I'm Miranda Vetter," she said as she took Lilly's hand and shook it. "Dad's filled me in on your idea and I already love it," she quickly scanned the booth and looked squarely at Lilly. "You're Lilly?"

"Yes, I'm Lilly Carter. It's nice to meet you." Lilly answered robotically, her face still a mask of shock.

"And you're the professor?"

"Yes, Eilene Hendricks." PH put out her hand professionally, "It's a pleasure to meet you."

They shook hands and Miranda said, "My father tells me we will be your first angel investors. We just want you to know that we're happy to work through the process at your pace, we're in no rush at the start but once the ball gets rolling we're going to want to outline a fairly specific timeline and set some hard deadlines for productivity and for getting to market."

Lilly didn't even know if Miranda had stopped for a breath.

Mr. Vetter put a gentle hand on her arm, "Lilly?"

All of the color had drained from her face. Her head was spinning. "Yes, Mr. Vetter?"

"Are you ok?" His bushy black eyebrows were furrowed with concern.

"I'm ok," she shook her head and took a deep breath. With a smile of disbelief, "I'm just surprised."

He nodded encouragingly as he spoke, "This is really good."

"Yes, thank you," Lilly said with a laugh.

"Good. I'm glad." Mr. Vetter smiled warmly, "Miranda likes to talk shop, that's why she's our CEO."

Miranda deferred to her father with what felt like a familiar refrain, "I'm not CEO yet, Dad. This is still your company."

"I like to handle the people part," he said to Lilly. "Miranda is a wonder with numbers and strategy. I like the part where we just talk as friends."

"I do too," Lilly confessed, feeling comforted.

Miranda spoke authoritatively, "If you're both available we'd like to meet in our offices on Monday. We realize you're still in school Lilly and we're very supportive of your education."

"Thank you." Lilly answered.

"We're eager to get started but we want you to be comfortable first and foremost, right, Dad?" Miranda gently placed a hand on her father's shoulder and gave it a squeeze.

"Now she's doing it my way. We're really excited to take the next step with you, Lilly." Lilly blankly extended her hand for a hand shake and Mr. Vetter took it into both of his papery hands and squeezed gently. "Is a meeting on Monday good for you, Lilly?"

Lilly looked back to PH who nodded her support, "Yes, Monday would be just fine."

"Good," he squeezed her hand again and let go. "We'll see you both on

Monday. Miranda will text you a time?"

"I'll have my assistant make sure all the details are covered," Miranda explained with a firm handshake.

"Really, that's great," Lilly said in disbelief.

Lilly turned to PH with large astonished eyes. A look PH returned with calm composure. Once the Vetter's had gone, Lilly started talking quickly, "What just happened?"

PH smiled, "Well, it looks like you have some interest."

Lilly took a deep breath. She could see stars on the insides of her eyelids as she blinked them hard to be sure she was awake. "This is insane!"

"It's pretty exciting," PH agreed.

Lilly sat down and pushed her head into her hands on the cool plastic conference table. "I can't believe we have a potential investor!"

"This is phenomenal," PH said frankly, shaking her head. "I'll admit, I thought you would do well, eventually. I did not anticipate that we would find someone willing to invest today."

Lilly stood up, suddenly full of pent up energy, "What do I do now?"

"We figure out start-up costs. You've built the software, you've written your business plan, now you've got to figure out a way to deliver," Professor Hendricks laughed. "We'll figure it out. You're doing great. Tonight you need to relax and celebrate."

"Thank you," Lilly said, "for everything," and hugged PH. "I couldn't have done this without you."

PH smiled dotingly, "It would have taken a little longer but you would have figured it out."

They tore down the booth and packed all of their supplies into PH's car. PH drove Lilly back to campus and dropped her off near her dorm. The air was sweet and cool with the earthy promise of fall. The sun set as Lilly walked across campus in a daze. She was excited and happy. This was real. She was thinking about where to pick up dinner when a dark shadowy figure walking the opposite direction announced, "Hey, Carter!"

"Drew, hey," Lilly answered, startled to see him.

"What's up with you?"

"I have my first investor!" Lilly announced, amazed that she was saying those words out loud.

"That's awesome, are you going out to celebrate?"

"I was just going to pick up dinner."

"I'm going to this little bar to grab a burger and beer. Do you want to join me?"

Lilly put up her hands in refusal, waving off the idea, "You're going to meet up with your friends. I don't want to crash."

"It's just me. Are you in or are you out? I'm hungry."

"Ok, one beer," Lilly agreed changing directions to walk with Drew.

"Ok, one rule," he replied.

"What?" She looked over at him as they walked.

"You need to take off that stupid jacket, you look like a banker."

"This is J. Crew! I don't look like a banker." She said, pulling the jacket tighter around her body.

"You look like a banker who spent way too much money on a jacket that makes you look like a cheap couch."

"I look like a couch?" Lilly laughed.

"Really cheap couch," he affirmed with a solid nod.

"I hate you," she laughed.

They walked into Professor's bar. It looked like a grandmother's basement, except for the fully functional skee-ball machine in the back corner. Drew picked a table and ordered two PBR tall boys. The waitress didn't card them and Drew's relaxed demeanor led Lilly to believe he was a regular.

The waitress quickly delivered the beers and took their orders with vague disinterest.

Drew raised his can, "to investing in your project," he said with a broad smile.

They clinked cans and both took a long drink. There was an extended and awkward silence. Drew took another gulp and looked around the room.

"Thank you so much for making those posters and the logo. They were perfect," Lilly offered gratefully.

"I'm glad you like them." Drew answered and returned his attention to the room around them.

Lilly tried to force conversation. "You're really talented, Drew. I can't thank you enough. Seriously, this dinner's on me."

"Not a big deal. I'm happy to help," Drew smiled. He added, "I will let you buy me dinner though."

"Thanks," Lilly laughed tracing a trail of condensation forming on the outside of her tallboy. There was another extended break in the conversation. "Why is this weird? We're friends, why is talking to you right now so totally awkward?" she asked unable resist her desire to take the conversation into more intimate territory.

"Talking about it being awkward does not make it less awkward," he informed her, adding, "You know why it's awkward, Lilly."

The waitress brought out their burgers, Drew waited for her to leave before speaking. "It's awkward because you're here and your boyfriend doesn't know it. And I'm here and you know I like you but you don't like me," he said.

Lilly interrupted, "I like you, Drew."

"Yeah, you like me. But you're never going to date me and that's cool. It just makes this weird and uncomfortable."

Lilly knew he was right, "I'm sorry, Drew."

"No, don't do that. Don't act like you're sorry for me. I'm not some lost puppy out in the rain," he said with an adult tone of voice. "I'm not miserable and alone without you. I'm fine, you can just acknowledge that what I said is true and we can move on."

"I'm not cool with a puppy in the rain," Lilly said with a flirty pout.

"You're such an asshole," Drew said with a laugh rolling his eyes. "I don't even know why I like you," Drew grabbed Lilly's face with both hands and pulled it towards his across the table. Inches from her face he said, "You are a moron."

Lilly shoved his hands off of her face. "I hate you," she said with a laugh. "Can we just talk about something else?"

"Like that catsup stain on your shirt?" He said and took a swig.

"Are you kidding me?" Lilly looked down at her blouse.

"Nope," Drew said, taking another healthy gulp of his drink.

"I'm a mess!" Lilly did the best she could to get the stain out, blotting it with a wet napkin but it only seemed to make the spot larger. "It's right in front too," she whined.

Drew shook his head from side to side slowly, "Carter, you are a hot mess."

"I know," she agreed as they both laughed.

They were back to making fun of each other and laughing. They played skee-ball and after dinner Drew walked Lilly home. The fall air was cool and chilly. They passed a gaggle of girls chatting loudly. Lilly recognized Amy, the girl who had broken into her dorm room las year and heard Nicole, Drew's girlfriend, *of course they were friends. Were Nicole and Drew still dating?* Nicole's voice rang out from the crowd. "Lilly Carter, is that you?"

"Hi, Nicole," Lilly said and kept walking.

"Are you and Charlie Abbott seeing other people?" she asked as she eyed Drew.

"What kind of question is that, Nicole?" Lilly demanded aggressively.

Not intimidated, Nicole stuck to her guns icily, "Well, Charlie seems to be having a great time at the lacrosse house. We just left him with three girls holding him up," she added. "And you two seem to be having a good night."

It felt like the wind was knocked out of her. Lilly didn't want to think about Charlie and another girl. Her mind was racing for a comeback. Finally, she sputtered, "You know, you're a real nosey bitch, Nicole," and marched away.

"Not cool," Drew said to Nicole as he followed Lilly.

Amy chimed in, "You're an asshole, Drew!" she shouted after him.

Drew caught up with Lilly, "Are you ok?"

"What did I do?" Lilly asked empathetically, her arms up in exasperation.

"Nothing, just ignore them."

"Easy for you to say," Lilly replied.

"Why?"

"Because you don't care what anyone thinks, you just say and do whatever you want," Lilly explained.

Drew was confused, "Shouldn't I? Should I do what someone else wants instead?

Lilly looked at him fiercely, "I don't know, maybe consider other people's feelings before you speak."

Drew rolled his eyes and shook his head, "You think everything is about you and everyone is interested in you. Here's a news flash: nobody cares. You're not important and you're not happy." He yelled, "You're not happy, Lilly, because you're lying to yourself and that is so much worse than anything I could ever do or say to you."

Lilly lashed out in anger, "You know what, no. No, what you're saying is not ok. No, it is not accurate. I get that you have a bruised ego because I'm seeing someone else but that does not imply that if he were out of the picture I would be dating you."

"That's cold Carter, really fucking cold."

"Yeah it is because you say that I shouldn't pity you or treat you differently

268

but the second I don't you throw a fit. So which one is it Drew? Because I'd like some clarification."

Drew turned and walked away.

She walked the rest of the way to her dorm alone, her shoulders slumped and her breathing shallow. Drew was right, she was unhappy for a lot of reasons. She spent all her time working on her project and didn't have any time for herself or her relationships. She and Charlie were on the rocks. He had spent all of his time focused on law school applications and any time spoke he seemed bored and disinterested. Her own mother didn't want her in her life anymore, Lilly had tried to feel strong and empowered about her decision to move on, but it still hurt. Melanie was the only parent she had ever known and she only let her stay in her home because Lilly paid rent. Tears streamed down Lilly's face. She wanted to do well on her project if only so there was one thing that she wasn't failing at, one piece of her life that wasn't falling apart. She had worked so hard just to get this far, she didn't let Melanie get in her way and she sure as shit wasn't going to let Drew. As she opened the door to her apartment her phone rang.

"Hey," she answered with exhaustion in her voice.

"Lilly!" Charlie drunkenly yelled into the phone.

Lilly pulled the phone away from her ear in discomfort.

"I'm coming over," he asserted with slurred speech. The same drunken arrival that had become his routine this semester. Lilly had been so hopeful over the summer for their relationship but every weekend Charlie seemed to want to get drunk with his lacrosse buddies, come over to her dorm late at night, and leave in the morning without an apology. Charlie spent all of his free time during the week applying to law schools and playing lacrosse. And even when they did have some time together he only wanted to talk about lacrosse or his applications, he showed no interest in her or her work and usually zoned out or fell asleep whenever Lilly brought it up.

She didn't have the energy left to argue with him, "Fine. You're not driving. You can walk," Lilly answered with irritation. He showed up 20 minutes later, still hammered.

"What happened to you?" Lilly asked when she met him in the lobby. He was leaning on the door frame and clearly intoxicated. The question was general but it rhetorically implied how vastly different he was now from the boy she had fallen in love with so easily.

"Nothing, what happened to you?" he slurred.

"I'm fine," Lilly's tone was clipped. She took his hand in hers and pulled him behind her toward the elevators. She was unamused by his state of complete inebriation. Lilly wrapped her arm around Charlie's waist, trying to support and guide him like she had done for Melanie so many times before. As the floors rolled by in the elevator, Lilly looked Charlie over. His hair was a mess, there were remnants of a red lipstick kiss smeared on his cheek as if he had clumsily attempted to wipe it off. She sighed loudly. *How long had this been her life? Supporting some drunk long enough to put them to bed seemed routine.* Lilly looked at her own distorted reflection in the metal doors. Last year she had worried that Charlie wouldn't understand her emotional messiness, this year he seemed to take it as a personal challenge and made himself and their relationship just like the home she left behind.

"I'm going to clean your shirt," he loudly mumbled under the jarring florescent lights.

"You can clean it tomorrow. Let's get you to bed." They stepped off of the elevator and Lilly guided Charlie to her room.

When Lilly woke up in the morning, she thought about what Drew had said. He had a point, she worked so hard to project a pristine image of herself to the world. She hadn't told anyone about her father dying and she could have, she had friends. She didn't need to be perfect all the time but she did need to be open with the people who were actually there for her, like Emily and Celia. *What would make her happy? What did she want? Independence. Financial freedom. To be done with Charlie.*

Lilly pulled out her computer. She would negotiate a role with Vetter where she maintained ownership of the project and a salary in exchange for a percentage of the profits. That way she was still in control of her program but Vetter would pay for the hardware and technical staff Lilly was sure she would need. She was going to take care of business and herself. She would put herself and her own needs first.

28. AWAKENING

Within the month Lilly was working with Vetter and her time with PH was limited. She still turned to her mentor for guidance but Lilly's work was no longer a school project, it was a growing business venture. She and PH would discuss smaller pieces of the software so Lilly could keep her scholarship but the major components were shared property with Vetter. The time Lilly had usually used to talk through ideas with PH was quickly replaced by meetings with software engineers at Vetter.

Lilly did still talk with PH about the challenges she was facing. They had formed a bond that Lilly cherished and she still looked to her mentor for guidance and support. "I'm just not sure that I have feelings for Charlie anymore," she confessed on a blustery October morning. The sky was grey and overcast. She pulled at the sleeves of her oversized red sweater, covering her hands and fingers to warm them.

"Then why don't you end it?" PH asked logically, her dark eyes clear and steady.

"Because I feel selfish. He needs me," Lilly admitted out loud for the the first time.

PH shook her head slowly. "Lilly, you should never be with someone because you need them or they need you. You should be in a relationship with someone because you want to be together."

"I know..." Lilly shifted in her seat and looked uncomfortably down at where her hands were hidden in her sweater sleeves.

"And to be honest, now is the time for you to be selfish. You're twenty years old, you need to put yourself first. You have the rest of your life to think about other people and worry about them. Right now, it's your job to take care of yourself."

Lilly nodded her agreement. She knew that was the right answer but had somehow put off admitting it to herself. She didn't want to break Charlie's heart but she also knew she didn't want to carry him home again or listen to him puking in the bathroom after a party.

"Speaking of being selfish and putting yourself first, you need to learn all you can from Miranda Vetter." PH said firmly, looking into Lilly's eyes. "You need to ask her to mentor you."

"But I still feel I have a lot to learn from you," Lilly said defensively, afraid to give up her already limited time with PH.

"I'm not saying that our relationship will end or that we should stop meeting. Lilly, you know I will always be here for you," PH reassured her.

Lilly nodded up and down. There was a lump in her throat that she was fighting to keep in check. PH was one of the few strong female role models she had and really the only mentor she truly trusted.

"Come here," PH stood up and walked around her desk, giving Lilly a warm hug. Two tears slid down Lilly's face silently as she hugged her professor. When the embrace was over, PH returned to her seat and Lilly wiped her face with the sleeves of her sweater and sat down again. Clearing her throat PH started again, "You need to ask Miranda to mentor you. Don't be afraid to push for what you want. You need to pursue your goals doggedly and I think Miranda can show you how to do that best. I will gladly continue to talk with you and mentor you but for the sake of your progress and growth, I think it's important that you let Miranda know that you want to learn from her."

"Ok," Lilly agreed hoarsely.

"I also think that you could point out the value of reverse-mentorship and how you can help her too."

"How could I do that?" Lilly asked, recovering her composure.

"Well, you're young and younger people know more about technology and what's cool. By entering into a mentoring relationship you're showing

Miranda that you value and respect her knowledge and what she has to share. When you offer a reverse-mentorship you're showing that you're willing to give back and that it won't just be another obligation or meeting in her day but an opportunity to learn. Which is something I think she'd be receptive to trying," PH led.

"Ok. Next time I talk with Miranda, I'll bring it up."

"Great." PH beamed at Lilly.

"Oh," just remembering, Lilly asked, "You said in your email that you had some news about Don Inglesbury?"

Taking a long breath, PH replied, "I did. He is no longer with the University."

"You got him fired?" Lilly was shocked and amazed, there was an incredulous laugh in her tone.

"No. He retired." PH said with some disappointment.

"What?"

"He apparently started working here while he was still enrolled as a student."

"He went to Vanderbilt?" Lilly asked with disdain.

"I don't know a lot but I can tell you that I made no headway when I attempted to speak with the IT department regarding the confrontation between you two last year." PH took a deep breath, "I imagine they expected him to retire and thought it best to let the situation resolve itself without any intervention."

"But he was a complete asshole." Lilly said quickly.

PH didn't flinch at Lilly's language, "What he said to you was completely out of line and inappropriate. However, he is no longer a university employee so there is nothing more that we can do at this point."

"I understand," Lilly said with a wrinkled forehead, "it's just so frustrating and anti-climatic."

PH nodded her head slowly in understanding, "That's life sometimes."

"Yeah," Lilly agreed quietly.

"He's gone and that's a good thing. And your focus needs to be on your work with Vetter and school."

"Right," Lilly nodded quickly.

"I want you to do well and succeed in your education and your career," PH shared. "Just remember that success is not an end unto itself, Lilly. You need to see the world, experience life, build healthy relationships. To live a full life you need to be a brave and whole person. That means getting out of the office and out of your comfort zone."

Lilly nodded, she was finally starting to understand what PH was talking about.

That afternoon she was supposed to meet Charlie's parents for the first time, she needed to break up with him before they arrived. Unfortunately she arrived at the lacrosse house as they pulled up in their town car. Lilly slowly walked down the street trying to look serene and welcoming.

"Dad, this is Lilly." Charlie's father was a tall and burly man with a full beard.

"Hello, Mr. Abbott. It's a pleasure to meet you," Lilly beamed as she stuck her hand out for a handshake.

"Hello, Lilly. Charles Abbott, glad to meet you," Mr. Abbot's hand engulfed hers as he pulled her in for a hug. She was physically wrapped in an embrace that felt like the Heimlich maneuver. Mr. Abbott then stepped aside to reveal his wife.

Charlie's mother was a petite woman with short blonde hair sculpted into a helmet of curls. She wore a wool coat and camel trousers over brown leather boots. Mrs. Abbott said, "Estelle Abbott. How do you do?"

"I'm great! Thank you so much for asking." Lilly replied, "It's a pleasure to meet you."

Estelle nodded, her Botoxed face unmoving.

"We just stopped by to see the place and then we're heading over to the hotel," Mr. Abbott announced.

"It's not that big a place." Charlie explained leading his father into the lacrosse house. Lilly smiled and hung back hoping to strike up a conversation with Charlie's mother.

"Did you have a nice flight?" Lilly asked politely.

"Yes, thank you." Mrs. Abbott clipped.

"Charlie speaks so fondly of you both." Lilly smiled eagerly.

Charlie's mother nodded and said nothing. Her hands were clasped in front of her. Lilly and Mrs. Abbott lingered in the uncomfortable silence.

"This is a fun house you've got here, Sport," Mr. Abbott announced as he and Charlie bounded back outside.

Lilly sighed, relieved to have Charlie there to break the tension.

Mr. Abbott continued, "Time for us to head out."

Lilly was confused, *They had flown from Denver and they already had to leave?*

"Nice meeting you," Mr. Abbott hugged Lilly again clasping her in a bear hug that was slightly less crushing. This time Lilly could breathe shallowly, the scents of woodsy cologne and stale cigarettes filled her nose. After he let Lilly go, Mr. Abbott held the door for his wife.

"We'll see you for dinner at seven, Charles," Mrs. Abbott commanded.

"Yes, mom," Charlie replied dutifully.

Mrs. Abbott spoke like a cruise director, "Please remember to dress appropriately. We will be dining with your father's clients."

Charlie smiled condescendingly down at his petite mother.

"See you later, Sport." Charlie's father clapped him on the shoulder as he left.

The door closed, leaving the street feeling empty without them. Lilly hissed, "I didn't know we were going to dinner tonight."

"Yeah, my dad has some big client meeting. You don't have to come."

Lilly crossed her arms defiantly, "Why wouldn't I come?"

"Fine, come. Jesus, I don't care." Charlie turned his attention to the sound of cheers coming from his teammates in the house. He turned to follow the sound.

She didn't bother pursuing him and instead rushed back to her dorm to prepare. She called Emily on her way, who had a pile of dresses spread over the couch when Lilly arrived. Celia showed up an hour later with make-up and jewelry. Lilly settled on a sea green long sleeved dress with a deep V-neck. The dress was Emily's and Lilly was self-conscious about the fit but it was a designer dress which she thought Mrs. Abbott might notice. Celia pulled Lilly's hair up into a French twist and put a deep scarlet lip stain on her lips, Lilly felt glamorous and dramatic.

Right before Lilly and Charlie left her phone rang. It was a call from Miranda. She held up a finger to Charlie to show one minute, as she answered he rolled his eyes.

"Good evening, this is Lilly Carter. How may I help you?" She walked to her bedroom so that Charlie's annoyance would not distract her from her conversation.

"Lilly, it's Miranda," the voice said in a clipped tone.

Miranda never called Lilly on her cell phone. Lilly was terrified. "Oh, hi Miranda, I was just..." Lilly didn't get to finish her sentence as Miranda cut her off.

"Lilly, we've recently had a position open in our Palo Alto office. Our head of software development was just poached by Google."

"Jay's gone?" Lilly gaped. He had been really helpful to her as she started working for Vetter.

Charlie came in, dramatically pointing to his watch but she waved him off, "How can I help?"

"I know one of the conditions we discussed in your negotiation was giving you the time and the freedom to finish your education at Vanderbilt," Miranda said at a monotone as though someone was forcing her to speak. Lilly suspected that Mr. Vetter was sitting with his daughter as she made this call. "And we can look outside for someone else to fill this role but before we start that process I wanted to ask if you're interested."

Lilly's mouth went completely dry and she coughed. "Excuse me," she said more as a reflex than a comment.

"Director of software development is a full time responsibility, possibly 80 to 90 hours a week, as the role is integral to our operations." It sounded like Miranda was trying to talk her out of it but her tone changed in the next sentence to the calm and patient voice Lilly recognized, "We realize that you're young and you have limited experience managing a team but my father has offered to mentor you and assist with your acclimation to the role. Initially you'll work with him here in Nashville but once we're comfortable with your progress, you would need to move to California. The position in based in Palo Alto."

"Ok," Lilly said firmly, nodding her head up and down, even though they couldn't see her.

"We plan to start our external search shortly but if this is a challenge you feel ready to accept we could move forward immediately," Miranda was back to her formal tone.

"Lilly?" Mr. Vetter spoke up on the line, *she knew he was there!*

"Yes, Mr. Vetter," she didn't even try to keep the smile out of her voice.

"Miranda is going to send you information on the compensation package, which is quite competitive for the position. You'll want to talk to your parents, or Professor Hendricks, or someone you trust about this decision."

Lilly nodded, "Yes, of course."

He used a fatherly tone that Lilly appreciated, "Also, Stanford is minutes away from our offices in Palo Alto. If you wanted to continue your education, the school and its resources are all there."

Lilly smiled so hard her cheeks hurt, "Thank you."

"It will be a lot of work to bring you up to speed and it will be hard. But once you get the hang of things, I personally think you'll fly in this position."

Lilly nodded thoughtfully and tried to think of everything she knew that Jay did at work.

"Lilly," it was Miranda, "We'll send you a position description in a few minutes and we hate to rush your decision but we need an answer in the next 24 hours."

"Ok," Lilly said with cool composure, even though her heart was racing. "Thank you for the offer and the serious consideration."

"You've earned it." Mr. Vetter said and Lilly knew he was smiling too.

"I will get back to you as soon as I have my answer," Lilly said professionally.

"Very good," Mr. Vetter said with fatherly pride.

"If you have any questions Lilly, you may call me directly," Miranda added.

"Thank you, I will," Lilly said with excitement that was a significant step up. The phone clicked and they were gone. Lilly jumped up and down, unable to contain her excitement. "AHH!" She screamed and walked to the living room in her bare feet ready to announce her coup to the world. She found Charlie sitting on the couch alone, staring at his phone.

"Where are the girls?" she asked with disappointment.

"They left for dinner. Are you ready?" He asked anxiously.

"Oh," she had totally forgotten about their dinner with his parents in her excitement. "You know what, no." A moment ago she had wanted to tell him her news but his attitude made her want to keep it to herself. "I can't go with you tonight, Charlie."

"What?"

"I can't go, I have a work thing and actually, I can't go with you tonight."

"You're seriously not coming?"

"Seriously."

"Wow, you are so selfish." Charlie said coldly.

"No, I'm not," Lilly answered frankly. "Selfish is showing up at my apartment hammered every weekend and expecting me to take care of you.

Selfish is spending the entire semester making me listen to you talk about law school applications and never caring when I want to talk about my work. Selfish is assuming that what you do is imminently more important than what I do and expecting me to be fine with it. I am not selfish, I have been incredibly patient. You are selfish, and I am done putting up with it."

Charlie rolled his eyes, "Fuck you, Lilly," he said as he walked out.

Lilly pulled out her phone. *Fuck this*, she thought and called Drew.

29. DECISION MAKING

Drew answered his phone with a relaxed and intimate exhale, "Lilly Carter, finally called to apologize?"

"No Drew, I just need to talk," she said urgently.

"Of course you do," he replied smoothly. She could hear the smile in his voice. She told him where she was waiting. "I'll be there in fifteen minutes."

"Thanks." Twenty minutes later the rain poured down as an old car pulled up and the driver leaned over, rolling the passenger side window down by hand.

"Carter?" Drew yelled, leaning over the passenger seat, "What the hell are you doing?"

Lilly got into the car, the windshield wipers slapping away the rain at their highest speed.

"Are you ok?" Drew's face clearly showed his concern, "I circled the block like three times to make sure it was you. I didn't want to yell at a total stranger."

Lilly laughed easily, it felt good to laugh at something. "Stalker," she teased him.

"I'm glad you think that's funny," he said sassily. "I could have been following some heroin addict, inviting them into my car,"

Lilly gave him an unimpressed look, "Here? You'd be more likely to find debutants than heroin addicts."

Drew replied, "You don't think they're heroin addicts too?"

She laughed again, rolling her eyes.

Drew looked over his shoulder at her in the passenger seat, "Why were you standing in the rain anyway?"

"I had a rough night." She started plucking bobby pins out of her hair, letting the wet strands fall over her face on onto her shoulders.

Drew replied with false brightness, "I couldn't tell."

Lilly tried to explain, "I know, I look like hell. I broke up with Charlie," she said obviously.

"And you called me?" He asked with a smirk.

"I did." Lilly tried to keep the sides of her mouth firmly in line, not wanting to betray how much better she felt now that she was with him.

"Are you trying to have your way with me, Carter?"

Lilly laughed out loud.

Drew went on, "I am not some floozy you can call at the eleventh hour who will drop everything to save you from certain death on shady street corners just because you called. I am a gentleman." Drew finished with a flourish as he stopped the car at a red light.

Lilly leaned over and kissed Drew. It was awkward and soft. When she tried to pull back Drew caught her head in his hands and pulled her closer for a deeper kiss that she felt all through her body. The light flipped to green but instead of driving on Drew pulled to the side of the road as rain thundered down on the roof of the car.

He then reached over and kissed her again with even greater intensity.

She ran her fingers through his hair and pulled his face to hers. She arched her back pressing her chest into him, feeling the warmth of his body through his thin T-shirt. She could feel his heart beat and the warmth of his skin. She didn't care that her hair was wet or her dress ruined as he rushed his hands over her body caressing her skin, groping her breasts, and firmly grabbing her and pulling her over to his side of the car so she was straddling him on the front seat. She breathed heavily as she kissed him. Her blood was pounding but she wasn't totally out of control. She pulled away from him and raked her fingers through her wet hair, biting her bottom lip, she felt sexy and empowered. Drew's hands were still racing over her body.

Pausing to enjoy the moment she finally asked, "Can you take me home, please?" She was still sitting in his lap and looking up at him with a knowing vulnerability.

"I thought you wanted to talk."

"I did but we're not going to talk and I need to figure some things out," Lilly explained, voicing her needs honestly for the first time.

Resting his head on her breasts Drew said, "Sure."

"Thank you," she replied as she pulled his face up to hers and kissed him firmly. She laughed as she settled back into the passenger seat. He pulled out onto the road.

They rode in silence. Drew parked out front of the dorm. Before she got out he kissed her again, confidently and aggressively.

When the kiss was over she said, "Thank you, for the ride."

"You're welcome," he acknowledged.

When Lilly got home Emily and Max were watching a movie.

"Hey Lil, why are you home so early?" Emily asked barely looking away from the screen as her hand absentmindedly hovered over a bowl of popcorn.

"You alright, Lilly?" Max said seeing her full disarray.

Emily looked up, "Oh, my word. What happened to you?" Emily rushed to get up. "Stay still," Emily commanded. "Let me get you a towel."

"Where's Charlie?" Max asked only slightly concerned.

Lilly spoke calmly, "He's at dinner with his family."

"Did y'all have a fight?" Max asked suggestively, taking a sip from his beer bottle.

"You could say that," Lilly nodded. She was getting cold and crossed her arms over herself.

"Want a beer?"

Lilly nodded easily, "That would be good."

Max grabbed a beer from his backpack on the floor as Emily came back with a warm towel. "Here, wrap yourself in this," she ordered.

"Emily, I'm so sorry about your dress. I'll have it cleaned."

"Forget about the dress. What happened to you? Did I hear that y'all had a fight?" Emily asked as she dabbed Lilly's face with a dry washcloth.

Lilly paused for a moment and answered, "Not exactly."

"What happened?" Emily asked again, squeezing Lilly's wet hair with the towel.

"We broke up," Lilly stated as a matter of fact, as though the words left a bad taste in her mouth.

"Oh, Lil," Emily exhaled.

"It's not a big deal," Lilly said, taking a swig of beer from the open bottle Max handed her.

Coming back to herself, Emily demanded, "Max, did you not get her a glass?"

"She's fine," Max said calmly as he sat back down on the couch.

"I'm good Em," Lilly said taking another long drink.

"What happened then?" Emily asked steeping back, searching Lilly's face for answers.

"I just got tired of it always being about him."

Max chuckled his agreement with Lilly's statement.

"You seem to be taking this all in stride," Emily said quizzically, waiting for the other shoe to drop.

"Yeah," Lilly leaned back in her chair. "I don't really think Charlie's the guy for me."

Max said teasingly. "Well played, Lil," he raised his beer bottle in salute.

"You're encouraging this?" Emily asked Max with attitude.

"She's got to find the guy. Charlie's not the guy," Max said as a matter of fact.

"How do you know Charlie's not the guy?" Emily demanded.

"Charlie's great, but he's not the guy for Lilly," Max reaffirmed casually.

"How did you know Charlie wasn't the guy for me?" Lilly asked with genuine curiosity.

"Charlie's too perfect. He's cookie cutter. Not the guy for you."

"How can someone be too perfect?" Emily asked with hands on her hips.

Max explained gesturing smoothly with his hands, "Look at tonight, Charlie is at a family dinner with his parents because that's what he's supposed to do. He's dressed appropriately, makes polite conversation, he does everything right. But," Max raised his finger to make his point, "tonight Lilly was supposed to come with him and instead of making her the focus of his evening, like any intelligent man would, because obviously," Max gestured to Lilly as the whole package, "he left. He's eating surf and turf and talking about law school and that's just Charlie. He follows the rules, he doesn't make waves."

Lilly nodded her head, encouraging Max to go on.

"Charlie needs a girl who sits quietly at dinner and likes that he's there. Lilly wants someone who runs in the rain."

Max had described exactly what Lilly was feeling. She beamed at him. She loved that he seemed to know exactly what was going on inside of her.

"Oh, shut up Max!" Emily swatted him on the chest, "Lilly and Charlie are in love."

Max gestured to Lilly with his beer, "Lil?"

"Max is right," Lilly acknowledged giving Emily an apologetic shrug.

"Because he didn't put you first one time, you're ending it?" Emily demanded

Lilly looked at Emily incredulously. "But it's not just one time," she explained. "He dates me because it's convenient and I don't want to be convenient. I want to be special. And I want someone that makes an effort, someone who cares about me not just that I can be there for them."

After a moment's silence Max said, "I wish you luck, Lil."

"Thanks Max," Lilly said with confidence. "Alright, I need to get cleaned up. Good night." She took another long drink and put the empty bottle on the table.

Lilly woke up the following morning to a beautiful day. Sunlight streamed through the window as she stretched and yawned. Lilly reached for her phone and realized it wasn't beside her bed. She got up and riffled quickly through her purse. Actually, she couldn't remember seeing it after she called Drew. It could be anywhere. She quickly got dressed and decided to re-trace her steps.

"Where are you going in such a hurry?" Emily asked looking up from her yogurt and granola.

"I lost my phone," Lilly said with worry.

"Where was the last place you had it?"

"I called Drew to come pick me up last night. It's not in my purse. It could be anywhere." She knew almost instinctively where the phone was, Drew had to have it. It must have fallen out of her purse when she was with him in the car.

Emily spoke with comfortable authority, "Ok, before we get worried, let's tear apart your room. It could have fallen under the bed or something."

Lilly agreed, even though she didn't think it was likely. "Ok." The girls quickly ransacked the apartment, finding no sign of the phone. "It's probably in Drew's car." Lilly admitted when they finished searching.

"If that's where you think it is, come with me to the cafeteria and we can eat, then we'll find Drew. Ok?" Emily immediately took charge and comforted Lilly.

"Ok, thanks."

"Hey, was that a date you and Max were on last night?" Lilly asked casually.

Emily smirked guiltily, "You could say that. Let's just say I heard your point on our run and decided that it was time I took my own advice."

Lilly grinned at her friend.

Walking into the cafeteria, Lilly filled her tray with food and found the girls happily chatting around their usual table. She sat down, "Good morning."

Celia blurted out, "You broke up with Charlie?"

Lilly shot Emily a quick glare and answered diplomatically, "We're just not right for one another."

"Good for you," Porter said supportively.

"Thank you, Porter," Lilly said with a small nod. She took a deep breath and added, "I have another announcement."

The table looked at her expectantly.

"I'm accepting a job offer from Vetter. I'll be in training for a while with Mr. Vetter here in Nashville but then I'll be transferring to their offices in Palo Alto." She frowned slightly, "I'll be moving."

Silent stares surrounded her as they waited to see who would speak first. Emily, who usually set the tone in such instances, was wordlessly gaping.

"Lil, if you leave to go to California you'll never finish your degree," Celia reminded her softly.

Lilly replied. "Their offices are located ten minutes from Stanford. I'll transfer and take classes at night.

The girls still hadn't found their voices.

Finally Porter broke the silence, "I know I'm not always the most supportive," she started, "but, I'm proud of you."

Lilly laughed and rolled her eyes which made Celia giggle.

"Congratulations," Emily agreed.

Celia started to cry but hugged Lilly with joy.

After an emotional breakfast, Lilly walked to Drew's apartment. He was loading the last of his things into his beat up old car. It seemed to excite in her all of her feelings from the night before.

"Hey Carter," he said, placing a cardboard box in the trunk and dusting his hands off on his pants. "I thought you might show up today." He reached into his jeans pocket and tossed her her phone.

"Hey," she caught the phone and asked, "Where are you going?"

"Transferring, I'm taking the rest of the semester off and starting fresh at NYU in January."

"Why didn't you say anything last night?"

"I was doing better stuff with my mouth," he chided.

She ignored his joke. "Why are you leaving now?"

"I'm a New Yorker," he said with a confident sigh, "This slow shit isn't for me."

Lilly smiled, "Do you need a hand?"

"Yeah, actually, I have another couple boxes upstairs. Do you mind?"

"Not at all, that's why I offered."

They hiked up the stairs to his apartment. The wood floors sparkled with the afternoon sunlight streaming through the windows. The space felt warm and homey even though it was empty. Drew watched her walking through the space, his face a mix of laughter and adoration.

She wandered through the dining room taking in all of the details, the grain of the wood floors, the dents in the wall. She quietly shared, "They offered me a job at Vetter."

"That's awesome," Drew said with a congratulatory smile.

Lilly traced a fingertip over the window sill and quietly watched the dust fly up into the sunlight. More softly she added, "It means I have to move to California."

Drew gave her a perplexed look, "Don't you want to do it?"

"Well, I want to surround myself with people who are creating and building. And I could really learn a lot at Vetter. Other than eventually moving, there really isn't a down side. There's nothing holding me back right now."

"Carter, you have awesome opportunities all around you and all you have to do is pick one. It's kind of bullshit," Drew said frankly.

Lilly abruptly glared at him. "Seriously?"

"What?" Drew shrugged his shoulders, "You have this project that just miraculously comes together and you get a huge investor at your first event and now they want to hire you to run some team. And look at me, clearly the best thing that has ever happened to your life." Drew gestured to his body with a smirk.

Lilly gave him a doting look.

He continued boldly, "You'd be a mess without me."

"Thanks," she said sarcastically. "But this didn't miraculously come together, I've been working towards this my whole life. I earned this success and you just happen to be icing." She stepped forward and kissed Drew. Drew grabbed her hand and pulled her closer. His hands firmly grabbed her hips as Lilly kissed him back and let the sunlight warm her skin as their lips pressed into one another. After several intense minutes they tumbled to the floor in each other's arms. Lilly did not anticipate the intensity and care he gave to her as they made love. It was passionate, pure, and slow. His kisses lingered. The touch of his fingers sweeping over her skin felt infinite and eternal. The early afternoon seemed to last for hours as he carefully caressed and attentively cared for her. Drew was tender in a whole new way, Lilly relaxed languidly as he massaged her shoulders in long luxurious strokes and pampered her body with his affections.

When it was over they lay on the floor with the afternoon light dancing through the air catching little specks of dust in its glow. Drew's arm was under Lilly's head as she played with his fingers and stared into the beautiful space. She was content, satisfied, and exhausted.

"You're leaving," she finally said.

"Yep, I'm leaving."

He rolled over onto his elbow and ran his fingers gently over her jaw line and lips. "You really are beautiful, Carter."

She smiled.

"I really like you," he confessed.

"Even though you don't want to," she finished for him.

"Yeah, even though I don't want to," he agreed.

Lilly kissed his naked shoulder. "This never would have worked out," she joked.

"It could have," he started. "Well, if I were rich..."

"Shut up," she shoved him away and began to put her bra back on.

With sudden honesty, Drew shrugged, "You just needed a push Carter. Once you got out of your own way and stopped looking to other people to validate you and your decisions, you could only succeed."

His kindness felt bittersweet. "Thank you."

"California is a good place for you. You're not worried about all the competition out there?" He teased with arched eyebrows.

"Should I be?" she dared him.

Drew smiled down at her, "I'm sure you'll be fine."

"Thanks, Drew," Lilly replied sincerely.

"Don't let it go to your head," he pushed her away lightly. "You're still obnoxious."

"Thanks," she said with a familiar laugh that bounced off of the empty walls and filled the room.

Getting serious he asked, "Why did it take you this long to figure out what you wanted?"

Frowning, Lilly thought for a moment. She looked down at her hands and twisted her signet ring, "I think I knew who I was and what I wanted, I just got lost. Coming to college, I felt really unmoored. And it was nice to be with new friends, a new boyfriend, and the Wilson Scholar. I felt like I had a place and even though I was uncomfortable in that role I wanted so badly to fit in somewhere, that I just became this canvas that let everyone else paint on her. I let my new friends and Charlie paint whatever they wanted and then I became that." Lilly shrugged, still staring at her hands, "I became a reflection of their wants and desires. I thought it would help me to be accepted and I wanted a home." Lilly looked up into Drew's eyes, baring her soul to him honestly, "I've wanted a home all my life and I thought if I just became whatever it was that everyone else needed, I would have that." She shook her head from side to side, "I became someone else, someone I'm not, but I think I'm done."

"You do?" Drew asked cautiously.

"I like who I am and I don't need Charlie or the girls to validate me. I like that I don't know where I'll be in five years." She smiled to herself, "I'm not a canvas. I'm the paint. I'm bright and messy, and beautiful." She laughed lightly, "I am a Jackson Pollack explosion of emotions and ideas. My thoughts are like fireworks that explode and bleed into one another." She smiled as she finally admitted this out loud.

Drew smiled at her as she spoke.

Touching his arm she said, "Last night and today really made me realize how much I had compromised in the name of fitting in and belonging. I wasted a lot of time."

"What are you going to do now?" Drew kissed her hand tenderly.

"I lost myself, to pursue the wrong things. I pursued what I thought I should have and not what I truly wanted. Vetter is giving me a chance to change all that and I'm going to take it." Lilly spoke with determination.

"You should take it." Drew stared into her eyes with admiration.

"I will," she smiled and kissed him. They lingered in the moment, quietly absorbing its energy.

Finally, Drew said, "I need to get on the road," as he traced his thumb over her shoulder, longingly.

"Sure. Let's get going." She shook her hair over her shoulder, closing the conversation with a grin.

Once they dressed Lilly walked Drew out to his car and quietly waited by the curb for him to pull away. The sun was high in the sky as the evidence of its beaming danced through the leaves of the trees above. It was cooler than it had been when she first got there and Lilly crossed her arms to stay warm, wishing she was back on the wood floor of Drew's dining room. Standing on the curb he kissed her hard. The look in his eyes was clear and honest. Before Lilly could catch her breath he quickly ran back to the car and drove away, his old car grumbling with resistance as he changed gears. Lilly hugged her arms to her chest more tightly and watched his car disappear around the corner.

Lilly pulled out her phone and promptly called Miranda, "Miranda, it's Lilly Carter, don't post the job I'll take it."

59949067R00181

Made in the USA
Lexington, KY
20 January 2017